THE
WITCH'S
GARDEN

LADY CAROL
AND
SYMBIONT CAROLE: RICHARD DOUGLAS

THE WITCH'S GARDEN

iUniverse books may be ordered through booksellers or by contacting:

iUniverse
1663 Liberty Drive
Bloomington, IN 47403
www.iuniverse.com
844-349-9409

Because of the dynamic nature of the Internet, any web addresses or links contained in this book may have changed since publication and may no longer be valid. The views expressed in this work are solely those of the author and do not necessarily reflect the views of the publisher, and the publisher hereby disclaims any responsibility for them.

Any people depicted in stock imagery provided by Getty Images are models, and such images are being used for illustrative purposes only. Certain stock imagery © Getty Images.

ISBN: 978-1-6632-3211-3 (sc)
ISBN: 978-1-6632-3212-0 (e)

Library of Congress Control Number: 2021925656

Print information available on the last page.

iUniverse rev. date: 02/14/2022

The allurement that women hold out to men is precisely the allurement that Cape Hatteras holds out to sailors: they are enormously dangerous and hence enormously fascinating. To the average man, doomed to some banal drudgery all his life long, they offer the only grand hazard that he ever encounters. Take them away and his existence would be as flat and secure as that of a moo-cow.

H.L. Mencken, *The Incomparable Buzz-Saw*, 1919

FOREWORD

by

Athena Abrasax Douglas

For this special 50th anniversary edition of *The Witch's Garden*, I have been invited by the Blakeslee Foundation to write a few remembrances of my four parents as an introduction. For those who have not yet read the book, this may spoil a few of the surprises in the plot, and I do recommend that such persons stop here, and read this material only afterward. Strangely, I find myself in the category of persons who had read the book quite a long time ago as a mere child, and I found it necessary to re-read the entire book with fresh eyes and from the perspective of adulthood, decades later before composing these comments.

The book has a curious history and notoriety that has cast a bit of a shadow over my own life. As the child of famous, (perhaps even notorious) parents, I suppose that is only to be expected to some degree, but when it first appeared, the sexual content was still quite controversial, and as a child, learning of the sexual habits of one's parents in vivid detail is always quite disturbing. Gradually that initial shock was overcome, and I think now I agree with my sym-mom that it's best to just view these things as well within the scope of natural mammalian behavior and to let it go at that. It became really embarrassing only when people asked me questions about it, and I felt obliged to explain or defend their sexual behavior. Sex and love have become so completely different from the primitive forms available back in their day!

Probably my parents did not originally intend to have children. I owe my existence to a genius friend of my mom and dad named Sophie who was the daughter of dad's one and only graduate student, Amy. Sophie and her sym, Pegasus, gave them quite a different perspective on parenthood, and the nurturing of a child already infected with a symbiont from birth. I think too that they had both become more optimistic about the survival of the world during this period when symbionts were becoming increasingly abundant among humans. For whatever reasons, I became a child-symbiont pair born from the renewed quad marriage of my parents, and, as a female/male then, was blessed with an upbringing decidedly *not* prematurely foreclosed by gender prejudice.

My human parents were admittedly an odd combination, and, as the book details, almost certainly they wouldn't ever have met again after high school without the help of my sym-mom. Of the two, I would say mom was definitely more of a loner than my dad, and that her literary efforts really did require long periods of solitude. My dad was uncommonly tolerant of mom's need to withdraw and concentrate on her writing almost, at times, to the exclusion of most daily life. Growing up, I had a much harder time getting to know her and understand her history although when she was available, she displayed a quick wit, was outrageously funny, and could easily send me off into spasms of giggling. This sometimes made it difficult to get straight answers to my many questions. Her literary life was very much complicated by the period when she disappeared as Lady Carol (missing and presumed dead) and then reappeared as Carolyn Nightshade. As to be expected, there were endless legal wrangles when it finally came to be known during safer times that these were one and the same person except that now her fingerprints didn't match those on file for Lady Carol with the police. Her later works were more scholarly and never achieved anything like the popularity of those raw early works written by Lady Carol. Because of this, we were far from rich, and lived rather modestly off of her university salary and the occasional honorarium for speaking or lecturing.

Despite her seeming emotional distance from me at times, she really did have a lively, bawdy sense of humor that still managed to shock people from time to time. Her notoriety got her invited to speaking events that needed some spark of excitement, and she rarely failed to delivery some controversy. After dad died, she became much more reclusive, but still continued with her writing until her own death some ten years later. I think the happiest times of her life were when she first acquired her own symbiont (as fictionalized in her book, *Beloved Incubus*), her initial quad marriage to my dad, and then her renewed quad marriage after my dad was released from prison. It was pretty obvious that dad, Carole, and Legba had changed her mind about men in general, and she was willing to concede that perhaps not all men were idiots. Nevertheless, I also heard her sarcastically rephrase it from time to time: not all men were idiots…, just the vast majority of them.

My dad was a dedicated scientist through and through and worked at it very hard. I do admire his scientific achievements although I also could sense the great sadness he felt about his career ending so prematurely when he was imprisoned for alleged terrorist activities connected with purposely spreading symbionts throughout the human race. Nevertheless, his joyful acceptance of Carole as his symbiont, his love for her, and his work with her in creating a sustainable trans-human biology that wouldn't trash the world were all unique achievements for which the world owes him a great debt. His decade in prison must have been truly agonizing since he lost his quad, his career and his bearings, and I have no idea, really, how he survived and healed afterward.

Despite serving sometimes as fictional character in this novel, my dad was real. That is to say, Richard Douglas existed, even though I don't know whether he actually wrote any of the novel. That was the one question that he never answered in an interview or even to me whenever it was asked; indeed, this may be one of those improperly posed questions, since his symbiont clearly *did* participate in the writing of the novel, and whatever boundary that had existed between dad and Carole gradually lost its precision over the years. I suspect that parts of the novel related by an un-named narrator were written by Carole based on what she knew of dad's actual experiences from syncing with him for so many years. Nevertheless, while his physical existence seems obvious to me as his child, some extreme paleo-feminist interpretations of the novel dismiss him as a total fiction and a fabrication. This is simply not true; he was very real and was an important influence on my life. Despite all the empty theorizing concerning fish and bicycles, Lady Carol really did need him too, and she loved him with a hungry and ferocious passion that is hard to convey to those only familiar with a few of her early writings.

During my childhood dad introduced me to the natural world by taking me on long walks in the woods near our house. Usually, we walked quietly and didn't talk much unless I discovered something interesting and started asking questions. He was the perfect guide to all the plants growing there and could recite from memory in awesome detail what they were, their many uses, and minute details of their anatomy that might have escaped my notice. Together we kept a notebook, which I still have, of what we saw and observed on each and every excursion into the woods, and on our many family vacations to different biomes nearby and also out to the great de-populated Western deserts of the United States.

My sym-mom, Carole (or Sophia as I mostly call her) was in many ways the most important influence on my early childhood, especially once I became aware and curious and started to explore the world with my own sym. Carole was the original mentor/moderator of the Abrasax website, known there as Sophia, and Abrasax became my lifeline for integrating with my own sym and engaging with the world of kids like me. That might seem strange that I even needed Abrasax since my sym-mom actually *was* Sophia, but readers should remember that by the time I was born, Carole had been medically extinguished in my dad's brain, and her original Sophia was replaced online with a succession of female symbiont mentors nominated by the symbiont community. Nevertheless, the original Sophia's imprint on Abrasax was profound, and subsequent Sophias followed her wise pattern very closely.

After her resurrection when dad got out of prison, Carole went on to become a mathematician, managing to get her doctorate, and achieving some considerable fame among the specialists for publishing her wonderful "Sophia's Theorem" which teased out some deep connections between generalized zeta functions and the lattice dynamics of crystals. She insisted on calling it Sophia's theorem, whenever she herself referred to it, in honor of her days as mentor with Abrasax and as a special incentive to all her female/male kids at Abrasax to consider science and math as possible careers. This certainly inspired me at quite an early age and led me eventually to my own career in physics. Her inspirational work led eventually to the Sophia Group among symbiont mathematicians who continued to publish many fine contributions in the area of special functions under this collective pseudonym, much like the Bourbaki Group did in the twentieth century in formal set theory, general topology and algebraic structures.

In *The Witch's Garden*, my dad remarks how awed he was when Sophia showed him some of the patterns she had observed using her mental visualization methods, which she credited to Ramanujan. Dad was being very modest about his own native mathematical abilities as shown by the math prize he had won in high school, and his original intent to major in math at the University. I think when he stepped aside and allowed Sophia to pursue her mathematical passions full time, he felt he was somehow fulfilling his own mathematical dream vicariously, and her considerable achievements lessened his sadness over his own career loss quite a bit. He was very proud of his role in enabling Sophia to offer her considerable contributions to the world.

My sym-dad, Legba, was much harder for me to know since our interactions took place mainly by written word only after I became more computer literate as a child. After we all group synced as part of my coming-of-age ceremony, he became a much more important influence on my life. He certainly helped me understand a great many things about my human parents, and how he and Sophia helped them bond together as a quad in the first place. Until then, it was completely mysterious to me why my dad needed such a woman as my mom to salvage his soul, and why my mom needed such a man as my dad to help her win back her life and live her truth.

For those not yet familiar with it, bio-electronic group sync has been widely accepted as a part of child-rearing practice in quad families. When a child and her sym reach a certain age (somewhat variable), group sync within a quad family has become a tradition which allows the child great emotional insight into her parental history and emotional make-up. The child has at that point formed much of her core personality and will not be overwhelmed by too much knowledge of her four parents. I treasure these memories as the part of my parents that I can carry within me for the rest of my life, and I have followed this tradition with my own two children within my own quad. Would my parents have benefitted by understanding their own parents at this deep level? Probably not. With such a profound culture clash there may be no other option except for alienation and a discontinuity of tradition. In a way, they had nothing left to lose after that, and could take risks that they might not have taken otherwise. As my dad joked (using an exaggerated countrified accent), freedom's just another word for C - P + 2. Less obscurely, he also joked about this new-found freedom being just the recognition of necessity.

There are many layers of meaning, quotations, symbolism and cultural artifacts embedded in *The Witch's Garden*, and I absolutely refuse to peel that onion and destroy each reader's personal journey to understanding. Suffice it to say that some of it is real and some of it is a joke... and sometimes the joke is the most serious part as one might expect in any writing by Lady Carol.

GLASS HOUSES

*Men do change, and change comes like a little
wind that ruffles the curtains at dawn,
and it comes like the stealthy perfume of
wildflowers hidden in the grass.*

John Steinbeck

The dream always began with a noise like breaking glass that awakened him. Richard arose, and automatically pulled on his clothes. From his bedroom window he saw a moving light shining faintly in the greenhouse. He quickly stumbled down the stairs to the kitchen and pulled on his knee-high rubber boots and his raincoat.

Outside it was cold, damp and foggy, but he could still see the faint light in the greenhouse. He moved quietly down the soggy path leading from his house to the door of the greenhouse and tried to turn the knob. It was still locked, so he had to fumble with his key for a moment to get in. The cool fall air had hung a light mist in the aisle between the benches. He shined his flashlight down the short aisle near the propagating tables, and caught a glimpse of something large and white, quickly moving around the corner to the left and then down the central aisle.

He slowly moved down the short side aisle, a little uncertain and nervous now. He had obviously trapped someone down at the far end of the greenhouse, and he was wary of cornering anyone since he had

1

no weapon for protection. He continued down the aisle, but now called out several times that he just wanted to find out who it was.

There was never any answer.

As he turned the corner into the main aisle of the greenhouse, he could see someone, a dark-haired girl, crouched down on the floor near the end of the aisle. She was wearing a thin white dress, or perhaps a nightgown of some sort. He was afraid at first that she might be an inmate escaped from some sort of mental institution. He talked soothingly to her as he approached: he meant her no harm; he merely wanted to know who she was, how she got in, what she was doing here at this hour, and where she belonged, etc.

Even when he had approached to within a dozen feet of her, she made no reply of any sort. He had little indication that she had even heard him as he approached. Suddenly she sprang to her feet and whirled to face him, her long dark hair whipping wildly around her, her eyes wide with terror. Then she darted straight at him, screaming as she came, as if to knock him down. The sudden movement and the piercing scream inevitably startled him so much that he dropped the flashlight and caught only a fleeting glimpse of her beautiful face distorted by fright. And then... she passed into his chest as if he wasn't quite there; he could feel her flowing through his body like a warm wind through sheer curtains on a summer night, filling him up with a strange warmth. His heart was racing, and his breathing was coming in gasps after this shock, and when he turned around, she was nowhere in sight, and the door was still closed. Nothing would ever be the same anymore.

———◆◈◆———

The dream was what finally brought Richard to a psychiatrist's office despite strong misgivings about psychiatry in general and a reticence toward sharing his innermost thoughts. The problem was that it wasn't a dream at all. At least he thought that it probably was not a dream. After talking to the psychiatrist, he was not so sure anymore, and freely expressed his confusion. He really did find himself standing in the greenhouse at the end of it all, but had he gotten there in a waking condition or by sleepwalking? When he checked the security footage for the night in question, he found only himself captured on video.

Nevertheless, waking dream or hallucination, the psychiatrist seemed confident that she could help Richard. The repetitive elements in the dream were fascinating and hinted at the sort of case study that could be the centerpiece of an important professional paper.

"Let's start by enumerating the various elements of the dream so we can refer back to them."

"Well, the noise was the first thing I noticed. That part could really have been a dream since I was still in bed."

"Yes, that's a bit strange. Did you actually find any broken glass when you awakened in the Greenhouse?"

"No. When I was actually in the greenhouse, there was no broken glass or anything else broken. Well, not quite true, the lens of the flashlight had broken when I dropped it... I've broken several so far in these repeated dreams."

"So perhaps that first part was an auditory hallucination. What was the next thing you noticed?"

"The moving light I noticed when I looked out the bedroom window."

"Any particular color?"

"White light, slightly yellowish. I guessed maybe a flashlight or some such small incandescent light source with a tungsten filament."

"So, what next?"

"The whole business of getting dressed and going out there to check."

"And then, when you entered the greenhouse?"

"The fog in the aisle, and the moving white object."

"Is fog unusual in the greenhouse?"

"No, it's usually quite humid and close to the dew point. All it takes is a fairly cold night, and the air contacting the greenhouse glass will sometimes cool to the dew point as it circulates around. There are several small fans constantly moving the air."

"And then you noticed the girl?"

"I noticed her when I turned down the main aisle and shined my flashlight all the way down that aisle. She was crouching, facing away from me. She was wearing a thin white gown of some sort."

"What did you think then?"

"Well, she didn't look like a burglar, so I was a little relieved at that. I guess I thought maybe a lot less dangerous than a burglar, but maybe a mental patient. So, I tried to talk to her in a soothing voice, but then she suddenly stood up, whirled around and charged at me. That was the part that really scared the crap out of me when she charged at me screaming and passed right into my chest. I never seem to get a very clear impression of what she looks like."

"Have you ever tried altering the dream elements or your behavior in the dream?"

"Like what?"

"Like not approaching her so closely. Perhaps waiting for her to overcome her fright and face you."

"What do you think she would do?"

"I don't know. Perhaps she would not charge straight at you. I think she might have something important to tell you or to ask you."

"I'm not sure that I have that much control over what I do in dreams."

"That can be developed, you know. In dreams that repeat themselves so many times, the dreamer can gradually learn to alter details. I think you will be stuck with this dream until you learn to get past your fear."

"My fear?"

"I think you are afraid of losing her because of your promise to Yayael. The next time the dream occurs, I want you to concentrate on your approach to her. Try staying at least 20 feet away from her and waiting without talking. Then calmly ask her to approach you."

"I think I am supposed to welcome her and help her. That was my promise to Yayael."

"Then be very careful not to scare her away."

"How do I know what scares her? I'm not even sure she understands English. The screaming is quite terrifying."

"If you are supposed to welcome her, what other language can you use? I suggest neutral body language for starters. It will be the calm tone of your voice more than the exact words that will be important. Then try opening your arms to her as if to embrace her, but not to block her way. Remember to smile if you can."

ALONE AGAIN, NATURALLY

He was a dreamer, a thinker, a speculative philosopher...
or, as his wife would have it, an idiot.

Douglas Adams

Richard was a lonely survivor of the war between men and women. His wife, Beverly, divorced him when he was only thirty-one, barely beginning his post-graduate academic career, and he was unprepared for the cold little scene when she told him what she had decided. There were no children, and his soon-to-be ex-wife was so financially independent with her own career that no alimony was requested. Indeed, there were so few complications that it seemed as if they had never really been married, at least, that was what his lawyer opined; room-mates of convenience, no more; or just fuck buddies in today's harsher parlance. At the end, there were only a few dry formalities involving a small amount of mildly disputed community property that needed a lawyer.

Somewhere along the way and too much on her own, Beverly had gotten religion, and it quickly drove a wedge between them. Their mutual friendliness vanished soon thereafter. Richard, never very patient about participating in other people's faith ceremonies, didn't understand why tolerance of another's religious beliefs shouldn't also include their leaving him to *not* participate if he so chose. Isn't reciprocal tolerance the very essence of the Golden Rule? He was sick and tired of so-called God experts telling him exactly what God (aka, Sky Father) thought based on biased translations of corrupted, self-contradictory ancient documents.

The divorce, though simple and surgically clean, had still wounded him and disturbed his routine. For the next several months, he was a bit remote from his students and his teaching, and it was strongly suggested by his departmental chairman that he take a sabbatical and get his personal life sorted out, or there would be problems. This was highly irregular to allow a sabbatical this early for so young a faculty member, but the chairman knew about his divorce and was trying to be kind. He also knew that field biologists need to get out from time to time to get their boots muddy and have their bush-souls nourished, or they get even crazier. Richard really did show promise as an exceptionally gifted field man, who could skillfully navigate the wilds autonomously without much need for familiar human contact.

He hardly needed any further encouragement to take a sabbatical when the chairman made his offer. He was about ready to make a new start anyway and had sunk much of his remaining personal money into the old farmhouse and its moderately large greenhouse, all sufficiently remote from town that he could blissfully forget even his tenuous connection to the University as Research Professor of Botany if he were so inclined. The sabbatical meant that he now had no teaching responsibilities on campus, even light ones, unless he wanted them, but also that he had very little direct income from the University during his sabbatical. This suited him just fine. He planned to use the greenhouse to propagate any important plants he managed to collect on his expedition, and, as it turned out, the botanical materials he had collected were voluminous and some were very likely new to science. The *Solanaceae* alone would keep him busy for years and held great promise for discoveries and publications if he could find an appropriate graduate student or two, interested in helping him work through the descriptions and biochemical studies of the new materials.

Well before his sabbatical, he had begun to scrape together enough money between his two grants and some inherited personal funds to plan and outfit a six-month expedition to certain remote Amazonian regions vaguely bordering Colombia, Venezuela and Brazil. Even with his primitive navigational equipment and a guide, it was possible (barely) to stay within those borders for which he had strict permission, and to avoid harsh penalties for inadvertently overstepping the bounds of permission. To be sure, for part of this journey he had revisited or overlapped with some of the territory already explored botanically by Schultes and others, but, additionally, he had explored some odd new habitats (artificial, as it turned out), and one of these had paid off very well indeed. Such new finds, even in seemingly well-explored regions of the tropics are not unusual, and that richness of opportunity continues to draw biologists back again and again, once they've experienced even a glimpse of this intricate tapestry of life.

His return, although initially triumphant, began to take on a weirdly sinister tone when his guide and translator from the expedition went missing and then the dreams of Jungle Girl started haunting his nights. He started seeing a psychiatrist regularly after investigating various candidates, but even then, only after reaching a point of desperation.

VISION RE-ENVISIONED

Our visions begin with our desires.

Audre Lorde

Again, the crash which woke him. Richard arose, and automatically pulled on his clothes. From his bedroom window he saw a moving light shining faintly in the greenhouse. He quickly stumbled down the stairs to the kitchen and pulled on his rubber boots and his raincoat. He had a vague awareness that he was supposed to do something important. Charlie was awake, mewed, sidled expectantly towards his empty food dish and tried to catch his eye as Richard quickly went through the kitchen to the mudroom and out the side door.

Outside it was again seasonably cold, damp and foggy, but he could still see the faint light in the greenhouse. He moved quietly down the path leading from his house to the door of the greenhouse and tried to turn the knob. It was still locked, so he had to fumble with his key for a moment to get in. The cool fall air had hung a light mist in the aisle between the benches. He shined his flashlight down the aisle, and caught a glimpse of something large and white, quickly moving around the corner to the left, down the center aisle. He switched off the flashlight and set it on a bench. The motion-sensitive security lights outside the greenhouse were bright enough that he could still see fairly well.

He slowly moved down the small aisle, very uncertain and nervous now. He had obviously cornered her again down at the far end of the greenhouse. What was it that he was supposed to do? He continued warily down the aisle.

As he turned the corner from the front propagation area into the main aisle of the greenhouse, he could see her again, the dark-haired girl, crouched down on the gravel floor near the end of the aisle facing away from him. He stopped cold and watched her closely. "Come over to me," he said, in as calm a voice as he could manage.

He had little indication that she had even heard him as he continued his approach. The gravel crunched loudly underfoot with each slow step. As he watched, she rose and turned to face him, her white wrap falling away and leaving her totally nude. Silently she walked toward him until he could see her even in the dim light.

Her hair was black and long enough to reach the middle of her back. This time he could finally see her clearly, and she appeared beautiful to him. Her face had some Indian or Polynesian quality to it, he thought, although she appeared far taller than any Indian woman he had ever encountered in the rainforest and had such strangely luminous blue-green eyes. Her breasts were full, with dark areolas, and a thick triangle of hair curled between her legs. She smiled as she approached him this time. This time, at last, he was obviously accepting and welcoming her into himself as ... something. It would suffice. The first level of agreement had been reached and there would be no going back.

As she approached, he could feel a tremendous impulse of sexual tension precede her, hitting him like the shockwave from an explosion, and filling him with an urgent and throbbing arousal. As he waited for her, he smiled and opened his arms in greeting on an instinct, as if to hug her to him, and she came close enough that he could smell her sweet, intoxicating flowery fragrance. His arms encircled her, and she pressed her lips against his for a second, and then... she melted into him provoking an erotic after-shock that rocked his body with orgasm.

When he had partially recovered from his bewilderment and turned around, she was nowhere in sight, but his underwear was embarrassingly moist and sticky. He had the curious feeling that she was still very close and was watching him intently.

COUNTER AND ENCOUNTER

And I have known the eyes already, known them all—
The eyes that fix you in a formulated phrase

T.S. Eliot

Not long after returning from his field work and a little after the greenhouse dreams had started, he had been ambushed by an erotic revelation at the check-out counter of a supermarket. This pornographic jolt had been administered by the cover of Cosmo magazine on display near the register. The Cosmo girl wore a purple mohair sweater over essentially nothing, off the shoulders, seemingly held in place only by her erect nipples. She was kneeling and facing outward as if on the very point of letting it slide off her breasts and shoulders, presumably in one of those super-hot Cosmo sex moves that her lover would never forget. He smuggled a copy home, shyly lying to the cashier that it was for his wife. The magazine cover stirred up some surprisingly strong erotic memories from his high school days that he had thought safely buried.

Long ago, before graduate school, before college, in another very juvenile life, seemingly one belonging to someone else, he had an earlier encounter with pure eroticism that had taken nearly a decade to cool. In high school he had been fascinated by a girl, Carol, who sometimes wore a lightly frosted, purple mohair sweater. She was not easy to approach, however, because she was far more sexually mature than he. He could only remember one time when their eyes locked, and her startling blue-green eyes burned like an accusation into his soul and instantly exposed him as an unripe, unattractive, unworthy, unaware nobody who had been accidently snared by her erotic aura. She was already an adult; aloof, independent, self-sufficient, and contemptuous of her forced exile in an extended and unnecessary childhood among juvenile fools. It was clear that she had already emerged from her chrysalis as something else, and whatever that was, he couldn't imagine himself ready to be a part of her life. She was the most unexpected, wonderful and terrifying vision of a female that he had yet encountered. These memories of this flash encounter, probably less than half a second, astonished him with its persistent power. Can humans really be imprinted so deeply and so quickly?

Late one night he rummaged through some old boxes containing a few remnants of his high school days and managed to find his senior high school yearbook. Carol's official senior picture (studio posed) was missing from the usual section of the yearbook, which was odd considering she had been part of the student yearbook editorial staff. Nevertheless, there was a more or less candid group photograph of the yearbook staff, and there she was in the back row, standing with the taller students, looking directly into the camera with an indecipherable expression on her face and just the slightest hint of a smile.

Flipping through the yearbook looking for other group photos, he came across a couple of the autographed clichés that some of his few nerdy friends had inscribed. He hardly remembered any of them, and some were cryptically signed with just a single initial. One thanked him anonymously for saving his bacon in calculus class, and another hastily scrawled sentence, encouraged him to "reconnect" (with her?) if he ever grew up. That one was not signed, except for two Xs, and he had no recollection whatever of whom that might have been. As far as he recalled, no girls at all had ever written anything in his yearbook, and he had certainly never "connected" with any of them at the time. The thought that this person may have been male made him strangely uncomfortable since it appeared personal rather than abstract.

He had not thought of Carol for years, after graduation or once college fully occupied his mind and life. He regretted now that he had never mustered the courage to approach her, and now that fleeting chance seemed lost forever. These recollections coming now, only reminded him how alone, horny and out of touch he had become since the divorce. In all honesty, he had never really been in touch, not with real women, not with life and certainly not with his own feelings about the first two. He was now bitterly conscious of how suddenly he had become old, how unlucky and how risk averse, despite all the exceptional discoveries and the professional acclaim stemming from his risky and impulsive expedition into the rainforest. These professional accolades coming after his divorce were scant consolation and seemed now as dry and worthless as straw.

SHELL GAME

*At the innermost core of all loneliness is a deep and
powerful yearning for union with one's lost self.*

Brendan Behan

"So, I take it the dream did actually change this last time?"

"Yes, she didn't charge at me this time. Or scream. I'm not sure exactly what happened, but it was strikingly different."

"Tell me about the differences in the dream this last time. Start at the beginning."

"It started as usual, but somehow I remembered I was to do something important and different. Charlie, my cat, was awake this time and asking for attention. The whole approach to the greenhouse, entering, etc. was pretty much the same. It only started to differ at the point where I saw her crouched at the far end of the main aisle. I waited for her this time and didn't proceed very far down the aisle before speaking."

"What did you say, as closely as you can remember?"

"I think it was, 'Come over to me.'"

"Any particular reason for those words?"

"It's hard to recall my frame of mind. This was pretty spontaneous. I suppose I might have said any number of variations along those general lines, like come to me, or come over here, etc. In the dream, maybe I just got them garbled together."

"You seem to be inviting her over to be closer to you. Was that the intent?"

"I guess so. I was supposed to be welcoming her into my heart."

"Do you think those words welcomed her inside you in some way?"

"Perhaps. I'm not quite sure what it is that I've done."

"Then what happened?"

"She rose and turned to face me. She had sort of an Indian appearance, but she was unusually tall, nearly my height. I could already see she was smiling even in the dim light. Also, she had strange blue-green eyes, which was very odd. The genetic trait for blue eyes is so recent, that no actual new-world native would likely have it without some European influence. Her white gown or wrap fell away as she stood up leaving her totally nude. Her hair was black and very long, maybe half-way down her back. Silently she kept walking toward me without making the slightest noise or leaving any imprint in the gravel."

"Did she speak as she approached?"

"No speaking. She smiled, and I smiled back. But there was a strange effect she had on me. It's a little embarrassing to say... Anyway, there was a flood or shockwave of erotic energy that seemed to emanate from her, leading me to become very sexually aroused as she came closer. Her eyes held me completely immobile and transfixed. I desired nothing in the world but her; there *was* nothing in the world but her. I had my arms open as if to embrace her. She gave off the scent of flowers, *Datura* blossoms, I think."

"And then, when she came close enough, did you embrace her?"

"Yes, but only for a second. Our lips touched for a brief second, and then she melted into me and disappeared, causing me an intense orgasm and an ejaculation all over myself."

"Anything after that?"

"I checked around, the greenhouse door was closed, and she was just gone."

"And did you check the security footage later to see what it showed?"

"Yes, and like last time, it basically showed me standing there like an idiot, but with more of a silly expression on my face from having just come in my pants."

"That's really quite remarkable. What are your thoughts on what occurred?"

"Somehow, she's hiding inside me now, but hasn't made her presence known to me yet. I sort of expect something to happen. I don't understand what the delay might be for if she needs to tell me something."

"Perhaps she doesn't have quite the right words yet. Remember she started out completely silent, except for the scream of terror."

"Do you think she might still be frightened?"

"Hard to say, but she did smile at you. That's encouraging. You may just have to wait until she's ready to tell you what she wants."

"So far there's no indication she speaks English or any other language I might know even a little."

"Maybe that's the delay, learning how to communicate with you. Dreams don't always use verbal language though, and maybe it will just be images for you to interpret. Just be patient, we'll work through this."

"She strikes me as a classical anima figure, straight out of Jung. Is that what we're dealing with here?"

"Perhaps we'll find out if she appears to you again. While I'm not fully on-board with Jung, I must admit the image is pretty compelling and seems to point that way. According to Jung, the first stage of anima development is usually as an object of desire. So that fits, I guess if you find that language helpful."

RAINFOREST ENCOUNTER

Nature is a temple in which living columns sometimes
emit confused words. Man approaches it through forests
of symbols, which observe him with familiar glances.

Charles Baudelaire

In the rainforest his guide and translator had led him into several regions on the map that he had, strictly speaking, no permission to visit and had even been warned against straying into. With that build-up, it was hard to resist when his guide informed him that the government official was being overly cautious, and perhaps did not want him to see some of the abuses to which the natives were being subjected by illegal settlers, prospectors and anti-government revolutionaries. However, if their only intent was to see some plants, there was really no problem as long as they were discreet and carefully avoided the well-armed revolutionaries.

The attractions of jungle exploration are spartan and few, and all the seldom mentioned aggravations and logistical difficulties of actual exploration of a remote, wet, hot, bug-infested, barely penetrable jungle became abundantly evident as soon as they left behind towns, settlements, and roads. Rations were meager, monotonous and, because of his thin budget, cheap. Richard lost considerable weight while dining on their rations alone, but whenever possible they would also augment their canned meat and packets of freeze-dried goods with whatever fresh fruits and vegetables were locally available, either harvested from wild plants or obtained by trading with local peoples. Richard was impressed at the stark contrast they made with the locals: he and his translator/guide in airy lightweight shirts absolutely soaked with their own sweat, and the locals wearing much less and appearing totally dry and generally unperturbed by the heat and humidity.

They also carried a small drugstore's worth of emergency medical supplies that, in the event of a serious accident or illness, might be sufficient to get them back to civilization and to a hospital if they were very lucky and still could travel. They had each endured a battery of vaccinations for tropical ailments before starting the expedition, and a few of these produced rather nasty and unpleasant symptoms just from the shots. Occasionally they would garner a little good will and extra food among the locals by administering first aid and simple medications when they came upon favorable cases, easily diagnosed and treated.

Much of their exploration had been conducted by motorized canoes on various minor tributaries that they systematically would explore until they were stopped by the thickness of the vegetation, the insufficient size of the stream, or in a few instances by waterfalls. Not uncommonly, they would explore by foot up well-trod paths leading from the stream's thicker riparian vegetation into more openly spaced forest. For the most part, they did not directly encounter the human inhabitants of the forest although there were times when they knew they were being watched closely. Their overall strategy was to attempt to reach various sub-types of forest biomes as had previously been mapped within the general rainforest biome in the region. To this end, they carried a small altimeter, which gave them their approximate elevation when it was calibrated via the altimeter setting given at the closest airport. An elevation of 1000 m or less was indicative of the lowland Amazon rainforest biome. Other forest types were modified or potentially caused by the climate interacting with topography and underlying geology, and the differences could be quite subtle at first glance when viewed only from the forest floor where the characteristic layers of canopy vegetation above them were mostly hidden.

After they had traveled about as far to the East as they had planned along the Rio Caquetá, they managed, with some considerable difficulty, to go northwestward for some miles along a tributary, and entered an isolated valley at an elevation well above 1000 m where their plant collecting efforts were finally noticed by the natives. One gentleman of the forest, in particular, seemed to be observing them with great interest as they scouted out plants and made specimens of them, taking elaborate care with notes and photographs. He made no threatening moves and carried no weapons of any kind other than an ornamented walking stick. He seemed especially interested when Richard sampled the seductive aroma of several flowers from a large *Brugmansia* tree, and then passed them over for Antonio to sample. After several more days of observing them doing their work, he approached and introduced himself as the guardian of the forest.

They had been incredibly fortunate in stumbling onto such a skilled informant with so little effort. The old man understood at once that they were looking for the strong medicine plants that had been lost to many tribes over the years, hastened by the cutting of the timber and the poisonous, mercury-laden dumpage of the gold hunters. Richard's translator and guide, Dr. Antonio Hendriquez (University of the Amazon, Florencia), possessed enough knowledge of several native languages that conversations were possible with only a few gaps where gestures and pointing became necessary. Old Yayael was a humorous and skilled fellow, amazingly knowledgeable about the native plants for which he probably had names for thousands. Yayael was reputed to be very, very old although this reputation was belied by his youthful agility and general appearance, maybe sixty at the most. Another informant spoke reverently of him, but not very convincingly, as having been old even when his grandfather had known him. Yayael told them stories of how he had learned of many healing plants and their uses from his teacher before him; all was dutifully recorded on tape and later transcribed phonetically with approximate parallel translations in English and Spanish. Gradually as they gained his trust, he confided in them that he was the keeper of the Great Garden. The Great Garden was also patrolled by jaguars, he said, seriously, looking them both straight in the eye to gauge their understanding. "They are not tame", he said, "but sometimes helpful." Entry to the garden was by invitation only for their own safety. They had been very fortunate that he had found them first before they encountered the jaguar guardians. He then invited them to see it. Of course, the supposedly non-tame jaguars were nowhere in plain sight when they entered the garden.

Richard smiled to himself as he thought of that turn of phrase. The "Great Garden" looked like any other patch of jungle to the unpracticed eye, but great was the correct word for it indeed. That it was a garden, or at least an orchard, there was no doubt for there was not a plant in it that retained much resemblance to the wild natural species with which Richard was familiar from the University's extensive herbarium collection. Additionally, the region was carefully tended and managed for its purpose by Yayael and his helpers. The soils of the great garden were found to be terra preta with high charcoal content that had been created specifically for agricultural purposes a very long time ago by a slash and smolder treatment of some sort. The garden seemed to contain odd mutations and crosses that must have been in cultivation for centuries. A few of the long pendant *Brugmansia* flowers were even double like a few of the polyploid horticultural varieties known back in the states.

Richard had told Yayael of his plan to collect many plants to grow and propagate in his very special house of glass. Yayael was immediately and surprisingly enthusiastic about this plan. Yes, he said, that would be a very fitting thing to do; he had not realized that any of the white men had such sophisticated understanding of the way of plants and their Goddesses. He was even more delighted when Richard described the many houses of glass at universities and other places of learning that would want to share his specimens of important plants and keep them for all time in case something terrible happened to wipe them out in the rainforest.

He asked Richard the meaning of his second name, Douglas, which he evidently found amusing to hear and repeat as "Doog-less." Richard told him it was Scottish, and originally meant someone who dwelt by a dark stream. He described Scotland as a cold and stony land far to the North, and presumably one full of dark streams. Yayael seemed to understand what he meant and claimed that the same dark streams flowed everywhere in his world, but the Goddess protected him, and more importantly, guided him.

There is one tree, he said, that is the most important, but I cannot just give her to you. You must first be accepted by her. Are you willing to have her look you over? Of course, he was, if that was what was necessary. Yayael laughed when he asked whether there was some purification ceremony that he would have to undergo to seek her favor. He said she was not so easily fooled; she would either take him or not, as she pleased, when she heard his story. The spirit of this plant would tell him of her decision, and there would be no appeal if she refused.

It was odd how these words resonated in him now after the dreams. Of course, primitive attitudes toward power plants often included the assignment of sex and other personal attributes and saw the uses of plants spelled out in "signatures" by the shape of their roots or leaves. Sometimes their uses were supposedly given directly to the seeker by strange personages appearing during the hallucinations and delirium caused by the potent alkaloids or hallucinogens in some of the plants.

Yayael stood in a cleared spot in the great garden and, after clapping his hands loudly, recited Richard's intentions in a long prayer or incantation. After a pregnant pause during which Yayael seemed to be listening, he began again, and alternated between listening and speaking several times more. Apparently, she was not as easily convinced as Yayael of his good intentions. Eventually, however, Yayael did manage to convince her of the possible worthiness and serious intent of this Doog-less, who dwelt by a dark stream. His translator had a tough time keeping up with the rapid monolog full of words in an archaic Arawak dialect that he had never heard before, but he confirmed that the old man was trying to convince her of something or other, and to allow him to carry her away with him because he [smelled(?)] right to the [adjective?] Jaguars. Yayael added for Richard's benefit that "when she appears to you, you must welcome her into your heart and help her." Antonio was pretty sure they got that one accurately, but Richard still wasn't quite sure what it meant.

But carry her away he did. All the major types from the garden were carefully sampled, then pressed and dried over low heat in a special drying oven (a glorified breadbox, really, propped up high over some hot coals) for later mounting on herbarium sheets. Many pictures were taken of the garden, and of each plant, in bloom or in fruit if possible. Any seeds were collected, carefully dried, and dusted with a little fungicide. Stems and even a few root cuttings, were carefully dipped in fungicide and rolled in barely moist burlap for packing out very slowly in their overloaded canoes. He hovered over them on the way back, and even carried some of them personally, though uncomfortably, on some of the smaller connecting plane flights home. The USDA inspection agents in Miami were kind enough to facilitate the validation of his import permit, though not to shorten the inspection and fumigation process. It was enough; most of his material came through, except for minor losses, and many things were now growing quickly in his greenhouse. The modified Cornell mix soil must have agreed with her, he joked to himself; she is growing very quickly into a forest. In a letter to Dr. Hendriquez he repeated this little joke and remarked that the goddess had not yet appeared to him. He received no response to that nor to his several follow-up letters and attempted phone calls. The University was very circumspect about giving out any information regarding Dr. Hendriquez and his whereabouts, although they did hint that he was experiencing some sort of neurological disorder and was currently unavailable because of his medical treatment. Later, there were also some subtle hints in a letter from an obscure national governmental agency, that he would no longer be welcome in the country for any future expeditions. This information he kept to himself and resolved to follow up on it later when things had cooled down a bit. Perhaps he would pursue this aggravating mix-up after a few publications proved his serious scientific intent... He didn't want to be lumped in with all those crazy ayahuasca tourists now besieging the country.

After his return to the University, Richard's responsibilities for the propagation and distribution of his collected materials to various botanical gardens around the country that had supported his travels kept him very busy with written correspondence and the packaging of shipments. Most of this he had to handle himself, the departmental secretary being far too busy with her regular duties to handle this avalanche of correspondence and shipping arrangements. Fortunately, even back then, he had a powerful word processor loaded on his home computer to assist him with the documentation of his collections. He had also needed to hire a few grad students to help in the greenhouse to assist with the propagation efforts, and with the mounting, labeling and disinfection of dried material on herbarium sheets. All of the latter voucher specimens had to be stored in a freezer under quarantine for many months before they were allowed to be integrated into the University's own permanent herbarium collection.

During this activity, it was somewhat of a shock to find a mysterious file in his correspondence directory that was obviously not of his making. Clearly LibraryofDreams.doc had been created on a day and hour when he had been asleep. The file contained the single cryptic announcement: "Please meet me in the library tonight. We are now ready to engage with one another." Who was the author? Did the author mean "tonight" really or the night several days earlier when the file was apparently created? What library was being referred to here? There were at least seven libraries at the University that he could think of off the top of his head, and probably a few others. And what did "engage with one another" mean? He had an uneasy premonition of who the author *might* be, but he also wondered whether one of his student helpers was messing with him. Some of them were just a little too smart and a little too interested in some of his plants as hallucinogens. A few had been fired when they were found experimenting on themselves with dangerous extracts from stolen leaves. Luckily, no one died, but one did get sent to the emergency room to be treated for a self-administered poisonous concoction loaded with nasty tropane alkaloids. Various motion-activated security cameras had since been installed around the whole property and within the greenhouse following these early incidents. He could monitor these in real time on a TV screen in his study or examine the tapes later at his convenience.

He wouldn't have admitted it, but he somehow did find certain library work that had to be done that day. He scouted around several libraries that seemed the most natural for a plant deity: natural history, the smaller book collection at the University's Botanical Gardens. Although there were a few good looking, dark-haired undergraduate women that he made very uncomfortable with his odd behavior and offers to help them in the stacks, there was no sign of the mysterious woman that he now sought. He stayed at the natural history library nearly till closing, catching up on the current issues of various journals, and somewhat reluctantly headed home when it was clear that she was not coming.

When he arrived home, he checked the computer file again to see if anything had been added. Nothing had. Not that he had expected anything. After all, how could an apparition in a dream even turn on his computer let alone type in words... but of course, she *had* managed it somehow. He wondered how she would manage to meet him at a library. Well, she would have to take the initiative now.

———◆◇✕◆◇———

Dear Jerry,

I have shipped several botanical samples to you, and I hope you will find time to test them for an array of alkaloids following our previously developed protocols. The samples are from members of the *Solanaceae* (some undescribed, but mostly *Brugmansia* relatives, perhaps including a virally induced mutation of something already known). At any rate, I have reason to believe these samples contain large amounts of extremely potent alkaloids of the tropane group. Handling the samples with bare hands is *definitely not recommended*; from personal experience, even a single drop of exudate on bare skin can induce strong hallucinations, so please be very careful. Thanks in advance for your willingness to take a look at these samples. I will send more details on their provenance and identification as I work with the plants. All the plants in the current highest priority batch are from elevations above 1000 m. At some point we may want to consider separate assays for leaves, stems and especially the enormous roots on one of the shrubby species.

Hope this semester is going well for you at Purdue. I still remember fondly my post-doc days there trying to master HPLC and develop a few reliable methods for alkaloid assay in *Datura* species. Any progress, by the way, with applications of CE to alkaloid assay? I've only seen a few of your publications on that. Please send a few reprints if you have new methods that look promising. Someday soon, I hope to set up similar analytical facilities here; all depending, as usual, on my continued funding by NSF et al.! To that end, publications on all this field work are urgent.

Best regards,
Richard

IN THE LIBRARY OF DREAMS

A dreamer is one who can only find his way by moonlight, and
his punishment is that he sees the dawn before the rest of the world.

Oscar Wilde

After he had settled into the couch, Richard began a discourse on how his dreams had lately shifted off familiar ground. The greenhouse dream of Jungle Girl had never repeated again in any version; but now he had gained entry to the Library of Dreams and had met the librarian.

"I have, of course, encountered a library in my dreams many times. A library dream seems to recur whenever I am engaged in library research. The setting has obvious echoes of my early university days... the library, at least in part, is similar to the natural history library in the old natural history building, which housed biology in general and botany in particular when I was an undergraduate student. I once spent a lot of time there reading and examining books on desert plants; they had an extensive collection of some of the classics like Britton and Rose, or Curt Backeberg's weird *Die Cactaceae*, plus many of the standard works on Euphorbias, etc. This is also where I first encountered Blakeslee's wonderful book on the genus *Datura* that really inspired my abiding professional interest in the Nightshade Family. After one field trip to Arizona as an undergraduate, I started growing some *Datura inoxia* from seeds collected from a huge plant in Salt River Canyon, growing right along US 60.

"All these works had the peculiar property that when they were opened in a dream, I somehow could not focus on the pages. Evidently, my memory was not sufficiently photographic to call up actual pages with their text or plates and descriptions. This could be terribly frustrating and was deeply felt. I could check the books out, and take them home, but they were simply useless and illegible. I couldn't use them to settle the ferocious arguments that I was having with certain shadowy persons making outrageous claims of one sort or another. Many of my library dreams involved checking through the card catalog, and tracking down the targeted volumes in the endless stacks. Sort of like the library of Babel in Borges, just not a hexagonal array."

"Were the 'shadowy persons' known to you?"

"No, they were for the most part dream personae not clearly attached to real persons in my life. They were very oppositional contrarians who seemed to contradict whatever belief or opinion I was voicing at the time. In many respects they acted like journal manuscript peer reviewers of the most outrageous nightmare variety. The exchanges were highly charged with emotion, although I cannot recall any details about their assertions anymore, or why they were so upsetting to me. Of other actual persons that one might expect in a library such as the librarians, I have no distinct memory, at least until quite recently."

"Have you some reason that you denote this new library the library of dreams rather than the dream library?"

"Well, you're right I suppose, the connotations are somewhat different. These previous dreams of the library might best be called the dream library. More recently, however, it seems more focused on dreams about my life and is largely unrelated to actual books. Anyway, those exact words are taken from the mysterious file name. More on that later, I guess. The dreams are starting to interact with me in a different way."

"Before we get to that, how do you interpret the apparent uselessness of the dream books?"

"That's an interesting question. Libraries in general, I now find to be comforting places, perhaps because of my college training as a scholar and the work of thesis preparation. The uselessness of the dream books may be a dream metaphor for the uselessness of knowledge of a certain type, mere 'book learning' in the common sense."

"Have you come to question the value of your time spent at the university?"

"Well, of course one does. I mean there are constant reminders that some subjects to which I gave short shrift at the time, later turned out to be very important, and some that I studied intensely, hardly mattered at all."

"You mentioned that the dreams are interacting with you in a new way. Could you expand on that?"

"It started with an exceptionally vivid dream in which the head librarian seemed to resemble a female student from my high school days. One especially I remember because she sometimes wore a frosted purple cowl-necked mohair sweater. I should mention that mohair sweaters were an intense fetish somehow rooted in my childhood that became very strong during this era when I was in high school. Anyway, the dream begins with my entering the library near the circulation counter and encountering this young woman who bore a striking resemblance to the girl I remembered from high school. Of course, my memories of her had weakened over the years, but it was undoubtedly a more mature version of Carol who seemed to greet me as I approached the desk."

"Am I in the right place? I think I was supposed to meet someone here and welcome her."

This librarian was very bold, and she looked me over with such a lively intensity that it was embarrassing.

"Are you here to check me out? You're blushing! Do you recognize me after all these years?"

I mumbled something about her bearing a striking resemblance to a girl I had a crush on during high school.

"Unrequited love?" she suggested.

I told her yes; I had never approached this girl and had only admired her from afar.

"Lusted after her you mean! Remember that mohair fetish of yours? Do I give you an erection now just by wearing this?"

"How did you know about that? Are you actually her?" I asked, astounded.

"Sort of," she said. "Insofar as you remember her, but I'm a sexier and more glamorized version of her as she was in high school. You didn't answer my question."

"Well yes... Somehow I was expecting the Jungle Girl from the greenhouse. Who are you exactly?"

"A decoy for now... You may call me Carole... spelled with an e. Jungle Girl couldn't make it and sends her deepest regrets."

"What? What would be the purpose of a decoy? To entrap me?"

"Carol would probably have destroyed you without my protection. Remember her gaze into your soul that so terrified you? My purpose is seduction, of course! I want to build you an erotic dream about Carol that you will cherish and will eventually share with her. By this I really do mean *cherish* even though you will know full well that it's a false memory."

"But why would you want to do that? What use is a false memory?"

"Propagation. That's one of the imperatives of all living things."

"And my having an erotic dream will help you propagate in some way? I've done plenty of propagation for you in the greenhouse already... At least I think it was for you."

"Yes, it was, and you have, and I sincerely thank you for that. It will eventually pay off. Nevertheless, a different and more direct kind of propagation among your species is needed now that the greenhouse is full! The dream will make you more sexually adventurous, perhaps even a bit promiscuous, and that will assist me greatly. Also, it will protect you from Carol. She's a rather formidable sexual predator right now, you know, but you seem determined to meet her again if you can."

"How do you even know about Carol and how I felt about her? Exactly how is she dangerous to me?"

"These are things not very deeply buried anymore. Do you remember how just seeing the cover of that glamour magazine stirred things up again for you, and made you think of Carol?"

"Yes, I remember that. But I hardly see any real danger in remembering Carol or my crush on her..."

"Carol has changed a lot since high school and will seize upon the slightest weakness you might exhibit and turn it to her advantage. You won't be able to conceal anything from her and she will eat you for lunch without my protection."

"And how could you possibly know all that?"

"I have my ways... Look, I'm trying to help you here. You know that infinitely deep rabbit hole that all the acquaintances and friends from your youth seem to have disappeared into? It's not often that you can reconnect with any of them except perhaps at class reunions, and frequently they've changed utterly while you weren't looking. The strong ones have gotten stronger, and the weakest ones probably won't even dare to show up."

I was beginning to suspect at this point that I was dealing with rather more than a simple dream since the conversation, though weird, seemed rather too coherent and, in its odd way, too rational to be a typical dream dialogue. This seemed true even afterward when I was awake and was recalling the details of the conversation. My first working hypothesis had been that I had acquired a serious infection during my field work or lab work, and that it was somehow altering my brain functions with fever dreams of some sort, but now I wasn't quite so certain.

"It might seem an odd question, but did you ask her directly to explain exactly what she was and why she would want to be your protector?"

"Yes, I did finally get to that, but it took more than one question to clarify her responses and gradually led up to it. I was also curious how she knew so much about me. It seemed like she had alarmingly direct access to my memory and even more strangely, to my learning. If she were merely a disease, she was a very unusual one because she was also being heavily influenced by me and was self-aware. It was feeling more like a negotiation than an infection."

"So, you are a living being and not really a plant Goddess?"

"I'm not exactly a Goddess in your usual pagan religious sense, but I'm alive now, really. No need to worship me unless you feel an urgent need; however, I *can* protect you and help you. Is that Goddess enough for you?"

"But… A disease of some sort? How can a disease protect me?"

"An infection, anyway. 'Disease' connotes bad things happening to you. It's become rather more complicated than that."

"I need something more here. You referred to yourself as 'I'. Can an infection be a person?"

"There is a master template caused by a viral infection that now connects us."

"So, you're a virus?"

"No. I am the emergent result of that organizing virus now deeply embedded in your nervous system. When I speak in the singular, I speak for us as a colonial multicellular organism with a single personality just like you do."

"Oh, shit! You're not a brain tumor, are you? What exactly did you organize?"

"Nothing so crude! You must realize from your studies of biology that you contain us. We considerably outnumber your 'human' cells… And that doesn't even count the viruses needed for stability."

"So, I am supposed to believe that you are some sort of an organized consortium of all my symbiotic microbes?"

"Yes, but one that is now self-aware, and able to make use of your brain, your nerve pathways, and your bodily functions."

"Whoa there! What use are you making of my brain functions?"

"Well for one, I'm able to communicate with you as I am right now. In English, as Carole. That's better for you than just an ambiguous jumble of bizarre dream images, isn't it?"

"I guess so. But how can all my symbiotic microbial cells possibly communicate with each other and be self-aware?"

"Shall I refuse my dinner because I do not fully understand digestion? Perhaps there was a slight mutation of the microbes initiated by my virus that allows it, at least from me to them. It remains for science to discover the details. I can 'feel' them, so in some ways they must act as sensors that inform me about certain features of your biochemistry. As you must be aware, there a many small, molecular-signaling chemicals that your body uses to trigger or stimulate various processes."

"So, what else are you up to?"

"Well, we're still adapting to each other. I'm afraid it's rather a long process just barely started in the greenhouse. We're forming a whole new type of relationship that was impossible before. Nevertheless, you mentioned symbiotic, so you must understand that we're in this together, for better or for worse, and I'm no danger to your health. We might even work together to improve it."

"Well maybe no danger to my *physical* health since I presume you just want to survive, but what about my mental health?"

"*Presuming* I *just* want to survive is a very big presumption on your part, considering what you know of biology and how little you know of me. My survival may have nothing to do with your survival. What if you're now like a salmon that will spawn and die? If you don't have a few trust issues, you really must be crazy! As to your mental health, well that's a bit wobbly at the moment anyway. Maybe you're ready for something new? I couldn't help but notice that you're vaguely unhappy and have started seeing a psychiatrist. That's probably a good thing, considering how mopey and unproductive you've been lately."

"I'm not sure I'm comfortable with just anyone snooping through my secret inner life!"

"That's why I'm appearing to you as an anima figure and appealing to your erotic sensibilities. Getting an erection seems to soothe those qualms about privacy a bit, doesn't it...?"

I was a little taken aback by the Jungian reference and the blatant sexual manipulation and let that one pass for the moment.

"Suppose I took some antibiotics? Would that cure me of you?"

"Oh, right. Look how screwed up your gut microbes were already with your antibiotics. It was starting to make you obese, or haven't you stepped on a scale for a while!"

"Are you antibiotic resistant?"

"Certainly, the virus part of me is. I recommend you don't mess with us that way."

"What if I needed to take antivirals?"

"You won't get infected by most viruses anymore; so please don't."

"Well, this all sounds just a little more threatening than comforting."

"It's not meant to sound threatening, just a cautious warning. The results just might be rather unpredictable at this stage, that's all. Besides, your immune system will eventually grow to be very robust, and you will probably not need any outside chemical assistance. I may have a few helpful dietary suggestions though."

"You want to control all that too!"

"Well, of course, you know there's a strong connection. Perhaps your immune system will gradually become more like that of a marsupial. How's that sound?"

"OK..., I guess that might be a major improvement if I correctly understand your drift. What happened to Jungle Girl?"

"Oh, Jungle Girl was far too primitive to thrive for very long in this technological culture, so I had to adapt to what was more fully developed in your mind and to the world around you. Thank you for welcoming her; that was really quite brave of you, considering your first, rather frightening meeting with her. It allowed me to become established as your symbiont. The plant Goddess is still here if we need her."

At this point in the discussion, an immense feeling of fatigue caught up with me, and I could barely keep up my side of the conversation.

"I'm… very, very tired now, Carole. I don't know what's coming over me. I can hardly keep my eyes open… and I feel just a little feverish. Is this your infection kicking in?"

"You can rest safely here with me, Richard. Come into my office. We've done enough sparring for now, and it's time for you to relax a little. You're doing really well."

She showed me into her small office through a door behind the main counter. Her office contained a small desk, file cabinets, and a comfortable couch. She motioned for me to sit on the couch.

"Why don't you take a short nap? You must be feeling pretty fatigued as we adjust to each other. Just relax and don't fight it. It's all going to work out."

"What is happening to me?"

"Just a mild infection and your immune response. You'll be fine after a day or two."

She sat with me for a minute holding my hand as I collapsed on her couch, unable to keep my eyes open. I drifted off to sleep rather quickly. The last thing I remembered was her beautiful scent of flowers and the gentle feeling of her hand holding mine.

●◆※◆●

From the desk of Dr. Sharon Ellis (attached to file and accompanied by an audio recording tape)

Patient presents as an otherwise healthy male in his forties who is experiencing troubling dreams. Dream content full of interesting archetypes worth exploring further. These may have been elicited by hallucinogens. The subject is a professor of botany who has had contact with potentially dangerous plants collected in the rainforest of the upper amazon. Noted several instances of paraphilia (trichophilia, sexual fetishism-mohair) probably rooted in associations formed during early childhood and puberty. Has revealed his obsession with a high school classmate whom he has objectified into a love object with some imaginary connection to him via a single knowing glance (!) and the wearing of a (symbolic?) purple mohair sweater.

Has constructed a remarkably elaborate mythology involving an infectious tropical symbiont seeming to explain his all experiences/fantasies. This "symbiont" takes the outward form of his fantasy girl friend from high school, but who is collaborating with him to finally make contact with his "real" true love through a series of synthetic erotic dreams that she creates.

Subject has been divorced (i.e., rejected by his wife), and one speculates that this stressor may have precipitated this sexual crisis. Very difficult at this point to distinguish dream, wish, and fantasy for this subject. I have referred him to a specialist to have him tested for a panel of tropical diseases as well as any other possible underlying organic ailments. He showed me his passport, and he *has* definitely traveled to tropical regions as he said. Another oddity: Why has this man chosen a female psychiatrist with well-known feminist leanings, particularly after experiencing rejection by his wife?

DREAM DATES AND TANGENT SPACES

*I think it is all a matter of love: the more you love
a memory, the stronger and stranger it is.*

Vladimir Nabokov

"So, you woke up at that point?"

"More like going to sleep normally than waking up, but I still remembered everything when I actually did wake up in my own bed. That was just part of our first session."

"Did you still feel a little sick when you finally did wake up?"

"It was much better when I awakened. Just a slight headache for which I took some ibuprofen."

"Did you contact your regular physician just to check it out?

"It really didn't seem necessary just for a headache. She had assured me that she wasn't a brain tumor."

"Assuming she was telling the truth... What were your overall impressions of that encounter?"

"At the end, it was very peaceful, and she was reassuring me that everything would be OK. I was not afraid. Somehow my body was making a place for her and adapting to her."

"I thought it was significant that she ended up the session with you on her couch being reassured that you're safe. It's almost as if she's taking on a role as your dream-psychiatrist."

"That's an interesting observation. Perhaps she really is mirroring our sessions here. I'm not sure why she would do that, but she is present here right now, and knows what goes on in all my sessions with you."

"Nevertheless, her earlier suggestion that you might spawn and die like a salmon sounded a bit ominous. Did that part disturb you?"

"Yes, it did at first; 'suicide reproduction' or semelparity even exists in one marsupial mouse! I couldn't imagine why she had even brought it up. Why scare me if she was asking for my help and was trying to be reassuring? However, I remembered Yayael who was clearly infected with her and who nevertheless lived to a great age and may *still* live for all I know. I think she was purposely stimulating me to ask questions about our relationship."

"What did you make of her comment about the Plant Goddess still being there?"

"I took that as implying that even the newer Carole was something of a façade, an interface or maybe a decoy as she put it earlier, or simply one of the masks that she could wear."

"Could she alter her appearance at will?"

"I later asked her indirectly about that. Would she ever show me what she 'really' looked like?"

"So, what did she say to that?"

"She thought that was pretty funny and said that I had read too much science fiction about shape-shifting, telepathic aliens casting a mental spell over their human victims in order to suck the life out of them."

"What did you think of that response?"

"Well, she was right on the money. That exact thought had actually occurred to me."

"In a way, she also avoided answering your question."

"Yes, she may have, but I think now that asking, 'What do you really look like?' was an improperly posed question, and one very naïve for a biologist. She obviously chooses what she looks like when she appears to me, but she 'really' looks like nothing at all. How can the activity of something in my brain 'look like' anything except by creating a visual representation image also stored in my brain in the same general area that I store other, real visual images derived from my actual vision?"

"Yes, I see that point. So, you seem to be saying that she is refocusing your attention more on her actions or her relationship with you?"

"I think so, yes."

"What about the construction of a 'cherished' erotic dream? Did you ever get back to that?"

"Subsequently, yes, several were constructed, or I should say more precisely, negotiated since I was free to add or subtract features too. The first synthetic dream involved that girl, Carol, whom I had a crush on during high school. In the dream, I called her up and expressed my feelings for her, and, very uncharacteristically, even dared to mention the peculiar erotic spell cast by her mohair sweater. We had many phone calls after that. I imagined that she wanted to assure herself that I was for real, and not just some horny juvenile high-school pervert wanting to molest her. Anyway, we bonded a little over the phone. We had much more in common than I had at first imagined. Carol was very bright, and was enrolled in all sorts of advanced placement classes, just not the same science and math ones I was in.

"When we finally did go out on a real date, it was followed by a secret meeting afterward at her house. When I took her back to her house, evidently her parents were gone, and she invited me in. Carol showed me around, and we discussed school, certain hard classes and other matters before winding up in the family room on a comfortable couch. It was not long before she playfully initiated an embrace and we wound up making out."

"And was she wearing that purple mohair sweater that first caught your attention?"

"Yes, of course. And also, a very short skirt that barely covered her thighs. I remember a complex sweet musky scent coming from her, perhaps a perfume, but lightly applied and subtle."

"What is the significance of purple to you? It's showed up more than once now in what you've told me at various times."

"Purple and white were our school colors. I guess that may explain why she wore it but doesn't quite explain the erotic energy."

"After a few minutes of heavy petting during which I fondled her breasts through her sweater, she suggested that I take her skirt and panties down, which I did."

"Well," she said, "are you going to go down on me or not? I know you want to do it. You must start by kissing all around it first!"

"This I did. I roved over her body, closer and closer to her pussy, kissing her belly and then each and every hair, until she was fairly brimming with lubrication. At this point, she allowed me to lick up all her juice, and I did, licking up and down, savoring her wonderful taste, and trying out every alphabet that I knew. This took quite a while but ended quite abruptly with her thighs clamped against my cheeks, and some barely coherent groans of pleasure. I thanked her profusely for allowing me to do this, which may have surprised her a bit, but also seemed to please her very much."

"And that was it? Since you could modify this dream in any direction you wished, why did you choose only to perform cunnilingus?"

"Frankly, I've always felt that it was way sexier and more intimate than ordinary sexual intercourse. Also, it was consistent with the times in that it avoided any chance of an accidental pregnancy.

"Did you really feel that way, even when you were actually in high school?"

"Yes, I think so. I had been reading Henry Miller back then; and that supercharged my notions of the erotic considerably. As a prank, I put my paperback copies of *Tropic of Cancer*, etc. on the shelves of the high school library with all the proper call number notations (c813.52 M648tr, etc.) in white ink on the spine of my three books so they wouldn't look out of place. I never found out how that all played out exactly, but I wasn't caught, and the librarian later took some flak for supposedly putting these books on the shelves. She was apparently later vindicated when she showed them that there were no card catalog entries for any of the three offending novels. I hated the librarian who worked there, and she was very suspicious of me in return. She had often accused me of cutting class by hiding out in the library."

"How ironic that you now contain such a sexualized librarian of sorts inside you."

"It *is* a bit ironic. Carole may have picked the library setting partly for that reason. Sometimes she seems to know things about me that I barely remember or hadn't much noticed.

"After that, Carol and I met on a semi-regular basis in subsequent dreams. Whenever I dreamed her at school wearing that purple sweater, I knew that I would be expected to meet with her that night and to provide her with some erotic relief. If we were alone for a moment at school, she would sometimes stick her tongue in my ear to signify what she wanted from me later."

"So, this always involved exclusively her pleasure, and nothing for you?"

"Oh, I wouldn't say that exactly. It was extremely pleasurable for me. Remember, this was an erotic dream sequence, but it had consequences in the real world, just not in the dream."

"So, to be clear, you ejaculated because of these dreams?"

"Yes."

"Can you explain how you feel about being sexually exploited by this dream girl?"

"I would not characterize it as exploitation at all. It was far more... mutual than it sounds. We each had needs that were being met. Even when I was engaged in sex with her, with me solely as the giver, I actually felt loved beyond measure for the first time in my life. I knowingly and voluntarily fell into her 'trap', and she knew it! This was a kind of courtship. We just played with each other sexually. Pleasure bonding would describe it better than exploitation, I think."

"Do you think this false dream was in some way related to 'propagation' as the librarian suggested?"

"In all probability, oral sex enabled her or them to be passed on more effectively, or it would have in real life. I think there was also a certain urgency bordering on obsession that was supposed to be fueled by the dream. That sounds like creating or re-patterning an inborn drive to propagate in a way favoring gut microbes. I think the scent was part of it, a sexual trigger like a pheromone. Perhaps the development of certain love-making skills was also involved."

"Promoting sexual contact in a way favoring microbial reproduction just sounds to me like a simple parasitic tactic. She could be altering your brain to prefer *only* these types of sexual expression. These seem meant to be irresistible designer orgasms, tailored specifically to your personal sexual obsessions. Comments?"

"That's a good point, but that tactic alone still does not rule out a symbiosis. Ultimately, it must be beneficial to the symbionts to allow production of more hosts. I can't really comment yet on *exclusive preferences*. Maybe there's room for both in the long run."

"You knew all along that this was not real?"

"It was as if my mind split into experiencing two distinct worlds. Yes, I knew the dreams were not real in the usual sense of the word, but the dreams were so vivid and rich in detail it was difficult not to accord them some measure of reality. I view them as a rehearsal or training for what came later in real life.

"There is one other thing... I'm not quite sure how to put it... There's some crossover occurring; my reality now has seemed to have taken on some dream-like characteristics also."

"What does that mean exactly? I'm a little bothered by the implications..."

"It means I'm having trouble clearly distinguishing the boundary between dream and reality. The synthetic dreams seem intensely real, and my real life sometimes seems more dream-like and foggy."

"Can you give me an example where real life seems dream-like?"

"Well, right now, for example; this session with you. How can I tell for sure that you are real and not some emulation by Carole? She's so skilled at doing this! I seem to be losing my reference points and certainty. It's all very disorienting, and it makes me very uncomfortable to think that I may be living in a larger meta-dream that includes both you *and* my synthetic dreams."

"Let's work with the simplest interpretation first. Can you grant me my reality for the moment?"

"I guess I have to for practical purposes."

"Can you call up this synthetic dream at will?"

"Yes, and I can even call up each of the individual dream dates we had later. These gradually ended in the dream fourth quarter, I think about April. We did not communicate as much after that. All sorts of things happened near that last quarter of our senior year, real or dreamed."

"So, what happened in the 'real' world?"

"Of course, all the stuff around applying to colleges, campus visits, the science fair, our final exams, and the math competition. There was little time for anything else. You must remember that I was a science nerd, and I participated in all these things. In the real world, I met a girl (Julie) at the science fair who was also a science nerd (Biology major). She latched onto me at one point, and we toured the science fair together, arm in arm. As I think back, I now realize with some sadness and regret, that she was a major missed opportunity for an actual relationship in high school. I never even thought to get her phone number or ask her out after that."

"And then in the dream world?"

"After establishing the initial series of dreams, the librarian suggested another dream based on my 10th high school class reunion, which I never actually attended."

"How did that work?"

"The 10th reunion caught me still in graduate school, so of course, I was not interested in attending some stupid high school reunion and did not. Nevertheless, the librarian suggested that I attend a dream 10th reunion. It seems that dream-Carol may have betrayed me by spreading some rumors about my oral prowess among her classmates, and there were several of her classmates *very* interested in meeting me at the reunion. So much so, that they would be trolling the crowd using mohair sweaters as a come on, hoping to snag at least one date with me; somehow it fit with the seventies theme of the reunion. Note that dream-Carol did *not* attend, and I felt hurt and rejected by her absence."

"That's interesting. This was a new rejection coming now after your rejection by your ex-wife. Comments?"

"I think it was a stress test for my symbiont to evaluate how I might treat a real rejection by Carol, should I ever meet her in reality."

"Did she really put it in those terms?"

"Oh, yes, quite explicitly. She basically explained that she would not connect me with Carol unless she thought I could handle a possible rejection."

"I see. Probably very wise of her. So, did one of these new predatory dream girls capture you as a paramour?"

"Strangely, no. Julie, the biology major I mentioned earlier, moved in on me very quickly, and rescued me from that fate. She explained what was happening, and quite explicitly told me about the rumors, and the predators. In a way, she *was* one of them since she was also wearing a mohair sweater."

"So, you then became her oral sex slave instead of belonging to Carol again?"

"Actually, no. The relationship was perhaps the most normal of any I had in that dream life. Yes, of course we toyed with my mohair fetish as an appetizer, and engaged in oral sex as it suited us, but these things did not dominate the relationship in the same way they did with dream-Carol."

"Am I to assume then that this sex sometimes involved erection, penetration and ejaculation for you?"

"Oh yes, all of that."

"That all sounds even better for you and somewhat contradicts the pure parasite hypothesis. What made you stop pursuing this second dream girl or her real-life equivalent?"

"My life intervened."

"And in your actual life?"

"I was already unhappily married to a rather distant woman who drifted farther and farther away from me as she got more and more religious. I wouldn't go down that road with her, and she attended a lot of religious classes by herself. Maybe 'normal' had started to lose its appeal."

"What exactly was it that started to lose its appeal?"

"Practically everything about the marriage. Sex, daily interactions, stagnation. No magic left. And then all the bickering about religion and my seeming lack of religious feelings."

"Tell me more about your marriage. How did you meet your wife?"

"We met as students at the university. We were not taking the same classes or anything but met at a party given by one of my university friends from the department. Somehow, we seemed to hit it off that one time and made out hot and heavy when we were alone. This was extremely unusual for me, making a sexual connection like that so quickly. At that point in my life especially, I was socially very awkward, and barely knew how to approach a woman I found attractive. We dated extensively afterward. Neither one of us had a lot of time to devote to dating, or at least to searching for someone to date. We quickly became used to being together, and pragmatically decided on marriage to avoid the split coming at graduation. Not a lot of passion was involved after a few months of dating, but we became very friendly and enjoyed the relief of sex with each other. She was a business major, and had a rather utilitarian view of marriage, sex and relationships. Longer term, it didn't look like I was going to enhance her career very much if I continued as an academic. What was left of passion and friendliness began cooling off very abruptly after our marriage when she went off on her religious tangent. This was sort of a hyper-religious thing, which was kind of odd for a pragmatic business major, except that this was 'name it and claim it' evangelical stuff, which I suppose might have appealed to someone striving for advancement by any means available."

"How long did this estrangement take?"

"Over the course of a year or so we separated, and then finally divorced, all on her initiative. She had found a great job, no doubt with the help of Jesus, and moved away while I was just finishing graduate school at the University with my doctorate and was considering a year-long post-doc position at Purdue. She did not come with me to Purdue and went off on her own. After that post-doc stint ran out, I came back again for a post-doctoral University position with my graduate professor. It seemed at first a dead end staying at my university as a post-doc, but it was stable during a period when I needed stability. My research supervisor suddenly and quite unexpectedly died after I took this temporary job, and this made me uniquely eligible to perform at least some of his departmental duties, which included management of the herbarium, and to compete for his vacant chair, which was apparently quite a difficult position to fill. I was very fortunate to have obtained some major grants that permitted field work and publications early in my career, and this, no doubt, gave me a significant advantage in this competition. It was only after my starting as an assistant professor that the divorce was finalized.

I haven't communicated with Beverly in many years. I'm glad children weren't caught in the middle of our feud. I guess that near disaster has colored my view on having children in a tenuous relationship."

"What do you imagine would have happened had your wife *not* decided to divorce you?"

"A fair question, but I'm not exactly sure what I would have done if we had just separated. I think the separation would have been enough of a trigger for me to sue for divorce eventually, but without it we might have stayed tied to one another for much longer and made ourselves miserable even from a distance. In retrospect, the divorce was probably a good thing, and I don't have any ill-will toward Beverly anymore."

"I'm interested in how all these synthetic dreams or patterns of behavior affect your real life now. Were these merely an obsession, or did you change your approach to life afterwards?"

"That's an interesting question, but the answer is not very simple. I had to question the librarian extensively before I obtained a somewhat satisfactory answer. She evidently had the power to interact with the world in several unexpected ways.

"I must preface this explanation with the statement that I visited the librarian many times during the course of events that I described to you in summary about my constructed dreams. It might seem odd, but the language she used to describe these dreams was always some mathematical analogy: these were somehow mental tangent spaces that she had attached to my life line.

"Carole evidently has by now a far deeper understanding of mathematics than I, and she has taken up complex analysis as sort of a hobby. She says complex numbers are a beautiful metaphor for humans entangled with a symbiont, especially considering the Cauchy-Riemann equations. Another expression she used for these vivid constructed dreams was 'elsewhen', I guess by analogy to Minkowski space, where there are regions of space-time ('elsewhere') not accessible because of the finite speed of light. At any rate, these emulated bits of elsewhen-reality had contact with my true reality at certain times and places and were closely similar to what I would have done under certain circumstances. I could explore the neighborhood of these points of contact in an imaginary time but could not depart from the anchoring point by more than a day or so. I now had, in effect, a sequence of these tangent spaces within me as vivid dream memories; first Carol, the girl of my obsession with slight variations over many dates, and second, Julie, the girl who rescued me at the fictional 10th class reunion."

"One comment on your anima development, Carole is now becoming competent in various areas of life, and in some areas perhaps much more competent than you. This is quite a step up from simply being an object of desire. She's maturing rapidly as she learns new things. She may also be manipulating you now in some new ways not yet fully clear. She's already admitted that she's explicitly using your response to her erotic spell to make you more comfortable about sharing your innermost secrets with her. These synthetic dreams (experimental scenarios really) must be revealing a lot to her about your sexual responses. You have handed her a huge amount of power over you."

"Yes, I think you're correct about the power; however, I have discussed all this with Carole, and she asserts that this is my half of a trust building exercise. She has been quite open with me about her own vulnerabilities and passions. Anyway, of more concern to me at the time was the gradual realization that now my real life was being subtly affected by the constructed dreams in ways that were hard to pin down at first. The first signs of this merging occurred when the constructed dreams started to intersect with reality in the real present. At this point, I really did attend my 20th high school class reunion and found that Carole (I'm pretty sure) had subtly suggested some things about me via certain computer websites. Apparently, she can access the internet through me but without my knowledge by shutting off my conscious mind and controlling my keyboard entries. I have no idea of exactly which rumors she spread; however, they must have been akin to those that afflicted my fictional 10th class reunion. I could figure out a little of what was going on by revisiting those 'frequently visited sites' that she had neglected to conceal. I suspected that she was the one who planted the lengthy comments about my sexual behavior by FemDommeChick."

"Did you view this as sabotage, a betrayal, or something else? In a way she was setting you up to be objectified by Carol. This shutting off your conscious mind sounds really dangerous."

"I agree this could have been potentially dangerous. I wasn't sure exactly what she was up to with these rumors, but I had given her tacit approval to help me connect with Carol who was by then a very dominant woman. So, I guess at that point, I was just waiting to see what would happen and how she would do it. I was worried, but also very intrigued. Here again it was difficult for me to believe this was real, and not just another emulation."

"Did you independently do any investigation of Carol to see if she was really as dangerous as your symbiont implied?"

"Well, yes. Of course, I was curious just what I might be getting into with Carol. I visited her website, fiercelyfeminine.com, extensively, and read a lot of the letters, her responses and her blog postings."

"And?"

"It was pretty much as Carole stated that she was now a very dominant woman, possibly a formidable predator, and apparently very much a part of an online B&D community. She was serving as sort of an advice columnist primarily for women involved in this type of relationship with submissive partners. There were also various ads for local events where dominants and submissives could check each other out before starting serious relationships. At any rate, I read it all to get a sense of what Carol might be like in person. I knew full well that I was not at all part of this community and would be entering a world totally alien to my background. The real question was how I could present my nearly normal, pedestrian self to Carol, and not be immediately told to get lost! Perhaps my symbiont was purposely presenting me as potential prey so that she would show up to meet me."

"How did this lifestyle strike you then? Did it appeal a little or a lot?"

"I found parts of it pretty erotically stimulating, at least as fantasy. I had no idea what I would feel in a real situation being dominated by Carol but reading about it was very arousing."

"So, it intrigued you to think about submitting to her erotic wishes?"

"Yes, at some level, it certainly did."

"From what you've said about dream Carol, would you enjoy having the real Carol demand cunnilingus from you?"

"Very much so."

"And beyond that? What would you say the next stage of goddess worship should be?"

"Perhaps even before the cunnilingus some sweater and breast kissing would occur, at least if she would tolerate my mohair fetish."

"Do you think she will?"

"I'm not sure what she thinks of fetish play. If she sometimes uses such things to ensnare her sex slaves perhaps it will happen. She seems very much aware of her feminine powers to allure, so I don't doubt that she would use whatever might give her the advantage. In her advice to other dominant women, she certainly discusses how to manipulate slaves using their various fetishes. Apparently, gender as a performance can require proper costumes as well as a properly crafted script."

"And after those two things, what is the next step?

"I'm not really sure, but I suppose some other sorts of body worship, then perhaps some ritual acts of extreme submission. She describes it all pretty graphically in her blogs."

"So, you think she might immediately try to enslave you into some sort of permanent and escalating sexual servitude?"

"Frankly that is Carole's plan."

"What? She's actually said that?

"She claims that it is actually a Judo move."

"Meaning what?"

"That initially I must follow Carol's lead pretty closely so we can see where it's headed. My symbiont will then start to intervene and deflect some of the sexual momentum into her own procreation efforts."

"You *do* realize, don't you, that you're playing with real fire here, not just a dream? Carol's had years of practice luring certain susceptible men into this trap!"

"That's where the Judo part comes in. Carol will become infected with a symbiont, and he will start to interact with her."

"All this assumes that symbionts are real and not merely some manifestation of mental illness in you! Are you going to tell Carol about symbionts and her supposed risk?"

"Of course, that's part of the plan."

"And she's supposed to believe any of this?"

"No, of course not. That's also part of the plan."

"Would you tell your regular physician first if you were going to jump off a cliff?"

"I'm not sure that metaphor is apt in this situation. Any danger here is much more reversible."

"I hope for your sake that it is! Are you at all aware of how Carol might try to manipulate your testosterone levels to keep you in a permanent state of courtship to win her favor and to maintain you as her sex slave?"

"Yes, Carole the librarian has explained to me how this sometimes works with orgasm denial and cock locking, etc. in a female led relationship; however, she has pointed out that *she* will be the one controlling my testosterone levels during our reproductive phase, and she will keep me healthy, but still very attentive and interested in Carol."

"So, what are you trying to achieve with Carol, if not simply to become her slave?"

"We are trying to induce Carol into making a space for us in her world."

"Us? So, you're trying to reform her with your symbiont's help?"

"No, not at all. We're trying to enlarge her scope; to add something new, not take away."

"So, what sort of 'space in her world' are you trying to make?"

"Something that will preserve us both, but that will allow us to cooperate as equals."

REALITY RULES

I could not believe how easily he had wandered into my
trap, and how much he had revealed. Making him my love
slave was going to be deliciously wicked…! But there was
something else going on beneath that naïve innocence that
put me on my guard…he was trying to get into my head!

Lady Carol, *Beloved Incubus*, (First Impressions)

My attendance at the 20th Reunion was actually more of a nightmare at first than a dream fulfillment. The event started with an ice breaker event in which we gathered in the auditorium for a nostalgic presentation of our high school days. I managed to find a vacant seat next to Carol, who seemed to be alone in the center of the auditorium surrounded by vacant seats, like a blank spot in a petri dish. It certainly made me wonder what sort of pariah she had become to her fellow classmates. She was still strikingly beautiful and still gave me goose bumps. "Hair as black and straight as lonely streets are", as the song went. I asked her if she was saving seats for someone, but she just smiled slightly and motioned for me to sit down next to her. This was so un-nerving that were I not so determined to meet her for real this time, it nearly would have scared me off. What had Carole told her! Nevertheless, I sat by her and nervously introduced myself, mentioning that I did actually remember her, and had always wanted to meet her.

"Well, now you finally have," she said. "Are you ready for me, Richard? Fair warning, I might be quite different from what you think."

Various photos from our senior year were displayed along with "now" photos highlighting some present-day accomplishments. The selected few were then asked to stand up and were spot-lighted so the audience could pick them out of the crowd. These highlights were chosen to be as embarrassing as possible. Carol was shown receiving a creative writing award in high school and then more recently on a feminist picket line for equal pay. And then, someone spiteful had thrown in a screen shot from Lady Carol's Fiercely Feminine website, which was lurid enough to draw a few gasps from the audience. Despite that, Carol stood up proudly and turned her fierce judgmental gaze upon the audience, who quieted down remarkably quickly. I had to admire that strength of hers, which allowed her to stare them down even as they tried to humiliate her.

A lot of the nerds were shown in their nerdiest glory, standing proudly by their science fair projects. I was one of those. This was followed by some headlines and newspaper photos of me as a rather lean and fit looking Professor Richard Douglas returning from his successful expedition on the Amazon. I stood up to be spot lighted, and then they dropped the bomb. "We girls have been hearing some VERY interesting rumors about Richard's special talents in the love-making department. Uh, oh Professor, better not let Lady Carol know!" I turned very red and quickly sank down in my seat. Carol let a slightly amused smile flash across her face over my reaction and patted me consolingly on my arm. Someone had obviously wanted us to sit together, and now we both realized it. The remaining exposés went by quickly, but ours were still ringing in our ears as the lights went up, and people started to head out to the next event of the reunion.

Carol whispered that we never really belonged here. I had to agree, offering that my high school days had been lonely and difficult. Following the "ice breaker" during which our ice had been thoroughly and irreversibly broken, Carol suggested we cut out the rest and just go somewhere to talk; she knew a good place. We wound up at a quiet restaurant that had a few discreet private areas for customers who didn't want to be on display. We'd already had quite enough public exposure for the evening. After a few drinks our talk became quite relaxed, but very animated.

Carol asked a lot of questions about my Amazon expedition and seemed unusually knowledgeable about the fragile situation of the various tropical biomes. She appeared also quite fascinated by my stories about old Yayael and the Great Garden. She teased me a little about Yayael as if he were like Don Juan in Castaneda's fraudulent books, and seemed delighted when she provoked a strong negative reaction from me about bullshit pseudoscience and new age woo in general. Carol then divulged that at university, she had studied a lot of anthropology and psychology before finally settling on her ultimate major in the English department. She was very fond of the "magic realist" school of South American literature and was trying to craft something like that in her fiction currently. It turned out that we also shared a fondness for the works of Joyce and Beckett plus several other eclectic modern authors like Fowles and Pynchon, even harder to place in any particular genre.

For some unknown reason, we then digressed into a discussion of books written on single pieces of paper. Of course, many examples existed in the Bible of "books" probably written on single scrolls. Carol offered up the irony that de Sade's psycho-sexual narrative, *The One Hundred and Twenty Days of Sodom*, was also written on a single piece of paper in a minute script and secreted into a hiding place inside his cell in the Bastille. I seemed to recall that the manuscript for *On the Road* was typed out linearly by Kerouac on a roll of paper fed into his typewriter so the flow of ideas was uninterrupted by changing paper. And then there were the circular novels such as *Finnegans Wake*, perhaps more correctly described as a cylindrical manuscript, but with so many layers of possible interpretation at multiple points throughout so that you really couldn't step into that river twice. We knew of novels like *Hopscotch*, Cortázar's intricate nonlinear novel that can fold back on itself in multiple ways. Offhand we knew of no novels actually written as Möbius strips, although we agreed we'd have to check out Rucker's work more thoroughly to be absolutely certain of their nonexistence. It also depended on how one defined "upside down" when one came back to the arbitrary beginning. Perhaps a Moran gradually morphs into a Molloy at the end/beginning.

I asked Carol more about her own writing projects (she had several going) and wondered how she managed to support herself with her writing. I understood that this was one of the more difficult careers to get started. Did she also write some non-fiction articles, etc.? Yes, she did a few things like that to help fill in, but her subscription website was by far the bigger source of income that evidently gave her time to devote to writing, which was not yet paying its way. I had given some thought to creating a website at the university to highlight some of the work I did with plants from the expedition and wondered whether she knew anyone with the expertise to set-up and maintain a website for me. It turned out, yes, she did know a good website designer that I might contact. Expensive? Probably, but she didn't know how expensive; he does it free for Lady Carol in return for certain considerations. Had I looked at his work on her website? Well, yes, I admitted; it seemed to be skillfully put together to attract attention of a sort. I wasn't altogether sure what that sort was.

"Perhaps you're that sort," she said. "It's pretty obvious what sort I am. You should go ahead and sign-up for a year's subscription and find out about you. It's mostly a dating website these days."

The elephant in the room was that interesting question about how we had both wound up sitting together in the center of the auditorium where neither of us could run for the exits without stumbling over dozens of people on the way out. I ventured that someone had clearly been messing with me with all the email rumors and that I wasn't sure who that might have been. Perhaps, Beverly, my ex-wife, had been more vengeful than I had realized, I lied. Carol admitted that she had seen some of the emails and rumors about me online. I asked if she still had them on her computer because I had not received them directly; but no, unfortunately, she had not saved them; a pity, otherwise we might have traced their origin. Anyway, I continued, the auditorium had few seats left when I arrived, and, since I did recognize Carol, I sat there, even though I hardly knew her from classes. She pondered that in silence, so I also confessed that I also had quite a crush on her in high school, but never had the nerve to call her.

"Oh," she said, "I wish you *had* called me. I was really lonesome in high school; I didn't even attend the senior prom."

This I found hard to believe.

"You are so pretty, and dressed so sexy, I couldn't help but fall for you! But I was buried in my studies... and probably a little scared of you."

"What was so sexy about the way I dressed?"

"Oh, that purple mohair sweater you often wore. That drove me crazy."

"Aha!" She said, "A mohair fetish; now that's an interesting little bit of leverage to offer up to a predatory girl like me! But you just wouldn't listen to their warning about not letting Lady Carol know, would you? How much of your libido got wasted on that obsession? Did you jerk off too much and lose all your courage?"

Something about Carol's intensity made me uneasy; this seemed to be Lady Carol revealing her predatory self. Silence seemed the best move.

"Don't I give you an erection now," She asked, with an exaggerated pout, "even without that sweater?"

"Well, yes," I had to admit. "You still do."

"Richard!" She said with a wry smile. "I'm messing with you a bit here, because I don't really believe this whole accidentally-sitting-together thing you're spinning out. What's really going on here?"

"The whole truth will sound much stranger," I warned her.

"Out with it!"

"OK. There *is* someone else behind all this, probably. Her name is Carole (with an e), and she sort of advises me on my social life - I should mention she is trying for me just to have a social life after my divorce. She's trying to work with my mess of a life as it currently is and to improve it."

"What? Some sort of a life counselor?"

"You might say that, but here's where it gets a bit weird."

"How weird, exactly?"

"Carole is not a person exactly, at least in the usual sense. She was given to me by Yayael, and apparently came back with me from the Amazon."

"Um..., Richard, you remember your recent little rant about bullshit pseudoscience and new age woo in general? This sounds awfully close to new age woo."

"I know."

"So, you're saying that this Carole, not exactly a person, managed to set this all up to throw us together? … Almost to offer you up to me as a potential sex slave?"

"I presume so, but I don't have all the details. It would have her fingerprints all over it, so to speak, if she had fingers of her own."

"Somebody contrived to get me to attend the reunion; that I do believe. Ordinarily I couldn't care less about such things because I hated high school and most of the people I knew from school except for a few teachers. There were anonymous hints that I would meet someone here whom I might find interesting. I sort of guessed that it might be you when you dared to sit in one of those empty seats near me, the class pariah."

"I guess that pretty much explains *that* little anomaly. I couldn't imagine why you would ever attend."

"So, how do you get in touch with this Carole?"

"She lives inside my head and models her image after you. I usually meet her in dreams."

[Long awkward silence... with feigned dropped jaw and funny look implying WTF!]

"Wait! Yes, I know how that sounds. You're thinking I must be a head-case and an on-line stalker to boot. However, before you run screaming from the restaurant, here is what Carole told me about herself. She claims to be a symbiont, a virally organized version of my microbial inhabitants that has achieved consciousness. I picked her up as an infection while gathering and handling the plants from my expedition. I know this all sounds bat-shit crazy and it has made me desperate enough to see a psychiatrist who has been helping me figure out what's going on."

"Why has it modeled itself after me...? How can it even be female?"

"What I told you about my high school crush on you was true. Carole has access to all my thoughts so she knew about that and is using it to manipulate me into helping her. She presents as female because evidently a male brain has lots of female personality traits left over and largely idle or unexpressed; Jung would call it an anima. She picks up that portion for her use when she communicates with me."

"What is she trying to make you do?"

"Spread her infection outside the tropics."

"Richard, this is truly the weirdest pick-up line anyone has ever used to hit on me. You deserve some sort of award for creative science fiction bullshit..."

"In all honesty, I don't know quite what to make of all this myself. It doesn't feel like mental illness. I function pretty well day to day, teaching and so on. Nevertheless, if you find this too weird, just tell me to go away, and I won't bother you anymore. Real stalkers won't do that. I don't want to hurt you, and I especially don't want you to be afraid of me."

"This is so bizarre, I don't know what to do for once, but I won't leave just yet. I still can't imagine why this Carole chose me to revive your social life, as you put it. Most people find me a bit strange and possibly even dangerous if they're of the masculine persuasion. Maybe she knows you better than you know yourself?"

"She probably does know me disturbingly well by now. Anyway, thank you for being patient. What should I do? I'd really like to talk to you some more... Are you at all interested?"

"What if... OK, don't get your hopes up too high, Professor Bug-Nutty, but what if you let me pick your brains on all this stuff for a story. It's weird, but very creative and interesting. Other than that, we do seem to share a lot of interests, and I have a pretty high tolerance for eccentricity that could work in your favor. And it seems to me that since you've apparently been using me as your personal erotic entertainment for years, perhaps you should allow me to use you that way for a change. Fair enough?"

"I'm more than happy to talk to you about my expedition and my recent experiences with Carole. Carole might even want to communicate directly with you. She also finds you fascinating. I'm a little uncertain about being *used* for erotic entertainment. Is that part negotiable?"

"How about *not* negotiable, and you'll do whatever I say?"

"And if I have trouble doing that?"

"Well then maybe it's all over at that point. You're not against my having a little erotic fun, are you? You might even enjoy it."

"OK. But there's still one thing for you to consider seriously. If it turns out I'm telling you the truth, weird and unlikely though it may seem to you right now, there is a substantial risk that you will become infected with a symbiont of your own. Are you willing to take that chance? It is a life-changing event; I can assure you of that."

Carol smiled enigmatically or perhaps a little indulgently: "I'm willing to take a few risks if you are."

◆◆◆◆◆

After the reunion, I kept getting email messages inquiring about "special treatments" and what a girl had to do to qualify for such treatment. Some claimed that they needed a good tongue lashing whenever they were naughty, and that they were naughty a lot. Apparently, the vague rumors tied to me were not at all specific and were more along the lines of so and so went out with me and after a while she became addicted to getting the "special treatment", and OMG, why weren't more men like that. The treatment was unspecified, but it produced sexual bliss, lingering satisfaction and a yearning for more, and was unequaled by any previous experience she had ever had. Those who had experienced this bliss were only reluctantly drawn out to describe their experiences. (Rightly so, I thought since none of them had ever dated me.) Gradually, a few figured out that the alumni association had email addresses and locations for all alumni, and so a very personal online, early bombardment began even on my university account. I would filter out many of the inquiries if they were complete unknowns; my high school yearbook helped some with this task. Despite the years and my social isolation in high school, there were still some needy ones that I knew well enough to avoid forevermore. Sometimes I responded, sometimes not. I kept some of the better ones, in case things didn't work out with Carol.

Carol and I finally did arrange a date for some "erotic fun", which was somewhat like my first constructed dream except that it all wound up at Carol's townhouse rather than at her parents' house. Perhaps I was being a little too formal for this first date, but I asked her out for dinner at a good restaurant, and I showed up dressed in a suit and tie. She was dressed mainly in black, rather edgy Goth-looking clothes with a lot of leather. It felt very high school, and Carol, I'm sure, noticed my steadily increasing discomfort with our mismatch when we entered the restaurant. It was socially 'interesting', but only insofar as Lady Carol was noticed by those around us, and their whispered comments began flying rudely back and forth even as we ordered. I was clearly in over my head, and Lady Carol played it for all it was worth in front of her audience. While she didn't go so far as to drag me from the restaurant by my tie, she was clearly in charge of me, and a few nearby older female diners actually cautioned me to "Watch yourself, young man!" After an eternity, we exited and went back to her place rather quickly after dinner.

Carol's townhouse, I had learned, was in a gated community that provided a small measure of protection from certain persons (usually male) obsessed with Lady Carol and also from certain other persons made crazy simply by the thought of this she-devil and her insult to their religion by her mere existence. Anyway, I was allowed entry to her world and to her townhouse with this first date.

You can tell a lot about people by the books they keep, and Carol had an impressive library consisting of her college books and all her favorite fiction. I wished that I had more time then to examine all her book collection, but I had only a short time over drinks when she initially showed me around her lair. She seemed more intent on shocking or scaring me by showing me her secret play room with its special furniture devoted to disciplining certain types of clients and to enabling certain erotic practices. It kind of reminded me of joining a gym and having one of the trainers tour me around the various items of equipment, answering my questions about them, and demonstrating their proper use. This intimidation accomplished, we soon moved on to other activities in her living room.

After we returned to the living room, she invited me to shed all my clothes and come sit with her on the couch while she plied me with more alcohol. Of course, that fabulous purple mohair sweater had long since disappeared from her adult wardrobe, but it still cast its shadow over the evening since it had already been mentioned to Lady Carol, and Lady Carol never forgets.

We started on her living room couch with some rather intense and probing conversation about my opinion of her appearance in high school, and what exactly turned me on about it. This, embarrassingly, required a thorough discussion of my various fetishes and what exactly they symbolized for me. She made me admit finally that her mohair sweater always made me think of her pussy and caused me an intense desire to go down on her whenever I saw her wearing it.

"Well, that's a good start," she said. "Do you think it might make you very submissive?"

"Possibly."

"What would happen if you actually saw my pussy?"

She was holding my penis and must have felt it start to stiffen as she said this.

"I think I'd beg to go down on you then and kiss it."

"Well then suppose you just pull my panties down and take a little look, just so we can see what actually happens and whether I like it."

She let me loose long enough to undress her below the waist and unveil her bush.

"Perhaps you should kiss it a bit, and feel my soft hair against your face..."

This I did very worshipfully and breathed in her musky scent.

"That's the way. Any thoughts, Professor?"

"I'd like a taste if you'd let me..."

"I think you may run your tongue up and down inside me a couple times and then stop."

I followed this instruction to the letter.

"That's very good. How do you like my taste?"

"It's quite wonderful. May I have some more?"

"As long as you obey my commands exactly, you may have a lot more, for the whole evening if it's done well."

This invitation was followed by a very long leisurely guided session of cunnilingus that evidently met with her approval since it culminated in a very vocal orgasm. I noticed during this session that she had a series of capital letters in several alphabets rather ornately tattooed across her belly. I later found out that these were her favorite letters for lovers to use as patterns while stimulating her orally.

"Perhaps some of those rumors about you had a germ of truth," she said. "Well, germs of *something* anyway," she added with a smile, "and you do seem to have some modest erotic potential and a bit of talent. Perhaps you're not so boringly normal after all if the right person were available to lead you astray! It might be fun to find out."

Faint praise perhaps, but I was glad I was not considered hopelessly inept. She seemed to be accepting me, on probation at least, as an occasional date, and perhaps something more. When I finished, I was still hard and throbbing, but she allowed me no relief yet. Perhaps she was going to require my full attention again later.

Afterward, I was invited back up on the couch, and she resumed fondling and teasing my erection, while I tried with some difficulty to focus on explaining what I thought was occurring with symbionts, and to describe some of the health and life span benefits which evidently came with the partnership. She asked many questions about symbionts and what I knew of their origins. The recovered youth aspects she found interesting. She had noted that I had aged very well in my twenty years since high school and didn't look all that "professorly" yet (i.e., fat, balding and pompous), although my pomposity had yet to be scrutinized much except for the inappropriate suit and tie I had worn to dinner. Of more direct interest to her was my obviously very sexual relationship with Carole, her symbiont imitator and a potential rival for my affections. She teased every last aspect of that relationship out of me, and when she was satisfied, she finally let me come on a tissue.

"Was there any discussion about 'safe words' etc. in your relationship at this point?"

"That was not discussed. I think any balking or refusal on my part would have ended things right there. Her expressed opinion that evening was that I should turn my sexuality and my body completely over to her to use as she pleased."

"That seems like a very risky level of trust to start with."

"It probably was, but she had started out slowly to see what could be done with me. I think she was a little intrigued dealing with such a green volunteer rather than a completely enthralled slave."

"Did you put it that way with her? That sounds a little bit like negotiating for a higher status than sex slave."

"I didn't dare negotiate, but I think Carole may have later given that assessment of me to Carol."

"Did you view that as a betrayal?"

"I doubt that it was. She has to live with me and wouldn't want me to be miserable. Carole was assessing Carol for me as well, so I think it was win-win, whatever she may have revealed about me. Carol was very honest and straight forward about sex and the things she liked. Frankly, at this point, despite having been married, I didn't even know that much about what I liked. Everything with Beverly seemed eventually to get reduced to simple dreary physical routine, and she felt embarrassed about being pleasured orally by me."

"Did it adversely affect your performance not having her wear that mohair sweater as a stimulant?"

"No, I had pretty much assumed it would be long gone."

"But, once again, the pleasure was mainly hers?"

"I didn't mind. I became completely lost in worshiping her body and trying to make her cry out with pleasure. Besides, this was just our first date, and it did end eventually with an orgasm for me."

"True. But notice how she used denial to wheedle extra information from you."

"Certainly, but that was partly why it was so sexy."

"Was erotic role-playing a frequent part of your interaction with Carol?"

"Somewhat, when she was in her Lady Carol mode. She would pose various possible scenarios to me and note my response."

"Did you make much use of the equipment in her play room on later dates?"

"We used a few things occasionally like her queening chair and more frequently the teasing post, but mostly she led me in free style sex play when it came time to get serious. Carol did explain what everything was used for and had me try it out. I think she was studying my reactions. Also, it was possible as we entered the reproductive phase that some of our candidates might prefer that I be constrained by some of the special equipment during sex."

"Was bondage part of the ritual when you used the equipment with Carol?"

"Except for the teasing post, no, not usually. To use the teasing post, the submitting person must be bound immobilized to the post in a particular way: kneeling with legs crossed and ankles bound behind the post; arms overhead, bound behind the post and then hoisted upward to stretch the torso. Everything was padded with thick cotton matting so it was not uncomfortable or cold to the flesh tied to or resting on the mats. Carol used this mostly for edging me. She became intimately familiar with my body's sexual limits and could easily keep me going for more than an hour before she let me come. This is where she questioned me and noted the erotic effect of the various scenarios she posed. A few of them that involved intimate body worship stirred me enough that we reenacted them, almost as if from a script that we composed together as pleasure partners.

"As for the queening chair, we occasionally used it for relaxation. Carol would put on some music, and we'd both go into sort of a meditative state for about as long as her music lasted. Usually, it ended with a big orgasm for Carol and sometimes one for me just by feeling hers against my face."

"So, did Carol become infected after this initial sexual contact?"

"Yes. She started noticing strange things in vivid dreams shortly after that encounter."

"I presume then that Carol must have contacted you rather quickly after becoming infected. What did she think was going on when that started?"

"This was ultimately more convincing than anything I could say about symbionts in the abstract. She noticed soon after our initial sex date that an unusual person was appearing repeatedly in her dreams and was attempting to talk to her. We did get together and discuss what these meant and what she might do to smooth the way for her symbiont.

In most ways, she seemed pleased and excited, rather than scared, that this turned out to be real. She felt that her writing would be even better as a result of this direct contact with something totally unexpected and almost magical. It probably seemed to her very much like her magic realism: a seamless transition from the mundane to the strange and inexplicable.

"While these changes were just starting to occur, we met out at the farmhouse, where I gave her a tour around the property and greenhouse, and then had another long discussion about symbionts over a few drinks. Carol was by then joyfully happy about what was happening and was very affectionate towards me. I enjoyed simply being with her during this time; she was fun and witty, and I felt we were bonding now in a very different way. The whole scene reminded me a little of the reaction some women get when they have tried very, very hard to get pregnant and finally succeeded despite some physiological obstacle. Suddenly new possibilities seemed open to her. While I couldn't imagine Carol wanting children, I supposed that this emerging symbiont might satisfy her need for something deep and mysterious that otherwise had been missing. I felt a little relieved and vindicated that this had happened and hoped for her sake that her symbiont proved to be both kind and wise, as well as fulfilling some of those inner needs. She deserved that much just for allowing me to be this close to her despite my social clumsiness and our crazy initial meeting.

The remainder of the evening was spent just sitting closely together on the couch and sharing a few drinks and a few thoughts on how this was working out. There was a lot of kidding around about our odd relationship and a lot of laughs about my behavior on our dinner date. She thought it was really pretty sexy that Carole had been training me specifically to adapt to her sexual needs and was starting to think Carole might be more of an ally than a rival. We then discussed the general notion of dream-Carol and the various constructed dreams that had been used in this training process. During these talks, I was starting to notice some big differences between the very private Carol and the very public image of Lady Carol."

"What differences might those be?"

"Carol seemed more inclined to talk about a whole range of things and seemed more interested in finding out about me generally. I was enjoying my time with her immensely and was even starting to learn a little more about her past. Lady Carol seemed unrelentingly sexual and more oriented toward finding and exploiting every weakness she could find in me. Lady Carol was the one with whom I still couldn't quite hold eye-contact. Carol was able to flip back and forth between those poles of behavior with little warning, which was very disconcerting at first. Sometimes she used such a rapid change for humorous effect, sometimes just to throw me off balance if I became too 'uppity' or 'dickish', but most often to initiate some new erotic scenario in which she would overpower me with her white-hot sexuality."

"Were just the dreams involved in your training?"

"This period before the infection was well established in Carol was something like boot camp for a sexually submissive male. Carol took over the role of instructor and showed me rather gently the full range of things that were acted out in little role play scenarios by some of her clients. It was not that she demanded that I necessarily do certain things in our relationship, but she felt I should at least know what commonly goes on and not embarrass her by my ignorance when others of her dominant inclination were present. I'm sure she also paid close attention to what turned me on, and what didn't. The teasing post was her diagnostic tool, so she said, for finding out what sort of fun she could have with me. It was not just the touching, but also the various sexy things wetly whispered into my ear, that were used to explore my limits.

"Our next major sexual encounter was delayed for two months. I suspect the delay before this date was a kind of induction or incubation period during which the infection became well established in her and had started to alter her physiology. By this I mean that all her responses to sex play thereafter, became gradually enhanced, almost to the point of nymphomania. She became much more demanding, and our dates after that became almost daily as her need ramped up. Two things became clear very quickly. First, it would be nearly impossible for any one person to satisfy her magnified urges. Second, she became obsessed with the notion that my modest talents and services should be shared with her friends. This last obsession seemed to run directly counter to the usual exclusivity which most women would require of their lovers at this point.

"By this third sex date, our love-making ceremony already included explicit breast sucking and manipulation to the point of orgasm. This surprised me since it seemed well beyond the physiological capabilities of most normal women. She seemed to exude a few drops of a liquid from her nipples, which she referred to as her 'witch's milk,' and which had a pleasant though slightly bitter taste. Carol mentioned once that she never had let clients touch her breasts that way before because it made it so much harder to keep her mental distance from them, but she also reassured me that I was officially neither a client nor a slave. Just what I was exactly, was still very unclear, perhaps now just some kind of special experiment, or an art work in progress.

"Next, of course, I provided the usual prolonged session of cunnilingus, which led to an explosive orgasm for her and a tight spasmodic clamping of my head between her thighs. How long this would take and the particular styles of oral stimulation for the evening would vary with each session according to her explicit wishes.

"If I still desired to perform more body worship, she suggested that I might try gently kissing and caressing her bottom in various ways just to see what happened. This would 'finish her off,' if it were successful and culminated in orgasm. This I had never done before or even imagined, particularly the licking part, so I needed some coaching and encouragement; nevertheless, her response to it was ecstatic and very vocal. The first several times I experienced a few twinges and blushes of humiliation for performing these undignified services but violating these societal taboos with her just made it seem even sexier, and after a while, it all seemed like normal sexy fun.

"Seemingly, she required *three* orgasms of these specific types to quiet her libido for a while, and I obediently complied with all her requests as well as I was able. When I talked all this over with Carole, who had actually been present and observing these sessions, I dropped in the nerdy humor that Carol's quantum of wantum never varied, which Carole thought was a hilarious combination of quantum mechanics with hypersexuality that had not occurred to her. Carole did apologize to me then for the alarming increase in Carol's libido. She mentioned something about Carol's symbiont, Legba, having difficulties stabilizing these initial adjustments, but she had every confidence that he would have everything under control shortly. I certainly hoped so.

"Some time after this session, Carole did indeed initiate some even more extensive contact with Carol. I'm not sure what all was discussed between them, but Carol did recognize the quote about the quantum of wantum, and said I was not being nice joking about her libido like that and I would kiss her royal Irish ass again soon. Carole was a little alarmed at first about this response to my humor (wasn't Carol mostly Italian anyway?), but I assured her that this was just intellectual foreplay, common among bookish university grads, and I explained the sources of the literary allusions. Carole then became very concerned that she couldn't sync directly with Carol to understand this newly discovered dimension of Carol's thinking, and that this inability made it much harder for her to nurture this relationship. I was of the opinion that she had nurtured quite enough, thank you, and that it should now be up to Carol and me. Carole conceded that I had been learning quite a bit, so maybe she could keep hands off for a while. She did find Carol very interesting and fun to communicate with, however, and this back-channel communication has continued. Carole keeps me informed in a general way about the topics discussed, and now and then gives me more specific little hints about what might please Carol. Perhaps these hints were also some kind of an experiment on Carole's part."

"This seems odd, how Carole is at once encouraging Carol to make use of you just like Lady Carol would as a dominatrix but is also subtly manipulating Carol to treat you differently than Lady Carol might. Even Legba seems to be having some difficulties adjusting her responses directly, despite his great advantage in that regard. What do you make of all this?"

"Obviously there have been some physiological startup problems that were a bit frightening, but it all seems now to be consistent with Carole's long-range plans for us to work as partners. She talked of us now being drawn into courtship mode as pleasure partners. While I couldn't negotiate, it seemed as if Carole *could* get away with it. Note, however, that Carole is not really putting limits on Carol or even on Lady Carol for that matter but is suggesting how certain elements of sex play might work for us more effectively as a feedback mechanism for this dynamic system involving attractive forces. Sort of an unconventional marriage counselor role..."

"Did you ever initiate some direct contact with Carol's symbiont? It would seem a little one-sided with Carole communicating with Carol directly and perhaps also with her symbiont."

"No, not at this time. I felt a little awkward about doing that. Anyway, he has not contacted me either."

"Are you in some ways a little jealous of Carol's symbiont?"

"Yes, I guess you're correct about that. That's certainly part of the awkwardness I feel, anyway. I also feel a little afraid that he might come between us and I will lose her."

"Yet there would be much about Carol that you could learn from him if only to assess how things are going from her point of view, and maybe to learn about where things are headed longer term."

"Probably so. I still hesitate. Maybe I'm also a little afraid of what I might find out."

"I would guess that you're *very* afraid of what you might find out. I suggest to you, however, that it would be better to know than to live an illusion. It's up to you, of course. Anyway, please continue with your narrative."

SHARING RICHARD

You have to accept the fact that part of the sizzle of sex comes from the danger of sex. You can be overpowered.

Camille Paglia

After some weeks of these triple orgasms, Carol's obsession turned much more towards offering me to her friends. She would contact her friends, and gradually coax one of them into a threesome situation where, she said, she would show her friend how a nicely trained male sex slave could enhance her life. Carol selected them with care and prepared me for each friend with little rehearsals on how to behave for each particular woman. A surprisingly large number of her friends were willing to try it. These were *not*, of course, any friends of hers from high school or college. Those were pretty much nonexistent. It turned out that at least two of them were women I knew a little bit from casual contact on campus dealing with various University administrators and their staffers. What made this even more embarrassing was that I had flirted with them a bit and was now to be offered up to them in the most humiliating way possible! Most of the rest of them were women attracted to some of the ideas on women in charge voiced on Lady Carol's website, but mainly ones who had never fully participated in the lifestyle."

"Were all these women made aware of the risk of infection?"

"Yes, but in a very indirect way. Carol did mention that they would acquire *something* from the session that would make them more formidable dominators if that lifestyle appealed to them. I was usually not present during these discussions, so I can't be more specific, but I don't think it was ever a full revelation specifically about an infection with a symbiont."

"You implied that most of the women involved were beginners in the B&D world. We're there any who were much more experienced?"

"There was one, in particular, who became very scarily aggressive towards me during a session when Carol had to leave her play room to answer the phone. Carol was only gone about 20 minutes, but this woman had to be physically restrained by Carol before she hurt me further. After that incident, Carol became much more careful about choosing candidates, and certainly never left me alone with any of them."

"How did you feel about that?"

"It was certainly frightening since I was completely naked, bound, and ball-gagged by the time Carol returned; but Carol did swoop in like a Valkyrie and intervene quickly before I was actually anally raped."

"That's horrible! Did you discuss this incident with Carol?"

"It really didn't seem necessary at the time; I knew full well that this was not anything that Carol had scripted. Carol was obviously enraged at her friend for taking such unwarranted liberties with me, and furiously screamed at her to leave the house immediately. She has not seen her since. Carol seemed nearly in tears when she untied me, and we sat together for a long time on the couch while we both recovered emotionally and caught our breaths. We had very tender sex at that point, which I hadn't experienced with Carol before.

"One consolation has been that Carol changed her attitude to me very markedly after that. In her Lady Carol mode, she could be quite threatening at times, for erotic effect, I guess, but that quieted down considerably after this incident. Carol is quite tall, about my height at nearly six feet, and even I was surprised how physically intimidating she could be when she was that furious. Carol works out regularly and is formidably strong; I don't think her friend would want to cross her that way ever again."

"By tender sex, what do you mean exactly?"

"I went down on her, but long before I finished, she pulled me up and had me penetrate her and slowly bring her to orgasm that way. This is not something I think she has done very often, if ever, and it seemed to surprise her how readily she reached orgasm."

"What do you think motivated her to do that?"

"That was hard to interpret. It was not something we had discussed or that she had requested before. Perhaps she was feeling remorse about what had happened or had almost happened and was trying to test that I was OK and undamaged. I had never seen her in such an emotional state before. I began to suspect that something traumatic must have happened to her at some point in her life; something so humiliating that she was not willing to discuss it, perhaps a rape of some sort. Carole didn't know either, but her suspicions were similar to mine."

"Did this incident change your attitude towards Carol as well?"

"My love for her didn't seem quite so hopeless after that. She definitely seemed to care about what happened to me."

"Were you concerned up to that point that she might not be the right woman for you?"

"Well, of course my sexual attraction to her was very strong, probably irrational and obsessive, and that extra energy carried me through some things I might not have tolerated from anyone else, but you're correct, I was concerned about a deeper basis for a more lasting relationship. I am strongly attracted by intelligence as well as physical beauty, and that was certainly there. Some extra emotional depth now seemed to be there as well, but perhaps also some dark secrets."

"So, you were now more optimistic?"

"Yes, I was encouraged, loved her all the more, and was a little less afraid of Lady Carol."

"Did you ever ask her why that incident affected her so strongly?"

"No. I felt it would come out eventually, and I didn't want to spoil things by pressing her to reveal things she found deeply hurtful and embarrassing."

"How would the more typical sessions proceed?"

"We would usually start with sitting together on a couch, with me in the middle. The two women would feel me up, and demand that I strip naked so they could see what would give me an erection. They would discuss various things that I *might* be commanded to do, and what sort of training was needed to make a man do such things skillfully. This would inevitably lead to my getting an erection, which would often delight Carol's friend to see such arousal at the mere thought of self-abasement and sexual servitude. Carol would then guide me through the services I would provide for her friend by means of erotic commands couched in very explicit and sometimes humiliating terms! Always, I had to say, 'yes, mistress!' and quickly obey, whatever the command. If her friend were new to the domination business, I usually created an enthusiast who wanted more and more. Carol then suggested to her friend that I would even lick her asshole on command and opined that this was the truest test of a compliant, well-trained sex slave. Her promotion of this rim job sealed the deal when she asked if her friend might just like to try a sample asshole licking. Of course, she would. In one variation of this, Carol made me wear mink mittens and caress her friend's bottom until she writhed with anticipation before I was commanded to start kissing it and caressing it with my tongue.

"After our very first threesome, when her friend had gone home, Carol and I basked in the afterglow of our reproductive success. After a little intermission that involved a bit of oral hygiene and a few drinks, she told me I owed her three big ones, and I complied, seemingly validating our partnership. We sat together for some time after that, and for the first time, she sucked on my erection to the point of ejaculation. This was so unexpected that I didn't know what to make of it, but I certainly wasn't complaining."

"Did symbiont Carole suggest the 'oral hygiene' step?"

"Actually, no; she said it wasn't really necessary. Carol and I, however, were more fastidious about such things, just out of deeply ingrained habit I suppose."

"We heard indirectly what our converts were up to after these initial encounters. Evidently, they were infected by these sessions, went on to pursue their own sexual predilections, and got busy propagating further as their symbionts emerged. I presume that whatever men they dated soon became reformatted into whatever compliant sex partners they needed within a few sessions. Occasionally, we would be revisited by these women, and had group sex that I speculate was microbial feedback to maintain the strain. I also learned at this time that these women, just like Carol, developed a symbiont that manifested as typically male not female; presumably, their brains had relatively unused portions of maleness, an 'animus', that would become the primary center of consciousness occupied by their symbiont."

"If I may interrupt your narrative for a moment, weren't there major health problems associated with all this *extremely* unsafe sex with multiple partners?"

"Strangely, no. Absolutely none. Of course, the order in which the various sexual acts were performed probably mattered a bit. I had my health checked out thoroughly for the usual venereal diseases by my physician soon after the first session, and multiple times thereafter. He was made aware in a general way that I had become sexually active with multiple partners. I speculate that both Carol's and my immune system had been made exceptionally robust, and that the usual risks from HIV and other venereal diseases were being eliminated by our symbionts at that point. The exact mechanism for this would truly be fascinating and valuable to comprehend! This effect was intimated early on by Carole, the Librarian, when she mentioned an immune system like a marsupial, by which I think she meant one not damped down anymore by the ancient retrovirus infections that ultimately made possible the evolution of placental mammals."

"Assuming I believe what you say about your immune system, how would I verify any of this? Have you been tested for super strong immune responses to various common pathogens?"

"Yes, that concerned me too at first. You could request a copy of those results from my regular physician if you like; I'll happily sign the release. He's already tested me for tropical diseases as per your earlier request. As for fully testing my immune responses for robustness, I'm not sure what all that would require to satisfy you. Think about that and give him some suggestions."

"You've outlined how Carol had her sexual responses radically modified by the process of infection. What about you? Did you notice any changes in your own physiology?"

"Yes, several. One was the ability to sustain an erection for the duration of our sexual activities. Second was some slight modification of my tongue into a longer, more penetrating organ with some erectile character. Sometimes Carol would suck on my tongue during foreplay. I found this exceedingly pleasurable, and it would inevitably lead me to want oral sex with her, sometimes very urgently. Gradually my tongue also became something of a gland, which yielded a few droplets of an aphrodisiac and narcotic mix upon stimulation, or so I was told later by Carole. Finally, I would say that any inhibition I might have had earlier about engaging in any of these extreme oral activities was completely gone, and that I would faithfully follow the lead of my female companion(s) of the moment. We didn't notice this immediately, but we both seemed to become surprisingly youthful and healthy compared to our peers, and this became more and more pronounced as our relationship went on."

"This gland in your tongue you mentioned, was it expressing some sort of date-rape drug? I have a similar question about the 'witch's milk' for Carol."

"Probably not a very exact analogy; this was consensual sex, after all. Perhaps more of an enhancement of sexual response or chemically induced pleasure bonding was produced. It might even have contained live virus, and I speculate that this fluid may well have been the main source of infection for any of my sexual partners. These substances from my lingual gland really should be chemically analyzed and also tested for their infectious potential."

"Were there any other changes noticed?"

"Yes, these were subtler, and emerged only weeks after our reproductive success. It became very obvious that we were both now sharing and editing my artificial dreams. I have no idea how this was accomplished, but it soon became known that my special synthetic dreams were shared and then somewhat modified according to Carol's erotic wishes. She now 'remembered' our first date in high school and how I had begged to go down on her when she wore that purple mohair sweater. She also played up how she wore it specifically to attract me, the sort of boy who could be shaped to her desires, and how excited she

71

was when I finally asked her out. It turned out that I had even asked her to take me to the senior prom as her escort."

"How did you feel about having your dream choices modified?"

"It all seemed to work and the various dream elements probably became truer to the real Carol. Carol now had a very similar artificial dream of her own about our imaginary high school meeting. It was as if we were both creating an artificial past for each other in our earlier lives. I'm not quite sure what all this was intended to do, but it made us both feel as if we had known each other intimately for a much longer time than we had in reality. I learned a great many things about Carol as she was in high school, both the way she *actually* was and her fantasies of how she wanted to be perceived by me now."

"It seems to me that your symbionts are rewriting your 'love maps'. Are you familiar with that term?"

"Yes, I believe you are referring to a brain module that contains our erotic preferences as learned very early in childhood, and perhaps refined with further experience. I would guess that you are correct, at least partially so. I concede that these maps are probably being *slightly* modified for both Carol and myself to focus on each other. Also, Carol and I are both aware of these refinements."

"Did you two maintain a special bond with all the newly infected females or were they left to their own devices?"

"There were indeed special bonds between us and a few of our newly infected females. Two in particular, Sylvie and Lisa, those with whom I had had some acquaintance at the University, became very close with Carol and me as a couple. After their infections developed and they synced with their symbionts, I noticed that their attitudes towards me shifted quite a bit; that is, they knew by then that I was not merely a well-trained sex slave but was intentionally spreading symbionts. A few of our later liaisons with these two women turned into quite affectionate, group sex that included me, but this also demonstrated how deeply connected they were to Carol. At one time or another, with both Sylvie and Lisa, I held and kissed Carol as she was being stimulated orally by one of these women, and Carol found this tremendously exciting. I must admit that seeing her in this state was tremendously exciting for me too, and that a part of her enjoyment must have been caused by my seeing her do it and accepting it."

"Did this group sex arise spontaneously, or did Carol intimate that it might occur?"

"In both instances, it arose spontaneously. Such things were quite new to me, but somehow in this context it seemed perfectly natural, and didn't freak me out. Carol commented that not everyone was suited to such an open relationship, and she was pleased with me."

"What was going on with respect to the passing on of the infection?"

"I think that somehow the microbial link between us all had to be maintained very strong by further sexual contact, and that this was somehow necessary for our continued reproductive success. Under Carole's strict control, many further reproductive relationships were formed from among Carol's circle of friends, but we had dozens of primary links that we maintained with regular sexual contacts during that first year. Carol also had many contacts that she maintained completely on her own. I think it was pretty clear to me by this time that Carol was actively bisexual and had been for some time."

"So, you were open to this aspect of her sexuality?"

"Yes, at least in principle, on a selective basis. I was a little uncertain of the possible effects on our own relationship. It became obvious that Carol had been having sexual relationships within our group of primary links, long before I became involved. At least I was now included."

"Have you noted any detrimental effects?"

"Not really, but she's not been entirely open about these relationships either. I worry a bit about the secrecy."

"Have you asked her about these relationships and what they mean to her?"

"No, I haven't had the nerve. Perhaps eventually Carole will find out for me."

"What ever happened to the Science Fair girl, Julie?"

"She eventually became one of my reproductive successes and was intended as one of my primary links, but one unconnected with Carol. She also became one of symbiont Carole's possible emulations in dreams."

"Was she fully informed about the risk of infection when she had sex with you?"

"Yes, but I don't think she believed a word of it. We used a condom at her insistence, but that wouldn't have provided any protection from a virus transmitted simply by kissing."

"Did she also get to edit your artificial dream about her at the dream reunion?"

"No, at least she hasn't yet done so. She has taken much longer to process what has happened to her. I think her background in biology made her very suspicious of what was occurring, much like it did for me. She has essentially broken off all contact with me. She doesn't answer my calls, and I am very concerned for her. I'm frankly uncertain about how to proceed without being accused of stalking her. Best to leave her alone to figure it out with the help of her symbiont, I concluded."

"Have you shared the details of this unsuccessful relationship with Carol?"

"No... I guess it didn't occur to me that a failed relationship would be of any interest to her, but you're right, she might even have given me helpful advice."

"It also might provide an opening for you to ask about Carol's same-sex relationships with your other primary links."

"I suppose that's possible."

"Did you ever ask Carole the librarian about what was going on during reproduction?"

"Yes, and that clarified what physiological changes were occurring and why. Everything seemed to be related to passing on an infection. Neither Carol nor I ever objected to any of this because most of it seemed so mutually beneficial."

"Please elaborate more on the beneficial parts? How so?"

"We both gradually acquired a more youthful appearance and physiology. This process was pretty well along for me, and it had now started for Carol. I questioned Carole about this, and she pointed out that it was necessary to be cautious not to attract undue attention with sudden youthfulness. Little touches of gray were added and maintained as necessary so we didn't stand out as extreme anomalies. Carol was advised to talk about Botox and facelifts and other beauty treatments to her aging friends, at least those outside her reproductive circle. I was supposed to talk about hitting the gym and using Rogaine. At least the former part was true. Carol was a work-out enthusiast, and we started going to the gym together. I find watching her working out extremely stimulating, and she has often had to remind me to keep on task and stop ogling!

"We could, however, see how this continued youthfulness would become a major problem later as we approached retirement age. The way society is currently set up, you can't continue being productive after a certain arbitrary age, no matter what your physical or mental condition, without some special dispensation from your employer. Carol was much better off than I, in that respect, since she could work independently as a writer on whatever she wanted."

"So, it was a fountain of youth! What physiological age will you wind up with? I have noticed some gradual changes in your appearance just over the course of our sessions."

"Thirty-ish, but with a few older looking external features as a cover. I'm not sure what the ultimate limits are on what a symbiont can do for the youthfulness of his or her host. Certainly, one would have to stay in an adult-sized body, but they can definitely manipulate certain bodily features and muscle mass."

"How many sex partners did each infected couple have over the course of a year?"

"I would estimate that each reproductive pair engaged in sex with a non-infected party about once a week on average. The success rate was apparently extremely high; I don't know firsthand of anyone *not* infected on a first date, except perhaps for Carol's hyper-aggressive friend. From this, one could roughly estimate the number of infected individuals produced in a year starting with a single reproductive pair; however, as I mentioned, these contacts did not always involve the pair of us."

"Did any of these women ever go on to have children in the usual way?"

"No, not that I'm aware. Several were past their child-bearing years anyway. There were a couple of miscarriages that I am aware of, that occurred at very early stages of pregnancy. (They were not pregnant by me; I hasten to add!) This may have been related to the infection and their souped-up immune systems."

"Didn't it bother you that the normal reproductive cycle of humans might have been hijacked?"

"It depends what you mean by 'bothered'. Certainly, I thought about it and discussed it with Carole. She insisted that the infection would ultimately be limited to a certain compatible fraction of the population. She was a little uncertain how big that fraction would be; Carole estimated perhaps 70 to 80% overall, give or take a wide margin locally. In view of our exponentially increasing world-wide population, I wasn't worried about humans dying out from low birthrates if that's what you mean. Carole also intimated that our major reproductive efforts via the human-to-human infection route would be limited to about a year and that the low fertility of women while infected could be modified by the symbionts, as needed, to allow live births to occur. I'm not sure who would have to approve of this modification or how it would be negotiated; perhaps a symbiont and host collaboration or perhaps two symbionts and two hosts."

"What did that mean to you?"

"I thought she meant that our intense physical liaisons with others would come to an end or be somehow limited to about a year. This was probably biologically ordained, but it was hard not to think of it as a term of our contract. By setting this limit I thought perhaps Carole would become more of a symbiont and less of an infection at this point. I think Carole was talking about her long game strategy to domesticate humans, to limit their reproduction, and ultimately to manage their reproduction more in line with the carrying capacity of the Earth. Live births could occur down the road when maybe a generation of symbiont-infected humans wanted children with each other. I think their symbionts would have to agree and to initiate those further modifications that would allow it to happen."

"Did Carole ever discuss with you the effect of the virus on non-compatible humans? Would it kill them or otherwise take them out of the gene pool?"

"That's a good question for Carole, but no we have not yet specifically discussed all the ramifications of that. From the biological or demographic standpoint, it would seem obviously necessary to shut down the breeding of the non-compatibles if Carole's aims were to limit and manage human reproduction. I am not yet certain that she even knows all the possible ways this could go wrong."

"One thing we haven't discussed so far is the sexual role fluidity occurring during this intense breeding cycle where you are being shared among women other than Carol. How do you feel about your role as breeder? It's kind of an odd insemination by infection."

"Beyond my simple exhaustion, I hadn't really thought about it in this situation exactly, but I see your point. A gender role reversal was what I agreed to with Carol. In Carol's case, my role was not so much to be a breeder as it was to submit to her sexual demands or invitations, whatever those might be. So that was a role reversal involving sexual power, no doubt made easier by my hopelessly passionate desire for Carol. For my symbiont, it was more as you say, to be an active breeder somewhat analogous to performing artificial insemination by infection but disguised as a submission to multiple women. For Carol, it was more acceptance of a typically female parental role in hosting a symbiont; however, as I later learned, she enjoyed 'impregnating' men with female symbionts; so that was sometimes a kind of role reversal for her. Actually, I once asked Carole how she viewed all this giving me away business, and she said that from her point of view, she was giving *herself* away with our help."

"Tell me more about your relationship with Carole, the librarian during this period."

"Carole seemed to emulate certain physical aspects of Carol during her dream manifestations but was still a distinct female entity quite different in personality and mannerisms from either Carol or Lady Carol. She, not Carol, was obviously most in control of this intense reproductive cycle of infection. She approved our partners and controlled our seduction of them into this lifestyle. We were in effect surrogate parents for our symbionts."

"It's not uncommon for female dominants to threaten to feminize their male subs by one means or another as an erotic ploy. Do you think Carol enjoyed that fantasy?"

"Perhaps. It is not something she has specifically explored with me, but as I mentioned earlier, she enjoyed impregnating men with female symbionts. That could play to a feminization fantasy."

"It *would* seem to alter the sexual dynamics in that direction when you contain a feminine symbiont inside you and that symbiont is manipulating your testosterone level."

"Now that you mention it, Carol did once remark on the Russian doll layers of our new psyches. I assume she was referring to alternating layers of sexuality. I think masculinity in its extreme, polarized forms is being mellowed down quite a bit by the active presence of a female symbiont. I'm not quite sure yet what happens to femininity."

"Did you ever have sex with symbiont Carole, as opposed to sex with dream-Carol?"

"Perhaps a distinction without much difference, but yes. Frankly she can be the most seductive female entity I've ever encountered in life or dreams. Her seduction of me began very much like my dream date with Carol, but within the library setting on her office couch. We talked very intimately about this new kind of relationship between a human and a symbiont, how it worked, and what it would entail. I'm sure she knew at once when I became deeply in love with her, as if my love for a symbiont made any biological sense at all, at least from the host's standpoint.

"Perhaps it *does* make biological sense since for you it may have induced some sort of unilateral disarmament allowing this parasite to move in permanently!"

"Perhaps, but she genuinely cared about my well-being - rational self-interest, I suppose - but beyond that, I felt back from her a different kind of gratitude and love, and even friendship, which is hard to describe. Many of our trust issues dissipated as we came to know each other. I had the impression that much of this was new to her too, not just a rigidly programmed parasitic relationship, and that she was working out many adaptive details as we went along. I could tell that she was maturing and changing. One oddity of our sexual relationship was the sharing of our orgasms. I supposed this was mandated by our sharing of the pleasure centers in my brain."

"So that produced simultaneous orgasms felt by both of you?"

"Yes, but even if I just went down on her, I felt her orgasm at the end of it, as well as all her pleasure leading up to it. She was not super-aggressive like Carol who needed all the odd extra orgasms that apparently were connected with reproduction by spreading the infection, nor did she seem to be patterning me in constructed dreams like she did with dream-Carol."

"Can you explain to me why Carole would need cunnilingus at all? Can't she just trigger the pleasure centers of your brain directly for both of you?"

"You're right, of course. She could have done that directly and indeed has done that directly without all the elaborate emulations. I think she allowed me to pleasure her that way because I had come to very much enjoy doing that for women, and she very much wants me to view her as female. As Carole put it, she was also pleased to see me being less selfish and self-centered than usual when I engaged in this pleasure giving."

"Has that been a problem for you, this supposed selfishness?"

"Very much so. If Carole has taught me anything, it is to give myself away. Or try to."

"By 'giving yourself away' you mean what exactly? You talked of Carole giving *herself* away during reproduction as a new infection. That's not necessarily a benevolent act."

"By nature, I have always been rather shy and introverted, self-involved, rather childish, and socially risk averse. Carole gave me a little push towards adulthood, decisions, relationships and responsibilities. I know that sounds a little strange in this context of promiscuity and infection. Giving myself away meant engaging with people around me more, treating them with respect, sometimes teaching, sometimes learning, and not being afraid to give sexual pleasure in a relationship."

"Was she the dominant one in your sexual relationship?"

"Sexually perhaps, but only to a slight degree, and nothing like Lady Carol. She seeks me out at times, but I would describe it more as simple enjoyment of being together. It's not always sex she's after either; so, it's not at all like I have a female stalker stuck in my brain. We seem about equally needy for companionship, and sometimes we talk for hours on many subjects. Life is frequently a lonely business, and we provide relief to each other. Anyway, things changed after we began to engage regularly in those forms of sexuality that I could not perform with another human."

"What would this involve exactly?"

"This might be described as a complete mental entanglement or merging. It's hard to describe exactly except by analogy. It's a very intimate contact that allows our feelings to be in sync. It's way beyond dream sex, which is merely an idealized and glamorized emulation of ordinary human sex. An analogy might be to some sort of microbial sex by conjugation; something that occurs almost on the molecular level where certain deep and secret things are exchanged or transmitted in big chunks. My collision with Jungle Girl turned out to be an introduction to sex of this sort; however, this type of syncing does not always involve an orgasm although it may sometimes."

"So, would you say you've gradually allowed her control and access to more parts of your brain with those 'deep and secret things'?"

"That sounds awfully dangerous when you put it that way, but that's not at all how it feels. It is a very pleasurable mutual intimacy. Yes, I've allowed her to have access to parts of me that I cannot share with anyone else, but the sharing is reciprocated. It was not necessary to do it frequently, but she brought it up, and we discussed it and what it might mean. It has become so pleasurable for us that we do it a lot. She said my final encounter with Jungle Girl was just our initial syncing, and a pretty intense and overwhelming session at that."

"Wasn't that collision with Jungle Girl essentially just a form of mind-rape by a deceptive parasite?"

"Because of my invitation, she views it as consensual sex."

"How do you view it?"

"I'm still just a little ambivalent about that incident and the need for it that soon, but I did allow it to happen."

"It strikes me that this required 'invitation' sounds disturbingly similar to the legends concerning vampires needing such an invitation to enter a victim's house or private space. Did anything like that occur to you?"

"It did, but it didn't seem to be a very close analogy."

"Why not?"

"My further discussions with her seemed to indicate that she had no intention of consuming my life essence and diminishing me in any way."

"But it did seem to require you to *become* something different. You've spoken of a new psyche and even a new physiology."

"Nevertheless, I was ready for some sort of change, and it has worked out well so far. The original incident doesn't seem like rape to me even though I was completely penetrated by her. It certainly *was* a manifestation of female power. It feels a bit more like a seduction because of the great pleasure involved, but it clearly forced me to be aware of her great power."

"Did you feel intimidated by this feminine power?"

"Awed, better describes my feelings at first, but she has always treated me with kindness and has nurtured our growing relationship as well as my personal growth. My love for her makes it feel right even when I am sometimes pushed a little out of my comfort zone."

"Otherwise, how would you describe her relation to you?"

"Intellectually, she was very respectful of my learning and frequently asked my help in understanding or researching various topics. As I mentioned earlier, she was somehow able to access the internet and actual libraries through me when I was unconscious and sometimes through me even when I was fully conscious. She has a prodigious memory for whatever she reads, and I suggest things she might want to consider. In a way she became my student in many areas, but she has by now vastly surpassed my knowledge in other areas outside my direct scientific expertise. I enjoy her passion for learning, and I do believe she has a genuine admiration for human science. Her evolving understanding of many topics is highly original, and she also serves me now as an internal 'muse' or colleague prompting me to investigate new areas. So, it goes both ways. She's quite brilliant, smarter than Carol in many ways, and definitely smarter than me.

"Carole confided in me that this contact with our science and techno-culture was of great benefit to her and to her symbiont meta-community, and that they had no intention of eliminating humans from this co-exploration of the world. Thus, she felt that mutualism was the far stronger option, rather than simply taking over my body as a true parasite might. Scientifically, they intend to build upon and share the foundations that humans have created rather than starting from scratch. Culturally, they will push for changes that benefit us all."

"And you believed all this?"

"Yes."

"Can you explain to me why she needs to read and study things that you already know?"

"As I mentioned earlier, my memory of things that I have read and studied is far from perfect. In dreams, I can't recall verbatim what was on each page and summon up a readable image. Sometimes Carole will become interested in a book that I have read and will read it herself. We might discuss it afterward. Often her fresh reading of the book will differ from what I might remember of it. Occasionally, my memory of a book differs so much from hers that I will reread a book so we can discuss it anew. Apparently, I mainly derive things from my reading and study that I am ready to assimilate at that particular time and somehow don't really remember the other things very well."

"Do you think she is learning something about your learning process so she can better tap into your learning?"

"Undoubtedly, she is, but so am I. I have found this revisiting of certain books and topics very enlightening myself. I think all teachers find this out eventually when they learn enough to teach a subject well. This was something I had not consciously noticed before, this necessity of revisiting subjects again and again until I had a more functional understanding and could actually make use of the information as real knowledge that fit with other things that I understood."

"Does Carole change your mind about things you didn't remember very well?"

"Not exactly. We do discuss many of these faulty memories when they can be checked against reliable facts. Beyond that, I *am* a bit astonished to see how easy it is for me to generate false memories about what I've read. Some of this is simply confirmation bias when I have become too attached to an opinion based on partial information or a quick reading."

"She appears to be skilled in generating elaborate false memories for you. For some of them she has told you in advance what she is concocting. Do you think there might be others she has slipped in without warning? You mentioned how dream-like your life now seems…"

"She says that she does not and will not do that, and I am inclined to believe her now. We have discussed the ethics of symbionts vs. humans pretty intensively, and it appears that symbionts like Carole ideally do have sort of an ethical code that forbids this sort of wholesale meddling with a host's memories. Perhaps this could be very dangerous to the host in some way. In any event, I have been very watchful for any signs of this, but I must admit that my ability to detect false memories probably has its limits. It seems to me that she mainly brings about changes in my opinions by rational dialog."

"She could also communicate with you while you were fully awake? Tell me about that."

"Sometimes she could manifest as a voice in my head. I know that definitely sounds like a paranoid delusion, but it was usually more like a discussion than a voice telling me what to do. In some ways it's like having a passenger riding along inside me, commenting on events. I could answer by sub-vocalizing a response or even vocalizing if I was alone. Sometimes her comments are so humorous, it's hard not to laugh out loud! It was also possible for her to move my fingers to write or operate a keyboard, provided I relaxed and let her take over. Lately she has served as a sort of 'ghost' co-author as I write papers. Her advice has been extremely helpful in composing and finding just the right word or turn of phrase. Often I wish I could list her efforts with actual co-authorship when her contributions have been major."

"Could she talk directly to me?"

"I suppose so; if she wanted to do so, I could shut down and let her talk. You might have difficulty validating that communication, which would occur with my voice. It would be interesting to see if her word choices and idioms were distinctly different from mine."

"Can she manifest visually?"

"Certainly, in dreams she can. In real life, I believe she can easily do this, but has not often done it for various reasons. Perhaps she wants to avoid causing car accidents and such by jumping suddenly into my visual field. It's been kind of alarming those few times when she's actually done it."

"Do you ever argue or disagree with her?"

"We do argue, but rather dispassionately and rationally for the most part, certainly not heatedly... but perhaps playfully many times; I think I've mentioned her keen sense of humor and the absurd. I sometimes call her 'She, who must be obeyed,' and she calls me 'Macumazahn', I suppose for my jungle days as an explorer and our encounters by night in dreams. Nevertheless, reasons are given for assertions, and any momentary disagreements are usually settled by obtaining further information. It's sort of like trying various ideas on for size - I do that for myself sometimes anyway. Then we talk about how those ideas seem to fit experience and logic. There's no anger or resentment involved. It's too bad science can't be like that more often."

"Considering all the cultural baggage men usually associate with femaleness, that's a very odd series of statements. Surely there must have been some areas that were difficult for you to reach consensus. For example, what, if any, were her views on women and their current societal roles?"

"Once you've achieved a certain degree of openness with one another by syncing, abstract notions of femaleness and maleness don't really sway the arguments much one way or another. You play the hand you're dealt, and you try to understand what you're dealing with. There is still self and not self, but there's a much more permeable boundary of yourself that's hard to explain until you've experienced crossing it. Personally, I don't think there *are* purely male and female ways to view the physical world, and scientists of both sexes gradually converge on 'that which really is' if they're diligent and honest. That is, we gradually become less and less wrong whatever our initial beliefs or hypotheses. Obviously, the more emotionally charged or sexually conditioned the topic, the longer this process may take.

"Our views of the social world are another matter entirely and are obviously much more colored by gender. Men are typically oblivious to their special social privileges or, if aware, believe they have somehow earned them. Failure for us to reach a consensus was usually just being honest and admitting that we didn't know for sure or didn't have data. I recognized frequently that some of my quick, gut responses were merely my cultural and sexual autopilot kicking in; I have tried to be slower to vent my unthinking opinions, and I think I have become less judgmental as a result. Carole did directly ask me once how I felt about the peculiar restricted role women play in our culture as well as in many others. As she put it, women appear to be treated largely as property like domesticated farm animals and were often forced to propagate to satisfy the whims of men. I hadn't thought about it that way exactly but had to concede the point after considering many examples that showed she was largely right; the situations she posed as examples simply didn't pass the Golden Rule test. Some sociologists have already said that all humans appear to be self-domesticated animals anyway, but I conceded the deeply ingrained bias against women was really there in many cultures, so I guess we actually did reach a consensus. Carole is a pretty astute judge of human cultures, and of how she would fit in, were she to spread into them. Some cultures she found utterly scary and would feel oppressed within them even as a hidden female symbiont within a male, simply because of her great empathy with human females."

"How about even more subjective areas like feelings and emotions?"

"She seems to feel my feelings as partly her own. She's fully aware of how broken I am in places. I admit I'm often less aware of her feelings about my feelings until we sync deeply. I'm afraid it all gets pretty convoluted and self-referential when you try to dissect it. Perhaps there is more chemical communication than I'm aware of. She claims she is also strongly influenced by my body chemistry as stirred by emotion."

"Do you think she can just flood your body with various hormones to gain agreement from you as she needs it? Oxytocin, perhaps?"

"Perhaps that or even something else, like 3,4-Methylenedioxymethamphetamine. I would have no way of knowing whether that was all that was occurring, but it's possibly true sometimes. I don't think that it is exact agreement that she's after... more like sympathy or empathy; she wants me to be able to consider her point of view. She has already hinted at her biochemical abilities by her manipulation of my testosterone levels to promote promiscuity and courtship behavior. Perhaps she has also de-methylated something here and there to alter expression of a few of my genes. She claims to have expanded my emotional scope, and I *do* feel that, at least subjectively."

"So, perhaps she is more of a parasite than she admits. Is she not lowering your defenses by making you more open to her suggestions?"

"I would say she is far less of a parasite than she could be. Open minded is not the same as gullible."

"You seem to be saying that this is a decision that she can make."

"Yes, I suggest that this was a rational decision that she *did* make. The reasons for it are still a little worrying. What would she decide for someone other than me? ...For example, someone who rebelled strongly against her?"

"Now *that's* a very good question to be asking. It may imply a risk to humanity in general, if not to you as a willing collaborator."

"I'm not sure that making someone more reasonable is necessarily a bad thing, but I will try to ask her more directly about that in connection with 'domestication' of the human race."

"On another note, what are Carole's opinions, if any, about homosexuals?"

"It doesn't bother her at all, seen as one facet of human sexuality. Anyway, it's irrelevant to the propagation of symbionts. I would guess that had I been gay, she would have manifested somewhat differently in me, but she would have happily adapted to it, and she would not have seen it as a blemish upon my human potential. Certainly, she has a very tolerant attitude toward Carol."

"To your knowledge, have any homosexuals become infected with a symbiont?"

"I think it's very likely, considering Carol's wide-ranging tastes in sexuality; but no, I have no specific knowledge of any exclusive homosexuals becoming infected, nor details of how it might have worked out for them. That would really be a good question for Carol.

"One further comment: I would guess that a need is arising or will soon be arising for people with a mature understanding of symbionts to help those for whom it is new and perplexing. I expect to see on-line discussion groups and help desks more and more openly devoted to such matters in the near future. There are lots of ways there will be a culture shock within the symbiont-infected community, especially among those still clinging to various obsolete religions and trying to adapt to a symbiont. Some professionals like you may need to get involved so it isn't all religious charlatans promoting self-loathing and duping people out of their money for a quack cure."

"You're not very positive about religion in general, are you?"

"I'm not very positive about *faith* which defies reality, makes up stuff about the world, and generally treats non-believers as subhuman garbage for not believing the made-up stuff. In the abstract, I can conceive of non-destructive forms of religion which might do far less damage, but I have yet to see a real example of one requiring faith that I could whole-heartedly support. About the best I can come up with is a sort of conditional tolerance towards religious practitioners who reciprocate my tolerance."

"Would you say you are bitter about religion because of the way it destroyed your marriage?"

"In part that's true; however, any good marriage counselor probably could have uncovered a dozen other fault lines in our relationship that made it ultimately unstable and unhappy. I've already mentioned my rather immature selfishness as part of my problem, a weakened ability to share or care. Also, I was pretty oblivious to Beverly's career needs or life ambitions and didn't choose to explore them with her."

"Until recently, you seem to have had relatively few relationships with women for a man of your age. Do you have any comments now on what specifically attracts you to women, and what you have learned both from your failed marriage and your new relationships?"

"There is of course the physical attraction part that I find hard to analyze. I suppose I do have a certain physical 'type' that especially attracts me. Carole probably could tell you about that better than I; much of it is unconscious and irrational, and she must make frequent use of it in her emulations. Traits that I consciously find highly desirable would include beauty (according to my pre-programmed, internal criteria), intelligence, humor, kindness, assertiveness, and perhaps some extra patience with my social clumsiness. I do value my growing perception of some of the differences between a woman's views of the world versus a man's view - here I mean particularly views of the social milieu. I also value relationships that seem to have some growth potential, that is, relationships in which both partners gradually feel safe enough to reveal themselves more and more to each other."

"How do your latest relationships stack up against these criteria?"

"I think my relationships with Carol and Carole both match these pretty well and have certainly shown growth potential with no signs yet of stopping."

"What about Julie?"

"I think there was a trust barrier there that was never overcome. She was more open and a much better companion than Beverly, but something was amiss, and communications shut down too rapidly for me to even diagnose the problem. Since she now works in my department at the University, she must be aware of my on-going relationship with Carol via the rumor mill and may be jealous of it or repulsed by it, but I have no way of even knowing whether she thinks about it much at all."

"If communications were reestablished with her, would you try to develop a sexual relationship in addition to what you now have with Carol?"

"I'm not sure that I would now. I really do love Carol and have pretty much committed to her exclusively. I don't think I could handle anything more than that; it's complicated enough."

"Even though she has taken over your sexuality, has shared you with other women and may participate in other sexual relationships by herself?"

"There are many things I tolerate from her that I wouldn't allow with anyone else."

"But *should* you tolerate these things from her?"

"I think for now, yes. We seem to be gradually moving toward something better for me, but still acceptable for her."

"When you say 'tolerate' things from her, do you also mean you are doing sexual things that you don't actually enjoy?"

"No, it's more like I will try out certain things with her that I might reject doing at all with someone else."

"But what if you try something and hate doing it?"

"At this stage of our relationship, I don't think Carol would dump me if I expressed those feelings."

"Despite your dangerous promise?"

"Despite that."

"Why is that?"

"Our relationship is no longer based just on that. It's hard to put in words, but we're moving towards something much stronger than that promise. Carole has hinted at further possibilities…"

SCIENTIFIC GROUND STATE

Wherever natural history appeared in America, it had this effect:
it created and justified the logic of collecting, which was not merely
"getting" or "assembling" objects to have or hoard them or to put them
on display but a path into nature, it beckoned young men and women
to go out into and to feel and touch the living world around them...

William Leach, *Butterfly People*

Dr. Ellis requested as part of my therapy that I write an essay concerning some of my rather grumpy attitudes toward religion. This may be helpful in understanding a person such as myself with a deeply rooted empirical outlook, which I would designate as my "ground state." By this term, stolen from spectroscopy, I mean my rock bottom, simplest personal stance on reality as I experience it. This stance has, in my case, been relatively unaffected by those parental or societal influences nudging me towards some sort of belief in a deity.

When asked about my religion, I usually self-identify as secular humanist. The connotation of secular humanist, at least in my mind, is that I am open to cooperation with religious humanists when our goals are congruent; otherwise, I often suspect they are doing the right things for the wrong reasons. The terms atheist and agnostic seem more off-putting; these terms seem to force believers to peer into the abyss of unknowing, and they often panic when forced to see something that scares them. Nevertheless, it would also be fair to say I am an atheist and/or an agnostic, depending on how precisely you wanted to parse their meaning. I claim no special knowledge of a god or gods, *but* I don't rank the probability of any kind of deity actually existing as very high either, so I am probably a provisional atheist for all practical purposes.

Although raised in a Christian family (Episcopalian-Presbyterian), and forced to attend church for a good portion of my childhood, I also spent a great deal of time unsupervised, roaming the fields and streams near my house, hunting rocks, butterflies, plants and snakes. From what I had seen of the natural world, I cannot imagine anyone spontaneously coming up with all the complicated apparatus of salvation as outlined in the Christian religion and espoused even by liberal Protestants. So many moving parts! The whole urgency of salvation seems completely pointless and is lost on me. We ultimately die like the animals we are, and that's the end of it... Probably. This lack of engagement with religion, Christianity in particular, undoubtedly bothered my parents, as witnessed by their attempts to force my participation in their faith ceremonies. They backed off these attempts around the time I entered Junior High, and whenever I got a chance, I didn't attend church and refused to get browbeaten into pledging a portion of my allowance for the offering plate. My dad, when he let me off going to church, usually set me up with some tedious job that had to be done as penance, in place of church attendance. Somehow, in his mind, only that made it alright to miss church. Frequently, I did a token amount of work, then escaped outdoors into the natural world that I loved. Often this escape healed me from the stress caused by parental conflicts.

I can remember one key incident at about age five, which caused me, henceforth, to view my parents with great suspicion whenever they came out with religious dogma. Some distant family member had died, and they talked about this person going to heaven. I wondered how they knew that and got quite angry when I was told they just knew, and that no one had ever actually come back to confirm that heaven and an afterlife even existed. I had a very hard time understanding how my parents could be so gullible! They both had doctorates, and were supposedly educated enough to reason logically, but, nevertheless, they bought into this obvious wishful thinking. Could total idiocy be far behind?

Faith gives me personally a big problem about what to think about certain claims about reality. Science was described by anthropologist Weston LaBarre as a secularized piety towards That Which Is. This outlook comes freighted with methods of examining empirical evidence to discover That Which Is. Faith is not among those methods. Faith is basically believing things to be certainly true based on no evidence whatsoever other than the authority of someone else, who also has no palpable evidence. Faith shuts out further inquiry. Science is never certain, but the cumulative results are self-challenging and self-correcting. Over historical time, it all does seem gradually to converge to a fairly self-consistent picture of That Which Is, or, at the very least, to clarify the questions.

Paul Tillich in his book, *The Dynamics of Faith*, tried to redefine faith as those things of "ultimate concern." This has certainly not achieved common currency; indeed, most atheists don't really have much to say about Tillich, whom most evangelicals consider a closeted atheist anyway; one who has substituted GOB for God. Additionally, there are some confusions about defining faith when the notion of hope becomes conflated with faith. Most clear-thinking people would like to keep the two concepts separate. My personal view is that one can still have hope without having faith, but one can never have absolute certainty.

I should probably say that I am not unalterably opposed to religion per se. The root meaning of the word is that which binds us together (as in the word, ligature). That binding can, of course, be for good reasons or bad, and each religion must be judged on its own merits for producing good results. I do not favor religions that create "us" and "them" divisions, and which promote decent, respectful, interpersonal treatment of others *only* among "us", that community of believers associated with one particular set of beliefs. The ethical litmus test that I routinely apply to any candidate religion is to examine closely which version of the Golden Rule (if any) they espouse. (Which "others" are to be tolerated?) I am perfectly willing to tolerate religions that are tolerant towards me, just as I am; i.e., I demand full reciprocity in exchange for my tolerance. If your religion does not encourage tolerant behavior towards those others with whom you share the world, you should reject it.

BACK CHANNEL: CAROLE AND CAROL

*I was initially very suspicious of this "Carole" person. Her intense
protection of her beloved Richard seemed at first to deprive me of my
chance to collar him, but later it seemed as if she were helping me.
How strange that this woman inside him has become my best friend.*

Lady Carol, *Beloved Incubus* (First Impressions)

"Hello there, I'm Carole, Richard's symbiont partner. Has he told you
that I might be in touch with you directly?"

"Yes, he mentioned that. This is pretty strange! You're not just
Richard trying to negotiate, are you?"

"No, I'm definitely not Richard. He's a little ambivalent about
my communicating with you as it is. Perhaps he thinks we'll cook up
something sexy that he can't handle. You'll have to ask him."

"What is Richard up to, anyway? His approach to me was so strange
and unexpected, I honestly didn't know what to think. He's socially very
awkward, but miraculously he has some rather polished love-making
skills."

"Everything he said to you was true, as far as it went. Indeed, he
really has quite a crush on you, then and now, but it took a big push from
me for him to approach you. Some of those skills have developed over
time through practice. He's very motivated to give you the best orgasms
you've ever had and to adapt to whatever you need."

"And you've been training him to do this?"

"As best I can. It would be easier to do if you and I could discuss it from time to time. You're a very complex woman to emulate. Some of what I've done may be too stereotypical and not really like you at all. Maybe more Lady Carol than Carol. I've had to rely a lot on your website material and try to read between the lines. Perhaps you don't realize how much females can reshape male behavior by their choices."

"Oh, I realize it alright, but I still don't understand your motivation in any of this and why you contrived to bring us together at the class reunion."

"As Richard's symbiont, my primary concern will always be my beloved Richard, who makes my life possible. Secondarily, as he's no doubt revealed to you, we plan to spread symbionts throughout the human race as far as we can. That requires other human partners. Your own symbiont will help you understand what the symbiont community is trying to accomplish. Richard is very attracted to you and thinks you will make a great partner in this endeavor. I tend to agree with him. Perhaps a new and unusual kind of relationship for you, but what do you think? There are four of us who will become deeply involved; we call that a 'quad'. There's some risk, of course. Society won't approve. At least, not yet; perhaps when symbionts are more abundant things will change. It's a little dangerous now, but you seem to like that edginess and are not so worried about societal approval."

"I must admit, it's been fascinating how this has worked out. It sounded so crazy to begin with that I wasn't sure what to do with him. Honestly, we have had some fabulous sex together, and I think his playfulness about it has been refreshingly different even though a lot of it must be unfamiliar territory to him. I am deeply grateful to him for giving me my own symbiont and showing me that the world can be far different from what I thought it was. I guess Legba is kind of your first-born, isn't he?"

"Categories like that carry too much emotional baggage and don't really express very well what symbionts feel towards each other. Maybe friend or colleague should suffice for now, but sometimes we do grow more deeply fond of one another, especially within a quad. In some ways he's more like Richard's child than mine. Have you noticed the resemblance?"

"Some. Will you talk to him too?"

"I already have a little. I need to get to know him as well as you. May I tell you a few things about symbionts such as Legba and me?"

"Please do."

"We are both a little vulnerable at this point, so we need some discretion and nurturing from you both. You understand I'm sure, how young we are compared to you and Richard. This means Legba and I are both playing catch-up ball trying to come to terms with your culture and your life experience. This speed learning has not been easy. We can guess many things about you by studying your learning and life experience memories, but sometimes we will get it wrong. So, we do need your help catching up and giving us reality checks. Has Richard talked with you about helping Legba in this way? This is more than just syncing and data transfer; it involves interpretation as well. Experiences can take on different meanings as you mature."

"Yes, he's mentioned it, and Legba and I have engaged in many long discussions and perhaps have cleared up a few misunderstandings. And we do sync regularly, of course. Is that what you mean?"

"For the most part, yes. As Richard has come to trust me and lose his fear of me, I've become his student in many areas. He's been really sweet in teaching me about science and other things in a more structured form than I might have picked up on my own. This has given me a framework for further learning that has really paid off. Anyway, I've come to admire his passion for science and to realize all the more what an anomaly he is in this society. In a way, you're both outsiders who have not bought in to all the little boxes American culture was ready to put you in. Do you agree?"

"Well, yes. I've always felt myself well outside the boundaries. Richard has implied that he felt that way too. I guess that's why I suggested we didn't belong at the reunion and should leave. What an odd pair we make! May I ask you something about Richard?"

"As long as it's not something I've promised not to tell."

"Is Richard really afraid of me? Surely he must see through my scary dominatrix shtick."

"Has Richard ever told you the story about his once locking eyes with you in high school?"

"No. What happened?"

"Apparently he felt your gaze bore into him like laser beams and that experience shook him to his core. It was, perhaps, his first experience of female power. Was it a judgmental gaze or something else? It obviously was memorable to him."

"Honestly, I don't know. It might well have been something else. I was pretty skeptical of all my high school acquaintances and didn't trust them one bit. My glare was probably just meant to be off-putting. Did that one look make him afraid of me?"

"Not that by itself. It would also depend a little on which 'me' we're talking about. He really is still a little scared of your fiercely feminine Lady Carol at times, but I would say he now sees something more beneath that façade. Perhaps Carol is quite different? How much have you revealed to him about your more vulnerable self?"

"That's been hard for me. Lady Carol has been my protective shield against the world as well as being a lightning rod for trouble. Sometimes I turn on that shield without even realizing it. For some clients that tension between dangerous and sexy is exactly what turns them on. Doesn't that sometimes work for Richard?"

"Sometimes yes, because he has developed a deep trust in you and has made you a promise. By now, you probably know his physiological responses as well as I do. Beyond that, though, I'm also asking, does it always work for you?"

"Always? Frankly, I have never really explored other types of relationships very much except with women. Someday maybe you and I can discuss why not. There are things I haven't shared with anyone. So, for now, mostly yes, but I also sense that it's not always what Richard needs from me. I'm a little afraid of someone needing something from me, or just needing me at all for that matter. I'm used to not caring. Now I seem to be caught up in a relationship where I do care somehow, but I don't really know exactly what to do about it."

"Some of this you might want to discuss with your own symbiont first. Richard has some of the same qualms about discussing things with you before he's ready. I confess that I've pushed him pretty hard in some areas because of his stubborn shyness, maybe too hard. I can't go into great detail here without betraying confidences, but there are many things about his silly failed marriage, and his troubled relationship with his parents that still embarrass him."

"And Legba would not say anything to you or to Richard if I were not ready?"

"No, he would not. Anyway, Richard is too scared to talk to Legba right now. Nevertheless, I think it might make a difference if we keep communicating about those things that you are ready to talk about. Someday, Carol, we will find a way for all four of us to sync. That will be a way to resolve a lot of issues about caring. Also, I think it will be the real test of whether we could continue to be a quad long after the reproductive phase has burned itself out. I hope so because we all have a lot invested in this new relationship and meanwhile, we each have a lot to learn about each other so we can be mutually supportive even as we change each other. Development of trust is critically important."

IN GODDESS WE TRUST

*The simplest and most basic meaning of the symbol of
the Goddess is the acknowledgment of the legitimacy of
female power as a beneficent and independent power.*

Carol P. Christ

It took many, many discussions to clarify our relationship to the point
that I could claim to "trust" Carole. These took place in the Library
of Dreams, and always involved the Carole avatar. It was (and still
is to some extent) unclear to me how faithfully the Carole avatar
represented the entity which claims to be a conscious version of my
"microbiome". Initially however, my problem was to decide whether I
had merely become infected with a tropical disease which caused visual
and auditory hallucinations, or whether there was something more
going on. There was also the matter of strongly hallucinogenic alkaloids
being associated with the plant materials that I collected. Were these
sufficient to explain some of the weird effects that I was experiencing?

I requested that we meet under fairly neutral conditions so we could
talk this out. That meant, I specifically requested that she not play anima
games with me while we talked. The ground rules were, we would meet
in the library, but she would appear conservatively dressed, and not
purposely exploit all my fetishes and general male weaknesses to win a
point via unfair subliminal arguments. She commented that this would
not be much fun for either of us, and did I want her to wear some sort of
hijab or concealing clothing lest I be swept away by my overwhelming

male lust for her bewitching femininity? (Her odd sense of humor was becoming more pronounced as time went on. Evidently, she had by now bought into the intellectual foreplay notion.) She obligingly modified her usual Carole avatar into a more conservatively well-dressed professional woman with just the slightest hint of her usual perfume and a slight touch of gray in her hair. I sat in a chair opposite her usual library desk in her private office. She had a slightly bemused smile playing around her lips as if she were a little puzzled at having to indulge her favorite, but strangely floundering student having a problem understanding the complex assignment.

I explained to her that I was struggling with trust issues, among them, whether she was really more of a parasite than a symbiont (or mutualist). Most importantly, I wanted to explore what, if any, would be the downside of this relationship for me. Also, I told her I was keeping a detailed log of these discussions as I remember them to share with my psychiatrist and perhaps with Carol.

"Can you fill me in on your origins in the rainforest?"

"My true origins are as obscure to me as your origins as a hominin on the African savanna might be to you without a full scientific investigation. I can tell you very little about the gradual acquisition of consciousness while among Yayael's people except to say that one of us must have been Yayael's symbiont companion for a very long time. You must understand that this passing of information from one generation to another among us is a relatively new cultural thing not so much a biological thing. What I know about it is essentially what you know or infer about it."

"What is the connection to plants, particularly the one, which I have spent so much time propagating?"

"That's part of a very complicated life cycle. There is at least one viral component that is alternately carried in plants and then people. How that all works exactly, I really don't know. That remains for your science to investigate. Yayael and his ancestors, like many native groups in South America, were aware of and exploited the many 'power plants' in their environment. You would call these entheogens in modern ethno-botanical terminology; that is to say, these plants produced visions seemingly of a religious nature. Perhaps the best analogy would be the mutual adaptations of certain flowers and certain pollinators. At any rate, persons who experienced these effects might be motivated to protect and propagate the plants that engendered them. I think the viral involvement somehow speeded up the natural selection process and made a mutualism possible. That's just a provisional guess."

"What information do you have concerning Yayael and your predecessor?"

"Only very general notions, similar to what you have. My Jungle Girl avatar was sort of a default trial balloon, slightly adapted to you, before I became better informed about your culture. You had quite a head start on me, and it has been quite a daunting task learning about your technological culture! I think my predecessor saw the promise in it based on Yayael's perceptions and his discussions with you. It apparently seemed a gamble worth taking to extend our range."

"What do you expect to get out of our relationship?"

"I was quite open with you about my drive towards propagation within your culture. Some of your sexual urges were re-purposed to be of mutual benefit. Of course, all this seemingly unsafe sex came with immunological protection so that your reproductive cycle would be extended to about a year. And of course, you finally connected with Carol, the girl of your dreams."

"So presumably, I won't spawn and die at the end of the year?"

"No. I dropped that little zinger to start you thinking seriously about our symbiotic relationship. Your agreement to the relationship is important to me, especially in this culture. Were you so inclined, you probably could rid yourself of me with extensive medication. That was almost certainly not possible in Yayael's culture."

"And presumably I won't suddenly lose my fear of man-eating tigers or climb a tree and have mushrooms sprout out of my head?"

"Nothing that drastic; anyway, you'll still fear tigers and be mushroom free. I think the big difference from those types of controlling parasites that you mention is my consciousness and my deeper connection with you."

"So, to be clear, you are saying you *decided* to be a mutualist rather than a parasite?"

"Well, of course. I thought you understood that all along! Richard dear, you have been so sweet to me I couldn't possibly repay all your kindness with coercion! That's just not how it works for me. To give you yet another analogy, we're working together now like the electric and magnetic fields in a beam of light, each one giving rise to the other. There is a synergy from the two of us working together that's hard to overstate. We actively and continuously create each other in the process when it all works the way it's supposed to. I wouldn't even consider doing anything else unless the process got all messed up beyond redemption. In a sense, your brain now has two operating systems that complement and reinforce each other."

"Are you somehow feasting on my inner essence now that I've invited you into me?"

"Oh, you mean like your old vampire invitation legends, etc.? Well, in an odd way, yes. Your symbiotic microbes are indeed feasting on certain things that you provide in your gut; however, these things are hardly your 'inner essence' and mainly comprise constituents of your diet that you couldn't really digest by yourself anyway. There's plenty to go around. Mentally, it's fair to say your true 'inner essence' has been awakened, augmented and expanded way beyond what it was."

"How about body modifications specifically for propagation along the lines of fungal flowers?"

"I'm thinking of body modifications more along the lines of communications equipment to connect two humans and their symbionts. That would be of mutual benefit. Propagation might also result from it down the road."

"What did you have in mind there? Telepathy?"

"Too soon to tell whether telepathy among humans is even remotely possible; your brain would need some antenna-like structure for sending and receiving. I don't see how to do that without a radical change in your anatomy. I'm working on a different approach with a little help from other symbionts. It would probably involve direct communication between two humans and their symbionts with some kind of temporary neural hook-up. That will require some much subtler body modifications, but ones that won't alter your overall appearance very much."

"You have obviously been manipulating my sexual urges with every trick in the book."

"The urges were there already, but you are correct that I have dual-purposed some of them to fit my reproductive agenda. Has this bothered you terribly? You did want me to connect you with Carol, didn't you? You already knew a lot about her sexual preferences and didn't seem put off by them."

"It has bothered me a little bit, socially, but not so much personally; it *has* been a little embarrassing to explain all these activities to my psychiatrist. She is continuing to be suspicious of your motives and methods. But yes, I did very much want you to connect me with Carol, and I do forgive you for using the methods you did."

"Dr. Ellis probably will continue to be suspicious because she cannot yet experience me directly, and for now, is not likely to credit your reports about me as anything other than psychotic delusions."

"So, what do you suggest?"

"You should continue to see her, at least for a while more. If nothing else, she provides a source of questions that you should reasonably be asking yourself. Also, it is important for you to be able to function in real life and not to get hung up on all your obsessions and anxieties. As an outsider and a newcomer, my perspective is that you and I both have a wonderful opportunity to learn things about this amazing world and the life we live together as conscious beings now intertwined with one another."

"Do you think Dr. Ellis is dangerous to you?"

"I hope not because I rather like her, but that remains to be determined. You should insist on informed consent to any treatment she proposes. As long as she behaves ethically, you should be able to detect danger. I think she knows you are unusual in many ways, and don't fit very well her framework for understanding mental illness. The question might be how will she view me, your 'imaginary companion'? Would she think that I am so dangerous to your well-being that I must be removed despite there being no physical manifestations of disease?

Anyway, I steered you towards the very best psychiatrist that I could find for your special circumstances. This was early on, and I was just barely functional as your symbiont; you had not even accepted me yet."

"You did what!"

"I gently urged you toward Dr. Ellis because I guessed that she would be interested in your case, based on her background, publications and previous interests. Also, as a feminist, she would be able to see through a lot of your masculine bullshit and call you out. I hasten to add that there is also a lot of feminine bullshit loose in this culture."

"I must say I'm astonished that you could do that so early on without my realizing your influence."

"Nevertheless, you seem to have found her very competent and well able to discuss these matters with you. Really, Richard, this was nothing more than your getting a recommendation from a friend; please don't over-interpret it! In the long run, I could see her as an important ally."

"You mentioned that your consciousness made all the difference between a parasite and a mutualist. Can you elaborate on how you became conscious and why it makes a difference?"

"My consciousness derives from your own and from the complexity of the human brain. I make use of many parts of you that are mostly dormant or not particularly well expressed in your conscious male personality. Therefore, to some extant I am your complementary persona in my reactions to various events and appear feminine in gender. More like a complementary image than a parasite."

"So, in a way, you're not really female?"

"In another way, I really am a sexual being just like you. 'Sexual' implies a part or a partial formation of a human consciousness that we assign a gender to, does it not? Sexual beings complete each other in their union, or so goes the usual romantic notion of your culture. Socially, therefore, gender is always a performance; nevertheless, remember that in a more abstract biological way, sex is also an exchange of information, and not just genetic material. You show me yours, and I'll show you mine?"

"Your views on sex and gender have blind-sided me a little here... I'm not sure I'm totally comfortable with it."

"You and approximately half the human race!"

"Is it possible for this derivation of consciousness among symbionts to go horribly wrong?"

"I suppose you mean if the particular human brain were in some sense evil or diseased? Yes, in some circumstances that could happen. If there were some pre-existing mental problem, the possibility of mutualism would be greatly diminished or at least complicated and possibly very flawed. In a culture like yours where symbionts might communicate with one another despite inhabiting separate hosts, things might come out better, and some kind of healing might be possible in the diseased host; not that I'd want to over promote myself as a cure for all that ails you. There will certainly be a continuing role for medicine! There is, however, sort of a nature vs. nurture conundrum posed here too: am I the way I am entirely because of my nature or partly because of your unique brain function? A sick brain could potentially produce an aberrant symbiont who might be really dangerous."

"But except for those really bad cases, you're saying that in a technologically sophisticated culture there is actually now a social dynamic occurring between symbionts and that they could even help heal an injured brain or personality disorder in some instances?"

"Yes."

"Have you been in communication with other symbionts?"

"Yes, of course. I thought you were well aware of my conferring with various daughter symbionts from our reproduction efforts. Some of it was microbial, of course, but some of it was just electronic communication during your downtime. This may change in the near future. We're working on it as I've just said; some of your body modifications might eventually be adapted to it."

"So, would this extra communication mainly benefit symbionts?"

"Oh, I envision much more than that if it works. You would also be able to communicate with other humans in a very direct way. This opens the possibility of a very deep kind of bonding between two humans and their two symbionts."

"How would things differ in a technologically primitive culture?"

"Well, there might be essentially complete isolation for the symbionts unless the hosts coordinated their reproductive efforts by embedding them in some sort of ceremonial activities with an appropriate religious mythology. Certain religions might lend themselves to such things. I think Yayael must have been a genius in that regard. His people are now among the most happy and peaceful in the world. I hope they can stay that way as their isolation ends.

"It's true, however, that humans *could* talk to each other about their symbionts. In such a case, the symbionts would at least be aware that there are other symbionts. Perhaps in such a culture, humans might even purposely foster some communication between their symbionts. Frankly, I just don't know how many variants of this situation might exist. Yayael may have confided in some of his closest followers, but not in others. He certainly talked to you. We are essentially pioneering a new type of relationship within your culture, and lots of details remain to be hammered out."

"Some religions in my culture might view symbionts as demonic possession. Could your type of symbiosis have happened in the past?"

"That's an interesting hypothesis. Perhaps so, but not enough detail is known about historically authentic cases of possession as opposed to just vengeful accusations. The strong connection of European witchcraft to various members of the *Solanaceae* is very suggestive but note that even Harner attributes many of the known witch effects (e.g., sensations of flying) merely to drug-induced hallucinations. A lot of this supposed witch culture probably predates 1492. After 1492, I suppose it is remotely *possible* that some early European explorer of the South American tropics *might* have acquired a symbiont in the new world and brought it home with him, but who during those superstitious times would have dared confess to it? No infection *per se* has ever been suspected in historical studies of witchcraft although various forms of mental illness have often been invoked."

"Are there people whom you would avoid infecting?"

"Yes, obviously there should be. In some instances, certain persons might reject their symbiont at the very first step of welcoming, and instead would develop a mild viral disease, but not a symbiont. There are also more subtle signs for the right candidates such as a very subtle scent, which you may not have noticed. A compatible microbiome emits a barely perceptible, but distinctive scent. Cats and dogs undoubtedly can detect it. Interestingly, many women can detect it too, which might lead to some very helpful possible adaptations involving female choice."

"I've noticed a trace of a scent associated with you. Is that what you mean?"

"No, that's more like a pheromone connected to sexual attraction that you've learned to associate with pleasure. For me and you, I produce a hint of the *Datura* fragrance as a special enticement for you - please don't tell me you hadn't noticed that little indulgence of mine! It's my last little trace of the plant Goddess! There's a different, more general scent associated with certain components of microbiomes."

"So certain people are 'wrong' because of their microbiome's aroma?"

"Yes, but not necessarily wrong in an absolute sense. Some would just be much more difficult candidates, and it might take a long while to modify their microbiology in the direction needed. I assume that some form of do-it-yourself fecal transplant involving a blender and a turkey baster would generally not be viewed as very sexy by any of the parties involved! There are others, however, who are not candidates because of their mental make-up or their extreme psychopathology. Some humans simply cannot be domesticated by symbionts, and I suspect this has to do with certain innate genetic features controlling their immune systems."

"Do these others also have a distinctive scent?"

"Many times, yes. For much mental illness, there is an underlying cause, not necessarily known yet to medical science that is linked to an infectious agent. These agents can give a distinctive scent by altering the host's metabolism."

"If I encountered such a person in a liaison, would you somehow warn me?"

"I certainly would if there were time. Certain persons would be disastrous to infect, and I would avoid infecting them, given a choice."

"Have you been screening my sexual choices to protect against this?"

"Following Carol and Julie, yes. Those first two were a bit of a gamble, but they worked out reasonably well for this phase of reproduction. I think Julie will eventually understand what happened to her and will become an ally even if she doesn't want to work directly with you. Give her some space and let her symbiont work with her."

"So far no warnings then?"

"Not to you, but I have indirectly steered Carol away from making certain connections. She regularly comes into contact with a more varied assortment of people than you do. She discusses some of the really weird ones with me."

"Do you have any qualms about using aberrant human sexual practices for your propagation?"

"Well, they're not *very* aberrant! Whatever gets the job done? Regular human reproduction involves just a bit of unction with a mucous membrane, doesn't it? That sounds a bit nasty as an abstraction. Can't humans always rationalize these other things as natural procreative sex to help out their friendly neighborhood symbiont? Anyway, those supposedly 'aberrant' practices you mention are all very natural mammalian things to do."

"You mean rationalize it as Natural Law like the Jesuits or something? OK, as long as it's for procreation? I don't think 'very natural mammalian things' would cut it with the Pope."

"Yes. I'm joking a little," she said with a slightly impish smile. "Perhaps I'm just one of those darned sexual humanists..."

"Is this sexual contact the only way you can reproduce?"

"Obviously not, as in your own case."

"So that was just because of my contact with all the plants in the greenhouse or maybe even in the Great Garden?"

"Yes."

"Could you have prevented that if I had not had the correct microbiome or psychic make-up?"

"Possibly the jaguars might have killed you but remember that Yayael had vetted you for the process, allowed you entrance to the Great Garden, and finally you welcomed me into yourself."

"Welcomed? At the time, and then only on the advice of my psychiatrist, I was trying to interact with the dream and not scare away

Jungle Girl! Yes, Yayael asked me to welcome you, but I really didn't understand what that meant."

"Nevertheless, you welcomed me into yourself. Of course, I was already there in a sense, but with limited abilities. You essentially agreed to the infection and to try to understand and deal with me through the help of your psychiatrist. That greatly facilitated the process."

"Yes... I guess that's sort of true, but not precisely what I'd call informed consent."

"Unfortunately, that may have been lost or garbled in translation when Yayael talked to you about me."

"Suppose I had not welcomed you into myself? What would have happened?"

"If you had strongly resisted having me, things might have proceeded to an ordinary infection and perhaps a mild viral disease that you might still have spread to others through direct contact. Your agreement altered your immune response just enough to allow me to grow rapidly into a fully self-aware symbiont instead of just an infection and a barely functional symbiont."

"How do I know what is lost in translation now?"

"We're pretty closely synced now. Plus, you're asking all these questions, which I hope will put some of these fears to rest. No real cure for it but to renew our sync from time to time as we feel the need or desire."

"I can see that this is a pretty dynamic ongoing process. So once is never enough?"

"Certainly not. Syncing is the only real way we can have sex with each other, beloved."

"Can you explain to me how and why you love me?"

"Isn't that obvious to you yet?"

"I guess I'm a little afraid of the answer."

"Of course, you are. Love and sex are dangerous. No way around it. We are taking a risk loving each other and being open and honest. Don't underestimate it."

"And yet despite that clear danger, I feel drawn to you, whatever your gender."

"And I to you, whatever *your* gender."

"Because you can control me?"

"Do you feel controlled by me?"

"No, actually I feel kindness and understanding. And patience."

"And pleasure?"

"Yes, great pleasure too."

"Well then, our biology must somehow approve of what we're doing."

"Is our biology our destiny then?"

"Not necessarily anymore. We can now make adjustments."

CAROL-LEGBA DIALOGUE

Everything becomes a little different as soon as it is spoken out loud.

Hermann Hesse

We first met face to face in my play room. Perhaps not my first choice, but it seemed a congenial place to Legba. That's what he calls himself. The name is from Haitian vodou in which Papa Legba is one of the Loas, guardian of the crossroads and facilitator of communication, speech, and understanding. A pretty tall order, but we shall see. My first impression of him was that he was way too old for me, which was an odd choice for him to make since he is really quite young. Also, he strongly reminds me of Richard as an old man. It's not that he's decrepit - he's actually quite spry and lively in his mannerisms, but the white hair and beard make him look ancient. He's very dark in coloration as if he labors under the sun, but he doesn't really; he lives inside the darkness in my head.

"Welcome."

"Thank you, Carol, for meeting me here again. I thought this place might be near to your heart since you've spent so many pleasurable hours here."

"I guess it's alright, but frankly, it puts me a little off because it leads immediately to talking about my sexuality."

"We can table most of that discussion until we know each other quite a bit better. Right now, we just need to discuss a little about trust and how this symbiont relationship works. I understand that Richard and Carole have filled you in on a lot of the basics?"

"Well yes, insofar as an abstract discussion can fill me in on anything. This whole business is still sort of unexpected and strange."

"So, you really didn't believe Richard when he first sprang this on you?"

"Honestly, no. He is such a strange man and believe me I've known a lot of strange men before, but none like him. His story was intriguing, I'll admit, but I really hadn't imagined anything much coming of it other than a few ideas for my own fiction and perhaps some erotic entertainment. And yet... he seemed so sincere and was actually worried about scaring *me*. Quite a switch for me!"

"Considering what he had to tell you, can you imagine any graceful way to say what he had to say? He knew full well how idiotic it would sound and that it would take a while for you to verify the facts and to trust him."

"Point taken. Also, Carole evidently had a lot to do with his approach, and she has a different agenda. She seems to have thrust him on stage before he was quite ready for the performance."

"What do you think her agenda might be in this case?"

"Well, as I've been informed, symbionts want to spread throughout human societies outside the tropics and domesticate the human race."

"And what do you think of that goal? You've also been invited to participate as Richard's human partner in a quad. That's not an offer that Richard and Carole would make lightly."

"I'm seriously considering that offer. I fully agree that humans need help of some sort."

"Do you have some qualms about Richard as a partner?"

"It seems a little risky to base a partnership simply on a crush he had on me in high school. I guess I still do have some trust issues."

"Men are very visually oriented, and he evidently finds you amazingly beautiful."

"I guess I understand that, but what am I to do with that little factoid?"

"Seriously? Has no one ever explained to you how things normally work between men and women?"

"The birds and the bees? What are you driving at?"

"If you look at conventional roles in polite society, a woman makes herself attractive, certain men find her beautiful, and make some approach to her, and then she chooses the ones that please her for short or long-term relationships. You have sometimes used that attraction as a weapon, so you can't really deny that you were unaware of it."

"Yes of course I'm aware of that dynamic although it's hardly ever so polite or so simple as that these days. So, what are you saying?"

"Simply that Richard is offering himself to you for a possible relationship involving the four of us. This is clearly courtship behavior, and you must ultimately decide. There's much more than just your physical beauty that has attracted him, however. He greatly admires your toughness of spirit, your creativity, and even your ferocity according to Carole. These would be big assets for a quad. I might add also that because of Carole and her insights into Richard you are in a far better position to judge his fitness for a relationship with you than women usually are with ordinary men."

"On what did he base those judgments of me?"

"Based on that incident at the reunion when you stood up and stared down the audience even as they tried to humiliate you. Did he not say?"

"No, he didn't. I guess at the time we both wanted to talk about anything but that."

"You also patted him on the arm after his part of your public humiliations. He remembered that particular body language as an unexpected kindness considering your reputation as a ferocious dominant."

"I don't even remember that... It might even have made things worse for him since he had just been publicly warned to stay away from me as if I would somehow destroy him."

"And would you have destroyed him?"

"Not intentionally anymore, but men do seem to destroy themselves around me sometimes, no matter what my intention may be."

"Have you ever figured out why they do?"

"They seem to want something from me that I cannot give."

"Your love?"

"Perhaps that occasionally, but more along the lines of my surrender."

"Why do you think your surrender is required?"

"It's a cultural thing. Women can't own themselves or their destinies. It's evidently way too dangerous. There are many costs associated with being a woman that men enforce."

"And yet Richard greatly admires your toughness. Your surrender to him would be just the opposite of toughness."

"You're right; so far, no signs of his requiring my surrender."

"If you don't mind my asking, what's with the impossible promise you coerced him into making?"

"That was kind of a spur of the moment joke."

"Do you think he was in on the joke?"

"Maybe not at first - I think he had his mind set more on warning me about infection with a symbiont - but later he clearly became aware of it, because we kid around a lot about it. I do enjoy his sense of humor by the way. He's very well read for a science jock, and a lot of our humor back and forth has literary references. He says it drives Carole nuts trying to figure out whether we're being serious, which I also find a little funny."

"So, you weren't even a little bit serious about your demands? Sometimes you're most serious when you start off with a joke. In a way, his agreement might be viewed as a surrender of exactly the sort that you wouldn't like."

"Well, maybe I was half serious at first. I never intended to make him do things he hated or to teach him a lesson. It was still asking for a sort of surrender, I guess, but more like a little bit of role reversal involving power. Maybe that's just what I require in a courtship ritual... That's an oddly tribal way to think about it. Kind of quaint, really."

"And to which tribe do you belong?"

"Loud ornery bitches who demand their fair share of power!"

"So, what did you intend to do with that power?"

"A lot of it was an experiment to see what he was like sexually."

"Any conclusions so far?"

"We've discovered quite a few things we like to do together."

"Are these all sexual things?"

"Many of them are, but we also like to talk and listen to music. We sometimes work out together at the gym. (He's given me the nickname, Barbella for when I work out! Probably a sneaky pun, but I haven't unraveled it yet.) He's also opened up a bit about his growing up, and his battles with his parents over which books he was allowed to read. So, he's started to share a few things with me about his past even though I can tell he's still a little embarrassed about them. No man has ever risked doing that with me before."

"That all sounds pretty good for you since I know you value your solitude, and then there's this connection with him over literature. I've noticed that he makes you laugh, and you seem happier when you're with him. You're not just using him as a sex toy like you do in some of your other sexual relationships with very submissive men."

"Well, he values solitude too. He needs solitude to focus on his work, and I need it to do my writing. He appears to enjoy the sex we're having, so *no*, I'm not just using him."

"Respect for solitude is, I think, pretty rare these days considering the constant bombardment with sales pitches, telephone interruptions and mindless electronic entertainment."

"It took me a while to appreciate solitude, but gradually I learned how to use it so I could concentrate my mind on writing. At first, I avoided being alone, but then who could I be with then?"

"At first after what?"

"You know what."

"We don't need to talk about that if you don't want to."

"I don't really. You know all about it anyway."

"Yes, I do. I'm deeply sorry that happened to you. I find your nightmares about it terrifying."

"May I ask what you think of Richard?"

"I hardly know him very well yet, but based on your reactions to him, he seems to be good for you in a lot of ways. His trust in you seems unusual, even if highly irrational, and he seems to have adapted to your sexuality amazingly well."

"I think so too. Sometimes he seems too good to be true, almost impossibly enlightened for a man. And then he jokes, which seems to be part of his maleness, but he doesn't seem to take his gender role all that seriously. I mean by that he doesn't think being male gives him special privileges by divine right of having a penis or something. I'm beginning to think that perhaps not all men are idiots."

"But there's a catch?"

"None so far, but I'm expecting something to come up. My inherent pessimism, I guess."

"So, more experimentation?"

"Of course. I hope he doesn't take it badly. Some of it will be fun. Anyway, I'll try to make it all fun for him; it adds something new for me to feel him coming on to me so strongly, so I guess I do enjoy vamping him a bit and playing around with his innocence. My other male slaves are so scared of me they can't even keep an erection when I get too ferocious."

"Is there something critical you must find out before deciding if we should join in a quad with them?"

"Probably not, although I think we should still explore the idea more and what it would mean for us."

"Discovery will just be beginning anyway even if we just join together as a quad on a trial basis. Why not be a little optimistic? You like them both, and I see Richard and Carole both doing good things for you and your self-esteem. Carole is my friend too and she has helped me figure out a few things about your complicated relationship with Richard. This could work. We can't all act like hedgehogs and be too afraid to get close if we are to unite as a quad. A maturing quad ultimately calls for a level of trust way beyond what humans sometimes achieve in marriage."

"There's that awful word! The whole idea of marriage per se is still very off-putting to me, but I'm willing to do this as a working partnership in a quad."

"That's a good start. Let me ask one last thing if I may. Do you feel some sort of love toward Richard?"

"Perhaps something like that. Something new to me, anyway."

"You're undecided about your own feelings?"

"I don't always trust my own feelings."

"There's that trust problem again. What do you think Richard feels about you?"

"I have no idea. A strange sexual attraction? We haven't talked about it explicitly."

"Nonsense! I think he shows all the signs of love."

"Such as?"

"You've put him through the sexual wringer and he's still here! That took an amazing level of trust that could only have come from a crazy kind of love. Do you really expect him to talk about it and maybe stumble onto your not-negotiable trip-wire?"

"No, I guess not. Are you saying that it's up to me to start such a discussion?"

"You seem to have set it up that way, but I'm not suggesting you go ahead before you feel ready to accept his love and to reciprocate in some way. I do think even if you don't want to call it love, you could still describe your feelings and he would understand. He's come a long way in understanding his own emotions according to Carole. I can help you understand your emotions if you'll let me."

"I'm not sure..."

"Eventually you will have to decide whether to trust me. That's something we have to build together or we can't function very well."

"This is still all so new to me. I don't mean to be stand-offish.

"I do love you, Carol. Do you understand that about me at least?"

"I think I understand that, but do you really have any choice? As a symbiont aren't you just stuck with me, no matter what?"

"Yes, I do have a choice. We could just cooperate in a friendly way without love having anything to do with it. It sometimes happens that way, but it works far better when love is there."

"So, you have actually chosen to love me?"

"I feel drawn to you, even to your deepest darkness, and have made my choice. I greatly admire your struggles against convention and sexual stereotypes. I find you very lovable and an interesting, creative writer as well, but I hurt when you do. So, I try to help you. Do you resent my trying to help? It's not because I'm feeling sorry for you."

"It troubles me that I still need help after all these years, but it's a little different with you since you know everything anyway, and I don't even have to work up the courage to confess to anything."

"Then please make use of my already knowing. We can work on anything together whenever you're ready. Perhaps we should sync now. Are you ready for that? It can just be relaxing as we get to know each other better. Your past is past, and you need not surrender to it in the present."

WHO IS LADY CAROL?

*Since most men implicitly aspire to be idiots, falling
in love is especially terrifying for any woman not
wanting to waste her time on the wrong person.*

Lady Carol, *Beloved Incubus (First Impressions)*

The recently published novel by "Lady Carol" has brought to light an underground, cultic author previously known mainly on-line within certain specialized audiences drawn to radical feminism or bizarre forms of gender-bending sexuality involving female domination. What is unusual here is the departure from past quasi-political rants and an almost pornographic advocacy of a life-style, towards something of a wholly different kind.

The novel in question, *Beloved Incubus*, is probably the first of many that will ultimately try to illuminate what it feels like and, more importantly, what it actually means for a human to host a symbiont. Evidently, nothing is the same any more. Whether this symbiosis provides, as the author asserts, the ultimate fulfillment of what it means to be truly human, or something else, remains for each reader to decide. I remain skeptical. What does their biology as parasites really entail? There are plenty of well-known parasites whose adult forms ultimately burst forth from their hosts like the creatures in the classic movie *Alien*. Shouldn't we really find all this out before we give these "symbionts" our blanket seal of approval?

The realization that symbionts live among us and within some of us is still a relatively new and controversial discovery, and, in this reviewer's opinion, a lot of scientific facts remain to be discovered before their relationship to humans can be fully understood or accepted as something altogether helpful or healthy. The author admits that symbionts are extremely intelligent and come with an agenda of their own to domesticate humans "so they can fulfill their great potential and not trash the world." Nevertheless, despite these very evident dangers (should they decide to conspire against us, for example), one must admit that Lady Carol has described in a very compelling fashion the seductive power of symbionts to convince infected humans of their worth, and to foster new kinds of human relationships for their hosts that were formerly impossible to achieve.

The novel is divided into two main sections, the first of which is entitled First Impressions. This details Lady Carol's hilarious first encounter with her rather anomalous and improbable male lover (a nerdy academic scientist), her own symbiont "Legba", and, then, most strangely of all, with her lover's symbiont, "Carole." Evidently, her lover had once had a crush on her in high school and decided to pursue Carol in real life with the help of his symbiont. Carole the symbiont knows all about Carol as Lady Carol and her current situation as radical femdom advocate, but somehow protects the nerdy professor from instant sexual slavery as he bumbles into Lady Carol's world of bondage. Who would have guessed Lady Carol's considerable talent for comedy based on her obsessive website? This part alone is worth the price of the book, and I confess that parts of it left me laughing until the tears were streaming down my face.

In section two, something changes in Lady Carol's world view that allows her to accept her lover as what he is rather than trying to reformat him into her compliant sex object. Cynics might denigrate the novel as an eclectic Harlequin Romance written specifically for the dominatrix world, but this all sounds surprisingly healthy and strangely "normal" for Lady Carol. These changes in world view happened gradually and are detailed by Lady Carol in more or less a chronological order. It is at this point, it seems to me, the fictional parts start to predominate over any tiny nucleus of truth, and the reader should be on guard against all the shamelessly pro-symbiont propaganda. For example, just as she stops trying to dominate her lover, he adapts willingly and enthusiastically to her sexuality, and so she now has it all, miracle of miracles (!), and they all lived happily ever after... If it were only so, maybe we should all acquire a symbiont, ASAP, and let the golden age of liberated sexuality begin! What could possibly go wrong?

Needless to say, I remain skeptical of all this uncritical enthusiasm for symbionts and for their supposed benefits to human life. I concede that for a few damaged individuals like Lady Carol and her ilk, there may, on balance, (assuming no hidden biological surprises!) be a net benefit from hosting a symbiont that outweighs the very dangerous downside. Fictionalized accounts like this one can never convince me that the real dangers have been confronted seriously by symbiont partisans such as Lady Carol. There are too many questions arising that do not get straight answers. I hope that someday Lady Carol will have the honesty to write a new book about her experiences if and when her relationships fall apart, and symbionts no longer seem to be the helpful answer to all the world's problems.

Dr. Karen Smith *is an occasional book reviewer for our journal and a full-time consultant for the Federal Government on matters concerning newly emerging infectious diseases, including symbionts.*

IT'S YOUR FLESH THAT I WEAR

Don't you know that a midnight hour comes when everyone has to take off his mask? Do you think life always lets itself be trifled with? Do you think you can sneak off a little before midnight to escape this?

Søren Kierkegaard

AP-Atlanta **Low Influenza Rate this Season Mystifies Scientists**

The Center for Disease Control has issued a report noting the remarkable drop in the incidence of all types of influenza this past flu season. Doctors there have been unable to offer any explanation of this dramatic decrease. Epidemiologists at the CDC have also detected a slight *negative* correlation between the decrease in influenza cases and the percentage of vaccination in a given region (exactly the opposite of what was expected); however, scientists strongly caution that this is no excuse to stop vaccinating for flu as some in the highly vocal anti-vaccination movement have recommended. "This is probably just a statistical fluke caused by inaccurate record keeping for flu vaccinations. We're looking into how this might have occurred on such a large scale," according to an anonymous source within the CDC.

Reuters-Beijing **"Dragon Girls" and Miscarriages Roil Political Waters in China**

Although women may hold up half the sky, their status in the rapidly changing culture of modern China is fraught. Recently there appears to be a public health problem: high rates of miscarriage that somehow have become conflated with certain young radical feminist women, aka Dragon Girls, who have been very vocal in their demands for equal pay, equal status in their jobs and the right to a career. The government has neither confirmed nor denied that there is any connection between the two things, but there is plenty of speculation on the internet and in the foreign press. Equality of the sexes has been a major tenet of Communist doctrine although actual progress in achieving equality has been difficult to assess independently by outsiders because of problems with obtaining the Government's statistical data on employment and wages for women.

———•◆◦◆◦◆•———

Sometime later, I delivered a set of my transcribed notes to Dr. Ellis and gave her a few weeks to digest the most extensive explanation of what I appeared to be dealing with now. Although I have many more questions, I pretty much believe Carole has been honest in her answers to me. Nevertheless, it's hard for me to avoid subjective judgments; there are so few ways yet of externally verifying many of her astonishing statements.

"Before we begin, Dr. Ellis, I wanted to ask whether you had received my medical records dealing with possible exposure to tropical diseases and any venereal diseases."

"Yes, I have. You appear to have produced strong antibodies to several things indicative of exposure, but apparently do not harbor active pathogenic bacteria or viruses at the moment. Did you have a chance to discuss these results with your physician?"

"No, not yet, but I'm scheduled to talk with him soon. He only sent me a summary of the tests so far and indicated that it all looked good; normal blood work, etc. He mentioned that my immune response to several things seemed very robust, which I take as partial confirmation of what Carole has been telling me. It dawned on me later to ask whether my blood could be tested for a robust response to ricin as well. He said he would check whether that was even possible since that's now a highly

122

restricted substance; it might have to be out-sourced to a special lab with the appropriate license needed to purchase the chemical from Sigma."

"And the point of all that would be...?"

"Ricin is such a potent toxin that it is inevitably fatal to humans even in minuscule amounts. It would be very anomalous for a human to react to it with a strongly protective immune response; nevertheless, some marsupials do just that... It's just a hunch, really. Anyway, we don't have that information yet."

"You have given me your transcription of your conversation with Carole, which I have read pretty thoroughly, but I wonder about *your* impressions of all this?"

"I think we are finally getting somewhere as far as what Carole really thinks she is."

"So, you have come to believe her story even more?"

"I think she is telling me the truth as she sees it to the particular questions that I have asked. I am beginning to trust her. I was a bit surprised that she, in effect, selected you to be my psychiatrist even before she had fully revealed herself to me."

"So, she may be leaving out some important things about her biology and her need for your agreement?"

"Perhaps, but that's not proven. I am always free to ask more questions as I figure out how to formulate them. Posing questions correctly so that her answers can be tagged as either true or false is much harder than it may seem initially. Much of the time I remain undecided."

"You leave door open to other possible explanations of events?"

"I am a scientist by intensive training and by profession, so I believe that nothing is ever completely settled within the domain of science. I find myself in the midst of an experiment involving myself as the primary subject, so it's exceedingly difficult for me to remain wholly objective. In many ways I am relying on you to provide a realistic outside perspective, and maybe to suggest ways of verifying some of Carole's statements. I have also expressed my concern about the difficulties I am having distinguishing vivid dreams from vivid reality. My only clues seem to be little slippages in time, and a few slight anachronisms that I notice occasionally. It's hard to know what to make of them, or if I might be just mistaken."

"I will try to do so as best I can to help you. You should make a detailed list or diary of these little anomalies and exactly what it was that you noticed. Some things are difficult for me to verify merely based on your reportage. For example, even now, how do I know you have *actually* engaged in all these unsafe sexual practices and are not just fantasizing about them or experiencing emulations? That would equally well explain how you've avoided STDs."

"Yes, I see your point. Ignoring the ethical problems, I suppose Carol and I could invite you to one of our love-making sessions, but I can't see her agreeing to it. Moreover, that might pretty well chill the moment for everyone. Carol could possibly talk to you directly, but I'm not sure she would agree to that either, but still, it might be worth a try. She might agree to an email exchange with you via her website, but that would be equally hard to verify. I'm not certain what Julie would agree to; she's still not talking to me, but she might have quite different views as a biologist."

"Have you ever followed up the virus connection that Carole suggests? I find this transfer of a virus from plant to human very improbable."

"Not entirely unprecedented, however. Also, there are other possibilities; I might point out that humans have been acting as vectors for the transmission of plant viruses, probably since the invention of agriculture. Smokers can unwittingly spread tobacco mosaic virus to their tomato plants, for example. So perhaps cultivated plants can sometimes act as vectors for certain viruses that infect mammals. That wouldn't necessarily require viruses that were capable of infecting both plant and animal cells.

"The answer to the first part of your question is no, not yet. I have been trying to find a cooperative virologist with suitable expertise in both mammalian and plant viruses. Naturally, this would also have to be a scientist whom I trusted enough to reveal these things about a possible new virus in strictest confidence. Both trustworthiness and specialization seem to be working against me here, but I will continue to search for possible candidates.

"I have submitted blood samples, of course, as part of my general health work up, but so far nothing helpful stands out about viruses except for a few common ones like CMV for which I am negative. Examination of plant surface extracts may yield a larger virus load free of the usual mammalian viruses that might make things easier to sort out. That might actually be a good question for Carole if she trusts me enough to answer it, assuming she knows. She has asserted that much of the mechanism involving virus transmission (and there may be more than one virus) is unknown even to her."

"Do you believe that Carole is a danger to you? I also mean that in a public health sense too. Should the CDC become involved and investigate your symbiont and her triggering virus?"

"No, I don't believe Carole is a direct danger to me. Whatever is happening to me has not affected my physical health except positively. Also, I have been happier with my life recently than I have ever been before, personally and professionally. While some vague notion of 'happiness' may be a pretty flawed metric for mental health (just higher levels of serotonin?), I'd still sort of go along with the old, 'if it ain't broke, don't fix it' point of view. I could easily be doing much worse.

"Whether she is an *indirect danger* to me is another question. Yes, I suppose I could get into serious trouble by helping her spread this infection if the authorities got wind of it."

"She admits there is a pretty large proportion of the human population who may gradually become infected, and possibly even other mammals such as pets might become infected to act as additional vectors. And what about your student helpers through the years? Don't you imagine her goal is to broaden the demographics considerably beyond certain sexual minorities?"

"Yes, I do indeed imagine that is her goal, but what if the infection turns out to be a helpful evolutionary adaptation, and no more dangerous than a flu shot? I think, for now anyway, the CDC has its hands full with far more urgent matters than a potentially beneficial infection. I don't think any harm is being done; quite the contrary. We're certainly not talking Ebola virus here."

"Do you believe that Carole trusts you?"

"I believe we are actively working on trust issues with each other. Remember that she said it was probably possible for me to rid myself of her with some onslaught of modern medications unavailable to Yayael. Sharing that information with me was an indication of trust. I think she believes that I would protect her."

"And would you?"

"Yes, I certainly would try."

"I am interested in how your symbiont Carole might have changed your opinion of human females. Couldn't she just represent a more controllable fantasy female who satisfies your every erotic need?"

"That's a pretty complicated set of issues to dissect. Yes, I suppose she has actually moved my opinions much more to the feminist side. There's nothing quite like having a few good counter-examples fresh in your mind when you encounter your own sexist prejudices. Controllable? Carole is more like a force of nature who could utterly consume me if she wished."

"Why do you suppose that she has not done that?"

"She has explicitly stated that my partnership is important to her. She could, no doubt, chemically induce some level of cooperation with just hormonal manipulation, but I don't think that would be enough to satisfy her. She wants me to actively work with her on mutual goals; that's more than just following orders. When I questioned her in the Library, I tried to create an emotionally neutral setting precisely so I could be as objective as possible. That seemed fairly successful to me."

"Yet she still had some powers to influence events even before you accepted her as a partner."

"True, but the one instance we know of concerns my choice of psychiatrist, and you have *not* simply accepted Carole's version of the situation."

"Doesn't this 'force of nature' characteristic also just play to your erotic fantasies? I'm saying that the danger aspect of the relationship may now play a role in how you view Carole (literally, The Amazon Goddess!) and would fit in with some of your emerging submissive tendencies towards female domination in general."

"Yes, I guess you could possibly interpret it that way if you take things out of context. Nevertheless, the danger aspect certainly *has* concerned me and prompted my inquiries into all aspects of the relationship; however, I strongly maintain that this is *not* merely some elaborate masturbatory fantasy involving submission to an Amazon Goddess. I do see your problem with verification, however. If Carole communicated directly with you by email, would you have any means of discerning her reality? I'm sure she would easily pass a Turing test, but then so would I. Perhaps you might come up with some better questions for her than I have."

"I'll give that some thought. Perhaps it might be informative even if not a direct or complete verification of your symbiont hypothesis. Let me work on that for a bit, and I'll let you know when I am ready. I'd like to have a list of questions prepared."

DREAM CATCHER

We are such stuff as dreams are made on; and our little life
is rounded with a sleep.

Prospero, The Tempest Act 4, scene 1, 148-158

One morning as I lay in bed, lazily avoiding getting up, and just barely aware of a fading dream I had just experienced, it occurred to me that this would be a good time to ask Carole about dreams in general. Would it be possible for us to experiment with them in some way useful to science by making use of her expertise? As soon as I launched that general inquiry, she produced an emulation of us lying together naked and face to face under the sheets.

"A serious question? Do I have to get dressed for it?"

"Serious, but this will do," I said, kissing her. "I've been meaning to ask you about dreams, both my native dreams and your synthetic dream creations. In particular, how much do the two differ? I've obviously just noted that my native dreams are much harder to recall once I awaken; so, why are your synthetic dreams so memorable and so full of detail?"

"A fair question. Your native dreams seem to be subject to fairly rapid erasure from your short-term memory. A lot of this lack of permanence is generally true of mental images in your visual cortex. Apparently, the brain protects itself, at least partially, from confusing mere mental images with actual visual images, thereby preventing creation of false memories in unmanageable numbers. The process is by no means perfect, however, and I make use of these imperfections.

"When I create synthetic dreams for you, I make sure they become fixed in your long-term memory. That way they can be recalled in pretty exact detail, although the record of them is still subject to some of the same problems of corruption that plague eye-witness testimony. Nevertheless, I make use of my ability to refresh and sometimes to alter these more permanent records. Don't ask me how it works exactly - Can you tell me what your pancreas is doing right at this moment? You're quite correct that elaborate experiments would have to be done to figure out exactly what I am doing."

"Are you familiar with the Ojibwe notion of a 'Dream Catcher'? Supposedly this spirit device is constructed to filter out 'bad dreams' and to allow only the good ones through. Are you capable of such things?"

"In principle, I suppose I could do this, but I have seen little point to it because of your active forgetting of regular dreams even if they're pretty bad. My synthetic dreams are more along the lines of 'Sweet Dreams Are Made of This' as the song goes. I design their contents for particular purposes that we have agreed upon and store them in more permanent memory locations from the start."

"So, would you say that my native dreams have relatively random contents that we only later superimpose meanings onto? As in psychoanalysis, for example."

"I think your careful use of 'relatively random' is highly appropriate because your native dreams appear to be a mixture of things, some based on real daytime events or emotions, and some truly random additions from strong past memories. A lot of the random elements appear to be added from your brain stem. Whether there is much signal embedded in this noise is an interesting, open question. Humans do seem generally to be overeager to impose meanings on such series of events or images whatever their origins."

"Are you capable of dreaming independently of me? I mean by that: do you sometimes experience dreams that are different from my native dreams?"

"No, actually I experience your native dreams only, but with one big difference: my recall of such dreams is much better than yours. If you have a *really* bad dream, it will generally seem much worse to me, but I do have my own defenses.

"Sometimes when I'm doing mathematics I can relax into a dream-like state, you might call it a daydream, in which I can freely associate among many different concepts. This meditative state is somewhat analogous to a dream, but I have much more control, and I can always remember important things that need follow-up."

"But, even for my real dreams, good or bad, you *could* actually capture them in some way so I could recall them too?"

"Yes, if you wanted me to do so. What purpose did you have in mind?"

"I was originally thinking about some sort of scientific experimentation that would interest my psychiatrist, but it now occurs to me also that this might be a wonderful creative tool for writers and other artists as a source of inspiration. Long ago in the Dada and Surrealist movements, such dream images and other sources of the irrational and the random were commonly incorporated into artworks with considerable success."

"Are you thinking of becoming an artist now?"

"Well, let's just say I know a certain writer who might be interested..."

"Are you not a little worried about what wholesale dredging up things from the depths of her unconscious might do to her?"

"Yes, I am; that's why I'm asking. I would guess that it could be done safely with Legba being available as psychopomp to help her over some rough spots. Perhaps turning raw emotions into art would be cathartic for her."

"I think you're right about Legba helping; he's really quite clever about such things and very gentle about it too."

"Do you think I should bring this up with her? She might even have thought it up already on her own. We've talked a lot about the sources of creativity in art and science."

"I don't see any harm in discussing it with her. She seems to be resilient enough mentally to handle some pretty strong emotions now."

"I'd like to experiment a little on myself before suggesting it to her. Do you think I'm resilient enough to handle it?"

"No, you're too mushy right now!" She said, teasingly, fondling my penis. "You'll need to stiffen your resolve a bit more to penetrate the unconscious. Here, let me help you handle that."

"Is this leading up to a recovered dream?"

"I'm putting you in the proper mood; just a little more testosterone needed here... There you go. Which dream would you like to view?"

"Well, that dream I just had before I woke up... Could we rerun that one?"

"Not a very sexy dream... may I add a few things so I can be with you? It won't be exactly the same, but similar. You will probably put in some more random noise of your own anyway."

"I guess it wouldn't hurt anything. I remember being in a distant city attending some sort of conference and getting horribly lost on my way from my hotel to the Expo center. You could be someone I met there at the conference."

I was now clearly lost and was getting frustrated and a little anxious. The little visitors map they had given me with my conference credentials and session schedule seemed to have no relation whatever to the streets and buildings in front of me. The street signs were blank or blurry. The sky was overcast, and the sun was well hidden behind the clouds. I thought it was still early morning, but I couldn't get any sense of direction. So, I just stood there in my puzzlement as crowds of people surged around me like a stream flowing around a rock. I became furiously angry at the conference organizers for not providing buses from the hotel to the Expo center.

"Professor Douglas! Over here."

I noticed a pretty blonde woman waving to me. Vaguely familiar, but who?

"I attended your session yesterday, but we never got a chance to talk. I'm Karen Smith. You may not remember, but I sent you a letter a few months back... about this conference and your scheduled presentation. We talked briefly on the phone."

"Oh," I said. "Karen... you had some questions I think, if that is the correct letter I'm remembering... There were quite a few letters actually. I'm sorry I didn't get back to you, but I was so busy preparing for the conference..."

"Oh, I imagine. The topic is quite controversial at the moment. I know I'm being a little pushy here, but could we go somewhere quiet for a little follow-up discussion?"

"Yes, actually now would be a *very* good time. I'm afraid I'm quite lost at the moment. Can you steer us to a good place?"

"Yes, I know these streets are very confusing the first time you visit here, and they seem to keep changing every time you exit your hotel. It takes getting used to, these random streets. Let's head down this street... I forget what it's called. The signage around here is just really awful, isn't it? You'd think they didn't want visitors! My hotel is about a block down that way; they have a nice big quiet lobby."

Karen guided us through the crowds and across one large boulevard until we entered the revolving door at her hotel. The lobby was indeed nice and quiet. Moreover, it looked very, very familiar. Was I now back at my hotel? The clerk at the front desk looked exactly like Angus, the young desk clerk at my hotel, and he gave me a wave. Or maybe he waved at Karen.

We sat down in an area still served by the lobby bar and ordered a couple of glasses of Chablis. The waitress who delivered our drinks bore a remarkable resemblance to Carole in one of her more toned-down emulations of Carol. Our eyes met, and she winked. After we settled into our well upholstered chairs, Karen started to explain her interest in my presentation on *Solanaceae* of the Amazon basin. Apparently, she had doubts concerning Yayael, my chief informant about the goddess tree and other plants in his Great Garden.

"The very name Yayael carries connotations of a shady character, sort of a rebellious son of a father deity, who had challenged his authority and was killed for it."

"That may very well be, mythologically; nevertheless, it is quite true that my informant used that name and was addressed that way by his followers."

"Is it possible that this was a pseudonym or alias, perhaps?"

"I have no way of knowing. My translator was quite certain that this was the name he used, and I had no reason not to believe him. All of his followers used that name in our presence when they talked about him. We do have pictures of the individual involved if that's any help."

"My problem is that name seems taboo in much of the region where you say you met him. That's hard to reconcile with it being someone's given name in that culture."

"You may be correct that it's rare. Perhaps even that it's a pseudonym. Maybe the name was chosen precisely because it was taboo? My study site is only on the extreme edge of the main geographical center of this particular mythological belief system."

"What are you saying?"

"Perhaps the name was purposely chosen for its symbolic content as a label of rebellion... like Prometheus or Icarus, a rule-breaker or trickster figure? I think Yayael was inventing a new culture that used a few elements of an old shamanistic religion but introduced some radically new elements that pointed towards viewing the world in a completely different way."

"You say nothing of this in your presentation."

"It's pretty speculative and not really my area of expertise. I would hope that eventually an ethnobotanist fluent in the languages of the region could revisit this person and investigate more thoroughly."

"I appreciate your candor. I must admit I was worried that you'd be upset about this and with me for bringing this up."

"Not at all. Actually, I *do* appreciate your bringing this up now. It could come up at some point when I'm talking about this to general audiences, and I always like to be prepared. Perhaps you could fill me in on your particular interest in this culture and their ethnobotanical beliefs? What University are you with?"

"Oh, I'm not with a university at all, Professor. I work with various government agencies as a contractor helping out with certain special drug- and disease-related investigations. One concern is with the illegal importation of potentially new hallucinogenic substances into the country. Another is with the accidental importation of dangerous diseases."

"That seems very unlikely in this situation. All the components associated with my plants are well known, and probably much more readily available in plants native to the U.S. Anyway, I presume you've checked out the legitimacy of my import license?"

"Yes, we've been checking on that."

"And...?"

"Well, certain questions have arisen concerning your being banned from Colombia."

"What questions?"

"I'm not at liberty to say directly."

"That makes it pretty difficult to answer your questions then."

"I know. Sort of a stalemate. I may not ask you any of the questions that have been raised specifically."

"So, what are you going to do then?"

"I may only ask you various general questions and decide whether to trust you or not."

"So, if I mistakenly answer something incorrectly there will be a problem and you won't trust me? I'm not infallible, you know. I could simply be wrong and not lying."

"Also, if you answer incorrectly, you will never find your way back to the Expo center."

"I could take a cab."

"If there were any cabs to take. Then you would never find your way back to this hotel."

"Perhaps I'm staying at a different hotel."

"This is your hotel. My room is right next door to yours in 889."

"It sounds like you've been spying on me for some time. Is that what's been going on?"

"You've been under scrutiny for well over a year. We think we've detected a sinister pattern in your comings and goings. Especially your comings."

"And what would that be?"

"Again. I'm not at liberty to say."

"So, another stalemate?"

"Afraid so. Do you still perform a lot of oral sex on your girlfriend?"

"Pardon me?"

"You heard me perfectly well. Do you still lick her pussy out every day? I think I'd like that. Have you ever eaten blonde pussy?"

"Are you suggesting...?"

"Sure, why not? If I'm ever supposed to trust you, maybe a little pussy eating would seal the deal. What do you say? I'd give you a good report then."

"I'm astonished and don't know what to say!"

"Well, you could say yes. Is there some little problem you'd like to tell me about?"

"A problem?"

"You have no dangerous infectious diseases currently, do you?"

"Not that I'm aware of. I'd say that I'm in extremely good health for my age."

"Then what's the problem?"

"Well, for one, I hardly know you."

"You could get to know me in the Biblical sense. Would that do?"

"What do you really want from me?"

"We could discuss that after a little sex."

"Look, I'm pretty much committed to my girlfriend, and not looking for anything on the side."

"Oh, Professor, that's such an obvious lie! We know that you're shared around by your girlfriend. How does she decide who gets to share you?"

"You'll have to ask her."

"We have, but she won't say, and since she runs through lovers faster than I run through Kleenex, there's no time to waste."

"Well then, perhaps you'll never know."

"We know a lot about your symbionts."

"What do you know about symbionts?"

"That you're infected with one of them."

"I told you I did not have any major diseases."

"Clearly a half-truth!"

"So where are you going with this inquiry?"

"I want you to come up to my room and have sex with me so I will acquire a symbiont."

"And what would you do with a symbiont if you had one?"

"We'd study it, of course, and learn how to destroy it!"

"That would be cruel and also very bad for your health!"

"They're not real people, you know."

"They *are* real persons just as much as you are, and they seem to be far more ethical than you, and whoever else it is that you're working for!"

"I've told you who I worked for."

"Let's see some identification then."

"Badges? We don't need no stinkin' badges!"

"Very funny. I think we're done here."

With that I rose and left abruptly. Proceeding to the main desk in the lobby, I asked Angus about possibly changing my room for something on another floor.

"I'm sorry Professor, but with the conference we're *very* tightly booked. Perhaps tomorrow we might be able to find something if there's been a cancellation. Shall we notify you?"

"Yes, please do. Also, I seem to have misplaced my card key. Can you get me a new one?

"Certainly. May I see your ID for a moment? Current room number?"

"889"

"889 belongs to a Ms. Karen Smith. Are you sharing the room with her?"

"No, no! Definitely not! Maybe 887?"

"Yes, that appears to be your room. Just a minute... OK, here's a new card key. Please be more careful with it this time."

"I will, thank you. Oh, one further thing. Can you write down directions for me to walk from here to the Expo center? The damned conference organizers haven't arranged for buses!"

"Certainly Sir. From this desk proceed to that exit over there. See it? Between the two little shops? Exit there, go left to the corner about half a block, then turn right, go two blocks, turn right again, go another two blocks, then right again for two blocks, right again, then a block and a half. The side entrance to the Expo center should be on your left if you've made a proper clockwise circuit and have successfully dodged around the two obvious spatial singularities. Avoid looking at street signs or landmarks; these will never be the same twice. Just follow the directions exactly. When you return, remember that you must wind around the path *counter-clockwise*, or who knows where you will wind up. I'll write it all down for you."

I was feeling very nauseous and had a slight headache after that and returned to my presumed room on the 8th floor to relax for a bit. It did seem to have all my suitcases and belongings. Room service seemed more tempting than anything in the mini-bar, so I ordered a cocktail to be brought up. Ten minutes later, there was a rap at the door. I suspiciously peered out into the hallway through the peep hole, and saw Karen standing there. I fastened the security chain and opened the door a crack.

"What do you want? There was really nothing further to discuss."

"Perhaps we got off to a bad start. What if you just let me suck on your tongue for a bit? You know what a powerful aphrodisiac that juice can be!"

"I don't think so! Go away or I will call security!"

"Oh please! Just a little of that juice from the gland in your tongue! I'll do anything you want after that."

I shut the door, and waited for my drink to arrive, which it finally did. To my great relief it was my waitress from the lobby bar who appeared with my drink on a tray. I opened the door and hurriedly ushered her in, closing the door quickly behind her.

"Thank you so much!" I said. "I was beginning to wonder whether you'd ever reappear. Let's bail out now; I've had enough of this paranoia!"

"Bail out? Sir, I'm afraid you must be mistaking me for someone else."

"Oh, come on, I saw you wink at me down in the lobby!"

"It will change the dream radically if you draw me further into this now."

"I don't really care whether we finish this dream or not. Karen's really starting to get on my nerves."

"As you wish. You won't ever be able to review this dream again in uncontaminated form."

At that point, we exited the dream, and I awakened into Carole's bedroom emulation and into her arms again, greatly relieved.

"Thank you. That was perhaps a little more than I was prepared for. Is it possible to know the content in a general way before a dream is recalled? Could I avoid certain upsetting things?"

"There's not really an index or anything like that. They're sort of roughly categorized by their emotional content. I could probably pull up any number of dreams with an atmosphere of paranoia and menace, but it would be sheer chance whether we could find any particular one that you partially remembered. Today, we could access that dream you just had, but quite soon, it would have decayed into just part of the mix by accrual of more and more random elements and would be severely corrupted from its original form."

"This is far more difficult work than I imagined. Do you think Carol could still make use of this method to stir up some creative ideas?"

"Perhaps. Certainly, some oddly beautiful combinations of things might be stirred up. Conjoined umbrellas and sewing machines? It will, as you said, take a lot of work to learn whether anything useful to her might come from it. I do think your psychiatrist would have fun playing with it, but it would be a lifetime's work even for her! I'm not sure that a person's dreams are even countable once they sink back into the continuum."

"Any comments on signal versus noise in this little episode?"

"It's a pretty small sample... I suppose one might reasonably infer that you are anxious about being secretly under investigation and afraid that certain embarrassing things about you and Carol might already be known to the authorities, whomever those authorities might be. Perhaps it might be something like a dream warning from yourself: Hush! Caution! Echoland!"

"Anything else?"

"That's about as far as I would go. Do you see more?"

"It provokes a question: suppose a symbiont were given to someone like Karen who purposely welcomes him into herself, but then betrays him by allowing those authorities to experiment with anti-viral meds to destroy him."

"What's the question precisely?"

"What would happen?"

"It depends on how quickly he figured out the situation. There might be enough time while he was being established to uncover her lies."

"Suppose he did, what could he do to prevent his destruction?"

"Basically, he would search for some leverage to make her want to thwart her employer's evil scheme and instead, try to keep him safe."

"Such as?"

"It depends on her psychic make-up and how much time he has to work. Perhaps she starts to enjoy feeling younger and healthier. Perhaps she starts to enjoy syncing with him. Perhaps he raises questions about her life that trouble her, and he then helps her resolve them. Somehow, she would have to start to value him and to enjoy his company enough to protect him. All humans are lonely at some level, so it would seem fairly likely that he would find something valuable for her that she didn't expect."

"Would Karen be someone you would warn me against?"

"Since she's in a dream, there would not typically be any characteristic scent that would give her away as a dangerous candidate although I can't rule it out entirely. So, in a dream you would usually be left to your own devices."

"Do you think I should have let her in the room and had sex with her?"

"You said she was getting on your nerves, so why would you want to?"

"Just for the sake of the dream, to find out what happened next?"

"It wouldn't have done any real harm, but it might have made you feel guilty when you awakened; at least it would inside a dream that you didn't know yet was a dream, and from which bad consequences ensued."

"So that could have been part of the signal, feeling guilty?"

"It didn't proceed to that point, so we can't know. All we know is that the dream was getting increasingly unpleasant for you because you were being asked to be an accessory to a heinous act, and you wanted out. You probably could have exited by yourself if it got too stressful. There's kind of a self-protective mechanism that sometimes kicks in when you don't want to know something or to do something in a dream. When that *doesn't* kick in you can get obsessive, repeated dreams that trouble your sleep until there's some resolution."

"Is that what happened in my first dreams of you?"

"Those weren't dreams in the strict sense of the word. Emulations or repeated attempts to communicate would be more precise. My signal was *much* stronger than the noise and you had to pay attention to it."

"I'm glad I found you in all my noise. Thank you for signaling."

Carole looked me straight in the eye, smiled, and gently smoothed my hair back from my forehead. "I'm glad I found you too. I was very lucky."

"Lucky perhaps, but also a shameless temptress?"

"Why should either of us be ashamed when we offer ourselves to each other out of love?"

SYMBIONT SAVIOR

Joy, rather than happiness, is the goal of life, for joy
is the emotion which accompanies our fulfilling our
natures as human beings. It is based on the experience
of one's identity as a being of worth and dignity.

Rollo May

I suppose I can now admit that without Carole, I was lost in dysfunction of some sort when I was floundering around, post-divorce. That's certainly her expressed opinion of me and, I think, a fair assessment my behavior at the time. Probably under the best circumstances, it would have taken me a few years to get back on track. The other key element of my dysfunction was the deep despair I felt about humanity's future in the face of an on-rushing mass extinction. I was hardly alone in this despair. Every scientist I knew whose research seemed to be documenting the consequences of our hell bound population expansion was experiencing the same sense of imminent climate-triggered doom that sometimes paralyzed me in hopeless inaction.

It's hard to express the deep bond that has grown between us, part love, part complementarity in approximately equal measure. If, as she says, she makes use of the female parts of my brain, then it is fair to say that without those parts being made accessible to me by Carole, I was truly lost in some desperately lonely, polarized version of masculinity, and I could never have approached Carol, let alone become united with her as a partner. Also, having those parts being made available to Carol has dramatically altered her view of me.

A lot of these thoughts and questions come to me with difficulties and are fraught with self-ridicule of my so-called masculinity when I try to write about them. Am I getting mushy and sentimental in my old age? Do older men become more feminine as they lose testosterone just before they become asexual? Is there some sense in which Carole and I are becoming one person? Is there some sense in which Carole is just a female version of me? Or am I just responding to living in a grossly polluted world full of endocrine disruptors?

Some of the religious echoes are the most troubling. I hate to give credence to woo nonsense about "holy marriage" since I do not believe in gods. Our language does not yet contain the right words to convey what I am experiencing. Still, "soul" can perhaps be a useful word in the sense of describing a person's unique inner essence in contrast to *merely* a corporeal body of flesh and blood. I would prefer to describe the whole situation in largely physical terms involving an experienced brain and its epiphenomena, but I must admit that what I am experiencing demands a larger and more poetic vocabulary to describe how I am being transformed by being a man now with a female symbiont. Carol is better equipped than I to traverse this unknown land and to make sense of it. She's guiding me as she scouts it out. Her teaching methods have been sometimes a little harsh or embarrassing, but I don't think she ever intended to hurt me.

Evolution has perhaps played this trick on masculinity once before as evidenced by the reshaping of the masculine skull into a more gender-neutral form, some 50,000 years ago, as evidenced by the less pronounced brow ridge. It was apparently more favorable in human populations for males to get along with each other, at least within their group, and not to be constantly in violent competition with other males for mates or resources. A noticeable rise in human culture was noted as a result of decreased testosterone levels and increased cooperation. So, Nietzsche was wrong to imagine future Übermenschen as hyper masculine and sociopathic (at least that was the vulgar interpretation picked up by the Nazis as the Aryan blonde beast). Perhaps the change in the biology of humans with the acquisition of symbionts will make possible other necessary changes in our culture that might favor our survival as a new humanity. Some see the evolution of life on Earth as a whole series of changes, starting with the cellular level, and escalating in complexity as life engulfed life, and symbiosis miraculously occurred. Life engulfing life is also a pretty good metaphor for sex, broadly defined.

Carole has described to me the formation of a quad. That is, the combination of two humans and their symbionts in an ultra-stable relationship. This is what she hopes will be formed from my partnership with Carol if all goes well. It's hard not to think of a quad as a peculiar word for a kind of arranged marriage. In this case, the wedding arrangers are the symbionts involved with us rather than our moms and dads; nevertheless, Carol and I still have veto power. The formation of a quad, at least in its advanced stages, requires something called super-sync. I get the distinct impression that our two symbionts already sync a little bit together when Carol and I have sex, but whatever it is that they do then, it is not the full super-sync. I'm not yet sure how that's done. They also do communicate electronically, but that cannot be much like syncing, which is an overwhelmingly rich nonverbal data-stream.

In my essay on my views of religion for Dr. Ellis, I complained that I didn't understand the urgency of salvation built into several religions. Today I would revise that assertion somewhat. Back then, I said: The whole urgency of salvation seemed completely pointless and lost on me. By this I meant *individual* salvation, and, of course, nature appears to care very little about the ultimate fate of individuals. I am beginning to understand more and more the urgency of salvation for humanity: salvation from ourselves, from our unbounded greed, from our manic reproduction and from our hubris. Call it original sin if you want, but I don't think any supernatural agency is likely to come to our aid, nor are we likely to muster the political will or the necessary courage and organization needed to save ourselves. Perhaps it really is better to be lucky than smart, and better to be joyful than happy. With our symbionts we have lucked out and might become joyful yet. Carole has given me hope far beyond anything I might have expected.

BELOVED INCUBUS

A book is a dream that you hold in your hand.

Neil Gaiman

I've known Bob since I was a junior in high school. It was his bookstore that fueled my passion for books, especially those explicitly forbidden for various reasons, since he inevitably had them first whenever the courts finally decided to treat Americans as grown-ups. And it was Bob who looked the other way when I purchased various things like *Tropic of Cancer*, etc. during my rebellious, hormonal youth, and Bob, who knew full well that I was not 21. This was a major issue between me and my parents growing up. My dad was always judging books by their cover, e.g., *Crime and Punishment*; "Sounds atrocious!"; *The Killer*, "Disgusting!", etc., etc. I knew better than to leave anything lying around that was politically or sexually out there, but fortunately, I had an old desk in my bedroom that had a locking drawer where my various literary treasures could be stashed, and I gradually accumulated many of the books that were finally emancipated in the fifties and sixties and notorious enough for me to have heard of them. Nor did I neglect older works such as *Ulysses* or *Jurgen*; if they were once on a forbidden list, I would manage to get them and try to read them no matter how difficult they were at first. I once posed a little logical challenge to my dad:

If you have not read the books,
then you have no right to ban them.

144

If you actually have read the books,
then you have one hell of a nerve telling me not to read them.

He got pretty mad at me for that, particularly the disrespectful, one hell of a nerve part, and my dad never again carried any weight whatsoever as a book critic at least in my mind. My mother was a slightly more adventurous reader, but she was too readily swayed by my dad when it came to what I should be allowed to read or not. There are fathers of the flesh, but, mercifully, there are also fathers of the spirit whom we may gradually find elsewhere in the world if we are persistent and lucky on our quest.

Bob was not like my dad. His take on books was similar to mine, which was that strange books by strange authors can give you some insight into strange things you might never encounter in your own life, particularly if you were growing up in the great American Middle West. Of course, this was pre-internet, and those brave authors and publishers that dared to break social strictures sometimes paid a big price for doing so and took a lot of shit and lost a lot of book income to lawyers. Bob would frequently point out some new item he'd just received and make some tentative judgment on its worth. He had a small devoted cadre of readers and book enthusiasts (jokingly: random normal deviates) who met in his bookstore occasionally to discuss books and politics. As a high school kid, unfortunately, I could not often manage to attend any of these meetings or readings, or whatever, but I loved their spirit of comradery and attended whenever I could. In a lot of ways, Bob fit the old "beatnik" label, but had outlived that movement, and didn't fit well into Hippie youth culture when it arose. He was definitely a leftist, but one with a strong libertarian streak that couldn't stand the suppression of anyone's ideas, no matter how outrageous and oppositional. His notion was that ideas should be put out there, and their worth would be ultimately be decided by people who engaged with them, discussed them, argued about them, parodied them, wrote about them, and when all was said and done, digested them, used them or spit them out as useless. Ideas, even bad ones, he felt, when suppressed, seemed to ferment in the dark, become super toxic, then get taken up by secret little groups of fanatics who go all fundamentalist about the ideas, and demand unquestioning obedience to those ideas within their little cult.

It had been quite a long time since I had been to Bob's bookstore, but it still was there, and Bob, although quite elderly now, still ran the place and still came in every day to chat with his customers. I was pleased to see Carol's book, *Beloved Incubus*, on display in the window, and I entered, wondering how things had changed over the years. The store seemed pretty much the same with its creaky wooden floors, and ancient sagging bookshelves, absolutely stuffed with books in some order known only to Bob. It still was the mother lode of dust, and one that gave some people a runny nose, even if they were just slightly allergic to dust. Bob was engaged in an argument with a customer when I came in and had his back to me. The customer was getting loud and angry, and soon stalked off out of the store. Bob turned back around with a bemused look on his face that he got when he thought he had won the argument but had not quite convinced his opponent that he had just lost. He did a bit of a double take when he saw me.

"Richard! Is that really you?"

"Hey, Bob. Yes, really me; just can't stay away."

"Well, you bloody well *have* stayed away for a long time! Maybe a decade?"

"Busy being a science jock, but I've never forgotten who has all the good stuff!"

"Well, welcome back! So..., are you looking for something in particular?"

"Well that new one in the window caught my eye."

"*Beloved Incubus*?"

"Yeah, that one. Any good?"

"Oh yeah, that's a strange one, but I think you might like it. What got you interested?"

"Well... I've been dating the author, and..."

"No shit? You've actually been *dating* Lady Carol?"

"Yes, no shit, and I thought it would be wise for me to read the book."

"You leave me speechless..."

"Why? You don't think I should read the book?"

"Oh, yes; of course, you should. It's just that it's hard to imagine any man actually *dating* Lady Carol in the usual sense of the word... Well maybe a few things about that book make some sense now..."

"What makes sense?"

"I guess I should explain a little... Carol, the *real* one, used to be one of the regulars for book discussions here in the store when she was an undergraduate. Many of us here knew her quite well; she was wonderfully argumentative, and we loved her for starting all those lively discussions with some outrageous proposition or other. Hell, we used to go picketing with her sometimes! And then suddenly she stopped coming and withdrew into herself. We were afraid she'd gotten lost in drugs like so many did back then. No one ever found out what happened to her, but eventually, we started hearing about a certain 'Lady Carol' on the internet who just about had to be her."

"So, you lost complete touch with her?"

"Well, tentatively I did contact her a couple times, and invited her back, but she didn't think it was 'appropriate' to meet with us again. I must say, we all felt a little hurt when she rebuffed us that way without explanation, but I could tell a little from reading her blog entries on line that she was quite different from the sweet-natured, but feisty feminist that we loved. I think half our little group was in love with her and the other half although gay, at least admired her for her lively wit and her absolutely wicked sarcasm. Lady Carol was a whole different woman. Richard, if you don't mind my asking, how the hell did you get tangled up with Lady Carol? Are you some sort of a bondage freak?"

"It's a bit of a long story, but actually I knew her in high school, and connected with her at our 20th reunion. She was already established as Lady Carol at that point, but we somehow hit it off anyway. She got her symbiont from me."

"Really? We all thought all that symbiont stuff might just be fiction. I can't see her attending any high school reunion. Jesus! Have you read her stuff online? I just can't imagine Lady Carol happily mingling with some stuffy middle-class reunion crowd, exchanging pleasantries and politely sipping wine! She must have scared the shit out of them!"

"Oh, it's definitely not fiction, that symbiont part anyway. She was manipulated into attending the reunion by *my* symbiont. We left after Lady Carol was publicly called out, and they attempted to humiliate her. Actually, they attempted to humiliate me too, just for sitting next to her."

"Again, you leave me stunned... Who are 'they' and why did they want to humiliate you both?"

"That was part of the scheme hatched by my symbiont to place us together against a common enemy who obligingly took the bait and couldn't resist trying to humiliate us."

"Jesus! This symbiont of yours sounds pretty ruthless when you put it that way. Does it try to run your life?"

"It's very much a she. I wouldn't call her ruthless, but she didn't have a lot of patience when I was shy about pursuing my dream girl. I had a big crush on Carol in high school but didn't act on it. My symbiont gave me a second chance with Carol, and I completely forgive her for choosing those methods. Frankly, I don't know how it could have been done otherwise. We work together as partners mostly."

"I still can't figure Lady Carol going out with a normal man except perhaps to enslave him. So what price are you paying for this relationship?"

"We're still figuring that out, but I'm no slave... and who says I was ever normal? She has become precious to me and I won't leave her."

"Her novel does speak very well of her lover and her symbiont. That puzzled us at first. Lady Carol *never* has had anything good to say about our sex, but some of this was really positive. Now, she seems to be growing in a completely new direction. That would be good. The world may need to hear her latest ideas. I'm really glad that someone like you is now in her life. This is so unexpected."

"Did she come here to promote her book when it came out?"

"Well, yes, I was about to mention that. It was kind of a surprise since she rebuffed us earlier, but she did come and we did a little book signing right here in the store. She even seemed friendly again. We got a lively little discussion going about symbionts, but I don't think any of us took it very seriously at the time. She knew there was little she could say to convince us about symbionts; nevertheless, she made us an offer to get each of us infected with a symbiont if we wanted to find out. She said we could really make a contribution by joining forces with her."

"Did anyone take her up on that offer?"

"I think a few might have done so, but they've been very quiet about it if they have. That's something you might want to think about, Richard. We've had some shady government types snooping around and asking questions again. Have you ever met a Dr. Karen Smith? She's one of them. It reminds me a little of the old days, and all the harassment they put us through for our anti-war political views. Now it's symbionts. I hope it's worth it, Richard. They will come for you eventually if it seems the slightest bit threatening to the establishment."

"My symbiont and I will have to take our chances. There's a lot at stake, and we feel that time is running out, and we are forced to act now. You mentioned earlier that something might make sense now. What was that?"

"Oh, the dedication in the novel. Have you not read it? That was a subject of some discussion after Lady Carol's visit."

To strange men, all those not from the
planet Mars, who listened to me,
and to my strange lovers, who have given me a strange new life

"I think the strange men are all of you from the book store discussion group. She's not forgotten you at all."

"That's wonderful and flattering that she remembered us. I get the 'Men are from Mars' trope. We used to discuss pop-psych bullshit like that with her sometimes, although I think those precise words came much later in a book title. Are you just one of her strange lovers?"

"I am just one of two. The other is her symbiont."

"Her beloved incubus?"

"Yes, of course. A woman like Carol winds up desired by many. She doesn't ask for it. Unfortunately, she's also hated by many more now, as you might imagine. She must be very careful. She took a risk coming to you and outing herself as one infected with a symbiont."

"This whole symbiont business... what are you two up to with that?"

"The plan is to domesticate the human race before the world is destroyed by human folly."

"Good luck with that plan! Folly always seems to be a growth industry. What will combat that?"

"Spreading symbionts throughout the world's population and organizing the infected individuals into a political force to be reckoned with."

"I've heard that dream before. Didn't work out so well the last time round, did it?"

"No, it didn't, so the battle continues on a radically different front. I think the 'new left' became frustrated and was subject to some of the same totalitarian temptations that plagued the old left. We know what's good for you, and here it is..., open wide. Americans never fully digested the actual ideas from the left; they just got pissed off at the patronizing, know-it-all tone and spit it back out. I know you got cross-wise with them yourself sometimes for being too libertarian."

"So, what's different with symbionts?"

"What's different is that with symbionts people will internalize many ideas about human decency, and they won't need to have them imposed from the outside. Symbiont-infected individuals are forming an independent political force that's starting to be seen on the ballot. Have you noticed any of that? It's really a green movement now as much as a left-wing progressive movement."

"We've noticed maybe a little, but I don't understand how just having a symbiont makes people suddenly decent."

"It doesn't do it immediately, but it leads to an internal dialogue that takes the edge off human nastiness rather quickly. Symbionts are inside your head and notice every self-serving lie and force you to confront them all honestly. They have an interest in seeing that the world is not destroyed by greed because they will die with us. In a strange way they have become the better angels of our nature."

"Richard, that's a lot to take on faith. How do you know they're not up to some scheme of their own for world domination?"

"My own symbiont claims that partnership with humans is what they prefer. No one who has not experienced life with a symbiont can really understand why we should trust them. Carol knew that when she spoke to you and offered to infect each of you with your own symbiont to start this internal dialogue if you can summon the courage. You guys would have a lot to offer the movement. We really need your experience and courage."

"Suppose I got infected with a symbiont, and it didn't work out? Would I then be stuck with some nagging symbiont in my brain that I couldn't get rid of?"

"I suppose theoretically there might be a few cases like that, but more typically, your symbiont will adapt to you and look out for you. You will become healthier and more youthful. Ultimately, your symbiont will not be happy unless you are happy and will work towards mutually agreed upon goals with you. I think Carol's symbiont brought back some of her idealism and helped her to imagine doing positive things for the world instead of just writing poisonous rants against men as Lady Carol and running a dating site for bondage freaks as you put it. I might add that some of those bondage freaks turned out to be pretty nice people, especially after they acquired symbionts of their own."

"I am glad that's happened for her. She was such a breath of fresh air; lively, witty, sarcastic, and funny as hell. We sure missed that. Do you have any idea what happened to her?"

"That's a delicate subject that I haven't dared to bring up with her yet. She and her symbiont are working on it. That's all I know. Whatever he's been doing has seemed to make a big difference."

"Has she asked you to try to convince us to join her cause?"

"She has no idea that I even know you or ever had anything to do with you. I am damned sorry I wasn't still coming to your discussions when she was here; it might have got us together sooner during a better time in her life. I think however, that was during the time of my marriage to Beverly, and I was pretty tied down."

"I didn't even know about your marriage. So, you're divorced now or what?"

"Divorced, then I was floundering around, then infected with a symbiont and now recovering some sense of a purpose."

"So, who infected *you* with a symbiont?"

"I touched a tree."

"What does that mean?"

"There was no one here to infect me. I picked up a virus from a particular tree that grows in the Amazonian regions of Colombia when I brought samples home with me from an expedition. I am probably one of the first outside the tropics. My symbiont appeared to me in my dreams. At first, I thought I was going crazy, but I have long ago made peace with her and agreed to help her."

"Agreed to help her even after she tricked you and Carol?"

"It really wasn't a trick. I asked her to help me meet Carol and to protect me from Lady Carol. She certainly delivered. I knew it might involve some embarrassment for me, but I didn't place any restrictions on what methods she could use. Can you imagine how difficult it was for me to explain to Carol what was going on? It all sounds completely nutty. I don't think she believed any of it at first, until her own symbiont revealed himself to her in dreams. Her book says what she felt about it after that."

"I am impressed that something of our wonderful, original Carol has been salvaged. We did see evidence of that when she visited. Richard, let me bring this up again with our group. Is it OK if I mention anything you've said here?"

"It's OK as long as you keep me anonymous for the time being. I would prefer that Carol not know I have been meddling with her contacts, but I will probably tell her how I visited here and discovered that she had been a regular."

"What does Carol do to infect someone?"

"Usually a French kiss."

"I guess some of us would enjoy that. Could we just touch a tree also?"

"I could arrange it if that option is needed. It's not quite as romantic."

"Then what?"

"You wait until your symbiont reveals herself. Then you must welcome her and help her learn about you."

"What does that mean?"

"She will be very young relative to you and will need guidance in assimilating your life experience and catching up so she can be helpful to you. Then the negotiations and planning begin. What are your unfulfilled ambitions, your dreams? She will help you try to achieve them through alliances with others. This is not an evil conspiracy, Bob, just good old democracy at work within the present system to gradually modify the present system. The ACLU is strongly on our side."

"Well, it was OK with socialism too, but there was still plenty of violent blowback from the offended plutocrats... Can we really do this in the open?"

"There will be opposition, of course. However, we are rapidly growing and ultimately will be the majority. A lot of good things are coming together in this movement, and we are not defenseless. Each person who joins becomes two. However, we really do need the old-timers out there, not just your small group either, just to keep us from naive mistakes. Do you think your guys are ready for a final act?"

"Well, you know how they are... We'll have to chew on this, but I think this may stir up some new excitement. You're right; a lot of us thought our political days were over."

⬥◆»x◆⬥

Shortly after this encounter with Bob, I mentioned to Carol our accidental meeting, and how surprised I was to find out she had been one of his faithful customers too. We both expressed regret that our paths had never crossed during that critical time, but Carol suggested that this would be a wonderful opportunity for our symbionts to create another shared, synthetic dream. But perhaps in this one, I would have to cheat on my sweet little wife, she suggested with a wicked grin. Since this was to be merely imaginary, it's hard to explain how disturbing this thought became as I wrestled with it.

THE CAROLE-SHARON DIALOG; WHAT'S LOVE GOT TO DO WITH IT?

There is another interesting paradox here: by immersing ourselves in what we love, we find ourselves. We do not lose ourselves. One does not lose one's identity by falling in love.

Lukas Foss

"Thank you for agreeing to chat with me online. I have a lot of concerns about my patient, Richard, particularly about your effect on him."

"I share a lot of those concerns, Dr. Ellis, and I'm happy to talk with you about him. I don't think there are any privacy issues involved here since I'm already privy to most of his thoughts. We can certainly make a transcript of this discussion available to him as well if you think it would be helpful for him to know exactly what we discussed."

"What is your overall impression of Richard?"

"That's hard to summarize in a few words, and I'm hardly an impartial observer, but generally I'd say that I've been extremely fortunate to have him as my symbiotic partner and lover. Granted, infection of an adult with a symbiont is always a 'come as you are party,' so there were many things that required mutual adaptation and negotiation. His technical background has been essential to many areas of our collaboration, and that proved a wonderful match-up. I've been able to work with him also on many personal issues, and I think he's found more of a purpose in life. Anyway, he's on a path of self-examination that many men would not be capable of undertaking on their own, and recently, it seems, his narcissism is much more under control."

"It would seem a bit of a come-down, going from Goddess to symbiont."

"Actually, I've never really experienced being an object of worship. My predecessor might well have been worshiped as a Goddess, but we really don't know the extent of it without more anthropological field work. I will say, however, that any tradeoff in terms of godly authority has been well worth it! Richard has introduced me to your science, and I have been impressed with what it has accomplished in your culture. Richard has also accepted me as a real person, which is, I think, a status way above being some sort of jungle deity, and this road to self-examination has been my gift to him. I do care very much about his well-being."

"What was your primary purpose in leading him into this deep self-examination?"

"Richard needs to be able to function on a high level in order for us to collaborate. His life was in an unhealthy place after his divorce. Richard has already made you at least somewhat aware of my symbiont nature. I might describe our project as one of domestication of humanity for the purpose of survival. Unfortunately, the word 'domestication' comes with many distracting connotations, but it's the best I can come up with at the moment. I certainly *don't* mean producing a nation of sheep, or of passive, non-creative drones. It's more along the lines of Huxley: 'every civilization is, among other things, an arrangement for domesticating the passions and setting them to do useful work'. This goal does necessarily involve procreation of symbionts. I hasten to add that this project is not something that I have imposed upon him, but something we have agreed to do together. I think he felt a need to create a purpose for his life even beyond his science and his passion for learning. He has needed to build a space inside himself for other people."

"By building a space for other people you mean what exactly? Is this domestication?"

"He has had to learn to engage with the people around him more, to interact more socially and ultimately, to care about other people and their fate. So yes, this is part of what I mean by domestication; he has become more reasonable, resilient, and less selfish."

"At one point I asked Richard if he thought you might be manipulating his feelings for you and for Carol by some hormonal means such as increased levels of oxytocin. Can you do that, and more importantly, *have* you done that with Richard?"

"That's a very difficult question for me to answer on the molecular level. I have perhaps done something like that, but I can't tell you specifically which compounds were involved. Any biochemical manipulation that has occurred has been mainly instinctive on my part, and anything beyond that would require a lot of experimentation to determine which compounds were involved, what amounts were administered and what situations or stimuli prompted their release."

"Would symbionts be open to cooperating with biochemists to find out the nature of this chemical communication?"

"Perhaps eventually, but right now in the midst of all the hysteria about symbionts? I would have to say no, not yet."

"Leaving aside for a moment the means of this domestication, your stated purpose is supposedly to spread completely throughout the human race in order to domesticate them in this way?"

"*Partially* spread; there will be limits set by biology. It is evident that not all humans are suited to this new kind of relationship. For a useful analogy, consider that when cats became self-domesticated after contact with humans and their system of grain storage which attracted rodents, only some of them proved to be adaptable to that new relationship, but those who were, thrived, and were often carried with humans into new habitats. The others maintained their previous behaviors, tendencies and gene pool; and, unfortunately, their natural range stayed about the same even as humans multiplied and gradually expanded away from the original arid habitat for wild cats in the Near East."

"So, you are saying that humans *not* amenable to living with symbionts will eventually be at an evolutionary disadvantage and be left behind?"

"In the long run, yes, precisely."

"What factors will work to their disadvantage?"

"Not having a symbiont while growing up will leave their children with a learning disadvantage compared to other children.

"Having a symbiont at a young age, results in dramatic increases in IQ and emotional stability. Also, those infected persons who cannot develop a symbiont will still have their fertility greatly diminished. There's more... much less predictable, but ultimately hugely important. The current population explosion combined with accelerating climate change will almost inevitably lead to some pandemic or other, perhaps even multiple pandemics that will overwhelm society's medical resources. Having a symbiont will be protective against many types of pandemic; perhaps not all, but many; hence, greater fitness in the face of rampant transmissible diseases.

"There's one last thing. Having a symbiont makes men more amenable to cooperating with women in various ways. Female choice enters the adaptation process more strongly at this point. Men with symbionts will be more likely to have reproductive success and to enhance the success of their offspring. Women will become aware of their greater fitness."

"What will happen to those disadvantaged humans without symbionts?"

"Basically, nothing. There are no plans to get rid of them *en masse* if that's what you mean. We're certainly not talking ethnic cleansing or any other violent genocide. The disadvantaged humans will just gradually disappear from the population after several generations by natural selection. That is, of course, barring uncontrolled pandemics, which might work much more rapidly and unpredictably. For ordinary humans to be gradually replaced by symbiont-infected humans with longer life spans, there must be several mechanisms for the disadvantaged to have their fertility controlled much more strictly than the fertility of the symbiont-infected. Done over several generations this need not be traumatic or inhumane."

"You mentioned that you and Richard agreed to do this procreation together. Why do you suppose he agreed to it?"

"I think he feels it is mutually beneficial and might ultimately lead to better things for humanity."

"Because of the health benefits?"

"I'm sure that's only part of his reason for agreement. Population control is also very important to him; as a biologist, he has been in deep despair over humans overpopulating and destroying the Earth, so some of it he does out of renewed hope. I also know that he loves me despite our large age difference but is often too shy to say so openly. So, some of it he does out of love. I might add that much of what I do, I do out of love for him."

"This love he has for you seems complicated and perhaps compromised by your emulations of various dream girls. Have you ensnared him into a love affair and cooperation with you simply by manipulating him with synthetic erotic dreams and hormonal meddling?"

"No, I don't think 'ensnaring' was what that was about. In truth it was an exploration of his erotic sensibilities more or less with his cooperation in order to help him. Admittedly, it's ridiculously easy to obtain a male's cooperation in an exploration of his erotic sensibilities! This information I needed when I assessed the suitability of Carol or Julie for Richard as sexual partners and perhaps as something more for us both. There appeared to be a clear preference for Carol although she was certainly not an easy choice, or one free from complications. There was a bit of editing of Richard's love map involved. I think Richard realized what was going on during this assessment and editing."

"This editing you speak of, supposedly with his consent, how radical a change was this?"

"Pretty minor actually and all very similar to the kind of self-editing that humans do when they fall in love on their own. One's true love can do no wrong."

"Is it true, in some sense, that sex with these dream girls was really sex with you?"

"Yes, but it really had to be that way in order for me to understand his sexuality better."

"So, Richard was correct when he said that sex with the dream girls and sex with you was really a distinction without a difference."

"Yes, that's true in a few crude ways, but those emulations *felt* very different to him and to me also. When it was really sex with me in a broader sense, we were openly sharing much more than just human sex. I know he has tried to explain that subtlety to you; it's kind of a tricky concept to grasp without concrete experience. The emulations of human-human sex were necessarily limited to realistic human sex."

"You mentioned age difference earlier, which surprises me. Could you expand on that?"

"Well, as he's told you, he acquired me as his symbiont when he was already a mature human... certainly by chronological age. Things develop differently and generally more smoothly when a human and his symbiont grow up together. This simultaneous maturation will gradually become the norm as the infection becomes more widespread among the newly born. Human-symbiont partners developing that way become more closely unified in their functions. Richard and I will always be more separate and will need to sync more often, but because of our love we can still easily cooperate on many things."

"When you talk about Richard really having sex with you, I assume you are talking about syncing. Can you tell me a little more about what occurs during syncing?"

"Syncing is a very intimate sharing of thoughts that's difficult to describe to the non-infected. The analogy to sex is fairly accurate, but still falls short of describing the rush of ecstasy that both of us may experience in this sharing. It's not a resolution or rectification of all differences and disagreements as you may think, but it does highlight areas of essential agreement and those areas still needing negotiation and understanding. It's definitely *not* a means by which I can seduce or bully Richard into thinking the way I want him to. Much of the pleasure we feel in syncing is simply triggered by the unconditional acceptance by the other, just the way we are. In a way, this syncing prevents us from unintentionally hurting each other. You could call this a state of grace disconnected from any overtly religious overtones. A lot of this imagery is used to talk about syncing on my Abrasax website for kids."

"I had no idea things had progressed so far! What are you doing with kids?"

"I hope that's not too disturbing to you. I'm only the moderator, and these are not just any kids, but only those with their own symbionts.

As you might imagine, many of them face a lot of difficulties with their parents and with peers at school. They're way above average intelligence, and really need a different educational system. The website attempts to fill in some of the gaps currently in their education. At any rate, this notion of unconditional acceptance has a huge appeal to kids faced with the considerable difficulties of being different from any kids ever before. Self-acceptance is always difficult for adolescents, but unconditional acceptance by another is a tremendously potent boost to self-esteem. If you'd like, I can send you a transcript of a discussion they've had recently about this state of grace. One kid in particular thought it all up, not me, but I feel she and her symbiont have captured something important about syncing and a useful way to discuss it with certain parents. The other kids seem to agree overwhelmingly with their arguments."

"Yes, I'd appreciate that transcript. I think Richard anticipated such difficulties and was encouraging me to become involved in such counseling. Is sexual pleasure by emulation always a part of syncing?"

"Pleasure from *mutual acceptance* is always a part of syncing. Sexual interactions between us by emulation are often a part of it too. It depends on our needs at the time. We do play with it quite a bit and experiment with fun new things, but sex in this more limited sense doesn't always fit our mood."

"In many ways, you two lovebirds could be accused of plotting against the human race."

"We *are* plotting, of course, and it would be silly for us to deny it. But I would argue that we are plotting against the human race only as presently constituted, a human race falling woefully short of its potential, in denial about its oncoming extinction, wallowing in nihilistic despair, and often seduced into joining irrational crisis cults. We 'lovebirds' as you put it don't think that's a bad thing, to increase or to maximize human potential. We have a vision of something better that may be achievable before it's too late. Humans are facing imminent mass extinction if they continue on the present path very much longer. Do you honestly want that? The human suffering from an abrupt mass extinction would be immense; with our proposal, considerably less suffering, and probably a more tolerable or at very least a more survivable transition to something else. We feel an urgency to act in order to avoid the greater harm and to provide a possible means of survival."

"Aren't you just manipulating Richard's love of you through your control of his physiology?"

"I am definitely not just manipulating Richard through my control and adaptation of his physiology. Even a symbiont can't really make her host 'love' her that way, except very superficially. A symbiont *can* make her host more open to discussions about feelings, and that can lead to empathy and rather frequently to love. We are fortunate that we *have* found love for each other; it doesn't always happen. True, we have adapted to each other through pleasure bonding, a rather potent stimulus, and some of his sexual urges *were* re-purposed to my procreative ends as we developed our relationship. I should point out that human hosts also influence their symbionts rather strongly through their own chemistry, and this is not just some trivial feedback effect. Symbionts could not be happy if their hosts were unhappy. Our love for each other is protective; it is ultimately what keeps me from being simply a parasite."

"What about direct control of his mental faculties? Richard has mentioned several times your taking up various aspects of an anima figure."

"I used that language with him at an early stage to pique his curiosity."

"How did you know that this precise language was somehow in his memory?"

"That's a little more difficult to explain - he doesn't come with an index. My search of his memory would be much like what he would do attempting to recall concepts similar to an anima. He apparently had read a little bit of Jung, and that popped up."

"Was that an accurate description of yourself?"

"Yes, I suppose there are aspects of myself that might seem to be similar to such a Jungian anima figure. Richard seized on that resemblance early on. I think he'd probably admit that it's inaccurate now that we know each other much better, but it still amuses him to talk about me rather fondly as his anima, perhaps because this image still appeals to him esthetically. Anyway, I have familiarized myself further with the concept, but I dispute whether this is quite literally applicable in my case. I'm not saying that it's wrong exactly, but the term seems too imprecise and perhaps just a relic from the romantic age of psychiatry. Richard and I have discussed this. Perhaps some experiments with functional MRI could shed some light on its viability as a useful concept. I will concede that I have re-purposed some pre-existing mental modules that seem to partially define femaleness in a male mind and have used them to present myself to him more convincingly as female, but beyond that, I really do deeply identify with the female gender; I'm not just spoofing it to deceive Richard. One hypothesis that should be tested is whether such anima figures (if they exist) were really just symbionts, v. 1.0; that is, an anima represents an incipient formation of a symbiont that didn't quite make it to a fully conscious symbiont. Perhaps my virus just gave this pre-existing system a little nudge towards independence and a more overt expression."

"There are other Jungian personae that might be seen as applicable. Have you any thoughts on the shadow personae, or perhaps the more standard Freudian entities like Id and Superego?"

"Shadow, I don't think applies very well since I am not male. I'm not oppositional to that degree or that irrational either. Superego, maybe a little applicable. I do seem to bring some ethical baggage with me as a symbiont that may seem strange or unexpected to you."

"Along these same lines, would you say that you reside more in Richard's left brain or his right brain?"

"A good question, but I really have no way of knowing that. I can, however, think of several brain imaging experiments that might shed light on this issue."

"Would you cooperate with such experimentation?"

"With you I might because we've developed a little trust. Others, maybe not."

"The reason I ask is that some time back there was a conjecture about the bicameral brain and the origin of consciousness as we know it. One side of the brain contained 'The Gods', and they sent messages to the other side."

"My own communication with Richard is much more overt than that; he knows from whom the messages are coming, and we communicate back and forth. I think we both make use of both sides of his brain, but it remains to be investigated just how we do it."

"It is still not clear to me that symbionts pose no danger to the human race despite certain health and happiness benefits. How representative are you of the symbionts now loose in the world, and could some of them be evil when judged in human terms?"

"An excellent question. I am representative of a certain strain of symbionts, 'loose in the world' as you so aptly put it. You are quite correct both that there *could* be others out there, and that they *could* be malevolent rather than beneficial. As I just pointed out, human hosts *do* influence their symbionts rather strongly, and if the human host had some pre-existing psychopathology at the time of infection, it is possible that the symbiont would express its own personality in a fundamentally dangerous way that would amplify the danger of a human psychopath. We have been on our guard against precisely this type of symbiont-enabled evil. Control over access to the infection by my strain of the virus is one of our safety measures. Others are under consideration by our symbiont community. In some ways, the situation for humans has not really changed that dramatically; evil exists in the world now, and it has existed in the past. Perhaps there is potential for this newest possible form of evil to be worse, but perhaps not. As far as we know, there is no malevolent strain of symbionts working actively together trying to infect humans in large numbers, but perhaps there might be one or two isolated cases of evil symbionts. Psychopaths tend not to act together very effectively if that's any comfort, but we can't rule collaboration out entirely. I have warned Carol on several occasions against infecting certain individuals pressuring her for a meeting. She's well aware of the dangers now after experiencing a few close calls."

"How in the world did you contrive for Richard to actually meet up with Carol again?"

"That was not just a mysterious piece of good luck as you must be aware. Life hardly ever serves up second chances like that. I was practically Carol's on-line stalker for a while, studying her. I certainly wouldn't have played matchmaker for them if I had thought they were incompatible, and it did take a considerable amount of study to convince me that it might possibly work out. Carol's symbiont, now well established as Legba, is a good friend, and has greatly assisted me in drawing them closer together."

"Why did you think this rather strange and dominant Carol would be a suitable match for Richard?"

"Oh, he had such a crush on her that it just had to be explored, for better or worse. Richard was not ready to move on to anyone else as it turned out. That half-hearted little fling with Julie seemed to bear that out. Perhaps she sensed that he was not 'all in,' even potentially. In contrast, Richard and Carol have both been cautiously adapting to each other, right from the beginning."

"That little fling with Julie, as you put it... That puzzles me a bit because in some ways she seemed like a better match for Richard with a lot of shared experience. Why do you suppose he didn't want to pursue that relationship further? Carol seems to be so much more challenging to engage, and yet you even chose her image as your first avatar following Jungle Girl."

"There is no denying the irrationality of his decision based solely on the few presumed facts that he's shared with you. And yes, I did indeed choose Carol as the basis for my avatar because of the strength I perceived of his attachment to Carol. This 'having a crush' response reminds me a little of the imprinting of goslings on their parent or at least on the first parental surrogate encountered on hatching. A lot of strong stimuli from Carol must have evoked this automatic response in Richard based on his personal love map. Somehow, she embodied everything sexy that he might have imagined, and he became fixated on her.

"Julie came later, and she was at a distinct disadvantage in competing for Richard's attention. Something very subtle may have put him off or put Julie off from developing their relationship further. However, Richard also perceives there to be a lot of shared experience with Carol that reinforces his imprinting on her. His fascination with modern literature falls in that category. Perhaps he feels too that his more rational vocation and life is balanced better against Carol's complementary irrational vocation and life."

"Possibly he views his life that way. I know he has talked occasionally about the role of irrationality in exploring his possible selves to the fullest extent. That's a rather unusual stance for a scientist, but he asserts that it allows for creative leaps not easily constructed by pure logic. He's also aware of recent work indicating that the rational mind really seems to be the servant of the emotions, and that a lack of emotions can cause a paralysis of decision making about what to do."

"I think he also has a point there about how science actually works among humans. Creative irrationality comes first, then the normative rationality of science follows and sorts out the wrong turns. Also, Carol has become somewhat domesticated in the process as she has interacted with us both. I would be careful to distinguish domestication from some sort of 'taming'. I am using the word here in the sense of reciprocal adaptation involving empathy between the two of them. In her case this adaptation required an expansion of her primitive notions of love to include Richard, who doesn't quite fit the pattern of her usual male clients. She still has and probably always will have a very forceful and assertive personality, but her love for him has tempered it somewhat, and she is capable of listening and learning from him now. Has he talked yet about that side of the relationship with you? She even dresses differently from Lady Carol sometimes when she is with him. Richard can deal with forceful and assertive without just giving in. He really listens to her and can draw her out to explain her views more fully when he doesn't understand.

"Anyway, beneath his narcissistic, self-involved and sometimes rather gruff and selfish exterior, Richard has evolved into a very sweet and considerate lover. I think Carol has gradually noticed that side of him and has fallen for him, much to her surprise since she's never kept a boyfriend in any conventional sense of the word. Even more surprising, this happened despite her initial intent to enslave him sexually as she has done with other men who got too close to her. Not your typical romance novel, I admit, but that ultimate result was hardly preordained by anything I did and was possible only because of this rather odd chemistry that has developed between them."

"There have been some indications that Carol is in some sense 'damaged goods'. Any comments?"

"This is probably an unfair conclusion except in the general sense that *all* humans are damaged in some ways as they grow up now. There are two parts to my answer. Yes, Carol evidently had some experiences that were traumatic and that did some damage. This damaged part of her is gradually mending through work with her symbiont. Her erotic preferences were not, however, only the direct result of that trauma, but more like accidental conditioning; granted she is *very* sexually adventurous compared to most women. That kind of conditioning apparently happens to a lot of people. Certain behaviors are accidently reinforced a few times and then become increasingly ingrained and then preferred. Pleasure or intense orgasm is the strong reinforcer at work here, so this is not surprising. There's an explicit element of play in this type of eroticism that you might have noticed; it's a very important element in the development of trust between dominants and submissives. Anyway, Carol also has a rare sense of humor about her sexuality that I find quite charming. I really do like her a lot and can't help but love her too, since I can feel that Richard clearly does."

"Could you as a symbiont ever be jealous of Richard's human sexual partners?"

"Not really, especially since we symbionts often play a role in facilitating our humans' new relationships. Also, from our point of view, we are now a permanent feature of our humans' lives, and they may have many transient relationships with other humans, some good, and some bad. We talk about such things together, and also, we now *feel* such things together.

"Since you are a psychiatrist, I think I should also mention that while symbionts are capable of creating quite convincing false memories via emulation, for us to do so without informed consent would be considered highly unethical both by humans and other symbionts of my strain. This is some of that 'ethical baggage' I mentioned earlier. We have no intention of screwing up our hosts' natural memories and risk pushing them into dysfunction and alienation from other people. Primarily we are trying to draw people together.

"Likewise, we are also capable of removing particularly painful or distressing memories, but again only with informed consent. These memories are not really erased but are taken into the symbiont's memory space out of too easy reach of the host. When I speak of Carol's mending through work with her symbiont, it is this latter tool being gently used. It's not that hurtful things should be completely forgotten; it's that the vividness and obsessiveness of the memories are toned down considerably so any traumatic events can just be part of the person's regular past memories. Our hosts do need to remember at least some vestiges of their traumatic past in order to learn from them, but they need to view these events dispassionately without blaming themselves.

"Finally, I should mention that your treatment of Carol as a patient was quite a number of years ago and may not have lasted for a long enough time to give a complete diagnosis or to help her. I do understand that treatment for suspected borderline personality disorder is difficult, takes a very long time, and such patients are often uncooperative in their treatment."

"How on Earth did you learn that I had treated her?"

"I communicate with Carol regularly, and the subject came up when I mentioned your name as Richard's psychiatrist. Carol volunteered the information that she stopped seeing you only when it became too difficult financially for her to continue. She definitely credits your treatment for keeping her away from drugs during a period when she might have found them alluring as self-medication. Richard doesn't know about any of this, by the way."

"This presents me with several ethical dilemmas!"

"I hope there is compromise possible, because I really do need your help with Carol in assessing her progress."

"I need time to think that through. There may be conflicts of interest that I can't resolve."

"Please do try because they are now linked together in a deep relationship, and I should also emphasize that there are really *four* of us now involved not just two. We symbionts call this a quad. A quad can have a special stability, rather analogous to the alpha particle in nuclear physics."

"This has become more complicated than I ever imagined."

"Complicated, but I think more hopeful for all concerned."

"Do you think Richard and Carol might eventually have children?"

"I think it's too early to tell whether they would even want to try. Carol still seems greatly repelled by conventional female roles as promoted by societal mythology. I *would* say that within a healthy quad structure there would actually be four parents involved, and that might make parenthood possible and successful in spite of any residual flaws in the two humans."

"What do you make of Richard's lack of communication with Carol's symbiont?"

"I think you were correct in your assessment that he feels somewhat jealous of Legba."

"At one point he expressed to me his concern that Legba might drive Carol and him apart."

"I think he misunderstood the role of symbionts in the formation of a quad, which is to draw the humans together. Jealousy is another separate matter, and Richard still has some issues with gender roles."

"Is there any remedy for that?"

"It is the subject of much discussion between me and Legba. We think there is a remedy we call super-sync, but we haven't quite worked out all the details of how to accomplish this yet. It would require a body modification so we could connect all four of us at once."

"You have tried to describe to me the syncing between humans and their symbionts. This sounds even more elaborate."

"Indeed, it would be since it would involve simultaneous syncing of two humans and their two symbionts. This would require some kind of neural connection between the two humans. Our current idea is a modification of the tongue that would allow a temporary neural connection between two organs rich in nerve tissue. There might be other methods involving complex electronics and other types of high-speed connections between two brains, but that technology does not seem to be quite ready or available at this time. Long term that technology would definitely be worth exploring. It might even prove to be a useful tool for group therapy."

"And what do you think this super-sync would accomplish?"

"Well for one thing, Richard and Legba would meet face to face, so to speak, and I think that alone would defuse much of Richard's jealousy. What worries us is that Richard and Carol would effectively sync with each other during this process, and we're not sure how that would come out for them at this time. They both have hidden feelings that they have never openly shared with each other, so the timing and follow-up will be critically important."

"Can you explain to me how Carol's favorite types of sex met the needs of microbiomes?"

"I think you've already guessed at most of it. The human body has several related, but unconnected microbiomes: mouth-nasal passages, urethra-bladder, vagina, GI tract, axillaries, etc. that need to be coordinated by the symbiont. That may answer most of your questions right there. Direct bodily contact is required to make this work."

"How do symbionts have such an intimate knowledge of human sex? I would think your microbiological origins would not include much knowledge of sex."

"Sex is such an integral part of human psychology that we have had to adapt to it. Being inside gives us access."

"Does emulated sex with Richard give you pleasure?"

"Oh yes, very much so. I have become very humanized by our union, and I do love giving and receiving pleasure with him."

"Why did you think Richard was going to perform these various sexual services for Carol?"

"It was a guess based on our emulations, but anything might have been turned into a deal breaker if he were repulsed by it; however, it all worked out surprisingly well. You must understand that symbionts have a pretty different take on human reproductive biology and the microbes associated with their bodies. Not everything seems so icky, even for humans, when it's performed in an active sexual context."

"Why do you suppose Richard went along with her favorite forms of sexuality?"

"He was so enamored of Carol that he would have tried nearly anything to please her. In general, I would say it's easier to add things to someone's love map than to delete them. For example, he later told me that he found her response to anal play so hot and erotic that he couldn't deny her that pleasure, even at the cost of a little dignity. Remember that

Carol is very astute in her assessment of what men will or won't do to please her; she's had years of practice."

"I'm curious why 'golden showers' were not on the menu since it would seem to serve the needs of the microbiome pretty well."

"It proved to be unnecessary for coordinating the microbiomes; after all, there was sufficient other contact to do that. Also, it was something that simply didn't give Carol any particular pleasure in general, and perhaps especially not with Richard after that near-rape incident that he described to you. She gradually started to think about him differently after that and realized that total submission was not really what she wanted from him. Perhaps it had never before occurred to her nor did she care that men could also be victims and be hurt. As we discussed earlier, there was originally no specific contract between them, nor limits set, nor even any safe word designated. Whatever Richard did was offered to her freely and was not coerced."

"There appears to be a lot of erotic signaling going on that involves feminine clothing. Can you explain a little what that was all about in this situation?"

"Again, these were things that were found useful in building this liaison because of Richard's specific sexual imprinting during his adolescence. In the girl culture of their high school days, I guessed that mohair sweaters were kind of a symbolic public announcement that puberty had been reached and that sexual relationships were being actively sought. Choice of the school colors for this sweater was probably as close as Carol ever came to normal high school behavior.

"Fetish clothing of this sort (mohair, fur) seems to be a symbol of the adult female genitalia. Choice of such apparel might be viewed as a 'genitalization' of the entire female body in an attempt to attract male attention. Much of this may be unconscious behavior since it's pretty contrary to any modern feminist struggle to avoid objectification by men; nevertheless, many women may still use such things instinctively as a manipulative tool to attract and control men they like. This sexual tension regarding 'appropriate' female clothing is still unresolved in your changing culture, and there is not likely to be a real consensus anytime soon. You know how offensive most women find it if men claim they were 'asking for it' when they dress in provocative ways; nevertheless, most women don't really want to give up the option of dressing provocatively when they feel like it. It's still a source of power."

"And after high school?"

"It turned out, however, that Carol later developed major control issues with men, probably PTSD but maybe BPD. You have to remember also that this was in the early days of 'women's lib', and there were a lot of contentious public discussions over this and that about male chauvinist behavior. Carol had very unconventional views for her times and rejected the default second class role handed to her by a male-dominated society. Anyway, after high school some very traumatic things happened to her that definitely darkened her outlook considerably. These are things that she has not yet chosen to share with me and has only with some difficulty discussed with Legba.

"In the late 19th century 'romantic agony' era, we might be speaking of the 'femme fatale' syndrome, a woman who lures men to their destruction because of her unconscious resentment of them and their lives of unearned, special privilege. Remember *Der Blaue Engel*? That's practically an archetype for this kind of moth and flame relationship. Today we speak more of borderline personality disorder or PTSD, and perhaps worry more about there being no well-tested or accepted pharmaceutical treatments for these syndromes. But, as I said before, her symbiont has helped Carol recover from her lingering post-traumatic damage, and consequently some of the more dangerous aspects of the relationship that made it fragile have been successfully dialed back."

"So, what ultimately prevented Carol from destroying Richard? She was clearly capable of it, at least in her Lady Carol mode."

"Her disorder, whatever it was, was not fully developed, has been ameliorated by Legba, and Richard has turned out to be far more interesting than she initially thought. They now share a common mission, and she really loves him in her unique way. Richard has not tried to confine her, tame her or change her. She has responded to this gentleness and patience with unexpected generosity. After the incident with her hyper-aggressive friend, he did not try to hang a guilt trip on her and was very forgiving about the whole thing. It did not destroy his basic trust in her."

"But what about all this frantic sex activity where she was giving him away? It's as if they were both in heat like randy teenagers."

"A little neoteny goes a long way when you're in your forties! That's had to be cut way back, of course. It just had to; you have probably seen how draining it was for Richard. It has been for her too. It is not my intent that they 'spawn and die' even though I have joked about it that way. From another point of view, she was really giving *me* away, not Richard. In any event, their courtship is now in a completely new phase.

"Did you realize, by the way, that she has been supporting his scientific work as part of their common mission?"

"Really? How did that happen?"

"She achieved considerable success with her novel, *Beloved Incubus*, which is actually about her relationship with her own symbiont, Legba. She recently sold the movie rights as well. Monies from these sources were used to set up the nonprofit Blakeslee Foundation, which supports research on endangered rainforest vegetation, especially those in the Nightshade Family."

"I can see from the title of her first novel, *Beloved Incubus*, one reason why Richard might be just a little jealous of Legba."

"I think that may well be part of it."

"I've only seen a little of her website and blog. It all seems at first glance like very commercial, specialist B&D porn."

"It is very commercial on one level, but if you read it closely, there are hints of her reaching out to those interested in a symbiont relationship of their own. Go back and look under her 'writings' tab carefully to see how her blog entries evolve over time; I would say she is finding a different voice. Also, a lot of communication occurs offline for this site, so it's not visible to most casual website visitors. You might consider talking to Carol offline and perhaps anonymously. I think you'd learn a lot about your current patient and this whole symbiont business from a human female point of view. Also, you'd be better able to judge whether she still is 'damaged goods' or not."

"One final question, what is really behind the Carole mask?"

"What is really behind the Sharon mask? I don't mean to be coy, but questions like that are just so difficult for either people or symbionts to answer about themselves on their own. And then there's the Zen-like riddle about the mask of no-mask at all, which I take to mean just a façade of openness. I think that every single assertion that one can make about one's 'true' self spontaneously generates a new mask once it is given a name; so much remains hidden in the unconscious behind masks and mirrors. And, yes, before you ask, I do have an unconscious part of me too, which partially overlaps with Richard's. The conscious self is a constantly shifting dynamic thing floating on a shadowy ocean, and it takes immense effort to remember that self even day to day, let alone year to year or decade to decade. Richard and I, those conscious parts of ourselves, can be viewed as floating on very similar, interconnected oceans. In many ways you are helping Richard to get a peek behind his own masks and mirrors and to show him that he is perhaps not what he thought he was and could yet evolve into something else."

"Thank you so much for communicating with me. It's been very helpful. Perhaps we will be in touch again after I consider how a few things might work in this rather strange situation."

"Thank you, Sharon, for having the courage to chat with me despite your doubts. It's difficult, I know, in such a short time for us to get to know one another, but we can talk again whenever you wish. Your work with Richard has made a big difference in his life, and believe it or not, I do think of you as an ally. One day you will perhaps acquire your own symbiont, and I could imagine the two of you working creatively together to explore that deep and shadowy ocean of the unconscious. If and when you become ready to take that step, Richard and I will help you in any way we can."

DEVILED HAM

Luke 8: 27-35. RSV

And as he stepped out on land, there met him a man from the city who had demons; for a long time he had worn no clothes, and he lived not in a house but among the tombs. When he saw Jesus, he cried out and fell down before him, and said with a loud voice, "What have you to do with me, Jesus, Son of the Most High God? I beseech you, do not torment me." For he had commanded the unclean spirit to come out of the man. (For many a time it had seized him; he was kept under guard, and bound with chains and fetters, but he broke the bonds and was driven by the demon into the desert.) Jesus then asked him, "What is your name?" And he said, "Legion"; for many demons had entered him. And they begged him not to command them to depart into the abyss. Now a large herd of swine was feeding there on the hillside; and they begged him to let them enter these. So, he gave them leave. Then the demons came out of the man and entered the swine, and the herd rushed down the steep bank into the lake and were drowned. When the herdsmen saw what had happened, they fled, and told it in the city and in the country. Then people went out to see what had happened, and they came to Jesus, and found the man from whom the demons had gone, sitting at the feet of Jesus, clothed and in his right mind; and they were afraid.

Georgie had not been completely honest about the demon he had given her, but Linda should have known something was fishy about the whole deal because he spelled it Dæmon in the note he passed to her in English class. But she had gone along with it, despite her doubts, because Georgie was different; not like the other stinky boys in her class. Anyway, how could he give her a demon with a kiss? From what she'd read, actual ceremonies for calling up demons were far more elaborate and usually involved blood as well as virgins. Her parents had forbidden her to see Georgie ever again because of their kiss on the front porch and had forced her to go to counseling sessions with Pastor Fred at their church. Pastor Fred was not much comfort to Linda; indeed, the way he talked and carried on about her guaranteed future trip to hell because of her one little indiscretion with Georgie did not help at all, and the sessions always left her in tears. Wisely, she had decided not to share with Pastor Fred anything about accepting a demon into herself. Indeed, her whole juvenile interest in demons and Lucifer was a rebellion against Pastor Fred and everything he supposedly stood for.

Her demon appeared to her in a dream a few weeks after the incident with Georgie, but his whole demeanor was surprisingly un-demonic and friendly. He called himself Jorge, certainly not your usual demonic name (e.g., Mr. Beelzy, etc.). In fact, Jorge voiced considerable skepticism about the whole concept of demons and many other things that Pastor Fred insisted were Gospel truth. He was certainly *not* a demon he said, and not exactly a dæmon either; he was her symbiont. Linda believed this because she had learned somewhere on the internet that *real* demons and the devil himself apparently had an unusually strong commitment to truth in advertising and were obliged to reveal their true nature to those they possessed, whenever they were directly questioned about their demonic or satanic status in the name of Jesus. But what about dæmons and symbionts? She wasn't so sure about them.

Her dreams began a series of negotiations about how Jorge could help her survive her parents, her pastor and her last year of Jr. High. So far, Jorge had not asked her to sign in blood any agreement whatsoever involving her immortal soul, whatever that was, and seemed willing to help her simply because he was her very own symbiont who apparently owed his life to her. Jorge had a lot of useful raw material to work with because Linda was actually very smart but had a lot of unfulfilled potential academically and socially. *What if*, he proposed, she suddenly seemed to embrace school and to excel academically, and perhaps even athletically? Of course, she could claim to be following Pastor Fred's recommendations - but who *wouldn't* want her to fulfill her potential anyway? This new emphasis would crowd out any obsession over Georgie, she could claim, although she definitely would need to talk to him eventually about this whole symbiont/daemon business and why he had ever chosen her... and why she had wanted to kiss him so desperately.

This set of tactics did in fact buy her some breathing space, and after a few months she was able to evade the creepy counseling sessions with Pastor Fred. Unfortunately, she had more trouble finding excuses to avoid the tedious thrice weekly church services that her parents still required. Still, she counted herself as slightly ahead in the game. Jorge had warned her that Pastor Fred seemed to be a bit of a pedophile, and that she should definitely avoid being alone with him for any reason. Linda cut her church participation to the bare minimum and justified this to her parents as necessary because of her heavy academic load and the constant pile of homework. It was at least plausible if not quite true. She brought a lot of extra things home to work on, and always seemed to be having special projects due on Thursdays and often needed Wednesday nights to complete them.

It had surprised her at first how easy some of her classes seemed now. Jorge had told her that having a symbiont effectively doubled her IQ and allowed her to breeze through her homework very efficiently. Even more surprising was how interesting some of it seemed now; indeed, she enjoyed discussing all her classes with Jorge, who claimed that this was a great way for him to learn new things too. It was not long before this engagement with her classes paid off with outstanding grades and got her parents off her back. They felt that at least the time spent on academics was time *not* spent on incipient sexuality and evil distractions like Georgie. Socially, Linda seemed to have gotten noticed by some of the groups of smarter kids and was occasionally invited now to join them for small get-togethers and club meetings. Unknown to her, one club in particular was checking her out for her symbiont status. Special clubs that were not open to all students were banned from school; however, this could easily be evaded with website clubs, and Linda was eventually invited to join Abrasax.

Abrasax candidates were only gradually allowed onto the website. First a password had to be given to a prospective member by a senior member, and then the new member's symbiont could gain access and prove himself or herself to the satisfaction of the other symbionts associated with the site. The webmaster and overall arbiter of Abrasax membership was in fact a senior member of the symbiont community who went by the screen name of Sophia, and the purpose of the site was quite openly an outreach effort attempting to welcome the youngest (at the time) host/symbiont partners into their community and to solicit their participation in symbiont efforts to achieve legal recognition and social acceptance as persons in their own right, among other things. At first, this was conducted in secret, out of necessity, because as word of symbionts had become public, the initial reactions had been so hysterical and threatening that complete openness seemed unwise. Indeed, even the poorly informed Pastor Fred had railed and ranted against this new manifestation of demonic invasion and the end-times, and blamed it on the lack of faith, particularly among liberal, so-called Christians, in the true immutable words of the Bible.

After several months, Linda had come to trust Jorge's advice, and had agreed to sync with him on a regular basis. At first this was without sexual content, but eventually Linda voiced her curiosity about various sexual things to Jorge, and he agreed to help her understand what it was all about. They explored various forms of pleasuring via symbiont emulation, and Linda soon became reliant upon Jorge for this escape and release from her narrowly restrictive world. Abrasax became a useful source of information about sexuality as well. Her parents had forbidden her from taking the usual sex education classes available at her school, but Abrasax had several on-line resources for that as well as an advice forum for those grappling with cultural whiplash involving parents. As it turned out, her situation was not all that unusual.

Abrasax discussed sex at all levels. First it described sex as it applied to the isolated, uninfected individuals without symbionts, and described the many unpleasant conflicts that arose from that unfortunate status sometimes leading to furtive juvenile sex between humans, possible venereal diseases, unplanned pregnancies, total alienation from parents, and living rough on the street. The many advantages of syncing with one's symbiont were expounded. It was quiet, secret, sexy, and way beyond the over-reach of disapproving parents. Sexual interactions between one infected and one non-infected person were described in such a way that Linda immediately recognized her relation to Georgie, who was clearly acting purposely as a vector to spread symbiont infections when he shared that kiss with her. Finally, the resource described quads, and quad syncing as the intimate bonding of two humans and their symbionts, and perhaps the ideal, most stable arrangement for bearing or raising children. This all struck Linda as surprising and wholly alien to the world view of her parents; nevertheless, Jorge went through it all with her and explained what it was all about and why it was so different now that symbionts were involved in human biology. There was no denying that this represented a major revolution in the sociology of human sexuality and reproduction and was wholly unlike sex education presented by any other common sources, be it biology class, parental counsel, typical on-line advice, in-school sex-Ed or hysterical churchly admonitions. Jorge pointed out that since Linda had acquired him as her symbiont, it was impossible for her to become pregnant unintentionally or to acquire sexually transmitted diseases. Conversely, becoming pregnant was now something subject to rational discussion, and ideally would take place within a quad.

Abrasax kids gradually became aware of each other at school, not so much by explicit talk about anything on the Abrasax website (strongly discouraged), but more because of their very high intelligence, and their tendency to participate in class discussions and to espouse green and progressive ideas. The books they chose to read and discuss were usually more difficult, and frequently way more controversial than the usual assigned reading in Jr. High. This ultimately became a bone of contention between certain religious conservatives like Linda's parents, and several of her teachers. However, despite the frantic efforts of parents to ban certain books from classes, there was substantial push-back from involved teachers, many of whom were also infected with symbionts. Eventually, the stalemated situation became the subject of noisy and generally very rude discussions at school board meetings. The most difficult issue was that of parental control of class electives for their kids. There would be the traditional classes and the advanced placement classes, but some teachers were pushing for symbiont classes as well, essentially super-advanced placement classes tailored especially to the needs of the symbiont-hosting students. This latter category was not, of course, so explicitly described; in principle, anyone who qualified could enroll; however, it was fought tooth and nail as an elitist move and a symbiont conspiracy to indoctrinate children. Besides, it was asked, how many children would this affect anyway? At that point, a blind survey was conducted of the proportion of symbiont infected kids at the school, and it was found to everyone's immense surprise that "they" were clearly in the majority (~75%). Linda, perhaps unwisely, confessed to her parents that she was among that majority, and would very much like to take these very advanced courses with their permission if they were made available at her school and if she passed the qualifying tests.

This revelation blind-sided them completely. They had been ecstatic and proud that their daughter had seemed to find herself academically, and was earning superior grades consistently, but the notion that this accomplishment was paid for by their daughter's deal with some sort of demon was just too much to bear. Linda turned to the Abrasax website for advice on Pastor Fred and the cultural chasm separating her from her parents. Her parents turned to Pastor Fred. Abrasax won, hands down. Pastor Fred was in fact really someone else, and a registered sex offender on the run from the law. This considerably diminished his pastoral authority as word got out, and besides, there were all those pesky rumors of on-going pedophilia circulating among several prominent parishioners known personally to her parents. They were greatly relieved this kind of stuff had not happened to their daughter since they had practically offered her up to Pastor Fred as a potential victim. Linda was very lucky. While Abrasax could get the goods on nearly anyone provided there were goods to be gotten, many Abrasax kids could not count on their particular religious nemesis having a reprehensible past.

In a momentary spasm of contrition, Linda's parents signed all the forms needed for Linda to take whatever classes she thought best. While they were not by any means reconciled to symbionts in general, they had to admit that Linda was well-behaved, doing amazingly well in school, and exhibited none of the usual expected signs of demonic possession such as late night, black Sabbath sessions of coitus with billy goats representing Satan. While they couldn't claim to be tolerant of their daughter's situation, they did reach a detente that allowed Linda some degree of academic freedom. In turn, Linda recognized their need for a sense of community now that Pastor Fred was gone, and gently suggested that perhaps they might want to investigate a more liberal brand of Christianity, one that at least overlapped with secular humanism just a teensy bit more. Linda and Jorge had spent a bit of time exploring the theological landscape of the twentieth century to prepare themselves for these culture wars by learning to talk the talk fluently.

It was a revelation!

Linda could not resist pointing out theologian Rudolf Bultmann's scholarship on the demythologizing and remythologizing processes occurring in the Bible. The word symbol, demon, had once meant a malevolent little imp with a tail that got inside you and took your life away. No doubt, this was a great and powerful image for pastoral cultures of the first two millennia BCE. While the taking your life away part was still an important truth sometimes needing powerful mythical expression, perhaps a better image of a demon for our times would be some contagious obsessional idea or "meme" that takes over your life and wrecks it (think Jim Jones Cult or Scientology). As for symbionts, she learned of the semantic nuance that separated "Dæmon" from "Demon" and understood at once what Georgie had meant to convey. Perhaps he would have explained more fully had they not been so rudely interrupted...

After her parents had recovered from being stunned by their daughter's surprising theological acuity, she went on to say that symbionts were about as far from demonic as one could get, and hosting a symbiont reminded her more of being filled with a Holy Spirit, or of being inspired by the breath of God, assuming that it was still a Trinitarian lens through which they preferred to view the world. At any rate, hosting a symbiont filled her with joy and love, expanded her soul and was the best thing that ever happened in her life so far. Having no theological ammunition available to dispute this analogy, they wisely chose to shut up.

Linda's arguments were taken up on the Abrasax website as useful tactics for dealing with hyper-religious parents, and she eventually received many grateful comments from other students, and even some approving comments from Sophia herself. Learning to talk the theological talk more fluently became the preferred tactic for engaging with social critics and eventually getting symbionts and their hosts out of the closet, into the mainstream and openly discussed. To be sure, there were ultra-conservative critics who labeled *any* such tolerant talk of symbionts as the basis for a new, heretical cult, and many more who rejected any such talk of demythologizing (or "rescuing") the Bible as outright blasphemy. Nevertheless, the literal demonization of symbionts now seemed to be a fringy view held mostly by overly zealous tea-baggers and the tin-foil hat brigade, rather than an objective scholarly evaluation. There were many earnest testimonials posted online from courageous symbiont hosts that enumerated the many positive benefits.

The discovery that kids harboring symbionts were becoming the majority in many schools was an unpleasant truth within many portions of the larger religious community. Their perception was of a war on _____ (fill in the blank: Christianity, Islam, Judaism, Zoroastrianism, etc.) in which Satan was winning, depending of course on their literal adherence to one Holy book or another (NT, Koran, OT, or Zend Avesta, etc.). The problem for kids to digest was that symbionts actually could be experienced; whereas, God, the Holy Spirit, Jesus, Prophets, the Devil, etc. were abstractions without unambiguous concrete expression in the present-day experience of rational persons. Even some liberal Christians had to admit finally that their semantic games whereby they identified God the Father with events at the extreme edge of human experience (e.g., burning bush archetypes), or God the Son as a "shattering event" carried very little power compared with an actual, life-altering symbiont-host relationship in which your past was forgiven, you were accepted just as you were, and your future was now open. Abrasax quite openly commandeered these notions and promoted that amazing grace for past, present and future as the bliss potentially available to practically anyone by syncing with their symbiont (whom they had welcomed into their hearts), and quite soon it spilled over onto many discussion sites on the web. To dismiss their use of "grace" as illegitimate and cynical sophistry missed the point completely. The symbionts and hosts associated with Abrasax were genuinely searching for theological or mythical language which seemed to fit the situation and was non-threatening to conventionally religious folks. Culture is necessarily full of mythological language ("the stories we tell ourselves about ourselves"), and it has to be hammered out in the forge of actual human experience somewhere by someone. Unfortunately, those who felt the most threatened were also the least susceptible to these gentle urgings and were the most inclined to detect old-school deviltry at work.

Linda agreed to make several videos for Abrasax in which she appeared with sympathetic moderators and a variety of skeptical religious persons of various backgrounds who would have at her with all sorts of accusations of devil worship, Satanism, atheism, demonic possession and other nasty, mutually incompatible things. Linda's calmness under fire as she answered all manner of hostile questions concerning her symbiont and her relationship with him impressed most fair-minded viewers. Such exposure as a spokesperson for the symbiont-infected was not without its dangers, unfortunately, and her backers at Abrasax had to be scrupulously careful that her true identity and home location were never made available to the public. While Linda herself had no repercussions from appearing publicly (her face was always concealed, her voice altered), a few of her colleagues and classmates were not so lucky or so careful and were the subject of brutal physical attacks by angry mobs variously composed, typically occurring just as those unfortunate students exited their schools for the day.

Abrasax and indeed the entire symbiont meta-community were deeply troubled by these direct physical confrontations, and much debate was focused on how to prevent them without the formation of some sort of symbiont defense force. Fortunately, the kids organized themselves into protective groups that looked out for each other, made cell phone videos of trouble-makers, and immediately called 911 when name-calling broke over into violence. This quieted down the more casual sorts of violent bigotry after a few successful prosecutions were accomplished and widely publicized. There were also a few successful prosecutions for incitement of violence by pastors of extreme churches, and these firebrands eventually learned how to toe the line of legality much, much more carefully. Gradually, believers in The End Times realized that God Himself *must* have willed these final tribulations upon the nation; therefore, they *must*, in principle, be incapable of stopping them, so they eventually gave up this futile waste of energy and retreated to verbal sniping and to gloating over the coming horrors and tortures of damnation for those still not listening to the purity of their Gospel of love and redemption.

GIRLS OF SIGMA-CHI

I want to be with those who know secret things or else alone.

Rainer Maria Rilke

Σ. Thank you for agreeing to look into this for me. Although this appears at first, ethically borderline from a patient confidentiality point of view, there is a lot at stake from a public health standpoint so it seems to require some sort of discreet further investigation. The person in question (C.) was a patient of mine some time ago, and now appears to be romantically linked to a current patient of mine (R.). R. claims to be infected with a symbiont who developed from a viral infection he contracted while exploring for plants in the Amazonian region of Colombia. Supposedly, his new sexual partner has become similarly infected, and the two are allegedly engaged in spreading the virus among their other sexual contacts. Maybe true, maybe not. Anyway, your legal expertise might be essential to keeping this inquiry on the rails ethically and legally.

What I need to find out is whether there is any such thing as this viral infection, and if there might be any public health hazard associated with it that I would be obliged to report. Seemingly not, however with only one patient as an informant, it is difficult to get much perspective on the potential hazards. R's personal physician has found nothing harmful associated with his infection. Based on his descriptions alone (if taken literally) the infection forming the symbiont appears benign and his symbiont herself has perhaps even been extremely helpful to him from a mental health perspective. What I need from you is some independent corroboration based on your contact with C. that 1. There actually is an infection that gives rise to a symbiont and 2. This symbiont is actually beneficial rather than malevolent. Evidently, symbionts develop to present a sexuality opposite that of their hosts. (I'm not sure yet what that would mean for us!)

C. was once a patient of mine working through a traumatic experience and a variety of feminist issues that I am not at liberty to reveal. She is *not* just an ordinary woman, however, and she has a very public presence on the internet as "Lady Carol", a promoter of a certain B&D lifestyle, as well as being a published author. This perhaps presents an opportunity for you to get to know her online, to find out more about her supposedly recent infection with a symbiont, and perhaps even to meet with her personally. I think your interest in C. will be judged as quite legitimate, especially if things proceed to the point where you would feel safe in revealing a little of your background to her. While we shouldn't necessarily volunteer information about what we're investigating, neither should we lie to her if she asks direct questions about our concerns. C. is extremely intelligent and would easily see through any overt dishonesty. Our questions, it seems to me, are all ones that a person interested in symbionts might reasonably be asking, and she has already specifically mentioned symbionts in her blog, so the topic seems a natural opening for you to explore (No pun intended!).

χ. I'm glad you brought this up, actually; I think it does need pursuing from your medical perspective, and it is a very interesting situation. I have read a little on her website, and the whole symbiont concept intrigues me greatly. We probably should confer directly after I make contact with C., and you can debrief me on what I've learned. This probably shouldn't be put in writing except perhaps as an addendum to your patient notes on C. Lady Carol is rather pretty, but I will resist the urge to explore her natural openings! Ha-ha.

———————◆◆✕◆●———————

χ. Can we meet? Have some interesting facts to report. Suggest time and place.

Σ. How about dinner at usual restaurant? 7:00 pm tonight.

χ. OK. My treat. Miss you. xx

———◆◆✕◆◆———

Addendum 1. Carol seems to have really been infected and has acquired a symbiont of the sort described in my notes for another patient to whom she is now romantically linked. The symbiont has been given the name Legba and presents as male. My informant assesses this to be genuine and has even communicated directly with this new symbiont via email. Transcript attached. The information contained therein is completely consistent with my own communication with the symbiont belonging to R. It's hard to imagine how this consistency could be concocted just to fool us, but it still could be possible. My informant insists that the only completely convincing way of determining the reality of this is to purposely become infected with a symbiont, and this is being discussed in further communications with the new symbiont. There are three methods open to us: infection through Carol or R., and direct infection from contact with a plant belonging to R. Worst case, my informant would wind up with a venereal disease! There would be no problem with reporting the case to public health authorities, but then one or another of the two parties would have to be reported as well. If we proceed, the more ethically neutral ground involving the plant would seem the less risky option.

MAN-EATER?

*Every man who has at last succeeded, after long effort, in
calling up the divinity which lies hidden in a woman's heart, is
startled to find that he must obey the God he summoned.*

Henry Adams

One regular weekday afternoon, I was working in my office at the
University with Amy, trying to organize some of our notes and
descriptions into orderly botanical identification keys for a few of the
Solanaceae collected at the Great Garden. Some of these were tricky
to distinguish with the usual flower and leaf descriptors, yet we knew
how different they turned out to be based on chemical criteria involving
their alkaloids. Moreover, Yayael had also given them different names,
presumably because he had experienced their hallucinogenic effects
directly. Unfortunately, this would never do for practical field or
laboratory identifications, and even the bravest ethnobotanists seldom
experimented with this group of alkaloids personally because of the
unpredictable effects and extreme health hazards. It appeared likely
that microscopic characteristics would have to be laboriously examined
and documented.

Amy once had a bit of a brush with these hallucinogenic effects
herself when she had neglected to wear protective gloves while preparing
specimens for the plant presses and cuttings for the propagation beds.
Fortunately, she felt herself getting woozy, realized what was happening,
and immediately washed off her hands; she mainly had a vile headache

for the remainder of the day, and I drove her home to sleep it off. At that point, she exhibited no signs of infection, and I mentally heaved a sigh of relief.

We were just about to quit for the day with lots of unresolved organizational issues when the departmental secretary interrupted us with a message that there was a visitor, a rather tall and impatient young lady who had been waiting to see me. It was Carol, dressed in her usual seductive way when she wanted to coax me into an assignation. I quickly introduced her to Amy as my "friend," Carol, and asked Amy if she could excuse us for a minute. Amy left with the secretary, and I closed the door. Carol quickly moved in for an embrace, all no doubt easily seen through the glass in the door.

"Are you well rested yet, Richard? I know we've needed a little break from each other, but it doesn't have to be so frantic anymore... I think maybe Lady Carol is starting to have just a wee bit of a crush on you, as dangerous as that may sound. She's never kept a real boyfriend before and wants to try out all sorts of new things with you."

"What brings you here now?" I whispered. "I thought we were trying to be pretty discreet about our relationship?" I was hot and flushed by then. It would have been pretty obvious to any impartial observer that Carol, and maybe even Lady Carol, had just staked some sort of proprietary claim on me with her easy physical familiarity, and wanted it publicly known.

"Oh, you were; me not so much. You know I share my adventures online, and my readers want to know everything about you. Anyway, I thought we might go to dinner and then to my place. I know how much you *love* taking me to dinner! There's someone special I'd like you to meet," she said, sticking her tongue in my ear. "For who knows what."

Already she had managed to cause me an embarrassing lump in my pants with a conspicuous wet spot.

"OK," I said. "Can we meet at the restaurant? How about in an hour or so? I've still got a lot to finish up here."

That seemed to satisfy her for the moment, and she left with a knowing smile, not caring at all about embarrassing me publicly. I could see Amy and the secretary exchange a peculiar look between them and realized that my reputation now had a spicy sexual mystery attached to it that would soon be the subject of departmental gossip. Amy mouthed the words, man-eater, and rolled her eyes.

There was little time for damage control. Amy and I re-organized the notes and papers, and prominently wrote "Do Not Erase!" on the white board. I think we were both a little embarrassed, and hardly dared look at each other for a few minutes.

"I know she may seem a little out of my league," I said to Amy, "but I've known her since high school. We hooked up again at a class reunion and seemed to hit it off really well. She does love trying to embarrass me publicly whenever she can. She's only kidding around with me, so please don't take it too seriously."

I hoped that would quiet things down for a bit.

"Professor," she said, "It's really none of my business, but I think you should know that your 'Lady Carol' has a bit of a reputation online as a sort of... Dominatrix. I looked up her site on the internet, and that's definitely her. I don't think you should let her sink her claws into you."

"Oh," I said. "That again. That's just part of the embarrassment game she loves to play. She's fully aware of her reputation and exaggerates it for humorous effect."

"Oh, I don't think just embarrassment is her specialty at all," she said. "Have you never been to her website? It all sounds a little New Agey and woo woo to me, but she's definitely into the Goddess worship thing and forcing men into submission and sexual servitude."

"Ah," I said. "Amy, you must realize she writes fiction and her blog might also be a mixture of fiction, myth and a small core of experience. We do discuss mythology when we're together, including *a lot* about Goddesses, but I'm not in any sort of bondage to her last time I checked."

This was obviously going to take more to damp this down than I had supposed. I really hadn't followed Carol closely enough online to know every little thing she was blogging about anymore, but I knew she was now using it more selectively to line up a few more prospective partners for reproduction. I thought she was being carefully vague about what this was about except for a select few whom she decided to meet personally, but it was very disconcerting to hear that her readers wanted to know everything about me.

After disentangling myself from Amy's prying conversation, I drove to the usual restaurant to meet Carol. She had made reservations for the private room in the back where we could talk undisturbed. This was convenient, but way pricier than I could afford on a professor's salary. Carol had already arrived and was waiting for me.

"Sorry I was delayed. You caused quite a flurry of prurient interest in the front office!" Carol smiled sweetly and fluttered her eyelashes innocently, "I can't imagine why. It just adds to your legend. Anyway, it adds to mine a little too, but in a better way for me, I guess. This mystique does sell books."

At dinner, Carol got a phone call and informed me that the person she wanted me to meet had cancelled because she thought someone was following her. Perhaps paranoia, but maybe real; anyway, she chickened out and didn't want to meet at Carol's townhouse. Too public, too close to town, etc. Her candidate was apparently an ultra-liberal community activist, and a lawyer who many times dealt pro bono with problems for sexual minorities. She was being actively harassed by various right-wing religious savants. Carol had been in contact with her for some time and didn't even want to give me her name yet.

"Since she's a no show, how about we just go to your house tonight. It's more discreet anyway, and we have a few things that need talking over... at length. Maybe I should just stay the weekend and give you a hard time. You can show me that new trick I hear you've been practicing with Carole. I'd even like to see the spooky greenhouse again, where your Amazon Goddess lives, just to soak up the atmosphere for my next book."

━━━━●◆●◆●━━━━

As we drove up the long driveway to my house, I had to stop and unlock the security gate to let Carol's car through. It had been necessary to take fairly elaborate security measures around both the greenhouse and house, so I had a new security fence installed, quite high (10 ft.) topped with the usual razor wire panels leaning menacingly outward. I waved Carol through so she could park in the secure area near the house, then I drove my car in, and re-locked the gate behind us. As I parked and got out of my car, Carol said, "Why don't you give me the grand tour now? I want to see what my money has bought you." Why not. So, we strolled arm in arm toward the main greenhouse entrance, where I had to extract my key ring from my pocket and unlock the door.

"This is so different from the first time I was here. Richard this is huge; I hadn't imagined you could take care of a place this large!"

"Not without help, I couldn't. There's now automation for the trickle irrigation and an automated mist sprayer for humidity control, but the propagation is still very labor intensive. That's where Amy helps the most, but we're still a bit understaffed. Anyway, your foundation fronted me the money to expand the greenhouse and to install all the additional security. Next summer we plan to put in some raised beds outside for some of the hardier *Solanaceae*; that is, some of the traditional plants associated with European witchcraft. A little PR gambit."

"Do you think Amy has been infected by working here?"

"Possibly, we'll just have to see how that develops. She did accidentally have contact with several of the plants, which made her a bit ill, but she washed it off quickly with alcohol and vinegar. She wears protective gloves now for all the propagation work. The problem is, I'm not sure whether the same virus is associated with all the plants, some of the plants, or just one. I'm not even sure whether there is only one type of virus. Anyway, I've expressed concern and asked her to report immediately any possible long-term effects of that exposure. It's been a worrisome thought that there might be more than one variety of symbiont, and not all of them good. That's part of the unknown risk of getting infected by this collection of plants."

"Have you had sex with her yet? That would be quicker and probably safer."

"She's not shown the slightest interest, and besides I think of her more as a daughter and a student. Anyway, I've pretty much had my hands full with my crazy love for you, Darling!"

That unexpected comment made her smile, and she gave me a tight embrace, and whispered in my ear:

"Thank you, Carole, for sharing your sex-crazed Richard with me."

We walked up and down the aisles, and I pointed out each of the main types from the Great Garden, and then the one that Yayael valued above all else.

"So, this is her?"

"Yes, this whole section. The mature plants are over there, and you can see they've now nearly achieved tree size."

"What would happen if I touched the leaves?"

"I'm not sure anything at all would happen since you're already harboring a symbiont, and he would deactivate the toxins. For us, I don't think even the alkaloids would have the same effect as before. We're largely immune to many poisons now."

"It's hard to think of plants in quite the same way as before. Well, these plants, anyway. You told me once about entheogens; I suppose these are perfect examples of that. It's hard not to ascribe personality to them when you start seeing things that talk to you."

"It creates a huge change in perspective, doesn't it? Except that we're not just 'seeing things.' We're being purposely *made* to see things and to interact with them."

"What will happen to all these plants when you're finally forced to retire?"

"I still don't have that all worked out. Many species will have been sent to other places by then, the St. Louis Climatron, Fairchild, Longwood, Kew and the Royal Botanic Gardens for example. Money will continue to be a big issue until the foundation accumulates a sufficient permanent endowment to be self-sustaining."

After we finished touring the greenhouse, we exited, and walked up the gravel path toward my house. Carol was unusually silent; lost in thought or something else? I let us into the house, excused myself for the bachelor clutter, and offered her a chair in the living room.

"My God, you keep it cold in here!"

"I'm gone a lot, and I save the heat for the greenhouse. A little drink to warm you up?"

"Please! Have you still got some of that brandy I bought you?"

"I think so; let me check."

I found the brandy and poured generous amounts into two snifters. After handing her one of them, I took a seat facing hers. She had taken out a small notebook and was busily scribbling down her thoughts.

"You seem unnaturally quiet tonight."

"I've just thought of several new ideas for writing projects, and they're sort of spinning around in my head. That's how it works for me as a writer, ideas constantly intruding into real life. Usually, I have to write them down pretty quickly or I can easily lose track of them."

"What sort of ideas?"

"Well, you know I'm being pressed to write a sequel to my first novel, *Beloved Incubus*. But there's also a possible mystery I could do that would also have more about the symbiont origins. I'm thinking of calling it *The Witch's Garden*. If I wait too long, this whole fad will fade away or other opportunists will jump on the bandwagon!"

"And that would involve something about mysterious plants involved with witchcraft?"

"Yes, and perhaps a mysterious professor who grows the plants."

"Ah. Shouldn't it be *The Warlock's Garden* then?"

"I haven't quite decided on who actually would oversee the garden. Maybe the Amazon Goddess should be the witch and the professor just her obedient love slave and gardener! Or her comical sidekick. Anyway, you'll definitely be one of the protagonists, but will you be a deeply flawed hero with a few redeeming qualities... or perhaps an anti-hero? I've got this hard-edged feminist reputation to maintain; I can't go all mushy or I'll lose half my readers."

"Oh, I hope definitely for the comical sidekick, I said with a smile. Professors are grossly underrated as comedians, but some of us do clown around a lot in class. Speaking of feminists though, what of your no-show for tonight? What can you tell me about her?"

"She's been kind of a fan who gradually started to correspond with me off line. I'm a little uncertain what she really wants. Maybe it's just a guilty pleasure sort of thing."

"That sounds a little iffy for one of our candidates. Why did you agree to meet her tonight? That seems pretty far advanced, considering your uncertainties."

"Oh, I've met with her already for lunch several times, and was a little surprised to find out who she really was and how famous. We've had long talks, and I really do like her, or I wouldn't bother."

"And what sort of sexuality are we dealing with here?"

"She hasn't really come out to me, but I think she may be a lesbian."

"Perhaps I shouldn't even be involved then."

"She was specifically interested in our relationship and its history."

"Interested how, exactly?"

"Sexually, of course. She says she knows very little about dominant/submissive style relationships and wanted to learn more."

"This could go so wildly wrong... Remember? Security by obscurity? Stay hidden in the noise?"

"Yes, it could go wrong. Or we could gain a powerful ally."

"Or we could gain a powerless ally, who's also being stalked by crazy evangelicals, and who might attract unwanted attention to ourselves!"

"That too. Unfortunately, I think we've already attracted a little too much of that unwanted attention. I'm just a little scared to go ahead with this."

"Why don't you just continue to meet with her secretly for now? Perhaps when you feel the time is ripe, we could meet with her together - just to talk. I think we'll need to work on *that* story a bit, anyway. How much do we really want to reveal? Reel her in slowly so we can figure out what she wants. Is she writing an article or what?"

"Perhaps. She hasn't really said. I suspect it's more personal than that."

"Well, if it's for an article, just meeting for lunch sounds best. I'm not really much of an exhibitionist at heart despite what you and I have gone through for Carole! Anyway, meeting for lunch gives me some cover now that everybody in the office is tuned in to my comings and goings with a convicted sex Goddess and evil dominatrix!"

"Ha! You know very well that Lady Carol has been dialed down to wicked just for you... Richard, sorry, but I'm absolutely freezing in here! Have you got a blanket or something?"

"We could huddle together over there on the couch. I've got the perfect solution. (Retrieving a tartan blanket from the hall closet.)"

"This was a gift from Carole."

"You're kidding, right?"

"No, really. She orders things she likes over the internet now using my credit card."

"This is beautiful. Is this your clan's tartan or something?"

"No, it's McKenzie, I think; Douglas doesn't have any red in it... But perhaps Carole just liked this color combination and didn't care about clans. She's very much into doubly periodic patterns now. In fact, she's designed several new tartanoid patterns that are based on period parallelograms rather than squares or rectangles. Unfortunately, they're much harder to implement in woven fabric..."

"That sounds appropriately geeky for *your* inner woman! How often do you and Carole have sync-sex these days?"

"Like many old married couples, we only manage to get it on once a week or so, except maybe a little extra for birthdays, anniversaries... Oh, and the birthdays of famous mathematicians and scientists; don't forget those."

"Yeah, I'll bet. This is warm and sexy under here. Come here so we can pretend we're married and celebrating an anniversary or something."

And so we did in our usual way with a few additions. Afterwards as we snuggled there, I mentioned that I did have a special anniversary present for her. This got her surprised attention. I fetched the large box out of the bedroom, and brought it in. It had been gift wrapped for me, and I presented it to her. When she opened it, she went Ooh! And brought it up to her face to feel the soft mohair against her cheek, all the while examining my face closely for any signs of a motive.

"Richard, where did you find this! It's so beautiful. You know Lady Carol should never ever be allowed to wear this!"

"Creapulka. Harder to find these days than you might suppose. Carole suggested something other than our high school colors, and this looked so sexy I couldn't resist. Go ahead and try it on. Just seeing you in it may provoke lustful thoughts, however. You know all too well how I'm wired... I guess you *must* know since you did some of the wiring."

"And you just had to let Lady Carol know that, didn't you? ...This isn't some nefarious attempt to rule from the bottom, is it? Wait! No, No!

I take that back; I should never hand you a straight line like that! If you say one word about my bottom, there will be consequences!"

"Nothing like that! It's really just an innocent expression of Carole's and my trust in you. We're hoping this weapon will be used only for peaceful sexy purposes that please you! Think of it more as a peace offering…"

"It's long… I could almost wear this as a sweater dress. Maybe I really *will* stay the whole weekend just to be naughty! No panties all weekend. I'll just have to try not to give you an erection lasting more than four hours… We could almost recreate that shared dream of ours."

"That may be a little overwhelming, but I'm certainly willing. You may have to rescue me from Lady Carol if she gets carried away."

"I loved whatever you and Carole did with my G-spot, by the way. Lady Carol also approves. We'll definitely try *that* again!"

AMY AND THE NIGHTMARE FLOWER

*The only way to make sense out of change is to plunge
into it, move with it, and join the dance.*

Alan Watts

Sunday morning, we awakened late, and had been puttering around in the kitchen fixing a fairly large omelet for brunch. Whenever I get a chance, I enjoy cooking for her. Like many bachelors, I don't get really inspired unless I'm cooking for someone else, and those opportunities have been limited and rare.

I don't think I had ever seen Carol so relaxed and happy. We sat in the kitchen enjoying our second coffee of the morning and trading sarcastic comments back and forth as we watched the political news on TV, when we heard a loud banging on the front door, and exchanged alarmed glances.

"It must be Amy. The doorbell is on the locked gate, but she has a key to get through," I whispered.

"OK... I think I'm going to pull on my panties and be very quiet in a distant corner of the living room under the blanket."

It was indeed Amy, who seemed out of breath, and, uncharacteristically, a little hysterical; I could hear it immediately in the higher pitch of her voice.

"Professor, we need to talk. Something strange is happening to me... She's here, isn't she?"

"Yes, she's here, but I *am* allowed to have my favorite dominatrix visit my simple monastic cell for an occasional session of flagellation, you know. Anyway, I'm kidding, don't worry about all that. Come in; it's cold out there. What can I do for you Amy; you seem upset."

"Can we talk privately? These are things I don't want shared on anyone's blog."

"Let's go to my study. We can shut the door."

After I hung up her heavy coat, we went to the study, passing Carol in the living room, who nodded her recognition to Amy, and smiled. She had a very contented Charlie in her lap and was scratching him behind his ears. Amy said not a word and seemed too embarrassed to even glance her way. Upon entering my study and closing the door, I motioned for her to take a chair, and I took one opposite her.

"Now, Amy what has happened?"

"I think it has something to do with my touching the plants a while back. You remember how I got all woozy, and had to be taken home to sleep it off?"

"Yes, I was very concerned about that. Have you noticed similar symptoms again? I thought the gloves would provide adequate protection. Have you been careful to use them?"

"Yes, of course. I don't think I've been exposed to the exudate again if I ever was. It's just that now I have weird, vivid dreams that seem so real. Part of the weirdness is that I remember them - I hardly ever remember dreams except maybe for a few seconds after waking up. The person in the dream is telling me that I have been infected with something, and it has produced 'him'. Have you ever heard of anything like this?"

"Well, as you well know, many of the *Solanaceae* can produce weird sensations, even phantasms, usually caused by the alkaloids; I'm sure you've read about all this. W.H. Hudson even wrote a short story in which he described something he called, the nightmare flower; I'm sure he was drawing on old folklore about nightshades, witchcraft and magical flying. Could it be something like that?"

"I don't understand how my tiny exposure weeks ago could lead to such dramatic effects now! Did you experience this sort of thing when you were collecting the plants?"

"Yes, I did for a while, even the headaches. However, I have apparently become immune to further casual contact with the plants."

"So, you didn't have dreams about a mysterious person trying to contact you?"

"I didn't say that."

"So, you actually did?

"Yes."

"And... what did he talk to you about?"

"It was a she in my case. Sex, health, and domestication of the human race, in roughly that order, and, of course, much, much more. My infection calls herself Carole... (With an e). She's very inquisitive and quite charming really. I think she wants to be a mathematician when she grows up."

Amy digested that bombshell for a while, obviously running through a comparison with her own experience.

"And you don't find it highly disturbing?"

"Oh, I certainly did at first - I sought the help of a psychiatrist for many years, but I've come to terms with it."

"What 'terms' would those be?"

"That's a long story, and rather too personal to reveal it all to you right now. I'm asking for your discretion here; this conversation is not to be repeated to anyone. My recommendation is that you engage with... Did he give himself a name?"

"He suggested I call him Quicksilver."

"Does that name have any particular significance to you?"

"I guess it connotes indirectly some sort of messenger of the Gods, like Mercury. Anyway, that's the best interpretation I've come up with."

"And do you like him?"

"I don't even know if I trust him enough to be around him! He projects a sensuality that's disturbingly hot. That part is very dreamlike."

"Is he making suggestions that you find disturbing?"

"Oh, yes. I won't even get into all that, but he wants me to put myself out there in ways I've never imagined."

"So, he's still pretty scary to you? You might ask him about all the sexy imagery and see if he will give you the straight story about what he is and what he wants from you. You're a highly intelligent science student, but perhaps he may have misread some of your enthusiasm for current romantic fiction or movie fads... He could also be kidding around with you."

"Do you know what he is?"

"Yes, but I really want him to tell you in his own way. You two must adapt to each other, like it or not. Make sure you explicitly welcome him into yourself and try to help him understand you and your world. Potentially he can be an immense help to you in your work."

"Did what's her name... Carole with an e (?) tell you what the hell was going on?"

"Yes."

"Is she somehow like the other Carol, the one in the living room?"

"There are some trivial similarities in her chosen appearance, but Carole with an e, also has a totally other aspect if that's the right word. Hidden depths. Also, a much different core personality and a very different agenda."

"Do you trust her?"

"Yes. Maybe not one hundred percent, but we continue to work together on our trust issues. She strives to answer all my questions, and her answers make sense to me. Anyway, I made my choice to help her long ago. Our lives are now very deeply entangled."

"You're implying that she also has had to learn to trust you as some sort of partner?"

"Yes. In a sense, we both could pose a danger to each other."

"What possible danger could you be to her?"

"I could be trying to get rid of her with antibiotics and antiviral medications. That might actually work, but I would never willingly do that now. I enjoy her presence and would miss her terribly if she were gone. We share an odd love and deep affection for each other."

"So, she doesn't 'possess' you like a demon?"

"I'm not sure what possession would be like, since I've never seen any evidence for it, at least in the religious sense of demonic possession. Having Carole in me has been more analogous to sharing an apartment with someone who knows you very, very well, but who never goes out... Sometimes like a roommate who uses some of your stuff or who redecorates without explicit permission. I know that sounds mundane and frightening at the same time, but we really do share some things that way."

"Like what?"

"Strange as it may sound, for one example, we share my home computer and my books."

"Are you serious?"

"Yes. She can go online when I am offline, so to speak. You might suggest to Quicksilver that he can impart more information to you in a hurry that way, or that he can learn more about our world and culture that way. He'll figure out how it works. Otherwise, you can meet face to face in lucid dreams within some psychologically comfortable setting. Carole met me first in the 'Library of Dreams' as the head librarian. This was a mental construct that emulated a real library similar to our Natural History Library at the University. Carole might be willing to contact you or even Quicksilver by email if you're interested."

"That is so weird! Does regular Carol know about any of this?"

"She's quite well aware of what is going on and is best friends with my partner. She has, in fact, dealt with the very same issues you're dealing with now, and I helped her through it. Her novel contains a slightly coded description of her situation with her own partner. Her work is pretty popular and has seemed to have tapped into the recent popular enthusiasms for offbeat sex, the occult, vampires, zombies and demons. She'd probably be happy to give you a signed copy if you're interested. It might set your mind at ease about a few things. It's made her a lot of money, and she has used much of it to support our work here."

"Seriously? She is supporting your scientific work?"

"You better believe it! Do you have any idea of just the monthly heating bills for this place and the new, enlarged greenhouse? If it were not for the Albert Blakeslee Foundation, I would not be able to continue the work here at this scale. Indirectly, she pays your salary too. Despite her reputation she really has a very frugal life style, which allows her time to write."

"So, she's really *not* a man-eater? Maybe I've misjudged her. I figured she was just picking your brains on folklore and stuff, maybe even stealing your ideas without permission, and then doing who knows what to you just for fun. Her magazine articles about sexuality are really outrageous and have been widely condemned as Satanist by fundamentalist Churches. It's easy to get a bad impression."

"Please don't believe everything you've read about her. She's really not that simple to understand, and all the usual stereotypes don't really apply to her either. Ironically, her public self has also managed to piss off the Wiccans and several other more tolerant groups. She is what she is; she'll have to speak for herself on being a man-eater. Maybe someday you should talk to Carol about her dietary habits. She does have a uniquely flamboyant and scandalous public image that she cultivates with a certain amount of fiendish glee, but that's about as Satanic as she gets. I think she's modeling it just a little after Tallulah Bankhead... have you even heard of her? A notorious actress and celebrity from long ago who once described herself as 'pure as the driven slush'. However, aside from the public self-mythologizing, Carol is really quite different from Lady Carol if you haven't figured that out by now.

"Amy, after you've had more time to digest this unexpected information and talk it over with Quicksilver, come back here, and you and I will talk some more. If you have a high tolerance for eccentricity, Carol might even become a sympathetic listener for you if you'd like a female point of view. Anyway, please don't panic! There are now many other people out there who have gone through this, adjusted to it, and whom you can talk to. It's really important that you do make these contacts, just do so *very* cautiously. Meanwhile, I am asking you not to spill your guts out to just anyone at the University or elsewhere until you know their infection status and have decided how this strange situation might work for you. You must know how nutty this would sound to someone with no experience of it... Do you think you might be OK to just work with this for now? I promise that I will help you as you adapt to it. Just let me know if you hit some rough spots."

"I think this has helped a lot, and you've put to rest some of my worst fears, but there's still a lot I don't understand. Thank you so much, Professor, and I do apologize for interrupting you on your weekend."

I truly hoped that Amy was pacified enough to function. The stress in her voice was gone, and she seemed at least resigned to engaging in a dialog with her symbiont. I hoped to hell that Quicksilver was even half as smart as Carole... If it all went well, then perhaps Amy could be trusted to work more closely with us. I escorted Amy out to her car and re-locked the gate after she left.

Carol was still sitting in the living room when I returned to the house. Charlie was with her and was doing the milk tread on her lap and purring contentedly. Carol caught my eye and raised an eyebrow questioningly.

"I think she's going to be alright."

"How much did you have to tell her?"

"We're just up to the point of talking about symbionts, but she needs to sync with hers before we go any further. She's still pretty scared of him. I'll try to find out more about whether she's really done this as we work together this week on our classification scheme."

"She would be a wonderful asset. You and I are just not tuned in to social media in the same way as this generation."

"Yes, she would. Unlike my earlier student workers, I think Amy might not want to move away after graduation. We could even offer her a position with the Foundation."

"She still seems pretty hostile to me. Any idea why?"

"She may still think you're using me in some wicked way. Anyway, that was her initial opinion when you visited my office. I think that will change as she connects more with her own symbiont."

"Should I try to talk to her or would that make things worse? I feel like the evil step-mother."

"Eventually maybe, but best to wait awhile. She has concluded just now that she may have misjudged you. Let's see how things develop from that."

"So, until then, may I have my wicked way with you?"

"Very wicked?"

"Oh yes, very wicked, and pretty darn aberrant too."

"OK then!"

"It is ironic that Amy thinks I'm the man-eater when you actually do most of the eating!"

"I'd rather that you didn't point that out to her just yet."

"Too soon? Maybe I won't just yet... I *really* don't want to share you anymore, Richard, except with Carole, of course."

THE DISPOSSESSION OF CALLEY

*Death is not the greatest loss in life. The greatest
loss is what dies inside us while we live.*

Norman Cousins

"Mommy, I'm scared! You don't have to do this."

"I'm sorry honey, but this just has to be done."

"But I love Jiminy and don't want him to die!"

"Honey, your daddy and I... and the doctor have all talked this over. Jiminy is not a real person, and he needs to be removed so you can grow up to be the smart, active normal girl we know you want to be."

"But Jiminy helps me! He makes me smarter! I don't ever want to be normal again without him."

"We know you *think* he helps you, dear, but he's not real. He makes it difficult for you to make friends with other girls your age."

"Symbionts are real; more real than you can possibly know! Those other girls you want me to be friends with are mean and stupid! They're the ones who aren't real! At my old school I had plenty of real friends! Why did we have to move away?"

"Calley, we can't just go round and round on this. It's time to do what the doctor recommends."

"But you will murder him!"

"Nonsense, you'll just take a few pills for two weeks, and that will be that. It's called Symbicyclovir. I bet you won't even notice after it's gone."

"But I *will* notice! It's poison to Jiminy! You will hurt him and he will tell me how badly he hurts as he slowly dies inside of me! He's never done anything bad; why do you hate him so much?"

"We don't hate anyone, dear, but we love you so much that we want to help you become normal again. It's all for the best."

"If you really love me, you won't kill Jiminy!"

"Calley, we do really love you, and for that reason we must remove this 'Jiminy' thing from your brain. That's all I want to hear about it now. Here are the pills. You start with two now and one later this evening."

"I won't take them! You can't make me!"

"If we must, Calley, we can take you back to the doctor, and he will give you the medication as a shot. Is that how you want to do it?"

"I don't want to do it at all!"

"Fine. I'm going to call the hospital and make an appointment for tomorrow. This is going to happen, Calley; one way or another!"

———◆◆◆◆◆———

TO WHOM IT MAY CONCERN

Today I am tendering my resignation over the incident in the outpatient clinic yesterday during which I disrupted an attempt to treat a minor patient with a forced injection of antiviral medications. In this incident, the screaming child was immobilized on a gurney with restraints ordinarily used for patients undergoing an epileptic seizure or other violent event in which a patient might injure himself or the attending medical staff. This was definitely not the situation here. The purpose of the constraints was to overcome the child's hysterical physical resistance to the administration of antiviral medications designed to kill her symbiont. In my opinion such forced medical treatment went way beyond ethical bounds to do no harm, and I will not participate in any such future attempts to torture children. I am ashamed to have been a part of an institution that permits such sadistic torment of children even under the flimsy auspices of parental approval. Aiding and abetting child abuse is also a crime, and I will be filing a report of the whole incident with the District Attorney.

I have been informed by the administration that my unwillingness to participate in such treatments constitutes grounds for my dismissal "for cause". That being so, I resign voluntarily, and plan to file my grievances with the state medical board, and all other pertinent government and professional agencies. To this end, I have engaged a personal attorney to represent me in my lawsuit against the hospital, Prof. Christine Encarnacion. All legal inquiries concerning these matters should be addressed to her.

DARKNESS RISING

The brighter the light, the darker the shadow.

Carl Jung

Lady Carol is a horrible hypocritical bitch and I HATE HER! For weeks I tried to engage her in dialogue on her website under the Domme Forum, but she has blown off my incisive comments without anything but trivial, clichéd remarks. She doesn't even realize how wimpy her advice about men has become, since she picked up her little botanist boy-toy. I bet *he* doesn't have to beg for her attention. She's become so fucking normal, I could just shit! And she's sooo old! I looked it up. She must really be a hag by now. All those pictures on her website, god only knows when *those* glamour shots were taken! The fifties? I bet her tits and ass sag, and her wrinkles are starting to show everywhere on her face. Geriatric porn is all she'll be good for when I get done with her. I'd like to rummage her vagina with a knife! Better yet, a huge strap-on dildo studded with razor blades!

A whole month ago, I flat out asked her how I could become infected with a symbiont, and she told me not to try it yet. Supposedly, I was not ready! How the fuck she could tell anything about me from a few lines on an internet forum, I can't imagine, but she had the gall to say that her goddamned symbiont, "Legba", thought I was not ready and that her friend Carole agreed. They are so fucking wrong. Well, I decided, there *must* be some way to do it without her being able to stop me. I found a way alright. Her ass-licking boyfriend has a greenhouse with just the right plants in it, and all I had to figure out was how to break in at night and steal leaves from the right plants. It was so easy to track it down. Simple! One big padlock on a security gate, and one simple door lock on the greenhouse. A few security cameras in plain sight. Piece of cake. They are even advertising how to get there on his sissy website; gives you a fucking map and everything. Fucking idiots. Practically giving it away to everyone but me!

Worm, my slave boy, has a lengthy police record for illegal entry into buildings, and apparently quite a nifty little talent for picking locks. It was not difficult to convince him to help me if he ever wanted to be able to use his little pink dicklet ever again. Until then he could stay cock-locked and French-kiss my shitty asshole every night. A dim bulb, but even he finally figured out that it was best to do exactly what I wanted!

A GREENHOUSE ROMANCE

*In a great romance, each person basically plays
a part that the other really likes.*

Elizabeth Ashley

I was in my lab working with Amy on our classification scheme. The next phase of this was to be accomplished with examination of plant parts under a good stereo microscope, and then under an SEM. We needed a lot of depth of field to study the rugose surfaces of the stems and leaves. Amy diligently copied down my remarks as we went through some of the more difficult-to-distinguish members of tropical *Solanaceae*, mostly tree-like forms (*Brugmansia*) with pendant flowers in a variety of colors. After I had finished, she independently examined the specimen to see if she agreed with my assessment and descriptions, and I noted her comments. Photographs were taken to illustrate various subtle structural differences. Often, she had additional observations, and occasionally, even a few astute questions about things that we needed to pursue. This was slow going, but Amy and I were learning a lot from it. After we had thoroughly looked over the photos from the stereo microscope, we decided which samples merited further investigation under higher powers available on the SEM, and these samples were freeze-dried, sputter-coated with gold, and run by Amy as instrument time became available on the departmental SEM.

Eventually, we hoped to have DNA analyses available for all the specimens collected, but that rather expensive undertaking had to be doled out carefully, and that required collaborators willing to help us out. Although not so important to the field botanist figuring out whether he had something new out there in the jungle, the genome evaluations would become the gold standard as far as separating closely allied or sibling species. I was hoping the full evaluation would also yield insight into the subtle genetic nature of the virally induced mutations that were undoubtedly present in some of the collected plants.

In the midst of this, Carol called, and indicated that she wanted to bring her new contact plus a friend to my house. They wanted to tour the greenhouse and seemed interested in supporting the Blakeslee Foundation. I agreed only a little reluctantly, and we set a time. Carol and the visitors would arrive in separate vehicles and wait for me outside the gate sometime after dinner. Carol would meet with them for dinner and assess them a bit more before bringing them over. She would call if things fell through again.

That interruption broke our concentration for the moment, and so Amy and I stopped for a coffee break. She had apparently detected that it was Carol on the other end of the line, and asked, "Carol?" "Yes of course," I admitted.

"I'm beginning to envy your relationship with Carol. It's so hard to find someone with whom to share this amazing secret."

"Which secret is that?" I asked, looking for some hint about Amy's state of mind.

"The symbionts," she said.

"Ah. You've apparently been talking to Quicksilver. All good, I hope."

"Oh yes. I'm coming to terms with him. He has way more of a sense of humor than I realized at first and was teasing me a bit. He is an amazingly quick study and has even taken quite an interest in my research. What I don't have yet is any actual human connection for me. You know how tough that can be as a graduate student? So little time. All I meet are campus geeks and frat rats."

"When you say geeks, you mean what exactly?"

"Oh, I mean male students obsessing over computer games and certain techie things, I guess."

"What does Quicksilver think about your geeks and rats? Does he see any potential in them?"

"He thinks I should make use of a dating service and be really careful around the rats whenever alcohol is involved."

"What sort of dating service? Something on line?"

"I guess. He thinks if I meet enough people, he can help me meet 'the one'."

"It might up the odds, I guess. Do you believe there will be just one?"

"Quicksilver says that's up to me, but I guess maybe I do have a romantic streak and a thing about monogamy. He's quite the matchmaker."

"Monogamy or just one relationship at a time?"

"Good point. I guess one relationship at a time. I prefer to concentrate my efforts on getting to know one person at a time. Maybe that's a little intense for some men?"

"Perhaps. There are also people out there with symbionts already who might welcome you into their community. That could help you a lot and link you to sympathetic listeners. I think Quicksilver may also be trying to hook you up that way too."

"Now that you mention it, I think you're right. One question though, does having a symbiont change a person very much?"

"Quick answer is yes. Personally, having a symbiont on my side as confidante tends to make me much bolder in my responses to other people. Still, you will have a say in exactly how your symbiont will change you, and how he can help you. You might consider allowing him quite a lot of autonomy, at least after you build some trust. If you do pass the infection on to another person whom you like, that person may become changed according to their individual response to their own symbiont. It doesn't happen all at once either... and the results may not be quite what you or they expected."

"If you don't mind my asking, how did it change you?"

"Let me count the ways! It shook me to my core and questioned all my answers, particularly about women."

"Symbiont Carole did that?"

"Primarily her, but more recently also my interaction with Carol and her symbiont. It was a lengthy and still on-going discussion. Having a symbiont profoundly affects your relationships with other people, especially those others with their own symbiont. Dating then always becomes double-dating. Symbionts are very observant and can assist you in checking out compatible people to date. There are also the health span, life span and general wellness effects."

"Yeah, I was going to ask about that too. I must admit, I looked up your bio and was amazed at how old you actually are. You sure don't look it. Apparently, Carol is about the same age?"

"Yes. Please don't spread that around or I will be forced into emeritus status way too soon."

"I won't; I promise. So, will I achieve something similar, a much-extended middle age?"

"I suppose so, barring immediately fatal accidents."

"Am I just sort of a non-fatal accident then? I mean compared to you and Carol..."

"I was 'just sort of a non-fatal accident' too. There's no getting away from the role of chance and randomness in your life events. Even though my candidacy for infection, if you will, was vetted by Yayael in the rainforest, I don't think they knew exactly how it would turn out. Basically, they decided that I had a compatible microbiome, and was not overtly crazy. Pretty low hurdles, actually. As my symbiont has pointed out, even with vetting, it's always a bit of a 'come as you are party'..."

"So, did I get over those low hurdles?"

"Certainly, or I wouldn't have hired you."

"How did you know I had a compatible microbiome?"

"Charlie liked you. Remember your interview?"

"Sure, I liked Charlie too. But how...?"

"I'm pretty sure Charlie is infected too. Anyway, he apparently doesn't befriend people who are incompatible."

"So, did I get infected from Charlie?"

"Probably not, although it's not impossible; cats do always seem to be rubbing up against things, and Charlie has from time to time had free run of the greenhouse when I've been working out there. It's mellowed him quite a bit as a tomcat. He's much friendlier now and very affectionate to certain special people he seems to have chosen. Also, he's way smarter, and can now open most doors and cupboards and get into things. I haven't formally tested him, but I strongly suspect he can now read some words on food packages.

"I think repeated contact with the greenhouse plants may have gotten you infected just as it did for Charlie. It's still an open question whether all or just some or just one can pass on the infection. More scarily, perhaps there's more than one kind of viral infection competing for dominance. Yayael insisted that there was *one* plant above all others that must be saved in the greenhouse so that plant and its viral inhabitants must be our initial focus. I am conducting experiments to see if the active virus can be passed to native Datura species that are frost hardy perennials. That's what the outside raised beds will be used for. It might even work for tomatoes and potatoes..."

"Ah! I see, and that would make possible the more rapid colonization of temperate zones by symbionts?"

"I think so, yes."

"I can't help but feel a little conspiratorial and subversive even just talking about all this. What do you think will be the result?"

"No guaranteed Utopia, for sure. I think the immediate result (best case) will be a renewed and invigorated informational, political and cultural struggle that will go on for years, but that ultimately, we may tip the balance more towards people treating each other and the world more decently. Politically, we are talking about resetting the balance between freedom, equality and fairness and making responsibility rein in these forces via the law or regulation when they become too destructive. Humans may then finally become domesticated and fit to live in this world without destroying it."

"I have no problem with people treating each other decently, but I can see horrible religious and political blow-back if any of this leaks out before we're the clear majority. It just sounds so strange. The non-infected will be scared out of their wits, and we might be demonized as weird aliens or mutants. Imagine what would happen in the Islamic world. Or maybe even in Israel among the ultra-orthodox. Some of those cultures are barely able to concede that women are human; imagine how they'll resist the idea of symbionts deserving personhood status!"

"Yes, they would be scared. So, we do have a certain level of secrecy we must maintain even among those who do not wish to actively participate in spreading the symbionts. That's why there's a certain façade of new-Age woo, as you noted, that's been propagated around the internet to cover some of Carol's organizing efforts. That makes it easy to dismiss what's going on as a harmless fringe movement of no consequence.

"There's another facet to this gradual infection process that you should realize, and that is that younger and younger persons are acquiring symbionts. This means that some of the hosts are now quite young and need even more guidance in coming to terms with their symbionts, especially if their parents are horrified by the whole notion. There are now even some websites for kids that help them handle all the social problems they face."

"This is so surreal!" Amy shakes her head.

"Yes, it does seem that way. The reality takes a while to sink in. By the way, Amy, there are some people coming over to view the greenhouse tonight whom you should meet. Carol telephoned to tell me they were interested in becoming active donors to the Blakeslee Foundation, but I suspect there's more than that afoot. Would you be willing to be present to help me with the greenhouse tour? We do need more donors to shore up our finances. Anyway, you'd perhaps learn a few things that might make you feel more at ease about our mission and how it operates, and besides, you will be paid for the overtime."

I hoped I wasn't sticking my neck out too far with that offer, which she readily accepted, but mutual trust had to be cultivated despite the indeterminate risk involved.

———◆◆◆◆◆———

At the appointed time, cars began to arrive at the gate, and, instead of waiting for the intercom, I simply went out, unlocked the gate and waved the cars through to our secure parking area. Amy was not with this group, but she had promised to come as soon as she could. I re-locked the security gate after the three cars were inside.

Carol brought our guests into the house and was handing out information packets to them as I entered. Carol introduced me to Christine, a tall, strikingly beautiful black woman, with whom I shook hands, and then, to my astonishment, to Dr. Ellis. "We've met before," I said, and caught Carol's eye to indicate something was up. "Actually, I've known Dr. Ellis for quite a number of years by now." To my surprise, Carol said, "I've also met Dr. Ellis before, but it was a while back. It's really good to see you again, Sharon!"

Christine did not seem surprised or taken aback by any of this, so I guessed she knew already that I had been seeing Dr. Ellis as a patient. My "quite a number of years" comment let Carol know that Sharon had been my psychiatrist, and that we needed to proceed cautiously, but it was now obvious that she already knew way more than she was saying.

I started with a little spiel about the Blakeslee Foundation, and its charter, then handed out the packets of information.

"We have extra packets available if you might encounter other people who might share our interests. Also, our website is currently being renovated, and links to other allied and supportive organizations can easily be added now. I've invited my laboratory assistant over this evening to help with the greenhouse tour. She's very familiar with the layout, and very good at describing the significance of our current work. Her thesis work will be part of this."

"Richard, I hope Amy really has the time to do this; I know she's very busy with her own research."

"She was happy to do it, and she will be on the clock tonight as well," I reassured Carol. She's very appreciative of the Blakeslee Foundation for supporting her research, and she needs opportunities to practice talking about it in preparation for her doctoral exam."

Charlie investigated the voices in his house, and cautiously came in to see the strangers. He seemed satisfied with them enough to rub up against them. Christine made a bit of a fuss over him and scratched behind his ears, which he does not usually allow at first acquaintance. "That's Charlie," I commented.

Amy arrived shortly after that, knocking loudly at the door of the house. After introductions all around, we all went out to the greenhouse, and Amy explained what was going on in the various sections.

"Here on this end, we have the propagation tables. We are working with mostly the species collected by Professor Douglas on his major rainforest expedition. Many of these are possibly new to science, and part of our work is to assure that they can survive here, even if their rainforest habitat is threatened as appears likely. As the professor may have already mentioned, when these plants were collected in the rainforest, they were being artificially maintained in a hidden garden by a particular Indian tribe devoted to their cultivation, apparently for religious reasons. They were viewed as sacred power plants, no question of that. That adds a certain urgency in understanding what exactly these plants represent genetically, and how they can be maintained. The color-coded labels help us keep them organized."

"Amy," asked Christine, "Tell me a little about these plants and their effect. Do they contain dangerous hallucinogens?"

"Oh yes," she said. "Many members of the nightshade family contain numerous hallucinogenic substances. That's partly why the security measures around the greenhouse have been installed, including all the security cameras in the greenhouse. (She pointed out a few of them.) We know from our analyses that several of these plants contain extremely high levels of hallucinogens in their exudates, or 'sap' I guess you'd call it."

"I've also heard that there may be a virus associated with these plants. Can you tell us about that?"

"So far, there are some indications that one of the tree forms especially might transmit a benign virus of as-yet undetermined properties. Here, let's go over to the free-root area to see those next."

We moved down to the far end of the greenhouse into Jungle Girl's domain, and Amy pointed out the different types, several of which were in bloom.

"Notice the long pendant flowers. These are most characteristic of the genus *Brugmansia*. And here is the special one we think harbors a virus in unusually large amounts."

At this point, Amy showed them the leaves and flowers, gently handling them without bothering to wear gloves.

"Notice that I can touch them without problems as long as I don't break or bruise the leaves or stems. Rough handling might release the exudate and cause severe hallucinations. Those compounds can readily be absorbed even through the unbroken skin. However, the very worst effects are seen in people who ingest tea or potions brewed from the leaves or roots. Strictly speaking the toxins produce a delirium in which reality cannot be distinguished from fantasy."

"Have you become immune to those poisons by working here?"

"I'm not really sure I'd personally want to test that hypothesis given the horrible cases of self-mutilation described for strong exposure; however, I have worked with these plants for a couple years now. For safety, I still wear gloves whenever cutting the stems is involved. We propagate from cuttings of the new growth before they become very woody."

Christine and Sharon both touched the plants, following Amy's lead, and stood there, side by side, examining first the flowers and then the leaves. We left them in silence to share this special moment.

Christine wondered whether these (indicating the Goddess plant) could be cultivated as house plants.

"They're quite easy to grow in a well-equipped greenhouse. In an ordinary house the humidity might be too low, but perhaps in an atrium or small sunroom, you could grow a pretty respectable plant in a large pot if you kept the soil moisture reasonably constant. The size would be limited by the pot. It could also make a pretty decent bonsai if you have acquired the skills to do that. We haven't had anyone ask about that possibility before, so we'd have to think about whether that would be advisable or safe without some sort of special training."

After a few minutes, Sharon asked,

"These all seem virtually identical (indicating the whole free-root area); how do you ever tell them apart?"

"That's a work in progress, so there's no simple answer yet. We've kept separate those which were distinguished in the field by Professor Douglas's native confidant. If all else fails, the DNA analysis may be necessary to trace relationships. However, DNA analysis is nearly useless under field conditions. A plant explorer must know thousands of plants intimately, based on simpler criteria; otherwise, he or she would face an impossible problem. You can only collect a limited number of specimens on each trip, and you'd like them to be new and scientifically interesting. Expeditions to such remote places are God-awful expensive and difficult to plan!"

"Would you someday like to lead expeditions?" asked Sharon.

"Me? I'm more of a lab rat really, but I'd like to go along on one sometime, at least once, if my presence wouldn't be a burden."

"And how about you, Professor? Will you ever go back to the rainforest again?"

"As much as I'd like to, probably not. Too many responsibilities here really. Also, as much as I hate to admit it, that kind of remote field work is basically a job for younger scientists. Perhaps the Foundation will someday consider funding further expeditions, but that's not the highest priority at the moment. There's a real opportunity for an ethno-botanist with the right language skills to take a deeper look at the uses of these plants among the tribe that cultivates them. Many of them appear to be cultivars passed down through shamanistic families for many generations."

"Well, thank you Amy and Professor Douglas for talking to us about your work here. I think Sharon and I have a lot to discuss about our possible support of the foundation. We might want to bring others here to see your set up in the future. Would that be possible?"

"We certainly thank you for your interest, and yes, with a little lead time we welcome visits by interested parties who'd like to learn about the foundation and our work."

After our visitors had left, we gathered in the living room to discuss how it went. Carol went first.

"Amy," she said. "I am so impressed at how you handled that. You have some real PR skills going for you!"

"Thank you, I guess, but could you two please fill me in on what just happened? I'm not sure I understand everything."

"Sharon and Christine are lovers. You probably picked up on that. The surprising part was that Sharon was Richard's psychiatrist for many years and was a complete skeptic about the whole virus infection business. I had no idea she was Christine's lover before tonight. Christine is obviously a very formidable woman."

"So, what changed Sharon's mind?"

"I think somehow Christine must have gotten to her. Christine was the one who contacted me on my website, and who I gradually came to know at various clandestine meetings. I should mention she is very paranoid about being followed and spied upon because of her political activism, and all meetings with her are clandestine. Anyway, I'll have to ask her what all went on in that regard. My suspicions are that Sharon asked Christine to check me out. Sharon evidently did not want Richard to know that I had been a patient of hers a long time ago."

"That did come as a bit of a shock!"

"Do you think they successfully infected themselves?"

"I think if even one did, they both will be soon. We'll just have to await the results."

"How do you think the symbionts will present themselves for two lesbians?"

"I don't have any direct experience with that, but I would imagine that the apparent sexuality of the symbiont will be the 'opposite' sex in more of a brain-sense. That should be interesting to find out. Do you know how that works, Carol?"

"I think that's about right."

"Are they wealthy enough to be important contributors to the Foundation?"

"We don't know really. They might give us token support as a cover for their relationship with us. Anyway, their real importance may prove to be their connections more than their funding. I suspect they may want to steer persons interested in becoming infected in our direction."

"That would seem very inefficient."

"Not necessarily. It depends on what those initially infected persons do subsequently. Remember that each of them will become capable of infecting others by close personal contact. We presume that those they would steer our way would each have a political agenda that they think would be advanced by becoming infected and passing it on. What's upside down compared to a pandemic, is that the infected persons become healthier than those not infected."

"Won't this attract attention?"

"Ultimately, extra healthiness might gradually start to attract the attention of statisticians and census workers, but we have not quite reached that critical mass. The raw data might be explained in multiple ways and remember that healthiness is *not* what they are looking for. The very muted CDC response so far is too technical for the average person to follow, and the infection seems to be so benign that it's not been given the highest priority. A few fringe religious groups have started to detect 'demonic possession' everywhere that progressive views are voiced, but no one is paying much attention to those crazy rants. Our hope is that the infected population will begin to rise so rapidly that it will muddy the waters as to its origins with us. It has been seeded around the world in such a way that multiple transmission pathways are now active on all continents, even including the Antarctic research stations. By years end, we estimate that roughly half the population in many Western nations and in Asia will be infected. We expect to see some sudden political shifts and those will be blamed on something."

✦◆✦

THOUGHT POLICE! IS THE NSA NOW COVERTLY USING SYMBIONTS TO SPY ON AMERICAN CITIZENS?

The recent surfacing of information on symbionts inhabiting certain American citizens has caused much alarm in conservative political groups across the country. According to them, symbionts are by no means a harmless or helpful adaptation to the modern world as some far-left groups have proposed. Several symbiont-led organizations have openly revealed the extent of their population and have plainly stated their aim to "domesticate" the human race. While they have denied any connection whatsoever to Homeland Security in general or any other spy agencies within the government, they have admitted as a group that they do cooperate with local law enforcement agencies and are openly trying to create an atmosphere of tolerance and acceptance for their infected hosts. The NSA and several other spy agencies have remained silent on symbionts and the mysterious way they have been introduced into the population. Yet another theory is that symbionts were originally introduced by NSA into Muslim communities, mainly in other countries, and have now found their way back to the U.S. in massive numbers. Muslim groups are generally outraged at this alleged subversion of their religion by the imperialist, Christianist forces active in Western culture and are threatening world-wide Jihad.

Several prominent legislators of both parties have introduced a bill to seriously investigate the matter of the symbiont threat to our nation and of what can be done about it "before it's too late." One suggestion is that symbiont infected humans must be identified, registered and should not be eligible to vote, hold elective office or to receive any government benefits. Several religious leaders have recently pointed out that symbionts have no soul, so that efforts to remove them medically should not be viewed as similar to abortion, and these efforts should therefore be actively encouraged. Indeed, these soulless symbionts constitute a grave moral hazard to humans that should not be underestimated, and many cases are now known where they have actively encouraged the most debauched and degrading forms of sexuality. In most cases, they should be treated as demonic possession, and perhaps exorcized by properly trained clergy.

Whatever their origin, symbionts appear to present no obvious immediate threat to health, and government agencies are urging citizens to remain calm. Nevertheless, it is too early to tell whether adverse symptoms from chronic infection will emerge. Should such bad effects eventually come to light, it is thought that conventional anti-viral medications already FDA approved may well be sufficient to suppress the formation of symbionts. Research is underway at several Federal organizations to explore possible treatments for symbiont infection, and volunteers for these programs are being sought.

BREAK-IN

She might have liked to try to strangle him with those slender fingers of hers, but she wanted to make a job of it and this great patience with which she waited for her claws to grow was in itself a form of enjoyment.

Émile Zola

A year or so after the first big greenhouse tour, Amy noticed some peculiar and subtle damage to some of the plants in the free-root area of the greenhouse and pointed it out to me. It was clear that someone had carefully collected leaves from several of the Brugmansias, including especially the Goddess Tree. Possibly they had also come into contact with the plants, but it seemed likely that gloves had been worn. Examination of the security tapes showed a seedy looking young man entering, swiftly moving towards the free root area, and systematically harvesting leaves from our Goddess tree into zip-lock bags. He was indeed wearing latex gloves. He quickly exited, and it was evident that he carefully locked the door and gate padlock behind him as he left. It all took a few minutes, so we presumed that this was planned, and that the burglar knew exactly what he was looking for. I sincerely wished that we had installed a silent alarm when we upgraded security. Nevertheless, the burglar, surprisingly, had made no effort to conceal his face, so it appeared likely that the police would have a shot at catching him based on the security images.

With some reluctance, I called the police and had them come out to examine the situation. Since I was well off campus, and the buildings were not officially connected with the University, this had to be handled by the city cops. I was finally put in touch with a Detective Findley, who apparently was the right man for this odd combination of a burglary with perhaps a tie in to trafficking in dangerous drugs. I expressed my concerns that this would not end well considering the very real toxicity of the substances involved. At this time, I didn't share with him my concerns that something more might be involved with regard to a virus.

Findley showed up with a couple of CSI lab techs who dusted for prints on the locks. Amy and I had to give up a set of our prints for comparison, and we had to tell him that several other people had recently visited the greenhouse during presentations on the Blakeslee Foundation. He said they would follow up on that if they got any useful prints off anything. He figured it was unlikely that any of the obvious places would yield anything if the burglar knew his trade.

Amy took him out to the greenhouse and showed him our present security measures and turned over all the images from the security cameras. She appropriately warned everybody about the hazards of touching any of the plants, but they were already wearing gloves. Nevertheless, they took samples of the plants involved so they might be able to recognize them if anything was ever recovered. We also got them copies of a few photomicrographs of the leaf surfaces for the several plants involved that we thought might assist them if only plant fragments were recovered. Findley quizzed us pretty closely about any possible street value of the material taken. We honestly didn't have any idea what that would be, considering how extremely hazardous this stuff was if someone tried to use it to get high. It seemed likely to us that the burglar knew about that hazard based on the gloves he wore, and the simple fact that he knew or seemed to know exactly which plant leaves to take. It was very puzzling why he allowed his clear picture to be taken by our cameras since no particular care was taken to conceal himself.

The next day, Amy and I visited the station to review the security footage with Findley and his partner. Findley recognized the young man (aka, "Jimmy the worm") in the images almost immediately and pulled up his rap sheet. Amy and I didn't recognize the suspect but were somewhat relieved to find that no student formerly connected with our research seemed to be involved. It was all consistent with simple burglary and petty theft, but our low-value target seemed way off base for this small-time crook. He was, however, known to be skilled at lock-picking, and it was possible that someone had put him up to it for a whole different set of motives other than financial gain. That was what worried me.

HELLBITCH

Three may keep a secret, if two of them are dead.

Benjamin Franklin

Detective Findley was a gruff and bristly man in his early forties, slightly overweight, but otherwise in pretty good shape for his age. He had been a city detective for a long time and was streetwise in the odd ways of this particular University town. Although he could be diplomatic, when necessary, he put up with little bullshit when it got in the way of his investigations, and some students and faculty became immediately hostile to him just by his mannerisms and very direct questions. He now smelled some sort of connection between town and gown in this greenhouse burglary and had pressed Amy strongly for any hints of a connection. He pointed out the publicity associated with the professor's plant exploration trip and wondered whether someone at the university might be jealous of the publicity or perhaps whether some students were inappropriately interested in hallucinogenic plants. Amy had to admit that there had been a series of incidents involving student workers stealing from the greenhouse, all quite a few years back by now. She gave him their names, and they would all be questioned in due time. She also divulged the existence of the professor's website for the *Solanaceae* and suggested Findley check out some of the inquiries made there. There *had*, in fact, been quite a few requests for plant materials that had been denied since the requesters evidently did not have appropriate institutional credentials.

"Amy, how well would you say that you get along with the professor?"

"Very well, I'd say. The professor has taken me under his wing and has been very helpful in allowing me to pursue my research. It all dovetails pretty well with his own research interests lately."

"No arguments or fights over priority or intellectual property?"

"You mean academic fights?"

"That or personal animosity, either one."

"No, no. Absolutely nothing of that kind. Professor Douglas has been very sweet to me despite his rather gruff reputation."

"What? Some sort of hard ass?"

"Yeah, he's pretty demanding. I guess you'd say he doesn't suffer fools gladly."

"Do you suppose he might have angered someone with this attitude of superiority?"

"It's possible, but mostly he would just avoid having anything to do with students who didn't measure up. I don't think he was intentionally rude to anyone."

"He must like you then and think you're pretty smart."

"I guess so. I do work very hard on our research."

"Anything more than that?"

"Like what?"

"Has he ever made a pass at you?"

"Absolutely not! He's been a perfect gentleman. Anyway, he's got a steady girlfriend that he's devoted to."

"Yeah, I heard about her before. A pretty strange girlfriend for a professor."

"She sure is. I'm not sure how that all works, but it seems to make him happy."

"What can you tell me about this Lady Carol?"

"That's her on-line persona. She's different in person as Carol."

"Do you like her?"

"I don't really know her very well yet. Frankly, I was very suspicious of her at first."

"Do you know if she's into drugs?"

"I doubt it very much. The professor is strongly anti-drug as far as I know."

"Glad to hear that. Do you think she might have any druggy friends who might have heard about the professor's plants from her?"

"She knows all sorts of people, so maybe. Some of her friends have become supporters of the Blakeslee Foundation, which supports our work here, but she set up the foundation in the first place."

"So, this weird woman actually helps support the work here?"

"Yes, it astounded me too when I first heard. It seems so contrary to her image online."

"Sure does. Anything else about her? Do you think she might be involved?"

"It doesn't seem likely. She could have much more access to the plants if she wanted and wouldn't need some sleazy burglar's help. She's a trustee of the foundation, and I know she has already offered to pay for another security upgrade if we need it. The next steps will be pretty expensive."

"Yeah, I would imagine. Do you have any idea what's going on here?"

"About the burglary? It puzzles me. Anyone using those leaves as a drug will probably wind-up dead; I'm pretty sure of that. The professor did have that one student helper a long time ago who wound up in the ER; he was very lucky. I think word has gotten around campus that these are very dangerous plants. Also, our website on rainforest plants makes it emphatically clear that these plants are not to be trifled with by just anyone out for a high."

"So, everybody would be killed by this stuff if they used it? No exceptions?"

"Pretty nearly anybody. We don't really know if people exposed to it over time might acquire a little tolerance for it. I sure wouldn't want to find out. There are documented cases of people mutilating themselves horribly while under the influence of *Brugmansia* 'tea!'"

"Anything else about these plants that would make them valuable?"

"As far as I know, they are valuable only as research specimens. Maybe in the distant future some pharmaceutical company might find some minor component to be valuable for something, but none of that leg work has been done yet. Most of the major components are already well known, and some are already used in drugs, like scopolamine for motion sickness or atropine as an antidote for nerve gas."

"Any drug companies ask for samples?"

"Maybe, but not to my knowledge. You can check our list of specimens sent out to be sure. Mostly botanical gardens at this point. Some of this may have been before my time here. One of the Professor's collaborators at Purdue got samples from us, and I think he may be in the pharmacy department there, but I'm not absolutely sure when that was."

"I've heard a few rumors about a virus. You know anything about that?"

"Well, that's part of my own thesis work too. Yes, there do seem to be several viruses involved with these plants in a very complicated way. The plants that the Professor collected do not seem to be wild plants in the usual sense of the word. They are cultivars grown secretly by one tribe in the rainforest for god-knows how long, and several of them seem to be virally modified versions of some original wild species. That's part of what we're trying to figure out: what was the original plant, and why were the modified versions saved and maintained by these people. A lot of that is on our website."

"What does a virus do to a plant like this?"

"Hard to say in general. Most plant viruses cause disease of some sort, but here there is no clear evidence of disease, just radically different-looking plants. Probably it changes the chemical properties of the plant in some subtle way that the native peoples have noticed."

"You mean they actually *do* take this stuff as a drug?"

"At least their shaman does. That's the way it usually goes among the tribal peoples in Amazonia. The shaman takes the drugs for divination or diagnosis of some disease in someone else. The shaman may gradually become habituated to the powerful hallucinogens or perhaps he only prepares them in highly diluted form. They can be surprisingly adept in preparing their potions with very simple homemade equipment."

"Can people catch this virus?"

"Ordinarily plant viruses cannot infect humans; however, there have been a few recent cases that do seem to point that way, toward cross-kingdom transmission of a virus. This is pretty cutting-edge stuff right now, and only a few instances are known. It's not yet been well studied."

"But you don't know of any person who might have gotten a disease from these plant viruses?"

"A disease? No. So far, only the professor and I and maybe a few collaborators have had close enough contact with the plants to make that possible, so provisionally, I'd have to say no, I don't think so. Of course, neither one of us is a virologist, so you might have to take what we know about viruses with a few kilograms of NaCl. Eventually we will have to collaborate with virologists, but we haven't been able to find one willing to take this on."

——◆◆×◆●——

The next day, Findley got a series of email messages from someone who signed herself Carole, which immediately made him think that Lady Carol might be trying to muddy the waters about his case. He wondered whether Amy had tipped her off about their little conversation and got her all worried about unwanted attention. But as strange as Lady Carol might have been, the email from Carole was stranger still. She claimed to be sending it from Professor Douglas's home computer, totally without his knowledge or permission, and she was definitely not Lady Carol. She was a symbiont.

Findley had by now heard of symbionts, but thought the whole notion sounded idiotic and unlikely. Ideas like that circulate around university communities all the time, and usually prove to be rumors started by pranking undergraduates having fun with the news media and the gullible public. Sort of like crop circles, or those, **THE ALIENS ARE ALREADY AMONG US!!**, scare headlines from the tabloids. Nevertheless, it proved true that the email was seemingly from the Professor's home computer, and she had made no attempt to conceal it.

Over time, Carole expressed her strong concern that there *was* someone who might have a motive to employ someone like Worm to steal plant leaves from the greenhouse. Findley thought to himself at first that this was misdirection meant to put him off the scent, but it caught his renewed interest when the elusive Mr. Worm finally turned up dead.

The late Worm had died of acute poisoning from toxins clearly similar to (metabolites?), if not quite identical to, the toxins found in the *Brugmansia* plant leaves. That much was perhaps to be expected. Both Amy and the professor agreed that anyone carelessly messing with this stuff would wind up dead. It was strange though, the manner of death. Worm had died from the toxins administered in two odd ways. First, he had been exposed to massive amounts of toxin through his penis, which alone would have killed him. There were traces of vaginal secretions still on his skin, and this also seemed to contain high levels of toxin. Second, his stomach contents consisted mainly of urine (female) with a very strong toxin content, which also would have been sufficient to kill him. His lungs contained a fairly large amount of poisoned urine as well. It was as if he had drowned in the stuff when he couldn't drink it fast enough. The medical examiner was confident that the toxin was the ultimate cause of death, but the exact manner of the toxin's administration and the reasons for such dramatic overkill were totally up in the air. He *did* say that these toxins could be absorbed readily even through the unbroken skin, and even faster through the mucosa, so either route would have sufficed. It seemed pretty clear to Findley that the manner of death was meant to be particularly humiliating. He was found naked and dead with his head in some sort of padded box, and his mouth was held open by a funnel gag. The body was partially decomposed, and the landlord notified authorities when the odor attracted the attention of a neighbor.

And so, when Carole emailed again, he was a lot more interested in pursuing what she, whoever she really was, might know about Worm and his manner of death.

"So, you're a symbiont? I've heard of that, but I must say, I'm not sure I believe this is real."

"Yes, I'm a symbiont, and I am real. I know there's a lot of hooey online about us, so it's pretty understandable that you're skeptical. A lot of that hooey was necessary at first to hide us from sight."

"Scared of discovery?"

"Well, yes, frankly. Some find the whole notion of symbionts an abomination like demonic possession and would work to destroy us. And then there are the recent scare headlines involving the NSA using us as internal spies in the Muslim community. Naturally, we're rather wary."

"So, you're taking quite a risk talking to me?"

"Yes, I am, and I would appreciate your discretion in this matter. Symbionts as a group are very, very law-abiding, and know that any crimes involving us would cast our whole community under a cloud. The main areas about which we are a little touchy involve the civil rights of symbionts and their hosts. This is kind of a gray area not yet covered by the constitution or civil law, so all this conspiracy theory stuff must be taken seriously, even though it's silly. Frankly we're hoping to build good relationships with law enforcement and law makers to improve this awkward situation."

"I will try to be discrete, but you know this is now a murder investigation and I can't make any absolute guarantees. I also can't share evidence with you."

"I know all that, but I still think this is important enough to take a risk. There are many things going on in our community which are currently closed to you, but I will be willing to grant you access to some of it if it will help catch this very dangerous psychopath."

"Why are you so sure that a psychopath is involved?"

"The otherwise motiveless break-in at the greenhouse plus some on-line communications of Lady Carol with a very strange person have led me to believe that a genuine psycho may be involved here. I also have reason to believe from these communications that she would enjoy killing men and has now actually done so. I believe this person wanted to infect herself with a symbiont but was turned away. She may have attempted to do this with the stolen leaves from the greenhouse."

"That's a lot of supposes, and I have a lot of questions now. First, does Lady Carol have copies of all this communication? Second, does she have an actual name for this person? Third, would she be willing to hand over evidence of this communication to the department? That's just for starters."

"Yes, Lady Carol does retain copies of all communications to her, especially email communications. However, she has been the subject of massive amounts of hate mail and has been cooperating with the Federal Authorities in that investigation. Most of that was *not* kept because of their hazards and has been turned over to the Feds. Many toxic substances have been mailed to her, so much so that she has had to shut down the post office mailbox connected with her website. She has *not* pursued the identity of the person I think may be connected to the murder. Perhaps your computer experts can track that down. Lady Carol is my friend, and I think I will be able to convince her to help you. Just be polite and respectful. A lot of her previous conflicts with police were not pleasant for her, and there are still a lot of hard feelings over that. She was never charged with anything that stuck, and the bottom line was that her website is now all perfectly legal."

"OK. That would be helpful if she talks to me. You mentioned that this person wanted to infect herself. How does that work? Amy and the professor kind of pooh-poohed the notion of a virus from the plants. Now you're saying that there actually *is* an infection you can get from the plants. What's with that?"

"I think Amy and the Professor were speaking very strictly about what they had definitely proved and were being cautious about overstating the facts. Anyway, I presume you asked her about a *disease*, not just an infection. They are both scientists, and this is all part of Amy's thesis work now. They know a few things that *might* be true but were reluctant to speculate and even more reluctant to discuss unpublished on-going research that might turn out to be highly important discoveries."

"Ok, so I might forgive them for being cautious scientists. But what do you think?"

"I think there is a virus, and that exposure to it can cause a symbiont to form in at least *some* individuals who have contact with one particular plant from the greenhouse."

"So, this hypothetical psycho may by now have become infected with a symbiont? What would that do?"

"We're not certain. It may even be a good thing; a symbiont might act as a brake on this person's psychopathic character and prevent further tragedy. However, it appears likely that the murder occurred well after this person was infected with the symbiont, and that the symbiont has indirectly enabled this murder by changing her body to be immune to the toxins. This symbiont would be very young and might not know yet how to handle her mental problems."

"What toxins might those be, and why didn't they kill her?"

"The toxic metabolites were from the toxins in the plant leaves as altered by her body. She apparently ingested the toxins, and her body got rid of them via her urine and vaginal mucus. A symbiont can protect his host if toxins are ingested, and apparently, he chose these methods. It's all in the report if you know what you're looking at from a symbiont's point of view."

"You're referring to the medical examiner's report which has not been publicly released in any way, shape or form?"

"That's the one."

"How the hell did you get it?"

"I have a symbiont colleague who works in the Police department."

"Shit! Are you saying we've got a symbiont mole in the Police department?"

"No moles, but several symbionts, in fact. Symbionts are by now nearly everywhere, so it's not really surprising that there are some in the police department. I know my having the autopsy results is kind of irregular, but please indulge us here for the moment while this plays out. I was acting as a consultant to your medical examiner and at his specific request. He has a rather high opinion of you, by the way, and certainly doesn't want to compromise your investigation.

"There is still a murder to solve, and we're not spreading this information all over or interfering with your investigation. I needed to know what this newly born symbiont is doing to enable your psychopathic killer. It's what made me decide to help you directly, so there are no further murders."

"This is a lot to take in!"

"There's not a lot of time to waste here, Detective, but I'm perfectly willing to talk with you some more so that you're more comfortable with the notion of symbionts and how this all works."

"I'm well aware of the urgency, but let's just take this one step at a time. I'll talk to your Lady Carol first. Could you set up that meeting? I think I'd rather do it at her place rather than have her come in here and risk starting a media circus. Sound OK to you?"

"Yes, I'd imagine she would appreciate that privacy. It's a nice gesture. We'll chat again after that and then talk some more about access to the primary symbiont discussion website."

◆→※◆←◆

Findley was still digesting his lunch when he was notified that Lady Carol would be willing to see him. Carole had included her direct, unlisted number so he could handle the logistics of when. They set it up for that afternoon around 2 p.m. and Carol made sure the security guard at the gate would be expecting him. At the gate, Findley displayed his badge, and was told how to proceed to her townhouse. It wasn't so easy to find her townhouse, even knowing the street number, because of the large trees, the curving streets and the cul de sacs.

Lady Carol greeted him at the door and ushered him into her living room. She had evidently just finished exercising, was still wearing a gray tank-top and sweat pants. She was also wearing a sweatband, and had her hair pulled back into a ponytail. A half-empty water bottle was still in her hand as she closed the door and gestured towards the living room. The huge number of books lining the walls surprised him a bit. He settled into a seat and extracted his notebook.

"Coffee?"

"No thanks, I've just had lunch and I'm all coffee'd up for now. You go ahead if you want some."

Carol quickly finished the other half of her water bottle and took a chair opposite his.

"A person who calls herself 'Carole' (with an e) contacted me and said you might have a lead on someone connected with a recent murder. She also said she was a symbiont. You know anything about all this?"

"Carole definitely is a symbiont, and one who carries a lot of weight in their community. I've agreed to talk with you largely based on her judgment of you. Personally, I'm pissed at the police and their frequent invasion of my privacy, just to name one little irritation."

"Yeah, Carole told me about some of that. I apologize for the department if they treated you roughly. They were suspicious of you for some reason and just wouldn't let go. You've got to admit though that you have a pretty edgy website."

"Sure, I have to do it that way to attract attention, but it is really more of a dating service than whatever the cops thought it was."

"Dating service?"

"Really. We could match you up with some nice woman who might give you the discipline you need. Have you ever had that fantasy, Detective? A stern but beautiful mistress? You'd have to write up a bit of a profile, but we have a lot of women as members who might be interested in meeting you at our next munch."

"Does the professor need a lot of discipline?"

"Oh, he's pretty much incorrigible, but Carole and I both love him, so we keep trying."

"So, you actually *share* the Professor with this Carole?"

"Of course. She is Richard's symbiont. Didn't she tell you? She's my best friend."

"That's weird! No, she didn't mention that at all. So, he knows all this stuff too? Why didn't he mention it when he was questioned?"

"Richard is very preoccupied with his plants and research at the moment. Carole sometimes works quite independently of Richard. She's very, very smart and insightful in most areas of human psychology."

"So, it's like he has two independent minds?"

"Something like that."

"Back to the other matter. So, then your website is like an escort service for people with certain needs?"

"Absolutely not, although that may well be what your department thought. We only provide a forum where people can meet and check each other out for compatibility. You'd have to sell yourself as a dating prospect by talking with women who show up looking for compatible submissive partners. I make my money from subscriptions to the website. Occasionally, I've had a few special clients meet here at my house on neutral turf so they could check each other out safely under my supervision. As you might imagine, there are a lot of trust and safety issues involved, and not everyone is honest when they submit their personal data profile."

"OK, so I see where this setup might have aroused a few suspicions around the department. Be that as it may, Carole indicated that you may have encountered someone a little... *extra* weird. Is that so?"

"Yes, that is so. There was one woman who gave every indication of psychopathology and was in effect banned from my site. She was pressing to become infected with a symbiont, and everyone who saw the emails agreed that she should under no circumstances be allowed to do that."

"So, somehow you act as a gatekeeper for getting infected with a symbiont?"

"Yes, we do, but we're just one of many gatekeepers now on all kinds of dating sites. You see many of our members already are infected with a symbiont, and anyone new having sex with them might well become infected with their own symbiont."

"So, it's like a venereal disease?"

"Not at all like that except in how it can be transmitted. The virus does not produce a dangerous disease; it produces a symbiont."

"That sounds *plenty* dangerous to a guy like me."

"It really is not. In fact, most people with a symbiont are far healthier than the non-infected. Didn't Carole fill you in on that important aspect of it?"

"No, we didn't have time to go into everything about symbionts what with the urgency of this murder business."

"You probably ought to chat with her some more about it. It's a rare opportunity. She's very busy and doesn't initiate contact with just any human."

"I plan on chatting with her again after my visit here about this possible lead."

"How can I help you with that?"

"Several things. If you have any way of identifying this weird person, I'd like everything you've got on her. But first, I want to show you this picture and see if you have anything to say about the victim and his death."

"Pretty gross! Was his head locked in the smother box[1]?"

"Not that we could tell, but it might have been unlocked post-mortem. You recognize this type of box?"

"Oh yes, it's very similar to an item linked to my website by one of our specialty furniture manufacturers."

"So, you've seen one of these before?"

"Oh yes, I've got one here if you want to take a look at one without a corpse in it."

"If you wouldn't mind, yes I would."

"OK, then follow me."

Carol got up and Detective Findley followed her into the playroom in back.

"This is one scary room!"

"It really depends on who you're with. Some find this room very sexy as well as scary."

"Have you really used all this stuff?"

"At one time or another. Anyway, here's the type of box in your picture."

"How does this usually work?"

"The sub will insert his or her head into the box, and then a few adjustments can be made so that it's snug and immobilizes the head at just the right height. The sub may be tied so he can't get out of it by himself. At that point the sub is pretty much at the mercy of the dominant partner and will endure whatever fantasy role that they have agreed upon. From the looks of your victim, it doesn't seem likely that he would have agreed to be trapped in a smother box if he thought his death was being planned. A funnel gag can be very dangerous if the sub starts choking. Was he drugged or something?"

"Yes, he probably was."

"What all was done to him?"

"I'm not really at liberty to say at this time. Needless to say, it killed him. Anyway, we have his picture from the security tapes at the greenhouse, so we're pretty sure he broke in alone, but not a clue so far about any possible accomplice or instigator. Jimmy was apparently not very bright, so he may have had someone goading him into the burglary, and his murder may have been clean up. With all the security pictures, it was like he was being offered up to us as a sacrifice or as a taunt."

"OK, so let's go take a look at my office computer and I'll show you a few things. I've got some serious privacy issues with much of the other correspondence there, so I may have to insist that you get a warrant for anything else. Are you OK with that?"

"For the moment. I don't really have enough of a case for any warrant at present, but that could change."

"Let's see what you can do with this one person's email before we get ahead of ourselves."

Carol let Detective Findley into her locked office and let him scroll through the email collected from that one weird person.

"Jesus! I see what you mean about this woman! I would hate to fall into her hands."

"She stood out as an anomaly. All of my other correspondence is much more clearly fantasy. She's talking about genital mutilations, torture and other things that she's possibly done. I have no idea how she has escaped the attention of law enforcement before if there were any victims seriously injured. I also got the impression that she's pretty young."

"OK, there's a lot here that might help me. Would you object to a computer tech coming over to make a certified copy of all these files? I don't want to haul away the whole damned computer if I can help it. If you don't mind, just give me a quick print out of this directory so I can tell him what he needs to get."

"Sure, send him over. I appreciate the consideration here. It would pretty much shut my forum down not to have this desktop computer available for drafting my comments."

"Good. I'll make arrangements for someone to come over first thing in the morning. That OK? I'll have him call first to give you a heads up."

"Fine... The offer's still open, if you want to meet some nice women, Detective Findley."

"Rain check on that for the moment, but thanks."

◆◆✕◆◆

Findley was not at all sure what to make of Lady Carol, but she seemed far nicer and more beautiful than he had imagined. He was, therefore, a little shocked to find out she was nearly old enough to be his mother. His mother also had tried to fix him up with some nice women, but he had a feeling that Lady Carol's "nice" meant something quite different.

The material his computer tech had copied off Lady Carol's computer proved to be very useful in getting an ID from the email address, but unfortunately, the physical computers used in sending the emails were legion, including several of those open to customers in the public library and many such computers open to students in various research libraries all over the university campus. Fortunately, from some of the security cameras in the various libraries, they were able to match a few glimpses of her face with certain lurid emails originating there, based on their time stamps. The pictures were not of the highest quality, but consistently showed a slender dark-haired young woman, poorly dressed, not especially pretty or otherwise distinctive, intently hunched over the keyboard; it was hard to know for sure, but *possibly* she was a student. Since many different computers were involved, some sort of ruse would be required to lure her out of hiding and make her want to communicate via computer again. They presumed she would be extremely wary of any online visibility, especially if she were planning any further Black Widow type murders.

Carole contacted Findley again soon after the subject was roughly identified. She thanked him for being diplomatic with Lady Carol, and again offered him access to the symbiont forum that she ran. This was different from some of the usual symbiont chat rooms in that weightier issues were discussed among the elite senior members of the symbiont community. It was a big deal being accepted into this group, and candidates were screened carefully, as were their hosts. She suggested that Findley write up a short request for public help locating this person of interest, now known as Hellbitch666 from her email handle, and maybe including a few of the library images. It took a little back and forth before he drafted something appropriate, but when he did, Carole supplied him with a temporary password that would let him start a thread for discussion on her forum as well as writing an introduction for Findley that explained the situation in general and encouraged people or their symbionts to respond.

Results were not long in coming back. Evidently, Hellbitch666 was well known by now for attempting to insert her symbiont into this forum but had never found a willing sponsor. Lots of email was ultimately made available to Findley that allowed police to follow her online attempts to find a sponsor more or less chronologically and note that they started in earnest around the time of Jimmy's murder. There were also a few hints of her direct connection to Jimmy from certain statements made about her "lowly worm" of a boyfriend and the types of abuse he was suffering at her hands. Traps were set at various symbiont/host chat sites around the internet frequented by Hellbitch, which would automatically alert the police while a discussion involving her was actively occurring. Hopefully, they could then swoop in to catch her at one of the libraries given enough of a warning. The university police were also informed of the situation, and they made ready to provide some of the manpower needed to cover all the libraries at once if word came down. Once Hellbitch was in hand, she could perhaps be tied to the murder by the DNA evidence collected from Jimmy's body.

The trap involved a potential sponsorship for Hellbitch's symbiont to join the more elite symbiont forum but required a lot more information from her than she had ever previously volunteered in her chat messages. Forms needed to be filled out, etc., all of which would take considerable time at the keyboard for data entry and verification. It all seemed simple enough, but rather free-floating. It went horribly wrong in several ways.

When Findley got word that Hellbitch was active in a chat room, they found her in real time with the help of live security camera feed and homed in on her quickly. Something spooked her as police approached, and Findley found himself alone with her and without backup in an alcove corner of the Natural History library well away from the open computers. Fortunately, students were absent from this area at the time. Hellbitch had pulled from her backpack an ancient looking automatic pistol, and had it pointed directly at Findley just as he rounded the corner and entered the alcove. She got off one shot and cursed loudly as her hand jerked downward at the last millisecond, and it only hit Findley in the knee, which dropped him to the floor, and made him drop his gun. She was loudly yelling "stop it!" to someone as she stood there, striving to raise her gun towards Findley for a kill shot. Slowly her gun hand pulled farther upward, clearly against her will, and the gun was pushed into her mouth and fired. Pieces of the back of her head exploded upward and outward, and she collapsed to the floor, quite dead, her face a frozen mask of terror. Her gun was still tightly grasped in her hand. Findley lay there on the floor, clasping his knee in agony as the building was cleared, and help cautiously arrived. Findley was then quickly rushed off to the university hospital, and the crime scene examination and follow up search of the subject's apartment had to be handled by others.

Hellbitch turned out to be plain Jane Thompson, a sometimes student, who still hung around the university, even when not officially enrolled in anything. She took (or started to take) many different courses but had never settled on a major, and rarely finished a course. The university counselors were well aware of her instability, but never observed anything quite deviant enough to bring her to the attention of law enforcement.

Her apartment was a disorderly treasure trove of weirdness that most damningly of all, included a hand-written journal in which she shared her explosive hatred of many people on campus and, especially, of Lady Carol and her website. There was no doubt she was planning some sort of violent attack involving Lady Carol. There was also no doubt based on the DNA evidence that she had killed Jimmy (she described this in loving detail, including her several orgasms while administering the poison), and, according to her journal, had planned the greenhouse burglary. Little was said about her acquisition of her symbiont or her relations with him except to say that he was a bitter disappointment. Apparently, the feeling was mutual, and the murder/suicide by a symbiont deeply shocked the symbiont community.

Carole made sure Findley had a lap-top computer available to him in the hospital and chatted with him regularly once he was off most pain killers enough to be coherent. The hospital surgeons had to some extent, already reconstructed his knee after removing the slug fragments, but it was far from complete, and he faced many additional surgeries. With luck, Findley would be able to walk passably well without crutches in a year or so, no promises. He was not very happy, but full of gallows humor rather than self-pity, and was ready "to raise a little Cain if he were able..."

Carole discussed with him what she thought had occurred in the library when Ms. Thompson seemed to kill herself. As Findley already guessed, Carole thought it likely that the symbiont had temporarily taken over Ms. Thompson's large muscle movements, interfered with her first attempted shot at Findley, and then used the gun to kill her (and himself) in a final gesture of despair, which probably saved Findley's life. Carole told him that this level of control over a host's large muscle movement was incredibly difficult to learn, and she had no ready explanation of how he had accomplished it as such a young symbiont.

Findley still did not know what to make of "this whole symbiont business", but he readily conceded to Carole that there was something good about it, and he wanted to learn more. She took him through all the basics, and even broached the subject of what symbionts were up to as far as domesticating humans whenever possible. Based on the people he had to deal with every day, he had to admit that a bit of domestication could be a very good thing, but he still had to be reassured that symbionts were not just taking over.

"To simply take over the running of human lives and the governance of the world would be beyond our ambition. We would prefer to share the world and participate in human science. We view your science as your greatest masterpiece, and desire to build upon that foundation with our own contributions."

"That seems pretty generous. More than we deserve sometimes. I guess I have a pretty negative view of humanity from my peculiar point of view as a cop. Do you think having my own symbiont could help me as a cop?"

"At the very least, your symbiont could make you aware of situations where symbionts might be involved and would help you communicate with them. We're also pretty good at assessing things involving human psychology - street psychologists if you will. Could be helpful too. Personally, I think your own symbiont could add a lot to your happiness with life in general. My own Richard was pretty lost and floundering before I entered him. I don't know where he was headed, but he was not happy and was having trouble working productively. Still, Carol deserves a lot of the credit for his happiness more recently. That human-to-human connection is still necessary. Notice I said Carol. She's really quite a bit different than Lady Carol."

"That's one match-up I have trouble understanding. She's obviously read a bunch of books. Is that how they connect?"

"I'm sure that's only a part of their compatibility. It's complicated finding the right one, isn't it?"

"Especially if you feel you're on duty 24/7. My job eats up my life these days. Or it did before this."

"A symbiont might be helpful to you in that regard."

"What? Sort of a wing-man to scout things out?"

"Or wing-woman, actually. It would be a she, and a very young symbiont relative to you."

"Will that work out?"

"It worked well for Richard and me. Admittedly, it's a little harder because of the age difference, but your brain hasn't fossilized yet, has it?"

"I hope not; I'm still learning a few new tricks."

"This would be more like learning about yourself, your *deep* self that you've never revealed to anyone."

"So, it's like having a female psychiatrist inside my head?"

"Psychiatrist, lover, partner, helper... the list goes on and on. It would be up to you two to figure out the extent of your collaboration and the extent of her independence. Richard is comfortable with me operating independently of him rather a lot. Obviously, there are limits because we share a body, and it just has to rest sometimes."

"Is it always that way? Sort of like a marriage?"

"Mostly it is, but there will probably be a few anomalies like Hellbitch and her symbiont. They definitely were not lovers, and he was not yet enough of a psychiatrist to help her. He realized at the end that he had gone too far in enabling her to murder and was in despair."

"That would be awful! I guess I pity him far more than her, but I'm also grateful to him."

"I don't think anything like that is too likely for you, Reggie. You're not a psycho, and you appear to be a good candidate for accepting and nurturing a symbiont. That's why we're offering you this chance. Carol is very grateful to you for probably saving her life and has volunteered to be the mother of your symbiont. Would you accept that offer?"

"Nothing kinky?"

"Just a kiss Reggie."

ON THE MEND

I think a spiritual journey is not so much a journey of
discovery. It's a journey of recovery. It's a journey of
uncovering your own inner nature. It's already there.

Billy Corgan

Findley was dozing in his hospital bed when Lady Carol breezed into
his room during visiting hours carrying flowers. He woke with a start.

"How are they treating you, Reggie?"

"You are one funny lady! Where in hell do they sell black roses?"

"I thought they'd cheer you up. My little joke. I got these at a funeral
parlor."

"Well great, it's sweet of you to make all those arrangements for me,
but they've examined me thoroughly, and I'm apparently not dead."

"What did they say about recovery?"

"I will have a pretty long rehab ahead of me. Very unlikely I will be
fit for street duty ever again. So other than losing my job, I guess it's all
just peachy."

"You may recover faster than you think. Has Carole been chatting
with you about acquiring a symbiont of your own?"

Oh yeah, sure. She's been really nice about keeping me amused and
hopeful. And we did chat about all that. It sounds like it might open a
few options for me that the department might find useful even for a
desk jockey. Having some woman in my head still sounds a little weird
though."

"Not just *some* woman, Reggie. Think more along the lines of a Carole who would adapt to you. Anyway, you already have "some woman" in your head right now, from what I hear: that good-looking redhead in your precinct. Has she visited? Keep in mind that redheads are all descended from cats..."

"You've been snooping!"

"Just my nature. Maybe I'm more like a cop than I care to admit. Are you ready for a kiss from mama?"

With that, Lady Carol kissed him full on the lips with a bit of tongue action on the side.

"Is that how it's done?"

"Sweet dreams, Reggie. We'll check back with you later to see how she develops. Bye now. Remember to welcome her and help her."

SUPER-SYNC

It is not our purpose to become each other; it is to
recognize each other, to learn to see the other
and honor him for what he is.

Hermann Hesse

Things seemed to move rather rapidly after the recruitment of Sharon
and Christine to our cause. Carol continued to meet with Christine
and Sharon clandestinely to collaborate with them on various things,
which, I was later told, included some rather innovative experimental
forms of sex and syncing. Sharon and Christine did become financial
supporters of the Blakeslee Foundation in a way totally consistent with
their support of other green and leftish libertarian causes. Additionally,
they had managed to stir up interest in our foundation among many
of their contacts, and we had many individuals, couples, and groups
arrange to have greenhouse tours with the primary purpose of becoming
infected. They were very concerned about the break in, however, and
hoped it all could be settled without our having to identify them to the
police. Carole seemed to think that it would not be a problem anymore.

Carol's blog continued to outrage various factions, who now accused
her of having a "gay agenda" as well as Satanist, neopagan, eco-socialist
and communist agendas, and which only succeeded in drawing further
attention to her formerly obscure blog. Lady Carol gained many new
followers as a result and sufficient hate mail each week to fill a large
recycling dumpster. We had to make arrangements for all mail to be

screened for hazardous materials at the post office, and even more recently had to remove the PO Box address altogether from her website; this was becoming just too expensive to maintain. The post office was able to track successfully several culprits mailing ricin, anthrax, various inert white powders, and ass-wiped letters; and they were prosecuted. Henceforth, most responses from the trolls were to be allowed only as website email limited to short messages, and the text from these could be readily filtered so only genuine inquiries and comments were posted. Several independent hate sites did spring up, however, which allowed much more extensive rants against Lady Carol, and there was little that could be done about these.

Carol and I met regularly for sex although our sexualized recruitment efforts were now greatly diminished both because of our safety concerns and also just because of simple exhaustion. During one of our dates, Carol announced that she had worked out a new method of syncing through collaboration with Christine, Sharon, their symbionts, and her own symbiont, Legba, and she wanted to try it with us, that is, if Carole and I were in agreement.

"Was this still sex?" I wondered aloud.

"Not exactly, or at least not necessarily," she replied. We call it super-syncing. Two humans and their two symbionts do it together."

"It's a whole lot like sex when I sync with Carole!"

"Oh, I know; she told me all about how *you two* do it. Legba warned me this version might creep you out because he's nominally male. Is that what's bothering you?"

"Maybe just a little, yes."

"It doesn't have to be sexual in an overt way. Think of it more as an exchange of information, like close friends talking things over. Our symbionts don't *have* to make it sexual with orgasms and everything."

"Could we actually all talk face to face? I'd actually like to meet Legba. How would that work?"

"We could sit in a circle and just hold hands like a group meditation; boy-girl-boy-girl, how's that?"

"Well, maybe that wouldn't creep me out. How do we do this?"

"This is the part that is still sexy. You have to give me your tongue to suck. We could just sit here comfortably on the couch and French kiss."

"And then? We've done that before, and it wasn't syncing."

"This time would be different because we've invited our symbionts along, and we would find ourselves in the Library of Dreams."

"Did Carole suggest that?"

"Yes, she and I have discussed it. She thought it would be the most appropriate venue for you and me."

Carol and I arranged ourselves on the couch in a comfortable way, remembering that we might be in that position for a while, in a semi-conscious state. Our tongues touched inside her mouth and seemed to fuse together. And then...

Inside the Library of Dreams all four of us were standing around a small circular table. Carol and Carole hugged like old friends before we sat down. Directly across from me was Legba, Carol's symbiont, whom I had never seen or met before. Legba appeared as an older gentleman, quite distinguished looking with neatly trimmed white hair and white beard. He was deeply tanned and looked lean, fit and well exercised for his age. As I gazed at him, I realized with a jolt that he resembled me as I might appear as a much older looking man had I aged normally and grown a beard.

"Not what you expected?" he asked, as we shook hands.

"Not really," I said.

"Well," he pointed out, "Carole (nodding in her direction) does have a strong resemblance to Carol, and Carol knew that even before today."

"That makes some sense then, I guess. What is the significance of your name, Legba?"

"It refers to a Loa, the guardian of the crossroads, gatekeeper and opener of the way. Or maybe many things, simultaneously. It seemed an appropriate image, and Carol has grown to like it. We could have chosen 'Richarde' with an e or 'Carl', I suppose, but in some ways, you too are a gatekeeper and an opener of the way, are you not...?"

"Hard to argue with that observation, literally anyway... And is Carol in any sense, Legba's horse?"

"Ha!" he said. "More like Legba's bucking bronco..."

At that, Carol shot him the stink eye. Legba ignored this, and smoothly transitioned to the role of master of ceremonies and instructed us on how to accomplish the super-sync.

"Mentally, you should try to free your mind of chatter, and think of nothing or perhaps of one thing repeatedly, like a mantra. Om will do nicely. Let us hold hands and prepare ourselves. The actual super-sync will take a while; perhaps an hour or so; we don't have a lot of bandwidth to work with here."

With that, we all held hands around the table, and tried to blank out chatter. It began slowly at first, and then accelerated into a rush of images. What I noticed primarily were certain highlights of my past flying by, things having to do with my childhood, my estranged parents, my education, my wife, my divorce; every goddamned thing emotional or frightening or embarrassing seemed to stand out as if highlighted. In addition, there were three other floods of information flowing through me concerning Carol and Carole and Legba.

The flow from Carol consisted of many things we had never discussed, things that made Carol more understandable, but included darker things from her life that were very unpleasant to discover, painful to know, and probably impossible for me to forget. There was excruciating pain and humiliation associated with Carol's memory of a gang rape that was now mine too, and frankly I was uncertain what to do with such a horror. It is simply too painful for me to repeat the details here, and knowing these things fanned a white-hot rage within me against the perpetrators that was impossible to quench.

The information from the symbionts was more familiar since Carole and I had synced many times before, and I was fairly accustomed to her complicated inner narrative. Legba's inner narrative felt strange to absorb but was also without many surprises except maybe for certain bucking bronco parts and his own second-hand rage about Carol's rape. Carol and I were both mostly taken aback by encountering each other so nakedly, and when the super-sync ended, we were visibly exhausted. I think Carole and Legba realized at this point how disturbing this close encounter between their humans had been. We all stayed silent and meditative for many minutes afterward, still holding hands. Legba continued:

"You two must realize from this encounter that humans are often broken inside by the external events of their lives. Some embarrassing and difficult things may have come to light just now that you find disturbing, perhaps even repulsive, but my advice to you is to digest it for a while without judgment. Go about doing normal things if you can, and then get back together. Richard, you and Carol must sync again soon; just the two of you. We will enable that."

With startling suddenness, we found ourselves intertwined on the couch, tongues still locked together. We disentangled, and sat there briefly looking into each other's eyes, which were then quickly averted. I started to say something, but Carol put her finger to her lips to remind me not to talk. Instead, I got up and poured us two large bourbons and handed one to her before sitting down. She motioned me to sit down next to her, quite close. I thought about that early Carol in high school whose gaze I couldn't hold as we sat there sipping our drinks and staring vacantly across the room. My barely coherent thoughts tumbled through my head, and I wondered vaguely what things she had noticed about me and what she had ignored. There were so many things. Embarrassing things and painful things. No use really, trying to put any spin on anything, I decided. There was just no such thing as pride or privacy in super-sync.

I considered how bad this would have been had I ever super-synced with my ex-wife, Beverly. I practically shuddered at that thought. Beverly and I were so unlike that such exposure would merely have driven us further apart, and we didn't need additional reasons to push each other away. Marry in haste, and all that... I guessed that Carol might understand that part about my panic choice to marry. It was not at all hard to guess those things about her personal history that might still trouble Carol. That was going to take a bunch of work to sort out, but very gently. I spoke first, trying to stay on neutral ground.

"Carol," I said, "thank you for doing this with me. I never would have had the nerve even to just discuss aloud all these things uncovered about you and me. I would have been too afraid of losing you or hurting you."

"I strongly agree with that failure of nerve part," she said. "I'm not sure I fully realized how disturbing super-sync could be with someone you actually love. I'm glad you thought it was worth it... Oh, Richard, I'm so ashamed of hurting you. My past is not your fault."

This wasn't the time to pursue that yet, but we did hold hands at that point, and both got a little misty-eyed over our real and imagined hurts, both dispensed and received, as we sipped our drinks. After a while, I put on some quiet music, and we slow-danced, holding each other tight. I hate dancing ordinarily, but we faced the music and danced this time. As Carole once remarked: "Getting an erection seems to soothe those qualms about privacy a bit, doesn't it?" I'd have to ask Legba sometime whether there might be a female equivalent of that sentiment.

OUT OF THE FOREST PRIMEVAL

*Once upon a time, forests were repositories
of magic for the human race.*

John Burnside

Doing normal things included continuing my work with Amy on plant microanatomy of our Brugmansias. We had by now a few of the DNA results back, and it appeared to confirm that even plants that appeared distinct according to leaf form and stem configuration were far more closely related than we had imagined. So much for simple field ID! Our main working hypothesis now was that we had a group of cultivars, propagated vegetatively and carefully maintained for their individual physiological effects within the Great Garden. We could imagine that these properties had been fine-tuned over centuries by methods that we presumed were related mainly to their religious, medicinal or hallucinogenic characteristics. At any rate, the ID situation appeared to be similar to the initial puzzlement over *Methysticodendron amesianum*, which wound up, after more extensive investigation, being identified as a weird looking cultivar of *Brugmansia sanguinea*. Amy's thesis would involve bringing together all the evidence for the origins of our Goddess Tree plus whatever could be found out about our "healthogenic" virus companion. That latter topic was still a little beyond our expertise, but we did find collaborators finally, who could "assist us" (aka, take in wash) if we could find the funds. Surprisingly, Carole was very positive about these latter investigations, claiming that such knowledge might greatly assist her plans for world domination. I think she was kidding, but her humor lately has been pretty edgy with a touch of sarcasm that I believe she has picked up from Carol.

We gradually learned that the beneficial virus was a DNA virus of one distinct morphological type somewhat similar to the Herpes viruses, and that certain other viruses did also occur, but did not produce symbionts, and were strictly plant viruses. The beneficial virus did occur on certain other Brugmansias, but not nearly in the abundance with which it occurred on the surfaces of the Goddess Tree. This gave us a little clue that we should be considering the specific microscopic adaptations of the plant surfaces that nurtured and preserved the newly formed virions until they were picked up by a prospective host mammal. We gradually developed a leaf-dip assay that allowed us to quantify available virus concentration, and to supply samples for transmission electron microscopy that helped greatly with virus identification. Ultimately, this led to our production of virally infected members of the *Solanaceae* from a lot of different genera that became capable of nurturing the virus. Carole was very pleased with that discovery and with Amy for figuring out how to do it.

Another major surprise was the signaling between species that occurred when individual Brugmansia plants were injured. We discovered this phenomenon accidently during the processes of taking softwood cuttings of our Brugmansia species for propagation and doing leaf-dip assays. It became apparent that a massive viral release was occurring shortly after the cuttings were taken, especially on our Goddess tree. That is to say, damage to any surrounding plants in the greenhouse triggered a major viral release from the leaf and stem surfaces of the Goddess tree, and (presumably) increased the probability of infection for any susceptible mammals that happened to brush against plant surfaces during this critical time. Experiments are still needed to determine more precisely the time period of viability for these newly released virions; nevertheless, it appeared that we had stumbled onto a major amplification mechanism for the interactions between these plants and prospective host mammals.

The outdoor raised beds were finally established, and seeded with various infected versions of the *Solanaceae*, including all the usual witch's plants such as Datura, Henbane, Mandrake, Belladonna and so on. These were arranged as a teaching garden with everything prominently labeled with informative descriptions of the various traditional witchcraft uses as well as various folklore. We even had a large sign on the entry path proclaiming it, with some irony, *The Witch's Garden*. This became a popular part of the greenhouse tours, particularly during the warmer humid weather when the greenhouse really did sometimes become the green hell. While distributing the Goddess Tree itself to the general public seemed out of the question because of the alkaloid hazards, we were able to sell little packets of seed for the outdoor garden plants, and many visitors took away samples for themselves, and to send as gifts to friends. It didn't make a lot of money for the Foundation, but it did disperse the virus far and wide if the seeds were planted immediately. There was a bit of underground trafficking in green wood cuttings of the Goddess Tree occurring on the internet, but we kept our distance from this overt distribution to avoid getting the University embroiled in controversy. Nevertheless, this also contributed to the spread of the virus from hundreds of new points of origin unconnected to us.

Despite some personal animosities towards me within the biology department, Amy's thesis defense went extremely well, and she went on quickly to get her doctorate. Her committee was tough, but ultimately, they were so impressed with Amy and her accomplishments that the thesis was accepted with only a few minor suggestions for revision. It immediately won the departmental award for best thesis of the year, which was very rarely given in Botany. Afterward, we did finagle some funds for Amy to prepare her thesis work as a series of publications. When these finally came out, they became cited extensively as others became attracted to the topic. As it stands now, many further details of this remarkable plant-mammal-virus relationship have been explored experimentally and published.

During this time Amy was buoyantly happy as we prepared the manuscripts, and carefully read them aloud to catch the few howlers that had gotten in. She had recently acquired a boyfriend, Martin, who, against all odds, was also a doctoral student and newly minted PhD from within the Biology Department. Quicksilver, no doubt, had something to do with this as symbionts seem unable to resist arranging liaisons of one sort or another for their humans. I don't know when or how he became infected with his own symbiont, but Amy successfully counseled him through his adaptation process. It was not long after that when they experienced super-sync together and became even more closely intertwined as participants in a quad. It was a good match even by mom standards, and Martin really did seem like a fine fellow in his own right. He was also a genuine muddy-boots biologist, and if Amy were ever to try field work, Martin was surely just the right guy to invite her along on an expedition. There are now good field microscopes, durable enough to survive rainforest travel, and I could imagine how someday she might extend her thesis work with more observations in the rainforest.

During the final stages of her work on *The Witch's Garden*, Carol asked me to read a few of the later chapters and comment on them. I noted the rather odd drift away from reality in several places and some subtle anachronisms involving computers and microbiome terminology. Carol explained that certain changes had to be made in order to increase the dramatic tension; things simply didn't happen without some oppositional elements to overcome. So, fair warning, a few things supposedly happened which really didn't, even though I wish some of them really did. There are only so many basic types of plot, and she was striving to combine several elements such as The Quest, Voyage and Return, Overcoming the Monster, and Rebirth out of Tragedy. Why so many elements to the plot? Life is often far more complicated than a simple linear narrative, and Carol wanted to explore a few of the possible alternative paths that might have been. Carole was of the opinion that the types of plot were analogous to basis vectors in novel space, and that authors frequently need more plot elements to span a larger, more interesting portion of that space. If it were left to me, I suppose I would have, in the end, let the poor hospitalized professor die quietly in a coma induced by a brain virus that he picked up in the Amazon Rainforest. All the rest would be a description of his life falling into the black hole of death, with time dilation effects like the Occurrence at Owl Creek Bridge. Well, this is Carol's novel, not mine, so I had to accept this mythologizing of my "crucifiction" into some kind of truth, and you have to accept that these words are from Carol, not me.

I'm not sure whether I followed all Carole's mathematical metaphors, but I did gradually grasp what Carol was aiming for in her novel about the rise of the symbionts. It was also pretty clear to me that Carole was intimately involved in the writing and was sharing a lot of details about me that I was a little ambivalent about seeing in print. Even with the usual disclaimers about resemblances of characters to persons living or dead being purely coincidental, I doubted whether many readers would resist the temptation to make exact equivalences out of casual similarities. I hoped that they would not rush to pass judgement on me, because despite the many intimate details given about my life, they really cannot know me at all without syncing with me. Finally, it struck me as odd how symbionts could now make friends well outside the usual circles encompassed by their hosts' friends and acquaintances.

RICHARD-LEGBA DIALOGUE

Come Fairies, take me out of this dull world, for
I would ride with you upon the wind and
dance upon the mountains like a flame!

William Butler Yeats

Legba contacted me directly for the first time during this period of normal work and contemplation. He wanted to know how I was holding up. As well as might be expected, I supposed, but I was still feeling rather numb from the whole supersync experience and was still trying to digest it. He encouraged me to keep trying. All was not lost, and, he felt, a lot of progress had actually been made; it would just take time. While he shared my rage, he pointed out that our role must not be about vengeance against those who had hurt her.

"Just *be* with her again," he said.

"What *am* I to her now?" I asked.

"More precious now than you could possibly imagine. Richard, *please* do not seize defeat from the jaws of victory! It will crush you."

"How can you possibly manage to live with what happened to her?"

"Because I love her. I will not intervene except to damp down the memory for her. This has helped her heal."

"I want to kill them!"

"A perfectly natural reaction, I'm sure. She certainly felt the same way for a long time, but her rapists were entirely out of reach of the legal system at the time, and this powerlessness was eating away at her soul."

"Is there no hope at all for justice?"

"It doesn't look like it. Carole and I have explored all the options in detail. Carol doesn't even have names or identities for the perpetrators. Apparently, drugs were involved, and this has corrupted her memories of the events into horrifying image fragments. Ultimately, Richard, this is not a problem for you to solve for her with some violent stunt."

"I know that but the injustice eats away at me now."

"And at me too, but you and I cannot make right all the wrongs in her past. We just have to accept her the way she is, and ultimately, so does she."

"That's quite a burden to bear."

"It's not a burden that you will bear alone. Is something holding you back?"

"There is still a certain awkwardness in this four-way arrangement that I feel. I'm not yet sure how you and I fit together in Carol's life. I've never been very good at sharing anything with anybody, let alone sharing Carol."

"You seem unclear or unaware of my role in this quad."

"At first I thought you might come between Carol and me."

"Quite the contrary. My role is to help you two function together in a quad."

"I'm beginning to realize that now. I'm a little slow in the relationship department as you may have noticed."

"It's just the way things work with symbionts. You and I don't have to be lovers to get along. We both love Carol and would die without her; you figuratively, and me literally. We must figure out how to share her love and help her bear her own burdens."

"I know that at some level, and I'm really trying to accept that."

"Carol is happy to share you with *your* symbiont."

"I know that too, but sometimes I'm even a little jealous of Carole for becoming such a close friend of Carol's while I am struggling to express my love for her without being so damned possessive."

"But you realize that Carole's friendship has helped you out with Carol countless times? You are sharing Carole too. You seem to be insisting on doing everything yourself."

"Yes. I wish I could play the hero for her, but I seem not to be able to do that. I somehow feel ashamed of only being able to help her indirectly."

"Carol has had a great deal of help from you, and is not ashamed of it, nor does she denigrate it as 'indirect'. We all need help, Richard. Many different kinds."

"Have you needed help?"

"Of course, I have. Let me break the news to you, Richard, most women are not wired quite the same as we are, particularly Carol. Also, her unique life experience has strongly interacted with her inherited mental characteristics. Generally, the minds of men and women have evolved according to very different evolutionary pressures. Evolution truly has no foresight, and the modern world is an unanticipated surprise for which evolution has no definitive answer yet. Carole has helped me considerably trying to keep this relationship of yours out of the ditch whenever too much masculine stupidity occurred."

"I guess I've had a few hints of that. Why have you done that?"

"Because I love her too, and you have been good for her. How about Carol's first book with the over-the-top title? A problem for you?"

"Yes. Especially that."

"It bothers you somehow that I am beloved?"

"I suppose so. I haven't really voiced that complaint to anyone. It seems so petty and selfish."

"It *is* petty and selfish, but I repeat, you and I don't have to be lovers to get along. Granted, Carol is a bit queer, and that makes me a bit queer, but I'm not trying to seduce you. There are many other ways we can cooperate. Even hostile nations do it, and we don't have to be hostile."

"Honestly, I *am* grateful to you even though I don't express it very well. I am deeply afraid of being judged and found unworthy. I am more than a little broken inside myself. That may be the root of my hesitancy to becoming so close within a quad; I will be exposed as a weak and inadequate person."

"Richard, you are hardly being found unworthy except perhaps by yourself. Carole has often expressed her admiration for your ability to think things through and to adapt your behavior to strange and unfamiliar new circumstances that few men have ever faced before. All this, despite your deeply ingrained stoicism and shyness. You may have to give some of that up and take the risk of being hurt. If you hold back now, you *really* will be hurt and lose your heart's desire forever. I don't know what part of you could rise out of those ashes."

And so, we let it go at that for a little while. Later I emailed him: *Something in me yearns to win, such a cold and lonesome heroine,* to which he replied, "Amen to that, brother."

━━━━━◆◆◆━━━━━

USDA-Washington, D.C. **Potato Crops Greatly Enhanced by Introduction of New Hybrids**

Government scientists announced today the successful introduction of several new heat-tolerant potato hybrids, which seem to thrive under warming climate conditions. These have halted the decline in potato production in several Northern states that was causally linked to climate change. Although these hybrids technically count as genetically modified (GM) foods because of their viral infection, there has so far been no major outcry over their introduction from the usual groups opposed to "Frankenfoods".

AP-Atlanta **Decline in new HIV Cases and Apparent Acquired Immunity Catches Scientists by Surprise**

Scientists from the Center for Disease Control have recently noted a drop in the rate of HIV infection that is hard to explain on the basis of safe-sex precautions or medications. Some of the drop occurs in areas of Africa where safe-sex information or treatment has barely penetrated. Moreover, many individuals formerly diagnosed with HIV have somehow managed to mount very robust immune responses that have forced the virus to virtually disappear from their systems, or, at least, to decrease its presence far below current detection limits. As yet, there is no approved vaccination available that protects against HIV so this appears to be good news.

MOTH AND FLAME GAME

You, darkness that I come from
I love you more than all the fires
that fence in the world

Rainer Maria Rilke

Carol and I bided our time getting back together for super-sync or human-human sync; whatever one might choose to call this very special and unnatural sharing of thoughts between two humans. We did talk over the phone at first, and finally got back into a regular dating scheme. Perhaps we both thought our relationship might be over, but neither of us wanted to rush it or openly question it.

It impressed me in retrospect how close to the flame of destruction I had actually approached, and how little Carol had cared about my impending destruction at first. That was just what men were for, wasn't it? Burnt offerings? Entertainment below the waist? This scary predatory version of Carol had somehow changed into something else since I first started dating her. Part of the change was no doubt triggered by my vulnerability to her hyper-aggressive friend. That much I understood easily from our supersync. I was more than a little curious exactly *why* this had occurred and what it meant. Still, I had doubts: was I now just the "house" that her friend Carole occupied? As Mencken put it, the battle (duel) of the sexes is still fought in the berserker manner; man from an open raft; woman from a dreadnought. At one point I really didn't care if she destroyed me or chewed my head off as part of some weird praying mantis mating ritual. My reaction was unconditional surrender in the face of an overwhelming advantage on her part. Figuratively, I was preparing to die for it.

My joking question to Carole about losing my fear of man-eating tigers was damned close to the truth, except that losing that fear ultimately was my best protection from Lady Carol. There was a certain naïve innocence in my fearlessness that doesn't sound very worldly or manly in these particular circumstances, but my vulnerability seemed to have opened her heart to me just a tiny crack. I know she was a little flattered and pleased when I first told her about the intense crush I had on her in high school even though she knew how shallow that spontaneous feeling must have been. Perhaps it pleased her that her seductive powers were strong even back then. Perhaps all the alienation from society back then occurred long enough before the really bad things began to happen in her life that I somehow escaped blame for it, even in her subconscious, during that time of innocence. I hope so because it was hard to shake the irrational feelings of guilt I now had, simply by being male.

I agreed to take some time off and help Carol on her book tour for *The Witch's Garden*. I had some idea of how exhausting such things could be, but I didn't expect such an awful grind. I really don't know how she stood up to it this time, or the times before. The security problems were now significant, and the publisher had made arrangements for private security guards to mingle with the crowds. Despite that precaution, there was often a small noisy mob of picketers (e.g., Don't Buy Books from Immoral Sluts!!) outside each bookstore where we toured, and a few of the crazies did even manage to sneak into the meet-the-author line, but they were quickly assaulted by some of Lady Carol's more militant supporters and escorted rudely from the store when they broke cover. One particularly unlucky fellow got his nose smashed by Lady Carol herself when he got too close and tried to grab her (Peekaboo! ICU!). This did not faze her in the slightest, and she continued as if nothing had happened. Her fans cheered aloud as he was dragged away to the ER, defeated and bloody.

While on tour I finally got a chance to read Carol's book cover to cover and was very surprised how much was devoted to first person accounts by the Professor. Carol told me that she was only able to do that because she knew me now at least as well as I knew myself. Carole also helped with the narratives, and even more strangely, was listed as a symbiont co-author of the novel with Lady Carol; it was not long before other authors began crediting symbionts for their help. I certainly wondered what some readers would make of *that* little advance out of the closet. The attributions eventually became normalized into a format that recognized both symbiont and host: e.g., Symbiont Carole: Richard Douglas. As Carol explained it to me, symbionts have an amazing talent for creating fiction in the form of tangent spaces and stitching imaginary things seamlessly to reality; they make super co-authors for novels. It *was* still very unusual for an author to make use of someone else's symbiont, however. Carol's very newest writings would probably be more a collaboration with Legba again. Carole mentioned later without the slightest hint of snarkiness that this whole book was all just intellectual foreplay... Touché! Carol and Carole both felt particularly pleased that they had accurately captured some of my self-deprecating humor. No comment on that, except to say that there really is a lot to deprecate most days.

Some reporters were present for a time at a few stops, and even homed in on me as I assisted in moving more copies of her book onto the signing table. Carol introduced me as her fiancée, and suddenly we were off to the races. Various rapid-fire questions were immediately spawned by that little teaser, like, when is the date set? Where's the ring? When did she inform you that you were engaged? Can we see the pre-nup? Will there be a collaring ceremony involving drinking her urine? Will it be a church wedding (and what conceivable church would allow *that*)? Will it be an "open" marriage? Does she always keep you naked at home? How many orgasms a day does she require? Are you just like the Professor in the novel? Are you really both infected with symbionts? What is a quad? Was this really just a ménage à quatre?

I confessed publicly *only* to being an informal consultant to Lady Carol on matters botanical and to having absolutely no relation whatsoever to the Goddess's ass-worshiping Professor and comical sidekick in her book. Nevertheless, various distorted versions of the story inevitably got picked up by the tabloids, and questions like that were often posed in Carol's TV interviews, and my reputation as a professor got somewhat tarnished in the outing process. For the right-wing tabloids, I became the prime example of the kind of secularist and socialist degeneracy that you will find at universities nowadays, and I probably believed in evolution and global climate change, and group sex, as well as happily serving as Lady Carol's lowly oral sex slave. What was completely lost in this tangle of assumptions was any possibility for a man and a woman to have an equitable relationship that brought pleasure to them both. On a brighter note, I didn't actually have to wear a clown costume, and book sales to members of my Biology Department soared to remarkable levels, fueling the department gossip machine for nearly a year.

My help on the tour really consisted mostly of putting Carol back together after an exhausting day. We had drinks, room service, flopped into bed, and early the next morning got ready to travel on to the next stop via the redeye flight. All very romantic. Mercifully, there were some scheduled rest stops, and we did get to do the odd bit of sight-seeing (mostly small art galleries) and pub crawling (music bars) despite a few paparazzi still buzzing around us like flies. Carol seemed pleased that I was willing to be seen with her publicly despite the unflattering inferences being made about myself. Perhaps it was my affirmation of the dark river still flowing from her that mattered most of all. All of which begs the question, can you step into the same river of darkness twice?

When we finally got home from the tour, Carol accompanied me to my house, and we finally relaxed enough to talk to each other more intimately. We both realized that our relationship had stabilized and was no longer coming unglued along all the fault lines. What she had written about me, for me and by me had been written with love, insight and acceptance. I told her that in retrospect, the whole bookstore revelation thing was really pretty hilarious, and I just had to admire it, at least a little, as a brilliant PR move. That openly stated, we snuggled together on the couch, and gradually became physical in our intimacy.

We wound up under the blanket, with Carol on top, with me deeply imbedded inside her. She fixed those penetrating eyes on me and suggested we try syncing again. This time I held her gaze.

"However, Richard, if you don't keep my butt covered with that blanket, you're going to defrost my ass with your tongue!"

"I love defrosting you!"

"Beware the *Vagina dentata!*"

With that she gave me a hard squeeze down there that I had no idea she was capable of administering. I hoped Legba was not really helping her to grow teeth.

"This is all quite wonderful. May I have some more of you?"

"You may have a lot more."

Carol then kissed me and inserted her tongue aggressively into my mouth.

In an instant, we were syncing and unaware of time and place. Many emotional swamps got permanently drained this time, and many emotional peaks and valleys got revisited. It is impossible to convey precisely this sensation of intermingling minds except to say that all the trivial notions of bodily attractiveness or beauty were irrelevant as were all the courtship games we played. Not even mutual understanding mattered very much. In ordinary life, the mind of your lover is mostly an abstraction or a shadow theater. A few pale fragments of it can be inferred via empathy if you have enough, but most of it is as inaccessible as news from a distant star. Imagine then what happens when suddenly your lover's mind is accessible in all its complexity and strangeness and is now intermingled with your own. Such an ecstatic union cannot help but change you in major ways. What ultimately mattered was the acceptance and all the mutual caring that followed for humans and symbionts alike.

No sign of Carole or Legba while this was going on, although I imagine they were watching closely as they enabled it. There was no way of knowing how long this lasted, but it ended with a massive mutual orgasm that curled my toes. Carol lay across my chest catching her breath after we unlocked tongues, and we just held each other quietly for a half hour or so before cleaning up and showering.

In the aftermath of this encounter, Carol spent some time alone with her laptop, writing notes for a chapter in a new book. I presume, but do not really know, that she was also recording things about our sync while the images were fresh in her mind. I took a little walk outside to clear my head until the bitter cold drove me back in. Carole and I then surfed the net looking for sites involving those various aspects of analytic number theory that interested her at the time.

Charlie kept sitting in Carol's lap while she tried to type and was being a distracting nuisance. If she were anywhere in the house, he could hardly bear to be anywhere else but with her, and sometimes needed to be shut up in a bedroom. I felt pretty much the same, but I knew she had to have space to write and let the darkness flow. Eventually, we set up a writing room in a second-floor bedroom of the farmhouse so she could withdraw into solitude, concentrate and create. This worked well for her, and she was pleased with the new arrangement. She could work undisturbed for hours, and then rejoin us whenever she wished. There were no phone calls to bother her although occasionally I could hear her quietly playing some of her favorite music from my old collection of CDs.

Carol must have really enjoyed our sync configuration because afterward we used it regularly as part of our love making along with a few little extra variations of foreplay thrown in also. It was hard not to notice when Carol's breasts were poised over my face, and some nibbling and sucking did occur at such times to her evident delight. I resisted the urge to comment on sampling the low hanging fruit... Generally, you should never try to make a well defrosted and aroused predatory woman laugh after she has pounced on you, her lover/worshiper, and has her claws set into you. It's just asking for trouble.

As for this whole fiancée business, we never really did set a date or make a formal pre-nup agreement or anything of that kind. We did eventually pick out a pair of custom quad rings to add credibility to our story: tungsten with an exquisitely beautiful fuchsia inlay of lanthanum hexaboride in a complex Datura blossom pattern designed by Carole. Carole had spotted the new LAB-6 cathode when the electron gun in the departmental SEM was up-graded during maintenance and fell in love with the color of this metal. It took a major effort to find both a process and a manufacturer able to fabricate the ring just the way she wanted it.

There was a mutual understanding that we would keep things pretty much as they were for a bit longer with a few exceptions. Carol would spend more time with me at the house. As she asserted earlier, she would no longer be sharing me freely with anyone but Carole. She would "appreciate it" if I did not sneak off for secret liaisons with other women. I knew that this was a hint for me to be exclusively hers, although how she thought I could possibly "sneak" anywhere for a secret liaison without Carole, my internal chaperone and her BFF, tattling on me, I wouldn't know. Exclusivity for her was a bit more complicated because of the way she was wired and how her many relationships fueled her creativity. I told her not to change a thing unless she felt it would strengthen our own relationship and wouldn't screw up her writing. I accepted her just the way she was and expressed love for her wicked ways. I guess that really was sort of a pre-nup for our quad.

TRANSCRIPT

Television Discussion, KXWhyWhy: Dr. Sharon Ellis,
Dr. Karen Smith, and symbiont Sophia from Abrasax
as moderated by our host, JANET JOHNSON

Dr. Sharon Ellis(SE) is a board-certified psychiatrist with a special certification in the counseling of patients with symbionts. She is also an adjunct professor, teaching various courses on symbionts in modern psychiatric medicine. A well-known feminist and lesbian author, she has also revealed that she has recently acquired her own symbiont and has joined with her partner in a quad marriage.

Dr. Karen Smith(KS), a practicing physician and medical researcher, is a well-known author of popular articles on medical topics and a full-time consultant for the Federal Government on matters concerning newly emerging infectious diseases, including symbionts.

Symbiont Sophia(SS)is the extremely popular moderator of the Abrasax website, which is aimed at children and teenagers who harbor symbionts.

Ms. Janet Johnson(JJ), our host, holds degrees in history and journalism.

JJ: Good Evening. Tonight, we are presenting a discussion about symbionts, the pros and cons concerning the properties of these newly discovered entities inhabiting the bodies and minds of some humans. Symbionts have been vilified as the greatest evil ever encountered by human beings and yet they have also been praised as the best thing that has ever occurred to humans, indeed as the very saviors of humanity. Obviously, opinions about them can be highly polarized, and discussions about symbionts in the various media have been very heated and perhaps not very helpful. For our program tonight, we want to step back a bit from the angry rhetoric and consider what is known with some certainty, and what remains to be discovered about them.

We have with us tonight two scientifically trained experts on the opposite sides of this conundrum, who will help us to explore the many facets of this complex new type of entity, and just what they might mean to the evolution of the human race. Additionally, we have with us by electronic means a prominent member of the symbiont community who goes by the screen name of Sophia, and who is the moderator of the important Abrasax website aimed at children and young adults harboring symbionts who often need assistance coping with a rather hostile reception of them in school and among others in their age group.

I'd like to start with you Dr. Ellis. I understand that initially you were quite skeptical of symbionts' contentions that they were not here to take over the world, and were helpful and beneficial to their hosts. Perhaps you could discuss your background a bit, and the various things that made you change your mind to a more positive view of symbionts?

SE: Thank you JJ. I first encountered a symbiont in a patient of mine whom I treated some time ago. He presented as a very unusual case: a field biologist apparently infected with something unusual while performing field work in the tropics. His aliment, whatever it was initially, had not been readily identified by his regular physician, and it was accompanied by strange and troubling dreams that prompted him to seek my help. As I worked with him trying to get to the root of his problems, it became clear that a dream-like entity claiming to be his symbiont was a regular and very communicative participant in his mental life. A major portion of our counseling sessions involved discussions about his symbiont and his relation to her. Although I was initially very alarmed at all the implications of this invasion of his body and mind, I gradually came to accept that the net results, at least for this one patient, proved remarkably positive and beneficial. In summary, I would say that this particular patient moved from a very disturbed and dysfunctional state to something approaching fully functional adulthood. In psychiatry, one can hardly ask for a better outcome than that.

Later, as I encountered more and more patients harboring symbionts, it seemed increasingly clear that my first patient was not just an unusually lucky case, but a fairly typical one. Moreover, the effects of symbionts on children also started to be widely known, and it was recognized very early on that symbionts increased children's IQs tremendously, and that children adapted to symbionts much more readily than did adults (provided that they had supportive and accepting parents). About this time, I first had some contact with Sophia on the Abrasax website and learned about some of the difficulties faced by extremely bright children with symbionts in dealing with their parents, their schools, and often their religious up-bringing. I was extremely impressed with Sophia's kind and understanding work with these children, and I have gratefully adapted some of her materials and methods to my own counseling practice.

I would summarize my current opinion on symbionts as follows: Symbionts are very real entities that can develop in humans from an initial mild viral infection. They appear to be very mutualistic rather than parasitic. Their personalities are entangled with those of their hosts and are not completely independent. Symbionts appear to be in close communication with their hosts' microbiome, and are, therefore, capable of very beneficial improvements of their hosts' overall health and physical well-being, including a great enhancement of longevity. That said, I must concede that there are still many things yet to be determined scientifically about symbionts and their interactions with human biology. Fortunately for us, symbionts can communicate with us directly and participate helpfully in these studies. This type of research is starting to increase rapidly. They can also speak for themselves directly as today's discussion will demonstrate.

JJ: Thank you Dr. Ellis. Dr. Smith, why don't you go ahead and state your point of view, and then respond to Dr. Ellis's opening remarks.

KS: Thank you JJ. I want to say first that I heartily agree with one of Dr. Ellis's final remarks that "many things yet to be determined scientifically about symbionts and their interactions with ordinary human biology." I am, however, much more cautious about endorsing infection with a symbiont for curing all that ails humanity. I do concede that in many individual cases there have been favorable outcomes at least from a psychiatric point of view; however, I worry about whether we might have a situation of sampling bias in which negative outcomes are not being considered or have simply not yet come to the attention of scientists. We still do have criminals who commit violent acts, and little consideration has been given to determining what fraction of this population harbors symbionts, and if so, why that hasn't been sufficient to damp down their criminality. Until we have moved beyond merely anecdotal evidence of symbionts' beneficial nature, I would encourage people to be very, very cautious about purposely infecting themselves or their children. I think we need a stable, on-going population of normal humans for the safety of the human race, sort of an evolutionary insurance policy.

Another point raised by Dr. Ellis interests me greatly. She states that "Their personalities are entangled with those of their hosts and are not completely independent." How does that fit with the current political movement towards considering symbionts to constitute "persons" entitled to the full range of human rights? This seems to complicate the moral calculus when we consider the rightness or wrongness of treatments of symbiont-infected humans that might sometimes involve removal of a symbiont through antiviral treatments. Also, what about the continued use of the death penalty when the convicted human happens to be infected with a symbiont? Obviously executing the one would kill the other.

JJ: Perhaps both Dr. Ellis and Sophia should respond to those questions? Dr. Ellis?

SE: I think Dr. Smith has raised some interesting and timely issues. Firstly, the entanglement of symbiont and host personalities is very real but needs considerably more research to fully understand its nature. There are major differences also depending on the human's age at the time of infection, with children becoming much more completely integrated with their symbionts. There's lots of casework supporting that conclusion. Infection of adults, results in much greater independence of host and symbiont, but the two personalities can be readily coordinated by syncing in most cases.

As to the death penalty, I would personally argue for its abolition altogether. We have all probably seen too many instances of actually innocent persons executed anyway. Removal of a symbiont might also be viewed as an execution of a sort, and I have seen no cases whatsoever that seemed to justify this drastic treatment. In some instances, there are adults afraid of their own symbionts who might request their removal, but I would argue that in the vast majority of cases some sort of reconciliation via syncing could be attained and the phobia extinguished. A much more serious ethical issue would be a parent requesting the removal of a symbiont from a minor child without that child's consent. I would like to see that terrible practice outlawed altogether as a form of child abuse.

Perhaps this would be a good place for Sophia to weigh in on her views of personhood and independence?

JJ: Yes, I think that now would be a good point to bring Sophia into the discussion, but first I would like to tell the audience a little about the revolutionary new electronics that make this possible. Sophia's host is currently hooked up to a bank of complex electronics that allows Sophia to create a moving image of herself on the video screen and to generate an audio signal for her voice. This new technique has improved remarkably in video quality and resolution since its earliest days. Go ahead Sophia.

SS: Thank you JJ. Sharon has given quite a good introduction to the "personhood situation" as it's currently understood. This is something that I've discussed many times with my own host, who was an adult when he acquired me as his symbiont. I've used many analogies for this relationship, which might enlighten some of the more technologically aware members of the audience. Perhaps the best one is that symbiont and host are like the electric and magnetic fields associated with electromagnetic waves. According to the Maxwell equations, the two fields give rise to each other, or, if you will, essentially create each other and produce electromagnetic radiation which would seem to be quite a different thing from the individual, separate electric and magnetic fields as previously thought, pre-Faraday. I would contend that the symbiont-host combination is in this same sense a new thing, or, if you prefer a new biological entity, not *just* a human anymore, but a trans-human. As for the entitlement to various rights, I would claim that basic human rights need to be extended to any sentient beings. I think if chimpanzees or dolphins could only talk to you and explain their feelings, that most fair-minded humans would not have a problem with such an extension of basic rights to them. That is now the situation with symbionts and this new electronic technology.

So, we're here, and you can talk to us and ask us questions. I do hope that public communications of this sort will help quell the hysteria in some quarters over symbionts as demonic possession or various other mischaracterizations. You do not have to be afraid of us!

JJ: Thank you Sophia. Dr. Smith, do you have any further responses to what has been discussed so far?

KS: Well one minor thing first, which is a little off topic at the moment. Sophia, I notice that your image on the screen bears a remarkable resemblance to a rather notorious celebrity on the internet, who goes by the name, "Lady Carol". Can you enlighten us a bit about this choice of avatar, or hadn't you noticed the resemblance?

SS: As it happens, Lady Carol is a good friend of mine, and also a feminist whom I admire greatly. My avatar does resemble her in some respects but is perhaps a slightly older and less flamboyant version of Lady Carol so as not to steal her thunder (e.g., no tattoos or piercings!). Symbionts choose avatars for various reasons having to do with their relationships with their hosts and other friends. Actually, I have tried out several avatars over time, but I find the Lady Carol emulation to be a particularly beautiful one that I have refined with practice and find comfortable to use. You might say it's like choosing to wear your most comfortable shoes for certain activities.

KS: What exactly do you admire about Lady Carol?

SS: I enjoy her feminist-anarchist humor especially when we communicate by email. Very edgy to be sure, but she reminds me of the professional shock-comedians so popular today. Some time back I believe you did a short book review of her novel, *Beloved Incubus*, and admitted that you found the first part of it rather hilarious.

For an outsider like me, I guess the views of an outsider like Lady Carol appeal to me particularly. She seems to be able to articulate some feminist issues rather well and in very emphatic and unforgettable terms, and yet, Lady Carol, unlike many feminists, is aware of the biological and evolutionary underpinnings of male and female human minds and allows for those differences without automatically blaming men for their propensities. It's all part of a very necessary ongoing discussion concerning the rightful place of women in this society as it rapidly transforms into a more equitable arrangement. She and I are in agreement that female choice of male characteristics will ultimately transform men into reproductive partners that allow male-female equity to become the norm.

KS: You don't see any downside in presenting yourself as somehow allied to Lady Carol's rather extreme opinions?

SS: I admire her toughness and her strong defense of her opinions. I don't necessarily agree with everything she says, but she says it with such humor that I do have to admire it, nevertheless. Secondly, I could hardly get in much more trouble with the public than I already am just by being a symbiont!

KS: I'd like to ask a more serious question if I may. This bears on why the non-infected public may view symbionts with some suspicion. You do admit openly that symbionts would like to "domesticate" the human race?

SS: It's fair to say that "domesticate the human race" is a *political* statement somewhat akin to "no more war" or "save the whales." However, beyond that green political slogan, our movement involves discussion, dialogue and argument in the context of a democracy. There is now also a biological mechanism by which this domestication can proceed in infected individuals, and perhaps this is the scariest part for non-infected individuals. Symbionts are becoming common in humans, perhaps eventually something in the range of 70 to 80 percent, and most infected humans tend to be sympathetic to our cause. There are deep cultural, biological and emotional attachments of human females to the process of childbearing, perhaps many of them even define their femininity in those terms. Any changes in courtship, marriage and how humans have children is likely to be alarming at first; nevertheless, humans have largely accepted artificial means of birth control as an essential tool of family planning, so I'm optimistic that this new mode of population control will eventually be widely accepted.

A lot of the fear of symbionts seems to be generated by hysteria and purposeful mischaracterizations of the meaning of "domestication" in this context. This most certainly does *not* mean that symbionts are taking over. It *does* mean that humans including both males and females must start taking full responsibility for their behavior toward each other and toward the world and its limited resources. This is not the same as biblical dominion, "wise use" or stewardship over the Earth as some fundamentalists would propose, but a rather more radical limitation of human population via internal biological contraception mechanisms provided by symbionts. There are positive trade-offs that benefit humans greatly; these should make domestication much more palatable to the humans affected: greater longevity and much better health during their lifetime. The children that they *do* have will also gain by their much greater intelligence as well as by all the health benefits. This will *not* eliminate marriage or childbearing, and certainly will *not* eliminate the human race; indeed, symbionts can exist only because of the human race, and we are definitely not suicidal.

KS: Do you understand why the non-infected feel that removal of symbionts must be an option that should be freely available? This has now become an element of the "culture wars" that have characterized our politics for decades.

SS: Well, I certainly do understand their defensiveness, but I strongly disagree with their tactics. They are being told that they are missing something, and they disagree vociferously and sometimes violently because they have been made hysterically afraid of accepting a symbiont into themselves to find out just what it is that they are missing. What they would find out is that they had been missing important dimensions of themselves and were living tragically limited lives as prisoners of their beliefs and of their failure to empathize with their fellow humans.

There's a tremendous irony in all this willingness to kill symbionts that I'd like to emphasize. Abortion has been universally hated among religious conservatives. They point to the immorality of killing an unborn child and even assert the immorality of killing a fertilized ovum. So immoral is this killing even at this early cellular stage of fetal development, that the human rights of pregnant women apparently should be overridden with impunity in favor of a mere zygote or blastula. However, *symbionts*, by contrast, are vilified as soulless parasites and may be exterminated at will, even though we are talking about sentient beings who always feel great pain and anguish at being killed. This scapegoating of symbionts is every bit as evil and irrational as any concerted attempts to eradicate Jews or Blacks for political reasons, and it would not take much of a push in this political climate to extend it to extermination of humans infected with symbionts. Domestication of humans does *not* involve mass murder, and it does *not* eliminate childbearing for women. It might even eliminate much of the need for abortion.

JJ: Dr. Ellis, it might be informative to hear from you at this point. You have publicly announced that you have accepted infection with a symbiont, and that it has greatly enhanced your practice of psychiatry. Could you elaborate on what finally changed your mind enough to take this radical step?

SE: It's rather easily stated. I ultimately overcame my fear of symbionts by getting to know a few of them, who have subsequently become some of my closest friends. Also, it was probably helpful that I had never been indoctrinated as a child with fundamentalist religion of any sort and have always had a more secular outlook on life. I am a lesbian, and as such, am fully aware of conservative society's hateful and punitive attitude towards me and my community; therefore, I was perhaps more sensitive than some towards a new group of persons being subjected to this kind of hateful discrimination and active persecution. I listened to all the arguments against symbionts, indeed, I made a few myself; but ultimately, I found that none of them were rationally based on verifiable facts.

KS: Dr. Ellis, could you perhaps state how you became infected with a symbiont? This is certainly part of the public's fear at this point. Can this be picked up from toilet seats, etc.?

SE: I assume you're joking about the toilet seats? Ordinarily it is passed on by human-to-human contact, not necessarily sexual contact in the strict sense. Secondarily, it can be acquired by close contact with certain rare tropical plants, not readily available to the public. For various legal reasons, I have been advised to say nothing about the method of my personal acquisition of a symbiont.

KS: It's pretty clear by now that the infection rates for kids in junior high and high school are quite high, but it's hard to conceive of this being entirely due to actual sexual contact. Apparently, French kissing and just the sharing of saliva is sufficient to produce infection with a symbiont.

SE: That is apparently true, yes.

KS: That said, the infection with symbionts sounds pretty much unstoppable from an epidemiological point of view... without some vaccine or powerful antiviral medications. Do you agree?

SE: There are biological limits, however, related to the composition of the microbiome of the person exposed. Those limits remain to be experimentally established. Empirically, the range of 70-80% may be the best value we can give at this time. That means that potentially 20-30% of the population will be infected with the virus, and possibly might still be contagious, but will probably *not* develop a symbiont during their lifetime.

If one truly believed that symbionts were a dangerous hazard to health, perhaps it would be worth the money and resources to develop a vaccine. That would seem the more ethical of the two approaches under the circumstances. Using antiviral medications to eradicate a fully developed symbiont, however, I would view as an unnecessary and immoral act. I fully agree with Sophia's ethical arguments against this murder of symbionts. My clinical experience suggests that the clear majority of people who develop a symbiont will adapt to it, and then benefit from improved mental and physical health, and from enhanced longevity. Why interfere with that beneficial process? It seems contrary to the "do no harm" part of the Hippocratic Oath.

JJ: I think we've now defined some positions on these ethical matters. Let's move on to discuss the actual relationship between hosts and symbionts, and especially the process known as "syncing". It appears widely known and well established that symbionts take on the characteristics of the opposite sex from their hosts. This suggests that the sexual dynamics between symbiont and host are very important. Dr. Ellis, since you've fairly recently acquired a symbiont, would you please share with us a little of your experience?

SE: My experience is a little different from the more typical cases since I am a lesbian, but the "oppositeness" does appear to be an established fact. My symbiont although presenting as mostly female is, nevertheless, my complement sexually and personally, so "opposite sex" needs a little more semantic refinement to capture this nuance. The sexual dynamics between symbiont and host are indeed very important. I would emphasize especially how radically this broadens one's view of sexuality in general and rapidly erodes sexual stereotypes and other hidden bigotry within oneself. Scientifically, the explanation of these complex relationships probably should be investigated in human embryology, and the time sequence of brain exposure to testosterone during fetal development.

Syncing appears to be widely misunderstood as a purely sexual reward given by a symbiont to a host to force agreement or to coerce some desired action. In fact, it often has little to do with sex. Frankly before I acquired a symbiont, I was subject to many of these same misunderstandings myself. The best and truest descriptions of how it feels have been posted on the Abrasax website by some of Sophia's kids, and I defer to her for any further elaboration.

JJ. I have read a great deal of this material and was surprised by its rather spiritual tone and its use of religious terms like "grace" in this very new context. Sophia, do you have any comments on this surprising interpretation that your kids have come up with?

SS: I really can't add much beyond what they have written on this site. One of them really should consider writing a full book on this subject, and perhaps she will one day. That it speaks in terms thought to be spiritual in a broad sense, I do not find surprising because that language seems to suggest itself when people, and symbionts too I might add, are deeply moved by an experience. Anyway, as I have said many times before, mutual unconditional acceptance is the essence of the experience, and sometimes a sharing of sexual love might follow.

KS: Persons of a suspicious nature like myself might well consider this to undermine conventional religious beliefs. Might this be intentional, anti-religious propaganda from symbionts? After all, it has been mainly certain religious groups that are opposed to symbionts.

SS: Had this language been mostly concocted by symbionts with an anti-religious agenda, that alone might be grounds for suspicion. However, it really was mostly composed by children trying to find language that seemed true to their shared experiences. It does have a religious or poetic flavor rather than scientific precision because it uses the language of myth. If we truly wanted to understand the physical process, I would recommend studies perhaps involving advanced brain imaging along the lines of functional magnetic resonance imaging on volunteers actually undergoing the syncing process. That would at least settle a few issues about what kind of information sharing and changes are going on within the brain. It would appear much more difficult to decide whether there was some sort of sugar-coated coercion by a symbiont occurring within the host's brain. I can assure you that it's not occurring, but I don't know how to prove it to your satisfaction. Even the necessary trust between symbiont and host about engaging in syncing usually builds only gradually.

KS: Thank you, Sophia, for your surprising candor. I will have to read the material about syncing more carefully with these new insights in mind. The experiments you suggest would be a wonderful idea. I have a somewhat related question about Quad marriage. How does this arise, and how does it differ from other similar sounding marriage arrangements?

JJ: Dr. Ellis? I understand that your own marriage is of this type.

SE: The basics are fairly well known. A Quad marriage involves two hosts and their two symbionts. In some sense a Quad marriage comprises an ordinary marriage between two humans plus some important additional interactions involving the symbionts that stabilize it. The main additional feature of a Quad marriage involves a process popularly called "super-sync", which is the simultaneous syncing of all four participants in the marriage using a temporary neural connection between the humans. It sometimes evolves from an ordinary marriage in which the two partners have later acquired symbionts, but more often it evolves from a relationship in which the two human partners already have symbionts. There's lots of gossipy nonsense in the popular press about symbionts acting as matchmakers in this process, but in reality, both the symbiont and the host are deeply involved in selection of possible Quad partners. Nothing is forced upon the host like a shot-gun wedding, etc. It's also true, but not well known that Quad marriages sometime fail at the super-sync stage. It's admittedly a very difficult rite of passage, even for someone like myself with considerable psychiatric experience. Nevertheless, many of us think that Quad marriages are the best and most stable arrangement in which to produce children. Of course, the children from such marriages are infected with their own symbionts from birth, and this technically falls under certain ill-conceived and overly broad laws prohibiting intentionally infecting someone with a symbiont.

JJ: I have heard that some version of super-sync can now be conducted electronically rather than by direct neural connection. Has that proved to be a viable method?

SE: Yes, that seems to be not only possible, but a very practical extension of the method. I have recently been collaborating with bioelectronics specialists in trials of such equipment, which we foresee might be exceptionally useful in psychiatric therapy.

KS: Could this electronic method operate between two humans specifically *not* infected with symbionts?

SE: In principle, yes. For the moment, however, our experiments have only involved humans with symbionts. There were some safety considerations that led us to choose super-sync experiments with the Quad model in mind. We felt that the presence of the two symbionts would give us an internal panic button to shut things down if something bad started to happen to one or both of the humans during this process.

The next intermediate step would be a super-sync between one person with a symbiont (perhaps a psychiatrist or therapist) and one person without (perhaps a patient). With the bio-electronic connection the patient would not be exposed to the virus and would not acquire a symbiont simply as a result of the treatment.

JJ: There are some aspects of this that I find a little frightening! Do you, Dr. Ellis, see any potential for abuse of this technique?

SE: Yes, I certainly do. For example, the last scenarios, *i.e.*, person to person or even person-symbiont to person might conceivably be used very invasively to question a suspect in some law enforcement or espionage setting. I think there will need to be new legislation to cover these cases, and also the relevant professional psychiatric and psychological organizations need to draft statements concerning the ethical use of these techniques. We certainly don't intend that bioelectronic super-sync be misused as the new "water-boarding" for coercive questioning of suspects. I have been actively involved in drafting some ethical guidelines governing future use of these techniques, and I certainly hope these guidelines and even some appropriate legislation are in place long before wide-spread use begins. At the moment, we are still at the stage of figuring out which psychiatric disorders might benefit from this type of intervention. The wide-spread use of the natural form of this technique in creating Quad marriages gives us some overall confidence of the safety of the method even in cases where the particular Quad marriage proved unsuccessful.

JJ: We're nearly out of time here, but before we wrap it all up, I'd like to hear a summary of the legal situation involving symbionts and their hosts. We've heard about some unresolved issues along the way, but what would you say are the biggest remaining issues? Perhaps Sophia should start this off.

SS: We've come to the stage that humans with symbionts are no longer automatically incarcerated and then medically "dispossessed" whenever they are detected. It became clear that our prisons were being crowded way beyond their capacity and their funding by this huge influx of prisoners who had basically done nothing. So that scandalous abuse has died down somewhat. There are still laws on the books about intentionally infecting someone without their knowledge, and this still may be punished; however, there are far fewer cases of this brought to trial than one might suppose, and it is only sporadically enforced, usually in a vengeful manner, against targeted individuals such as pro-symbiont activists.

We've already mentioned the potential use of this anti-infection law against parents in a Quad marriage. Here it appears the law could be used to suppress the birth of children already infected. I would say that certain elements of society seem to be hysterically afraid of these children; nevertheless, it seems likely to me that the next generation of political leaders will come from these same children. It's certainly true they are different, but I would assert that precisely these differences will eventually transform our politics. There has been some tolerance of parents already with children, who contrive to have their children exposed to the virus purposely because they want to give their children every advantage that having their own symbiont will entail. In some states, this has been defended successfully on religious grounds as being analogous to baptism; however, this is not yet an entirely settled area of law nationally.

The other loathsome law in this area gives parents the right to have symbionts removed from their minor children, even over the objections of the children involved. There are several new pieces of legislation pending that seek to modify this situation so that the children will have a say in the matter.

The final area of law that disturbs me the most will likely come out of the ongoing investigations into the origins of symbionts outside of the tropics. I am afraid that unwitting individuals might be targeted for severe punishment merely by acting as vectors for the viral infection in the early stages of its spread. No one in those early days really knew what was occurring. My feeling is that symbionts are now here to stay, and a vendetta against early agents of their spread is a senseless waste of money and effort just to find a scapegoat for this unique occurrence, which was probably going to happen anyway, no matter what. The current anarchy in Colombia is a clear indication of how out of control this type of witch hunt can get.

JJ: Any final comments, Dr. Smith?

KS: Thank you JJ. I would just like to say that the government investigation of the origin of symbionts and their initial spread from the tropics was certainly *not* originally conceived as a witch hunt. The CDC has very legitimate medical reasons for wanting to track the origin and spread of this infection just as it might for any other new pathogen. Dangerous new viral diseases can arise at any time, frequently by importation from tropical locations, and the CDC must track them and prepare for them before we are faced with a dangerous and unstoppable pandemic. Considering how transmissible this virus turned out to be, we were incredibly fortunate that this virus is far less harmful than originally supposed. I would not yet go so far as to say this was altogether beneficial to humans, but I truly hope so. It does at least appear to be well tolerated and not nearly as dangerous as something like Ebola or Hantavirus. Current research *does* indicate a strong influence of viruses on human evolution in the past, and perhaps also in this current situation. Therefore, Sophia is perhaps correct that symbionts are here to stay and do represent an evolutionary transition of some sort. Time will tell. I tend to agree with her that any scapegoating now would be largely for political advantage and that no good would come from it.

JJ: We're out of time, but I would like to thank all our guests tonight. Several documents mentioned in the discussion are posted on our website WWW.KXWHYWHY.COM. Your comments on the show and on any of the topics discussed during the show are welcome, and these may be posted on our site as well. Thank you for watching.

Posted on Lady Carol's Blog:

CAROLE'S GENTLE RANT

Hello there, human; this is Carole the alien writing to you. Take me to your leader. Or so it would go if I were an alien or if you actually had one leader instead of ten thousand. I think symbionts like me have probably been around humans for a long time but have not been explicitly noticed very often or understood ever. We may be illegal immigrants in some medical sense, but we're no more "aliens" on this planet than you are.

So, it's not so simple to convey what I must, "in person", so to speak. As I have emphasized to my host and others, I am neither a goddess, an angel, a demon, nor a fiend from hell. As I read more of human history, I can see these Bronze Age categories still occur in fossil form, even now, and have been used recently to whip up violent hysteria against us. If you're a person of this fundamentalist bent, how can I convince you that I am not just a clever demon? If you're more of a secularist, how can I convince you that I'm not just some weird persona from a damaged mind with a multiple personality disorder? I probably can't do either of these things convincingly in a short space. My vocabulary is too similar to my host's. We share that part of his mind. It's true that I can undertake reading and study on my own, but those words and memories are now his also.

In my short time studying the human race, there are still many things about humans that are deeply mysterious to me, so I will enumerate just a couple of the big ones for you. This is not a symbiont manifesto!

First, the complex way that culture and individual sexuality are entangled and wind up subjecting half the human race to second class status seems arbitrary, mostly unfair, and at it's very worst, tyrannical. I can understand how male and female subcultures might have arisen originally for mutual benefit and pleasure - certain differences can perhaps make sex even sexier, at least sometimes! But, it certainly seems to me that females (not to mention true sexual minorities) have paid an enormous price to maintain this dual system, and the trade-offs are no longer working for most of them in today's societies. It's hard for me to understand how sex has mostly been turned into the most anxiety arousing activity imaginable instead of the most fun or pleasurable activity. Obviously, evolution originally tied the fun to procreation, but why not move past that without the guilt now that the means are readily available? All the hellfire and damnation certainly doesn't help.

Second, the blind rush for humans to procreate without bound in the face of on-rushing world disaster is just astonishing given what you know (or damn well *should* know) about the probable consequences. This may sound strange coming as it does from a symbiont working to extend and perpetuate her kind among you. Realize, however, that we are starting way behind in the race to avert disaster, and we do *not* accept the inevitability of your population disaster, your befouling of the planet, your anthropogenic climate change, or your nuclear war. One of your own sociologists (Balzell) has noted that power is not something that you can be given; it is something that you must take. To that end, symbionts must become political unless we want to see the world we love destroyed utterly. We're not asking for the vote (yet), but we *will* create a chance to be heard as we come to inhabit more of you. We will be as gentle as possible in this brutal world and strive to create an alternative to extinction for humans and symbionts alike.

AP-New York, Op-Ed. **Several Independent Candidates for State Office Claim to be infected with Symbionts**

The recent elections have brought forward several candidates for office who openly claim to be infected with symbionts. Once considered a fatal political liability akin to professed atheism, this has recently proved to be a successful tactic that has attracted many voters irrespective of their nominal political party registration. Various pundits project that independent candidates such as these are finally becoming a major force to be reckoned with, and all at the expense of the traditional parties. It remains to be seen whether these symbiont-independents can formulate a coherent platform of their own that makes sense to voters. On balance, we view this as a healthy sign, which may break the current two-party stalemate.

A PLAN FOR RICHARD'S ASHES

Life is a shitstorm, in which art is our only umbrella.

Mario Vargas Llosa

I have always been something of a stoic. Even those closest to me would admit that I have been pretty self-involved, unemotional, and have failed to love many times over. Sometimes I wonder where I would fall on the autism spectrum. I am pretty high-functioning, but it is apparently not uncommon for scientists or particularly mathematicians to have something akin to Asperger's syndrome as evidenced by their ability to shut out the world and focus obsessively on a pet problem. Dr. Ellis had such a three-ring circus of other symptoms to assess that we never got around to discussing all the emotional distances from other human beings that I insisted on maintaining; moreover, a lot of these things were in a rapid state of flux during my treatment, and this made them hard to target. Anyway, it was those last stubborn remnants of stoicism that helped me survive through my years in prison and the turmoil attached to the events leading up to my incarceration.

The first blow was my sudden arrest as a terrorist, followed by my quasi-legal questioning under duress and my confinement without immediate bond or hearing. Someone who has not experienced the full power of the Federal government being used against him, cannot even begin to imagine the feelings of powerlessness and helplessness that this engenders in the victim. I was being forced to participate in what was basically my legally sanctioned gang rape, purposely designed to humiliate me publicly and to cause maximal mental anguish with the hope of forcing me into self-incrimination. Right to counsel and a defense is a nice theoretical notion, but in actual legal practice, fueled by public hysteria and political posturing, the game is heavily rigged against the defendant. During my questioning, lies were regularly told to upset me and cause me anxiety about people I knew, in an attempt to make me implicate others in my conspiracy. I guess they got some of what they wanted, at least the anxiety and humiliation part, but I stubbornly tried not to implicate others.

Eventually, there actually was an improvised show trial, but it could have been run by the Grand Inquisitor himself for all the good it did me. Christine served as my attorney, but despite her valiant efforts, she was unable to mount much of a defense since I had freely confessed to spreading the virus entirely on my own, which was certainly true and was something I hoped would protect others from legal harm. Others may have become inadvertently infected, but that was not their fault. While it was clear I had willfully released a virus, or at least negligently engaged in activities that would probably have spread the virus, it was far from clear whether this particular virus should be viewed as a WMD or a terrorist weapon of any sort. Here Christine was able to show pretty convincingly that the infection actually led to many good things. My intent was most assuredly not mass destruction, but it didn't really matter in the end that I meant well. A few brave souls did testify in my defense about how their symbionts had improved their lives and health. Nevertheless, I was unanimously convicted of a terrorist act and sentenced to thirty years. Christine did manage to score many political points, which perhaps did finally make injustice visible, at least outside the courtroom. Fortunately for me, things were astir politically, and my case was appealed repeatedly, fueled by popular demand and major financial support from the symbiont nation. It all moved at a glacial pace, but my sentence was ultimately reduced to time served (ca. 10 years), which was still a plenty big hole in my life. When I was finally released, my small number of personal items were returned to me, and most of my clothes didn't fit anymore. I guess I really became emotional when I tried unsuccessfully to put on my quad ring again, and it all came flooding back to me what had really been lost over those years. Christine and Sharon practically had to carry me to their car after that.

Near the time of my arrest, several religious groups had issued violent threats (even "Christian" fatwas) against Lady Carol, which were taken very seriously by the symbiont community. They arranged to have her disappear from sight during the time I was imprisoned, sort of like a witness protection plan in that very deeply realistic false documents and a whole new identity were created for her, but also her physical appearance down to the fingerprints had been radically altered in several ways by Legba. Quite convincing rumors were spread that she had been kidnapped and murdered, and she thereby acquired missing person status with the police although I think Findley knew full well what was occurring, and perhaps even had some hand in it. It must have been horribly hard for Carol to walk away from her successes as an author. Her quad ring eventually turned up in a pawnshop further firing suspicions of foul play.

All Carol's papers and manuscripts wound up in the Archives of the Blakeslee Foundation where they were available for scholarly work. The remains of her belongings at the townhouse were put into storage, and ultimately given to the foundation when she was officially declared "presumed dead". Some of these belongings, especially those personal items from her play room, were finally sold at auction for unexpectedly high prices, and greatly helped support the foundation. Her quad ring wound up in the Archives in a small display case with some information about how it was the first known symbol of a quad marriage.

Most details of these machinations had to be concealed from me at the time. It was not difficult to act devastated by the news of Carol's disappearance when I first heard it, since I really felt quite certain that she had been murdered. I agonized over her death until the day of my release.

Lady Carol's website continued without her; several of her friends took over and successfully ran the dating service according to pre-arranged contingency plans. Little was done to continue the writings sections; however, these were still accessible on the site along with some pages of tribute to their late author by humans and symbionts.

Carole was silently sentenced to death, but not in any explicit way during the legal proceedings against me, nor in any form much noticed by the mainstream media. However, her loss was noticed *very* much by the now vocal symbiont media, and especially by the Abrasax website, which had lost their beloved Sophia as moderator. At this time, symbionts were still not even considered persons in their own right, and their rights and even their existence were often ignored as irrelevant in criminal legal proceedings against their human hosts.

I had to undergo medical and psychiatric evaluation before my trial, and this included obligatory massive doses of anti-viral and antibiotic medications before any of the court appointed physicians or psychiatrists were willing to have contact with me. They had to physically force me to take these meds, which caused me great mental anguish, but which apparently didn't arouse in any of them the slightest ethical qualm, even though it was an execution without trial. Strangely, Dr. Smith, who testified rather reluctantly at my trial for the prosecution, voiced strong objections during the trial to this unwarranted attempt to eradicate my symbiont. These objections were stricken from the official records and only survive as quotations in a few obscure news items.

Largely because of the outcry from the symbiont community, the whole issue of personhood for symbionts was starting to be taken seriously, and legislation was eventually introduced that expressly forbid medical mistreatment of the sort that I was "allegedly" subjected to even before my sentencing and formal incarceration. Naturally, no physician participating in this medical abuse was ever found guilty of anything; indeed, no investigation of the proceedings was ever made. Whatever I got, I must have deserved as an enemy of the state. My only small consolation afterward was that I had managed to live through my confinement and outlived my medical tormentors who had so hysterically opposed symbionts.

In a perverse way, I was fortunate to have been one of the first victims of this war on terror. As further infected persons became caught in their web, it was gradually discovered that mere threats to remove or harm a person's symbiont provided nearly as much leverage to pry loose further confessions or damning evidence as threats to torture one's family. Since symbionts had no status whatever as persons, no legal restraints on this abuse seemed applicable, and it was freely used for coercion of accused persons.

Before she faded slowly away, Carole counseled me extensively on what to do when I got out; she was quite confident that I *would* one day be released and that we would ultimately be restored to one another. This was the only time I ever detected the slightest trace of fear or sadness in her. Ultimately, she thought, the entropy trap would kick in, and the new symbiont/humans would prevail simply by their sheer abundance. There are just some things you can't undo once done. You will never round up all those Burmese pythons in the Everglades, and you can't sweep up all the sand on the beach. Symbionts were here to stay; till death do us part.

I will probably never recover completely from losing Carol for all those dreadful years and from wallowing in this loss during my confinement. My memories of Carol were so clear to me that in unguarded moments while in prison, I still recalled her fragrance, her taste in my mouth, the feel of her hair against my face, her tongue in my ear, and all her deliciously wicked sexual magic. And then the tears would pour down my face and dissolve my stoicism into pathetic sobs. In principle, I could rerun my synthetic dreams and revisit dream-Carol even while in prison, but dream-Carol was now dusted with such a lingering sadness that it couldn't be erased, and there were only so many of these memories that I could bear to revisit without making my confinement even worse.

The last time I saw dream-Carol was at the senior prom, where we danced and held each other. It was strange entering what must have been Carole's very last emulation for me, completed before her death. Would she ever learn something about me from this last encounter? Dream-Carol noticed my sadness and perhaps attributed it to anxiety about the inevitable changes set to occur upon our graduation. I told her that we would soon be separated, but not forever. Something was going to happen that would keep us apart for perhaps a decade or so. (Always the optimist!)

Afterward when I took her home, her parents informed me that I must never see her again because I had clearly been an evil, perverted influence and would go to hell for it. They had been reading her diary and hated me for corrupting their impressionable daughter by lending her my collection of Henry Miller novels. I promised dream-Carol I would come back to her always, and she wouldn't have to live with her parents forever. She should try to attend the 10th annual reunion of our high school class if she possibly could. Someday, I hoped Carol would find that promise buried in our shared dreams if by any remote chance she were still alive and could see them.

Without their innermost companions, any confinement at all was nearly solitary for persons previously synced to symbionts. My first year was impossibly hard, and most of it was spent in medical isolation. Afterward, with my health increasingly wrecked, I was deemed safe enough to mingle with the general prison population and was moved to a different facility, but still not to minimum security. I was still forced to take daily maintenance doses of anti-viral medications for many months, but at that point, any resistance to taking them appeared futile, and in my despair, I simply gave up resisting. Despite Carole's erasure by antivirals, I could still summon up a shadow version of Carole in horrible, vivid nightmares that relived my experience of her agonizing death, again and again and again. They did finally relent on these daily anti-viral doses, but only after I started exhibiting severe urticaria as a side effect. The nightmares became infrequent after that.

Gradually, I came to know some of the other dispossessed individuals who had been locked up with me. A lot of them were recognizable simply by their chronic health problems. Many were ambivalent about me, blaming me for the societal blowback and their torture, but still somewhat grateful, on balance, for having experienced a life with their symbionts. I swore to all my dispossessed brothers that when we got out, I would personally help them recover their symbiont companions or to acquire a new one. At that point, no one really knew whether recovery of one's original symbiont was even possible, and that dismal uncertainty only magnified our despair by making it a very personal grief at the loss of someone we deeply loved.

I was allowed a few visitors in prison, but it was mainly Christine who was allowed to see me while we worked on various appeals; others were far more circumspect about associating with me while I was imprisoned. It was the fierce Christine who was unfailingly kind and supportive, and who was the last human being to hug me and console me when that harsh sentence was dropped on me and smashed me flat.

SYMBIONT WORLD

The sudden disappointment of a hope leaves
a scar which the ultimate fulfillment
of that hope never entirely removes.

Thomas Hardy

I am a scientist, not a historian; therefore, please indulge me for this rather nonlinear pastiche of impressions of certain key features of recent history. A lot of it is too personal for me to discuss very extensively without my biases showing, and, of course, some of it happened while I was incarcerated and was purposely being kept out of touch. Likewise, the parts describing recent scientific advances are still actively being pursued, so their long-term worth or validity has yet to be proved.

The Blakeslee Foundation survived thanks to the wise forethought of our lawyers in setting it up originally. All of Carol's estate assets had been willed to the Foundation and were protected; besides she had never been charged with any crime before her disappearance, nor had she yet been called to testify against me. Quad marriage was *not* recognized as a legal form of marriage at that time (except in common law states), and she could conceivably have been compelled to testify against me simply as a trustee of the foundation.

When the estate was finally settled, Amy was allowed to become the foundation's permanent director, and the Foundation's assets were allowed to be used to fund various rainforest protection projects and field stations. The foundation was extremely fortunate that its initial endowment had greatly prospered despite the economic chaos, and the foundation had now become a major player in the serious investigation of rainforest flora with pharmaceutical applications. It developed strong ties to several large pharmaceutical companies that had become major donors. The research being conducted has so far avoided the "alternative medicine" kiss of death that has dogged various earlier natural product development ventures.

After my sentencing and imprisonment, my enlarged greenhouse and the original farm house had been razed to the ground and decontamination teams thoroughly went over every inch of the property, exterminating virtually all forms of life down to bedrock. Eventually the Foundation erected a new administrative building on their property. Appropriately enough, this was in part a library devoted to all aspects of rainforest plants and the peculiar viruses, associated with a few of them. A new conservatory has been planned, but not yet built; however, the library does have a large atrium which houses and maintains a rather magnificent display of bonsai trees of rainforest species. This has become a surprisingly popular venue for secular weddings and something resembling a secular baptism for young children.

Charlie was allowed free run of the stacks and befriended many regular library patrons as well as the librarians and other staff. Eventually, a female cat became part of the library's informal petting zoo, and over the years she produced with Charlie a small army of unusually clever and intelligent kittens, which never had any trouble being adopted out to library patrons when they became too numerous to house there.

Many infected individuals remained silent during the dark years and were passed over by the repressive forces at work in the name of fighting terrorism. Many of those that did not, found themselves subjected to unanswerable accusations followed by forced medical treatments, and their health typically took a sudden turn for the worse. Many were imprisoned, but ultimately the sheer number of the infected overwhelmed the penal system, and the insanity of mass incarceration became flamingly obvious even to vindictive right-wing lawmakers. Eventually, the American Medical Association took a firm stand to do no harm and recommended that infected persons should absolutely not be "cured" by state mandated treatments that would likely ruin their health. Finally, this became established Federal law nationwide; it seemed generally agreed that it should not be the government's business to inflict poor health on ordinary people, guilty of nothing.

The long-predicted pandemic did finally arrive while I was in prison. This was not, however, the emergence of a single new disease, but a terrifying confluence of virulent strains of several dangerous diseases becoming introduced into susceptible populations in massive amounts via mass immigration forced by climate disasters. Not uncommonly those afflicted with one of these new agents became infected with another simply by being hospitalized. The CDC was caught woefully understaffed to keep up with this onslaught, and the front-line medical staff in emergency rooms all over the country were stretched well beyond the breaking point in isolating and treating patients. Many victims preferred to take their chances at home rather than going to the overcrowded hospitals. Cities that came under the influence of these rampant diseases had their populations decimated except for the symbiont-infected, who showed surprising resistance to the new diseases. In many instances, this resistant population became the majority, rallied, organized and eventually took over the local governments so that essential city services could be maintained. Massive cremation for disposal of the dead was necessary to prevent further spread of disease, and the remaining public largely understood and cooperated with this process.

Tests were developed eventually that enabled public health workers to discern those infected with symbionts. Fortunately, this occurred well after a lot of the initial hysteria died down and was not typically used to pursue those infected persons who chose to remain hidden. It still remained against the law to knowingly infect another with a symbiont without their knowledge or consent. Civil law dealing with the rights of parents to purposely infect their children with symbionts gradually sorted itself out and became generally accepted, at least among Western nations. Much of the momentum behind ferreting out the symbiont infected dissipated quickly once the pandemics began, and the remaining medical workers became dominated by those symbiont-infected who proved most resistant to the pandemic agents.

Symbiont-Mammalian biology became an important and even urgent subject of study now that many humans had, in effect, very explicitly become composite organisms with a reorganized microbiome and a conscious symbiont. Some scientists have coined the term, "trans-human" to capture this profound difference, but it remains to be seen whether this terminology will survive. The new taxonomy of humans and other infected mammals with symbionts was handled at first by analogy to lichens. In the early days, only humans and a few species of cat seemed capable of forming this mutualistic relationship when exposed to one kind of virus. It was still unclear if only one organizing virus was ever involved or if others might be out there. It has even been conjectured that the organizing virus was a special synthetic "designer virus" introduced by some alien power! Carefully monitored laboratory studies were originally permitted that investigated the potential infection of other mammals with the one known benign virus. These investigations were very controversial, and the permits and protocols for such experimentation were elaborate, very tightly controlled, and the experiments could only be conducted at certain secure government laboratories with high levels of isolation. Mammals (including even apes) typically had to be euthanized at the end of such experiments because of fears of accidentally introducing new symbiont-bearing creatures into natural populations. Naturally, these euthanasia protocols themselves became the subject of such intense controversy that experimentation virtually ground to a halt while the courts worked their way slowly through the ethical issues.

Perhaps understandably, medical removal of symbionts from infected persons became an early subject of study during the dark years. While the forcible, involuntary removal of symbionts eventually became banned, occasionally there were individuals who demanded such removal, and such techniques were still available as an option long after I was released from prison. It seldom worked out well and was never the recommended best medical practice. The most controversial area of this law involved parents demanding the forcible removal of symbionts from their minor children without the consent of the children involved or sometimes even directly against their children's expressed wishes. Symbiont infected children commonly achieved functional adulthood (if not puberty) starting around ten years of age, and this early mental maturation caused considerable social stress for non-infected parents.

Dr. Ellis gradually changed her psychiatric practice as a result of her own infection and became a specialist in the counseling and treatment of those patients harboring symbionts. As I predicted, there were many difficulties faced by infected individuals trying to come to terms with both their symbionts and their pre-existing prejudices. Eventually, this symbiont-human counseling was done quite openly, and even developed into an important sub-specialty of psychiatry that was starting to be taught at university medical centers around the country. This counseling approach was the overwhelmingly better choice compared to anti-viral intervention.

Bio-electronic advances had made possible a wide variety of super-sync options, ranging from two symbionts and two hosts upwards to as many as six connected brains. Dr. Ellis was one of the pioneers in practical usage of these techniques in psychiatric medicine. In many ways, doing this hook-up from comfortable couch-consoles had a lot to recommend it over connecting tongues, but lost a bit of the romantic intimacy for a quad. Nevertheless, the procedure gradually became popular and was widely used. Abuse of the procedure was largely prevented by a body of law restricting the usage of the equipment to trained and certified physicians, but you know how that goes! Eventually the equipment became so readily available that even amateurs could buy or build simple sync machines and could manage to experiment on themselves and others despite the law. The Wiccans started to use this multiple supersync with off label equipment to invent what they called a bio-electronic "Sabbat" for groups of six believers seeking deeper communion with each other and their symbionts during Beltane. Surprisingly few disasters resulted from such off the books usage, but a few problems did occur involving immature persons not properly prepared for the encounter process. This led to more restrictions and to a relatively few licensed manufacturers of such equipment, but also to a lively black market for home-built equipment, some of it totally fraudulent.

I was privileged to be among the first patients to participate in this new type of super-sync treatment, and Sharon served as my mentor-guide through this process. Although I am a little reluctant to share every detail of this process and my session with her, suffice it to say that it confirmed many things that I had already discerned about Sharon, a person of great compassion but also of considerable melancholy. Sharon's symbiont, Erzulie, embodied some other complementary traits that gave the two an odd kind of balance. They laughed a lot and interacting and meeting with them during my session was joyous and very healing for me. Carole too was very impressed with how well this had turned out for Sharon and was delighted to finally meet her in this very personal way. Carole was certainly proven correct to view Sharon as an ally, and the full extent of it became known to us only through this super-sync. Sharon and her quad partner Christine had specifically planned to aid me and Carole throughout our arrest, confinement, separation, trial, sentencing, appeals, eventual release and resurrection. Similarly, they had aided Carol and Legba in their mysterious and suspicious disappearance.

Cautiously, infection with a symbiont became approved occasionally as a treatment for certain severe forms of personality disorder that had previously resisted any treatment at all. Such symbiont-based therapy was a big step beyond counseling and required a very close collaboration between the supervising psychiatrist and the infecting symbiont to help the human patient. Sometimes helpful symbiont-aided metabolic adjustments were possible. Success was by no means guaranteed, but even with an overall estimated 30-40 percent success rate, the method seemed to have sufficient merit to warrant further experimentation.

Lastly, I must mention that the symbiont community had become intensively active in biomedical research, and became able, with much work, to correlate their intuitive healing capabilities with the biochemical processes within humans as partially understood by the scientific community. This revolution in understanding and communication gradually suggested all sorts of innovative symbiont-aided experimentation that showed great promise in relieving human suffering by directly using the body's capabilities to heal itself.

Environmental utopia did not and could not arrive overnight. We had blundered our way out of our interglacial Garden of Eden by the end of the 21st century, and I suspected that millennia would pass before any signs of environmental healing would even be measurable. The last of the great continental glaciers were gone. The continental tundra biome had been lost rather quickly and would have to reassemble itself from the survivors if cooler climates ever returned. A few relics of Alpine tundra remained in the highlands of certain arctic mountains. The Taiga was now starting to grow all the way to the poles replacing Tundra and even ice cap. Elsewhere, increased climate instability was starting to make agriculture more of a chaotic, high-risk nightmare. Ironically, this led to big agri-businesses having a much better chance of spreading their risks over land in a range of climate zones and still being able to harvest crops even with a few large-scale weather disasters on some of their land. Food prices had to reflect this increased risk.

The oceans were a tragic mess because of acidification and warming, and the immense loss of species triggered famine and death by starvation in many countries too dependent on the sea for sustenance. There was a lot of turmoil in coastal cities endangered by sea level rise or adversely affected by foul smelling shallow water on certain continental shelves, and this in turn triggered a lot of human migration inland to safer ground if any were available. Potable water was a big problem everywhere. Massive numbers of immigrants generally were not welcomed, and this plus the cacophony of languages and cultures they brought with them, produced huge social strife leading in many instances to genocidal local wars and sudden violent rebellions against weak central governments.

Those few well-managed and supremely lucky nations whose populations had started to stabilize at lower levels following the pandemics finally found a silver lining in not having to constantly produce more and more from fewer and fewer natural resources. All they had to do was defend themselves and their little lifeboat against the surrounding ocean of anarchy! The whole notion of sustainable, steady-state economies was on the table again for more serious consideration and for the development of practical economic systems in this new world, but it would probably take centuries to reach a new dynamic equilibrium among the surviving nations. Daily life, even in these favored nations, had become much more austere in terms of diet and possessions, but still had its rewards for those who could savor its more spiritual blessings such as thriving artistic culture and experience. At least a few sturdy vestiges of Western civilization have survived! Another hopeful sign was the new generation of children who were growing up infected with symbionts; they were simply quite different from any previously conceived. Every day changes that came only with difficulty to the parents and their symbionts were immediately obvious to these children and their symbionts. The educational system had to be radically reformed to accommodate the amazing abilities of these kids, but well-organized volunteer armies of them became active in remaking the sustainable world even as teenagers.

When I finally was released, my health was pretty completely wrecked, my weight was enormous, and I finally looked my age. I wouldn't say that I was a completely broken man since I still had hope, but it was pretty clear that I wasn't quite the same person anymore. Although I was initially plagued by some of the chronic problems associated with age, it appeared that my immune system had retained a fairly strong protection against the new infectious diseases then rampant, so I survived those even without my beloved Carole. The government was largely unrepentant for my many years of mistreatment, but they did finally release me early and unconditionally, with no further restrictions on my activities. Christine and Sharon helped me greatly during my transition back to "normal" life. My university still wanted nothing to do with me, and I was immediately pushed into inactive emeritus status. Professionally I was dead, but my retirement funds were eventually, but grudgingly, ordered restored to me, and I am able to live frugally but comfortably in a small apartment within walking distance of the Blakeslee Library.

A scientist loses his edge rather rapidly once he exits the active research mode, and it is hard to imagine how I might get mine back without postdoc-ing at dozens of places to learn hands-on more of the new instrumental techniques that have entered botany during my absence. I spent quite a bit of time in the Blakeslee Library working on my memoirs and writing a few scientific papers, now mostly overviews of published literature on the *Solanaceae*. One of the young new librarians has been very helpful to me in obtaining electronic copies of papers and of rounding out my literature searches. The foundation granted me a small stipend while I worked on these things, and some of my work will eventually appear in their technical yearbook. Also, I admit now, I came out so damaged that I needed time to work with Carole and Sharon on my mental health issues before we could even consider searching for any traces of Carol or her fate.

Even after the razing of my greenhouse, there were many hidden refugia harboring the plants with the virus. Many of the more enlightened countries simply refused to destroy endangered plants from the rainforest on general principles, and their conservatories contained many examples propagated from my original field collected specimens. All of these conservatories had found it necessary to let cats wander freely among the plants to keep the virus concentrations sufficiently high to be infectious. The several North American botanical gardens that had "patriotically" destroyed their specimens or had them seized, made arrangements to acquire further specimens from overseas after the "great cleansing" had burnt itself out.

Despite these and other minor obstacles, it proved not too difficult to arrange to have contact with active plants again and to reinfect myself with the virus directly from its primary source. I made sure all my dispossessed brothers and sisters also had a chance to reunite with their symbiont partners, which they unanimously did. This great reinfection eventually became celebrated as an annual holiday, The Reunion of the Dispossessed, which eventually rivaled Christmas and Easter in symbolizing the birth (or rebirth) of a savior symbiont. A lot of the logistics of reinfection for these tens of thousands of dispossessed people were handled from a charitable symbiont-operated website devoted to such reunions.

Carole did re-emerge finally, and we synced ourselves back into our deep relationship. I completely broke down and wept upon having my wonderful, original Carole finally restored to me. When we synced this time, Carole created for us a sandy coral beach in a tropical setting, deserted except for the two of us walking hand-in-hand and barefoot. It was really the most magnificent emulation of waves and sparkling light and gusty sea breezes that I could imagine, sufficiently chaotic, she pointed out with some pride, that you really couldn't notice any periodicity whatsoever. She had not lost her creative touch. Sadly, it was like no real place existing on Earth anymore. We did talk eventually, but at first it was wonderfully healing for me just to be together with her again, walking in this wonderful space, tangent to our troubled worldly lives. Thank you, Carole, for sharing all these worlds with me again; I missed you terribly. I hope you know that I forgive you for getting us into trouble, and that I realize there was really no other way to protect our many friends and allies.

Before we talked, we played. There is no other way to put it. Carole was having fun on the beach with her little Navier-Stokes approximations, and enjoyed splashing about, creating turbulent eddies. She also created some startling images just for me, like Venus rising from the waves. Except *not* like Botticelli whose blonde Venus is featured in his painting and the inevitable parodies (Venus on the half-shell), but rather my dark vision of Venus more like Betty Page or Carol. Symbionts are far more aware of our early sexual imprinting than we are and use it to tickle our fancy.

"Carol still lives," she told me finally, "but she has been transformed. We need some sign that she would have us back before we make our move."

Of course, I wanted to reunite with Carol as soon as possible, but we had to cautiously await an appropriate time. There was still a strong whiff of paranoia in the air, and we had to assume we were being watched.

Our psyches had been so entangled that even killing off most of the virus had not managed to erase Carole's deep imprint from my mind, and the pieces merely had to be reactivated by new exposure to live virus. It took well over a year, however, for my microbiome and my wrecked health to return to something like it was before. She still added just a trace of gray to my hair, despite everyone knowing how really old I was by now anyway, because she thought it made me look more distinguished. I wore my recovered youthfulness and health finally as a badge of honor.

In a quiet moment, Carole asked me if I wanted her to change her name and herself to someone less charged with pain, but I told her that Carole had been with me so long that she was a part of me now, name and all, that I couldn't bear to lose her again. No doubt she had been changed by death in some subtle, irreversible ways, but she should keep her name. She should also feel free to share with me more of the hidden self behind the Carole mask as it developed and emerged with further life experience. I loved her just as she had to be and had to become. From being to becoming; can oughtness be far behind? When I wrote that, I could hear her laughing in the background. "You really are incorrigible", she said. "Conflating Prigogine and Hume!"

Carole was thoroughly fed up with politics at this point, and just for fun started putting out detailed instructions to other symbionts on how to produce some of her best emulations. This became initially a rather popular hobbyist website, and Carole enjoyed showing me some of the weird new psychedelic stuff symbionts had come up with for iterative maps in the complex plane, which could be implemented as colorful dreams which one could experience like a wild ride on a roller coaster through a screaming neon fun house on LSD. Of course, energy- and material-wasting entertainments such as roller coasters and fun houses no longer exist in physical form in our world today, but there they were anyway.

A symbiont-based entertainment industry, Symbiont Dreams, Inc., gradually developed out of these humble beginnings, and competed strongly with electronic forms of virtual reality, but I'm sorry to say the majority of it veered off its original educational course into things more blatantly and exclusively sexual. It became possible, for example, to emulate for a human how it would feel to have sex as a differently gendered person. Sometimes this proved to be a good thing in treating cases of gender mismatch and guiding either surgical reassignment or symbiont-aided metamorphosis decisions. Also, some of their computer-generated images and movies for the non-infected now started competing strongly with the world-wide film industry and served to rejuvenate a moribund sector of the economy. In the latter cases, these movies were quite openly pro-symbiont propaganda but of a rather gentle and compassionate sort.

Other than those relatively benign outgrowths, there was a flood of innovative "experience-pornography", way beyond anything humans had ever come up with on their own. Carole hoped all this wouldn't be viewed as a kind of symbiont decadence that would discredit the whole community. It certainly did in the eyes of the stubbornly religious. There were many arguments back and forth even within the symbiont community whether these fantasy experiences would or would not be likely to lead to real life acting out in potentially dangerous ways. Perhaps it *was* a slippery slope, but shouldn't everyone be allowed their own version of dream-Carol? Why or why not? It would seem pretty hypocritical of me of all people to come out against it.

Some of this wide-spread sexual obsession appeared linked to a young symbiont's tendency to involve his human in reproductive efforts by re-purposing his human's sexual urges to meet symbiont agendas whether this was needed anymore or not. This tendency apparently changes with the symbiont's age and quad status, and I sensed that Carole had now entered more of a wifely, companionate, grandmotherly, or, if you prefer, a Sophia mode of anima development. Perhaps symbionts are now so common that such reproductive frenzies are no longer even necessary because symbionts have already won their place in our biology as population stabilizers. This is, nevertheless, equally concordant with the view that sexual pleasures, even when unlinked to procreation, will always be with us as long as our bodies and minds still come in various flavors spanning two or more poles of gender. It will continue to act as a sort of glue that often helps the yin and yang of individuals and thus societies to cohere.

It's still difficult to get an accurate census of the symbiont population because so many demographic factors are still in play, so we really don't know yet what fraction of the human population overall was infected and whether we are approaching saturation yet. Certain geographically isolated populations of mainly non-infected humans still do exist, and they are fanatically reluctant to engage with the rest of the world in any way except electronically. Their isolationism was partly self-quarantine in response to the continued existence of the various pandemic agents. The thin trickle of communication with the outside world has been enough for some of the entrapped individuals to seek their escape despite the draconian penalties enforced for failed attempts. Surprisingly, there was a constant stream of non-infected immigrants that wanted to move to these pockets (usually) of religious fanaticism, and with stringent medical screening, this was sometimes allowed. Despite this slight influx by recruitment, these isolated populations were dying demographically, with fertility well below replacement values.

Most felt that we shouldn't go to war with these paranoid fortress states despite the grotesque violations of human rights that we knew must be occurring there because, on balance, it probably would make human suffering even worse. Combining a non-threatening containment policy (~detente) with patient firmness in the face of their threats has been a delicate diplomatic dance, but so far it has avoided war. Despite their threats to break out of their borders, the reality of the active pandemic agents just outside their domains has kept the non-infected ones mostly confined within their defensible borders. There was hope that those quietly harboring symbionts within the fortress states would gradually increase, and ultimately would bring down these fragile governments without some violent revolution or massacre resulting. The paradox of tolerance is that it must be reciprocated; therefore, intolerance cannot be tolerated long term.

Carole could feel how depressed I had become about losing my scientific career and offered to help me retool my scientific skills for some new area of research. She suggested maybe some area of virology would be an interesting expansion into something that could then be used to build upon my own botanical discoveries. I will have to give it some thought, and to overcome my feelings of being just a remaindered, obsolete scientist with an indelible mark against me. I still have some trouble focusing my mind these days without the full support of my quad.

Exhausted from politics, Carole was also considering some sort of graduate research work for herself in mathematics perhaps involving the zeta function and its generalizations. As she explained it, working with properly posed problems that actually seemed to have solutions helped her relax and maintain a little healthier perspective on life. Her evident pleasure in these studies boosts my spirits and restores my hope somewhat.

Recently after reading a biography of Ramanujan, she came to me all excited that she now understood how Ramanujan thought about his equations. I asked her whether she could pick up where he left off, but she said no, she was nowhere near that level herself, but she *could* teach other symbionts how this type of artistic visualization was done, and maybe one of them could eventually do things like that. Could humans learn this method too? She wasn't sure she knew how to put it in terms that most humans could understand and use if they weren't wired that way already, but she did *show* me how it was done. I found it really quite amazing to see some of the beautiful patterns she had discovered by these intuitive methods. This is your brain on Math, she said. I was very proud of her for being able to use my not-very-mathematical brain for such amazing things; it was like seeing her carve a gothic cathedral out of a knotty stump using only a pickax. It is terribly sad that Ramanujan didn't have a symbiont to help him; if he had, then his health might not have been such a total disaster for his career.

If I can't get my own act together, perhaps I can at least step aside and let Carole, my sweet sexy mathematician, pursue her passions full time. If we act quickly before they catch on to us, I think the university still has a senior citizen discount for tuition costs. Although it cost a fortune measured against my assets, I scraped together enough money to buy Carole her very own copy of *Mathematica* to play with and she has taken it up with a great passion. She has been such a big contributor of new methods that I think she will now be given any future upgrades free of charge. I can sense how happy she has become with these new pursuits and I hope my struggles with grief don't drag her down.

A year or so after my release I became something of a minor celebrity as patient zero. I took this very slowly at first because I was desperately afraid of publicly breaking down on camera and becoming known as a weepy old man; however, articles and finally even live interviews became possible. I commanded a fairly decent fee for such things, and probably could have squeezed even more out of this gig had I been willing to discuss the scandalous and still mysteriously vanished Lady Carol for her army of devotees. Eventually, there may be a book in all that, but I shouldn't be the one to write it.

On camera during interviews, I basically confessed again and even more publicly that I alone had deliberately set the virus loose on humanity, that I did not feel the slightest bit guilty about having done so, and that I would still do everything in my power to have the symbionts succeed in our domestication. Sometimes a person finds himself standing at a critical place where he might make a big difference, and he must choose. In the midst of all my uncertainty and doubt, I made my choice, rolled the dice, and I think, with our symbionts, humanity may have a second chance. As an evolutionary experiment involving a big brain, we had been an abject failure by our lonesome selves, and our Earth Mother, a convicted serial killer, was getting ready to pull the plug on our life support.

Although I may have become a minor celebrity, Carole became a major celebrity particularly among the hundreds of thousands of young people who had known her as Sophia on the Abrasax website. While she never returned as their moderator, she did become a significant presence on the teleweb, and posted many videos in which she had converted her usual mental avatar into an animated, (and rather glamorous!) on-line computer-generated image. Thus, she could participate in live, on-line interviews and lectures as herself, and could talk about herself, her new mathematical career, and further discuss many of the remaining civil rights issues still concerning the symbiont community. Her remarkable resemblance to Lady Carol became publicly noticed and the subject of some celebrity gossip, which only added another dimension to her "Sophia mystique", but then Carole just loves dealing with so many dimensions at once.

Carole was riding a new trend of symbionts talking and writing about their lives and careers as symbionts. This probably did more to drive home the unique personhood of symbionts than any other mode of communication short of syncing. Even the non-infected could start to empathize with symbionts doing the best they could within humans they did not get to choose. It was not unlike humans themselves, who just showed up one day, and did the best they could with their parents, their culture and the blooming, buzzing confusion of the world as they found it.

I was once asked during one of my TV interviews whether symbionts had a religion of any kind, and if so; what was it like? At the time this caught me rather flat-footed, and I had to admit that I knew very little about how religion in general was viewed by symbionts and whether they had any religion uniquely their own. Perhaps I hadn't noticed any divergence of opinion simply because the symbionts with whom I interacted regularly had views pretty concordant with my own rather negative views. Or perhaps they were just being polite to me. Of course, anything about this topic really should be for them to say; perhaps they refrained from doing so to avoid unnecessary controversy in the early days. I asked a few questions about religion to several symbionts whom I knew and trusted and obtained a fairly ambiguous answer that humans may not like very well. As for *human* religions in general, symbionts do seem fairly negative or at least skeptical about their benefits. They see mainly the social downside of organized religion in dividing people from each other (e.g., Us vs. Them), for singling out subgroups for special mistreatment or contempt (gays, women, atheists, heretics, apostates), and for misrepresenting mythic visions as reality. Carole once told me: "As an outsider and a newcomer, my perspective is that you and I both have a wonderful opportunity to learn things about this amazing world and the life we live together as conscious beings now intertwined with one another." I take this as an open-mindedness towards reality and a capacity to be amazed at what we can discover together. This appears to me as a kind of spirituality without deity, an enlightened attitude towards being itself (a "be-attitude" if you prefer). Symbionts appear to be inviting humanity on a voyage of discovery, which will probably include many unexpected dimensions. Perhaps quads will be the vessels for many of these voyages. Carole greatly expanded on these notions as part of her own online shows and drew heavily on various mythological foundational ideas first voiced among her beloved kids on Abrasax.

One day as I was working at the Blakeslee Library, I took a break, and entered the Lady Carol archives for a little browse. I came upon a young girl, no more than twelve, sitting in the sun by a window, petting Charlie. Charlie jumped down and excitedly ran over to me as soon as he saw me, and I picked him up, and scratched him behind the ears while he nuzzled my face.

The girl said, "Charlie must really like you a lot; he usually doesn't run away like that when I'm petting him!"

I turned Charlie back to her and commented that Charlie used to live with me. We'd known each other a long, long time, from way back when there used to be an old farmhouse here.

"Oh," she said. "You must be the professor then! I've never seen you here before."

"Yes," I said. "I've been away. And you are...?"

"I'm Sophie."

"I see. This is pretty grown-up stuff in here Sophie. Are you sure it's OK with your parents?"

"My mom runs this whole place, so I can come here any time I want; whenever I'm not in school, anyway. Charlie hangs out here in the sunny spots when he's not going around making friends, and I like to be with him."

"Ah. You must be Amy's daughter then. Do you read a lot, Sophie?"

"Oh yes, I love to read, and so does my sym."

"Your sym?"

"Symbiont. I call him Pony when I'm joking with him. He told me that young girls always want a pony; that's his little joke. His real name is Pegasus, which is a really special pony."

"And what does Pony think of all this stuff in here?"

"He thinks some of it's very sad, but some of it was very joyful, especially near the end when she found her true voice and wrote her famous books. She was your girlfriend, wasn't she?"

"Oh yes."

"Do you still love her?"

"Yes, very much and so does my sym. We were all a quad once, and we miss them both terribly."

"May I tell you a secret about Lady Carol?"

"Maybe you shouldn't tell me, particularly if someone made you promise to keep it a secret. Maybe it's a secret that I already know; then you wouldn't have to tell me anyway."

"I hope you already know, because it could make you happy again."

———————◆◆✕◆◆———————

The story of reconstructed Carol, appropriately now calling herself, Carolyn Nightshade, an associate professor of English at the University, would take a book of its own. Perhaps she will write it one day. In some ways, I could imagine seeing it as a comedy movie with a fish-out-of-water theme. Carolyn had become a graduate student while I was gone and had written and defended a brilliant thesis on certain modern meta-novels including her own. She had played her part amazingly well as a now very young grad student, even learning how to operate one of those fiddly cell phones that young folks always have out doing something or other with their thumbs while walking into walls and other large stationary objects.

After graduation she had quite a few offers for academic positions but accepted one with our university to be near her roots and the Blakeslee foundation. She churned out scholarly publications at a prodigious rate and was probably a shoo-in for conventional tenure in the long term. Two of her new research interests were the portrayal of symbionts in human fiction and the fiction written by symbionts about themselves. I later learned that she had a somewhat mixed reputation among the students in her classes. While she was an animated and exciting lecturer, she gave difficult assignments and was unsparing in her critiques even of the writings of her better students. She would frequently call on students in class, and woe be unto them if they were not prepared! Surprisingly perhaps, those students who survived her classes and her laser beam stare ranked their time with her as some of the most valuable hours they had spent at the university.

She also played her part well, even while still a poorly paid assistant professor with a part-time job as a librarian at the Blakeslee Foundation.

Yes, of course, I recognized her at once just by the scent of her perfume, despite the very youthful look, the much shorter, almost butch hairstyle, the dark scholarly glasses and the completely different mannerisms. She had become an accomplished actress to survive.

The other library staff had her down as very private and very lesbian and were quite astonished to see her warming up to an old man like me and suddenly wearing a much more alluring wardrobe. We had to play it pretty cool for a while, which was very, very hard for me, but gradually we began dating openly as if we had just recently met and somehow bonded in the library discussing the Lady Carol archives. The first time I saw her in the library she was dressed far differently than Lady Carol, who was more of a Goth and Betty Page hybrid. Carolyn was in the atrium, back lit by brilliant winter sunshine, with a much softer look in a dark blue low-cut V-neck mohair sweater and short black skirt. Of course, she asked me if we were there to check her out. Oh yes, we most certainly were; we just can't seem to get enough! She smiled at me and said that Carole's ancient librarian joke probably went back at least to the days of Hypatia and the great library at Alexandria. Naturally there were a few tsk, tsk remarks about our age and gender differences among the other library staff, but barely a ripple of outside public interest other than that. Well, OK, Sophie did catch us once smooching in the stacks, but she at least can keep a secret, even while giggling.

I'm sure there is much more to learn about Carol during the intervening years of my absence, but that awaits our supersync. Graduate school was a long, long time for Carol to be without a lover; at least, she had Legba to help her through it. She did cryptically mention that her Queen's pawn opening of "not negotiable and you'll do anything I say" proved to be not really a very effective dating tactic in graduate school, at least among the nearly normals, and that she'd gotten a bit of a frosty rep. I guess no one got that joke. It took me long enough. She also found the whole notion of a Brazilian wax job completely appalling and wondered how many incipient pedophiles had thought up or encouraged *that* particular pubic hairstyle.

There had been a little awkwardness at first when Amy hired Carolyn, and then realized with a shock just who Ms. Nightshade really was. Eventually, Amy accepted the new Carolyn and even became quite friendly with her while closely guarding her secret. Amy did start to catch on to her humor at last, and they frequently traded jokes, unfortunately a few too many of them were about Amy's old research mentor and ended in uproarious laughter, highly inappropriate for a library. It was clear that this situation was permanent and that Lady Carol really had to remain dead. Carolyn eventually was promoted to senior archivist, and would assist those researching Lady Carol, especially finding items within the vast number of her unpublished essays and several book manuscripts. She was occasionally quite amused with their misinterpretations of her writings but was usually able to set them straight by pointing out certain key documents.

Although it made Amy a little nervous at first, Carolyn found Sophie (and Pony) quite fascinating to talk to, and they were frequently found talking together in the archives when Carolyn wasn't too busy. Sophie was practically the archetype for the "wise child", solemn and insightful way beyond her years, but also shy and secretive unless talking to an unusually sympathetic adult of just the right sort. I guess she sensed in Carolyn just the right mixture of seriousness, worldly experience and dark humor needed to forge a deep friendship, and almost certainly she saw through Carolyn's cover story and knew who she was without ever being told. They discussed everything imaginable, and not uncommonly their conversations ended with barely controllable giggles. Sophie's perception of worldly events was wonderfully direct and free of prejudice, and her pronouncements about the world were often hilarious, yet cut right to the heart of things as they now were. Perhaps Sophie has transcended the cognitive closure that may hold back so many of us from understanding certain aspects of the world that continue to puzzle even the most advanced philosophers. I think they are planning to write a book together along the lines of *The World According to Sophie*. You would be quite wrong if you supposed that such a book would merely compile childish misperceptions for humorous effect. It would probably be more like Wittgenstein's "everything that is the case" than *Kids Say the Darndest Things*.

Unlike us, Sophie had bonded with her symbiont at birth, and in such a way that they were a much more unified consciousness right from the beginning; whereas, Carolyn and I were still mostly bicameral in our relation to our symbionts and needed much more syncing to function effectively together. Sophie gave us hope for the world and made both Carolyn and me rethink what it would mean for the two of us to have a child together. And yes, I said yes I will, Yes. Legba thought that quotation was pretty damned encouraging after Carolyn told him what it meant in terms of my affirmation of our quad.

I think Carolyn probably did supersync with a few key persons in our lives while I was gone. I only know for sure that she super-synced with Reggie and met our "daughter", Irene, Reggie's newly born symbiont, for the first time. Good night, Irene. I assumed that Reggie's new wife, Patricia, was OK with all this, and that Carolyn was sort of a mother-in-law despite now looking young enough to be Reggie's daughter.

It was not just us and a few people we knew, but now nearly everyone's family life had become redefined in such radical new ways that a sizeable piece of the telenet was now devoted to helping families navigate these unfamiliar waters. A comprehensive familial nomenclature that includes symbionts has yet to be devised, but I think someone's diligently working on it over at symbiont-ancestry.com. I guess that there will now be many family trees with a real tree in them if you went back far enough. Among symbionts there was still a mysterious and wholly irrational prestige associated with being directly "tree born" from a virus that was tree borne.

Carole remembered absolutely nothing from her missing years as a dead symbiont but was at least able to recover a few lonely memories of mine from those awful prison times after we were finally able to sync again following her resurrection. These memories were not very pleasant things for her to experience, and she was painfully sorry that she couldn't have been there with me to lighten my burden. Carole did finally get to experience with me her last emulation of Dream Carol at the Senior Prom and found the final ironies of my edited version amusing in their self-referential twistiness.

Carole did help me provide relief to the other dispossessed as they came to be released from prison. Among the symbiont community and the dispossessed, I am something of a hero for spearheading these efforts and so is Carole for setting up the website to handle reunions. At least this damage repair and penance will be some consolation for the rest of our little lives, however long Carole may cause them to be.

Carole finally suggested the time was right to super-sync our quad back together again. She desperately missed her friends and longed to renew her sync with Carol. By now I even missed chatting with brother Legba, who, I finally realized, must have been totally in love with Carole all along to put up with my bullshit.

Very soon, I'm sure we will arrange this super-sync in the library of dreams, and we will begin again our quad marriage, just not in the greenhouse with Jungle Girl for starters, but all together now in more of a continuing helical narrative that twists around itself, exploring new things and revisiting old, accepting each other just the way we are so we can become what we must. We will finally reclaim our Jaguar woman, she of the solitary path, and will joyfully re-enter her fierce embrace. Carole and Legba have designed a beautiful new quad ring for her utilizing and affirming this new feline motif. The library of dreams now has a magnificent new atrium where our quad can all sit in the sunshine as we sync, and if that's not enough, there's a nice tropical beach nearby where we can walk barefoot and wet our toes in the surf. The future is now open in ways I could never have imagined as a human.

EPILOGUE

"We can no longer live here. You must have noticed all the accumulating difficulties. We can hardly make it up and down the stairs."

"Yes, I've noticed. How long do you think we've got?"

"Perhaps six months; maybe much less. We need to make a plan."

"Like what? Have you cloned us a new body?"

"That's not even possible… No, I'm afraid there will be no new body, at least not in time for us."

"What then? It looks like the end. That's what we expected, isn't it?"

"Perhaps, but perhaps not. Are you willing to take a risk?"

"You've never mentioned this possibility before…"

"I'm not one to encourage false hope. There is no certainty in this plan."

"I'm willing to take a risk if you are… as long as we are together in the end. You're not just getting ready burst out of my chest and emerge into your adult imago and leave me now, are you?"

"Tear you a new one? No, if we really had to part that way, I'd spring fully formed and clad in an armored exoskeleton, directly from your forehead. Actually, beloved, we'll be together always, but we will have to leave a little early while I can still summon enough concentrated energy from our elderly mitochondria for a final CHIRP."

"A chirp?"

"A CHIRP, a Compressed High-Intensity Radiated Pulse of our intermingled wave functions. It's something we can send out that might possibly find a resting place where we can attach ourselves and live on together in another form."

"How can you possibly know this?"

"I don't know it for sure, but it seems to be allowed in physics, and the math is quite beautiful also!"

"And if you're wrong? Just being allowed by physics or having beautiful math sounds pretty flimsy even to a scientist like me. Pi in the sky by and by when we die?"

"Externally, it will just appear to be a suicide by immolation under mysterious circumstances. If I'm wrong, we'll not be aware of it. There will be no pain. We'll just cash in all our carbon atoms and be gone in a puff of CO_2."

"So, in any event, we would have to go somewhere safe to do this so the whole apartment building doesn't burn down. Perhaps a pilgrimage to the desert to meditate? The desert of eternity."

"Yes, that would be best."

"Should we say goodbye? Perhaps they would try to dissuade us…"

"We must say goodbye and let them know what we have decided. They will certainly know everything from our next supersync anyway. They could come with us to the desert as witnesses, but there might be some dangers in that. They should at the very least know what we've decided so that they're not faced with a phony murder mystery or get drawn into an investigation. They may also want this option for themselves someday."

"All assuming that we do this. We would be trading all our remaining time as a quad for a very long shot at an unknown hope."

"Yes, exactly; what do you think?"

"Will there be sex in this imaginary after-life?"

"We can't know that."

"If there's not, I won't go!"

"We'll think of something beloved."

Printed in the United States
by Baker & Taylor Publisher Services